First Sun

by

Tara Tolly

To my mother's best
looking friend —
thank you for your
support!
Tara Tolly

F & I
by Melange Books

Published by
Fire and Ice
A Young Adult Imprint of Melange Books, LLC
White Bear Lake, MN 55110
www.fireandiceya.com

First Sun ~ Copyright © 2014 by Tara Tolly

ISBN: 978-1-61235-957-1

Cover Art by Caroline Andrus

To James and Bella,
my rays of sunshine

"After there is great trouble among mankind,
a greater one is prepared.
The great mover of the universe will renew time, rain,
blood, thirst, famine, steel weapons and disease.
In the heavens, a fire seen."
Michel de Nostradamus

Part One

Countdown: 153 Days
July 5, 2021

The stars twinkled in the night sky, serving as a reminder to all that no matter how big their problems seemed, they were small in the grand scheme of the vast universe around them. Andrew lay on his back on the red tiled Promenade atop the White House, gazing up into the stars, his phone turned off and strewn aside in frustration.

"Andrew!" his father bellowed from inside the glass-walled living room on the third floor of the president's manse known as the Solarium.

"Son of a bitch," Andrew muttered under his breath, recognizing his father's irritated tone. It was one that Andrew had become particularly familiar with lately.

"Andrew!" his father repeated, louder still.

Andrew sighed and reluctantly stood up. He pocketed his phone and with one final glance at the stars for comfort, hesitantly crossed the threshold into the Solarium to meet his doom.

"Hey, Dad," he said, futilely attempting to lighten the mood.

"Sit down," the president said curtly.

Andrew knew better than to argue. He plopped onto the red plaid couch inherited from the Obama administration and took a deep breath in preparation of his berating.

The president threw his phone onto the coffee table in front of Andrew. It was playing a video that Andrew was already pretty well acquainted with. He winced in response to the graphic nature of the scene playing out before him.

"Please tell me this is not you in a compromising position with Ava Jacobsen, the daughter of my opponent. The opponent I almost lost to because of you and your *publicity* stunts."

Andrew grimaced. This video was not one of his finest moments. He grabbed the phone and clumsily stabbed at it to stop the video.

"A little uncomfortable? Yes, I'd imagine you are. About as uncomfortable as I was this afternoon when my chief of staff played it for me." He retrieved his phone from Andrew and hit play again. Andrew leaned over and hid his face in his hands in disgust.

"Oh, no. You're not getting out of this that easy. You're going to watch the entire thing."

Andrew stayed hidden behind his hands.

"Andrew, watch it."

Andrew still didn't move.

"Watch it, damn it!" his father yelled.

Andrew removed his hands from his face and trained his eyes on the horrifying video. A single tear escaped his eye and slid down his cheek as he relived the biggest mistake of his life. He finally looked away, unable to watch another second.

"Don't you dare look away. You look at what you've become. Is this who you want to be? A joke?"

These last two words jarred Andrew out of despair. Now he was just pissed. He jumped up and glared at his father. "So I made a mistake. Big deal. It's just a frickin' video. It's not the end of the world." He turned around and stormed toward the ramp leading out of the Solarium.

The president chuckled ironically without an ounce of humor, halting Andrew in his tracks and sending a chill down his spine. "Actually son, that's *exactly* what it is."

Countdown: 109 Days
August 18, 2021

The sun shone through the blue sky, as it had done for billions of years, heedless of my gray mood. I squinted my eyes in frustration at its mocking cheerfulness, wishing it would just quit already.

"Dani, what am I going to do without you?" I asked, looking out of the corner of my eye in desolation at my best friend. She was strapped into the passenger seat of my rusty, decade-old jalopy on the way to the Ronald Reagan National Airport; the airport that would transport the last remaining piece of my home back to Iowa, ending her visit and leaving me to fend for myself in the unknown world of Washington, D.C.

"You're gonna rock D.C., that's what you're gonna do."

"I don't want to rock D.C. I want to come back home with you and rock Cedar Rapids."

"Eden, D.C. is *way* cooler than Iowa. The Smithsonian, Capitol Hill, the White House, the president and his gorgeous son..."

"It doesn't matter," I lamented. "Dani, Iowa is all I know. I'm scared out of my mind. None of my friends are here, and I have to go to school with a bunch of rich snobs, including the president's son. What the hell did my mom get me into?"

"Oh, Eden. We've gone through this a million times! First of all, she got you into school with the hottest guy in America."

I flashed her a dirty look. She knew where I stood in regard to this argument.

"Oh, come on, Eden. You'll be brushing elbows with Andrew Wellington, first son. Maybe more if you're lucky..." she said innocently, fluttering her eyelashes.

3

I couldn't help but laugh at her insinuation. "Yes, Dani. A drunken, womanizing meathead is exactly the kind of guy I'm looking for," I joked.

"All right, all right. Whatever. You're still going to one of the best schools in the country. You've always wanted to go to an Ivy League school. You know graduating from Sidwell Friends School with a 4.0 will be your ticket into the college of your choice."

"But what if the admissions departments just look at me as the kid of the academic genius who skated through her senior year at Sidwell because her mommy taught there?"

"They won't. They'll see that the apple doesn't fall far from the tree. Your mom is a genius, Eden. Nobody can argue that. My God, Dr. Mom created a freaking U.S. History curriculum from scratch and published a bazillion teachery books. But all the admissions departments have to do is take one look at your transcripts to see that you're just as smart as your dear old mom. Why is that a bad thing?"

"Well..."

"Yeah, that's right. You've got nothin'." She folded her arms and smiled in triumph.

"Danielle Louise Reider, what will I do without you to talk me off a ledge every five minutes?" I shook my head in misery at the thought of saying goodbye. Tears pricked the corners of my eyes, threatening to open the floodgates, spilling out all the fear and anguish that had been building inside of me for the past six months.

"I'll just have to talk you off the ledge over the phone," she said gently. "Now pull over."

"What? No way. Dani, we need to get you to the airport or you'll miss your flight. Your parents will kill me if you miss the first day of school," I said, shaking my head.

"Just do it," she said, annoyed by my usual stringent attention to rules.

"Fine," I grumbled, slowing down and coming to a stop on the shoulder of the highway, not too far from the Arlington Memorial Bridge. "This is really safe," I said sarcastically, turning to throw her a dirty look, but immediately softening at the intensity in her big, brown eyes.

"Look behind you," she ordered.

I twisted around in my seat to look out the rear window. The Washington Monument reached up to the heavens in stark contrast to the sky behind it, white against blue, towering over everything in its vicinity. I took in a sharp breath in response to its splendor.

"Tell me what you see."

"The Washington Monument," I whispered in awe.

"Yep. Now tell me what can match that at home," she challenged.

"I don't care about the view, Dani. As beautiful as this is," I said, gesturing behind me, "it's not home."

"Maybe not," she agreed. "But this is history, Eden. Your favorite. And you're about to become part of it. Plus, even if you hadn't moved to D.C. for your senior year, you would've left for college soon anyway. And last time I checked, there were no Ivy League schools back home."

I exaggeratedly rolled my eyes, prompting Dani to smile.

"You might as well enjoy what D.C. has to offer while you're here." She shook her head and softly added, "Iowa can't hang on to you forever. Neither can I. It's time to push you out of the nest, E. It's time to fly."

I hugged my best friend tight, and this time I didn't stop the tears from falling.

And just as I had suspected, once the tears began to fall, they didn't dissipate for much of the day. I cried the rest of the way to the airport, said a tearful goodbye to Dani at the gate, and sobbed the entire way back to the car. Throughout the drive home, I continued to shed tears as the comprehension that my entire life was changing in front of me hit me like an unstoppable Mack truck on the freeway. The vast expanse of the unknown stretched before me, threatening to engulf me in its void. I cried and cried as my car puttered along the streets of D.C. of its own accord, undaunted by its strange surroundings. I realized with a sudden jolt of anxiety that I didn't even know where I was. I scowled at my phone in fury, but it just lay there on the passenger seat, ignorant of its failure. "Stupid navigation," I mumbled, sniffling. I knew how irrational I was being, but I didn't care. It was easier to get mad at my phone than it was to face the impossible truth that everything I had ever known was about to change.

I spotted a gas station and pulled into the parking lot to get ahold of myself. This was not me. I was stronger than this. I glanced in the rearview mirror to check for any lingering tears and froze in amazement at what framed my tear-stained face. The tip of the Washington Monument blinked in the glow of the pink-and-orange-painted dusk sky. I stepped out of the car, entranced by its beauty, and stood there drinking in the magnificence of the manmade structure against nature's backdrop. Dani was right. It was time to end my period of mourning. I had indulged in enough self-pity to last a lifetime, and no matter how much I cried I would still be in Washington, D.C. when I finished. This was my new life. It was time to embrace it and make the most of it. I wiped my eyes with the palms of my hands and resolved to give D.C. the chance it deserved.

Deciding to take advantage of my little stop, I trudged into the gas station in search of some refreshment. After locating a Mountain Dew and thanking my lucky stars that not everything in D.C. was different, I grabbed a Snickers bar for good measure and headed for the cashier. Along the way, a photograph of Andrew Wellington on the cover of a magazine caught my eye. But it was not just one picture. It was a photo-collage starring Andrew Wellington in a double feature, cast as both the "First Disaster" and "First Charmer." The title at the top read, "All Partied Out?" Normally, I would have walked right by this display without a second thought. But with my first day at Sidwell looming, curiosity got the better of me.

Setting down my pop and candy bar, I plucked the rag out of its stand and thumbed through it to the featured article. When I found it, I was instantly repulsed by what unfolded before me. Picture after picture of the first son in rare form. Only it didn't seem to be so rare. In some pictures he was passed out amidst a litter of plastic cups and beer bottles. Others caught him mid-shot or cheering over a game of beer pong. One picture even showed him draped over a toilet, seemingly unconscious. I was about to throw the magazine down in disgust when I spotted a more becoming picture on the opposite page.

On that page, Andrew Wellington was portrayed in a whole new light. He was dressed to impress in every picture, accompanying his father to a charity benefit or cutting a ribbon during the opening ceremony of an inner city school library. My favorite was the one of the first son holding a sick baby during a surprise trip to an American-funded African hospital. Could this possibly be the same person? It was more like the hero and his doppelgänger. But one thing every picture had in common (devil or angel) was the famous Wellington looks passed down from his father.

The blurb under the title claimed the magazine was "unable to secure a picture of the first son partying for the last month." So what? He was probably just being more careful now. After all, the photographs the magazine *was* able to secure depicted a young man desperately trying to clean up his image. Holding a sick baby in a third world country? Puh-lease. How cliché could he get?

I dropped the magazine back in its rack and made my way over to the cashier to pay for my snack. It was time to find my way home. Both physically and emotionally.

* * * *

The next morning, I stood in the bathroom staring at the face looking back at me from the outdated bathroom mirror. Today was the day I would begin my new life. Would I fit in at the hoity-toity Sidwell Friends School? I certainly wouldn't be able to afford designer clothes or a two hundred dollar haircut every month. Back home, that kind of thing didn't matter. I had a bad feeling it did here.

I hurried through the shower, dried my long, dark blond hair and attempted to straighten it, even though I knew it would revert to its naturally wavy state the second I walked out into the late summer humidity. I threw on what would have been an acceptable outfit in Iowa, figuring I couldn't go wrong with jeans and a solid blue tank top. As a last-ditch effort, I slopped on some mascara and dark purple eyeliner I had been told enhanced my sea green eyes, and glanced in the mirror one final time. This was as good as it got.

Go get 'em, Eden.

I headed down the stairs wondering how Mom was doing and whether or not her nerves were wearing on her as well. She yelled up from the kitchen, "Eden! Get down here and eat your waffle while it's hot!"

It was moments like these when I realized just how lucky I was to have such an amazing mom. This was Mom's first day of school too (at least her first day with students), so she had to be just as nervous as me, if not more. But there she was, bright-eyed and well intentioned with the waffle iron beeping and the aroma of Belgian waffles wafting up the stairs of the historic row house.

"Mom, you really didn't have to do this," I said, shaking my head in amazement as I sat on a stool at the breakfast bar.

"Of course I did. I know this move hasn't been easy on you. But you have handled it with such grace. You've never made me feel guilty…this was the least I could do," she finished sadly, gesturing to our little feast.

I placed my hand on hers and said, "Thanks, Mom." She smiled thankfully and flipped a fresh waffle onto my plate.

We sat at the breakfast bar, eating in companionable silence, both lost in our own first day jitters. As I sopped up the last drops of syrup with my last bite of waffle, my stomach did a flip-flop. It was time to go to school. But this was not just any school. This was the famous Sidwell Friends School. The best of the best went there. It was known for educating the sons and daughters of D.C.'s elite. Presidents had sent their children there since its inception, including the current president. The thought should excite me. It certainly would excite most girls, Dani included, but as the drunken photographs of Andrew Wellington from the gas station magazine flashed before my blank stare, I shuddered. Drunk and promiscuous just didn't do it for me, regardless of how hot the offender was. He wasn't the type of person I wanted to associate with. Certainly Sidwell was big enough for the both of us.

My face must have exposed my uncertainty, because Mom placed her fork on her plate and softly asked, "What's the matter, E?"

"Nothing. I'm just nervous about going to a new school. That's all."

"I understand. It's a big change. I'm scared too. But throughout the last couple days of teacher workshop, I realized it's not so different from home. People are people. You'll be fine too. Just remember that you're special, sweetie. Don't lose yourself in the process of trying to fit in." She put her hand over mine for a moment and kissed me on the top of my head as she got up. "Now help me get breakfast cleaned up so we can get going. We don't want to be late on our first day, do we?"

Countdown: 108 Days
August 19, 2021

Of course he would be in my first class. And of course the only open seat would happen to be directly in front of him so I would get to be tortured by the sensation of his eyes boring through the back of my head the entire class. I had to hand it to him. Andrew Wellington was a hotty. His tall, built stature was noticeable even when he was sitting. It was almost comical how folded up he had to be to squeeze his long legs under the little desk he sat at. His short, dark hair was styled in a way that made it look messy even though every strand was articulately manipulated into a spiky coif. His tan skin glowed around a plain white t-shirt paired with expensive-looking jeans.

Andrew's big blue eyes watched me clumsily walk to the seat in front of him and plop down. My face radiated heat from the intensity of my embarrassment.

As I tried to compose myself, a voice from behind me said, "Hey, how's it going?" Surely he couldn't be talking to me. I sat as still as I could while listening for a response so as not to give away my eavesdropping. "Are you the new teacher's daughter?" he continued.

Okay, so he *was* talking to me. Why was he talking to *me*? I swiveled around as gracefully as I could manage under the circumstances and replied, "Yep. That's me. Famous already, huh?"

He smirked ironically and said, "Definitely the most famous person in the school, hands down."

"I work fast, but apparently not as fast as you," I answered without a beat. Oh crap. Why did I always speak before thinking? What did that even mean? I knew he burned through girls like wildfire, but he wouldn't know that was what I meant. He probably just thought I was crazy. Oh well. Who cared? He wasn't the kind of person I wanted to mess with anyway. And it was true. He did work fast.

He briefly looked startled, but then transformed his face back into a warm, heartfelt smile. It made my heart skip a beat. God was he gorgeous.

Eden, he's a total jerk. Don't forget that.

"Where are my manners?" he said, extending his hand. "Andrew Wellington. Welcome to Sidwell."

"Eden Warren." As I shook his hand, his eyes never left mine. It may have been my imagination running wild, but if I wasn't mistaken, he held onto my hand a little longer than necessary. The physical contact sent shivers through my body.

"Eden, huh? As in the Garden of Eden? Eden…" He let the name roll off his tongue. I'd be damned if I didn't love hearing my name slip out of his sultry mouth. "Pretty. Now I just have to figure out if you're the forbidden fruit." More smirking.

How did you even respond to that? I went with a simple smile, which wasn't so simple given the odd exchange. I probably looked like a deranged hyena. Luckily, the teacher, Mr. Yang, called the class to order with a clap and put me out of my misery.

The rest of chemistry went by pretty quickly. The first day of school was usually reserved for procedures and icebreaking activities, and Sidwell was no exception. I had to hand it to Mr. Yang. His little game of "What's your favorite element and why?" actually prompted quite a few smart Aleck remarks and responsive giggles. Some of my favorites were, "Helium, because it gives me the ability to sound like Alvin from *Alvin and the Chipmunks*, instead of Alvin from Alvin and the Camdens," (Alvin Camden, a robust redhead sitting in front of me), "Platinum, because it's precious, just like me," (Katie Chadwick, a cute brunette a couple rows over), and "Calcium, because some day it will help me grow up to be big and strong," (Sam Rogers, a very short and skinny freckle-faced boy in the back whom I could see being a fun guy to be around). Andrew answered, "Titanium, because you can try all you want, but you can't break me." What a typical meathead response. Yuck.

I decided to go bold and after taking a deep breath said, "Oxygen, because although you've never seen me before, you won't be able to live without me."

My first bell at Sidwell Friends School promptly rang moments later. I fiddled around in my backpack for a couple of moments in hopes of avoiding any more awkward conversation with Mr. Titanium on the way out the door. No such luck. I looked up to see if my little plan worked, only to find Andrew standing above me, waiting. Waiting for *me*?

"Where to next, Oxygen?"

First Sun

Crap. He is *waiting for me.*

"I can show you to your next class. I'm a Student Ambassador and happy to be at your service," he said with a swift, perfect salute.

Oh my gosh, that smile. His lips curled over his perfect white teeth in this mischievous, lopsided way that almost pointed to the twinkle in his eye.

"That's okay, I'm good. The principal took me on a tour a few days ago and showed me where all my classes are. I know where I'm going." He must have noticed my clipped tone, because he visibly blanched at my response.

His shoulders wilted and he quietly said, "Ah. So you *are* the forbidden fruit. I get it. See you later, Eden."

I was suddenly embarrassed by my behavior. Why did I sound so irritated with him? He was being really nice, and I was being so rude. Maybe he's not as bad as the press made him sound. It wouldn't be the first time the media had painted someone the wrong color.

As he slumped away, I noticed his secret service for the first time. They tried to be discreet, but they were about as camouflaged as peacocks in the snow. There were two of them, both dressed in civilian clothes, but their huge physiques and gun bulges gave them away. They were fascinating to watch. One never took his eyes off of Andrew, and the other one's eyes flitted expertly in all directions as if it were second nature. They waited until Andrew was far enough away to give him his privacy, but close enough to keep him safe, turned on their heels and followed him down the hall in perfect synchronization.

"Fascinating to watch, huh?"

Startled by the fact that someone was reading my mind, I turned around to find the cute brunette girl from class shaking her head in mock awe. "Yeah. I've never seen anything like it before. I didn't notice them in class."

"They don't usually come to class. The school is well monitored and safe, so they try to give him his distance and all. They stand outside the classroom to make sure no boogie monsters come in and then follow him from class to class. Fun job, huh? Babysitting the president's kid?"

"Yeah, real nail biter." We chuckled.

The girl stuck out her hand and introduced herself. "Katie."

"Eden," I said, accepting her handshake.

"Watch out for that one. You don't want to become his next flavor of the week," she warned, brown eyes gleaming mischievously.

"Don't worry. My flavor's way too plain for Andrew Wellington—you know, much too vanilla for his kind. He seems more like a Ben and Jerry's Half-Baked kind of guy."

Laughing, Katie snatched my schedule from my hand and compared it with her own. Luckily she was in a couple more of my classes, which helped

11

me make it through the day a bit easier. Unfortunately she wasn't in my last class of the day, Family and Consumer Sciences. I approached the room as if walking the green mile toward my death. Cooking was *not* my thing. Any concoction I had ever tried to make ended up dried out, burnt, or raw in the middle. The only food I could produce that would actually turn out edible was chocolate chip cookies. And I had a feeling they would not be on the menu. But when I crossed the threshold into the classroom, I smiled in surprise. It was the cutest room ever. It was divided into two sections; one set up as a classroom with rows of desks, the other with quaint little kitchenettes. Around the perimeter of the kitchen section were about eight stations, each with an oven/stove combo, a sink, and a row of cabinets with a counter on top. In the middle were two stainless steel refrigerators. A plethora of windows sent rays of sunlight streaming in through red and white gingham valances. Dividing the two sections were three circular tables topped with matching red gingham tablecloths and small white vases with a single red carnation in each one.

Maybe this class wouldn't be so bad after all. But as I pictured myself standing in front of one of those stoves with smoke billowing in the air and the piercing chirp of the smoke alarm alerting the universe of my adversity to cooking, my excitement waned and was replaced with trepidation. What horrors awaited me at the stove this semester? Fried chicken? Consommé? Or the worst of all evils…a soufflé? I shuddered at the thought.

"What's the matter, Oxygen? Cold?"

Oh, you have got to be freaking kidding. I looked up at the ceiling and rolled my eyes at God. *Nice one.* I made a mental note to kill my mother for talking me into taking this class. Her mocking words, "But honey, you might pick up a skill or two," echoed through me.

"No, just so excited for cooking I can hardly stand it," I said sarcastically.

"So this must be your favorite class then, huh? Me too! Who knew we had so much in common?" He smirked and slipped into the seat next to me as the teacher called the class to order.

Ms. Martin welcomed us to "FACS," as she lovingly called it, and explained that we would begin the semester with a study of kitchen utensils and their proper uses. She assured us, however, that we would begin cooking soon, starting with pancakes. I could hardly wait.

As Ms. Martin continued our welcome and went into her version of procedures and expectations, I looked beyond the spatial environment to the faces of my classmates. I was beginning to recognize some students, but still struggled with most of their names. I noticed Sam, the small, happy, freckle-faced boy from my Chemistry class right away, and he excitedly waved at me from a couple rows over. I grinned and waved back. As my eyes moved on, they fell on a strikingly pretty blonde whom I recognized from my Perspectives on American Government class. She was model gorgeous. Her perfect shiny platinum blonde hair hung in exquisite loose curls down her back and a skimpy sundress showed off a body any girl would sell her soul for. She had big boobs, a tiny waist, and flawless skin. The only thing I could find to criticize was how she exuded high maintenance. She wore too much makeup, even though she didn't need it, her skin was way too tan, and her fingers and toes were painted to perfection. She also had an air of over-confidence to her. The kind that suggested she knew how blessed she was and would use it to her every advantage. She looked awfully familiar, but try as I may, I just couldn't place her. Was she a celebrity or something? There was something about her that made me uneasy. I decided not to worry about her and turned my attention back to Ms. Martin.

"Okay. Enough with the first day stuff. Let's see who we're going to work with this semester in our kitchenettes!" She rubbed her hands together in excitement and retrieved a cup from her desk filled with craft sticks. "I have each of your names on a stick. I'll pick two at a time, and those two students will be partners."

The entire class focused intently on Ms. Martin. Her little lottery drawing could make or break the entire semester. I didn't care who my partner was, as long as it wasn't Andrew Wellington. Sam would be okay. *Anyone* else would be okay.

"Rob, you will work with...Leila!" They seemed content with their partnership and smiled at one another.

"Logan will work with...Cole!" They shrugged at each other.

She went on for another couple of pairings before pulling out Andrew's name. "Andrew, you will work with..." Every girl in the class leaned forward in anticipation. Except for me. "Ava." My stomach dropped. Did I actually want to work with Andrew? Because much to my surprise I was certainly disappointed. I glanced around the room, trying to locate the lucky winner. It wasn't too difficult to deduce that the familiar-looking blond girl was Ava, as she was the only girl left with a smile on her face. Only it wasn't really a smile. It was more of a sneer. She desperately tried to catch Andrew's eye to celebrate their pairing, but it didn't appear as though he was interested in celebrating.

Instead, he cleared his throat and raised his hand a little to get Ms. Martin's attention. "Um, actually, Ms. Martin, I was hoping I would get to work with Eden." The entire class turned to me in shock.

"Oh, well...um..." Ms. Martin was at a loss for how to handle this little request. I could see Ava fuming out of the corner of my eye. Lovely. Andrew was really helping me fit in.

13

Ms. Martin looked at me. "Would that be all right with you, Eden?"

"It doesn't matter," I managed to force out, trying to sound indifferent.

"Okay, then. Andrew, I guess you will work with Eden." She shrugged and stuck Ava's stick back into the cup and moved on. I could feel the disbelieving stares of my classmates linger and tried to appear as though I were interested in the remainder of the pairings. I refused to look at Andrew. What was he doing? It just didn't make sense. He didn't even know me. Was he just interested in me because I blew him off in chemistry? Was it because this was uncharted territory to him? I was the girl who didn't automatically swoon in response to his attention. After only one day of school, it was easy to see the effect he had on girls. They all wanted him and most, if not all, would jump at the chance to be the object of Andrew's affections. Heck, from the sounds of his extra-curricular "activities" perhaps most of them already *had* been the objects of his affections. I would not make the same mistake.

When the bell finally rang, I bolted out the door in avoidance of Andrew. Unfortunately he must have anticipated my escape and easily caught up to me. "Hey, Oxygen! Where's the fire?" he called, prompting every student in the vicinity to whisper and stare. It just fueled my anger. I ignored him and picked up my pace. Undeterred, Andrew easily kept my pace, strolling along casually beside me. I stopped in frustration and turned toward him, only to find an annoying little amused smile painted on his beautiful face. Oh, huh uh. I would *not* fall for his little tricks.

"Can't you take a hint?" I asked bluntly.

"I can. But I'm a little confused why you hate me so much," he responded.

"I don't hate you. But I do think you're a little arrogant."

"Ouch." His face contorted into a pained grimace.

"Plus, I'm just not into what you're into."

"How do you know what I'm into?"

"Take a guess."

"Ah, I see." He let out a long frustrated breath and ran a hand through his dark hair. "I'm not like that anymore. I'm going to prove it to you. It's my new mission in life." The twinkle returned to his eyes and he flashed a heart-stopping smile as he walked away, leaving me amidst a litter of nosy spectators.

* * * *

That night, as promised, I called Dani to recap my first day of school. But of course the only line of conversation she was interested in was Andrew Wellington, "First Disaster." I didn't disappoint. Even though I knew I would have to suffer through an "I told you so" speech, I didn't spare a detail in my rendition.

"Ha! I knew it!" she screeched into the phone. I pulled it away from my ear in preservation of my eardrum. "You seriously suck. Of course the one person who can't stand the guy becomes the one he wants."

"He does not want me, Dani," I tried to convince her, but in reality, I was trying to convince myself. She was right. For whatever reason, Andrew had taken a liking to me. But I was not about to become his latest weekly conquest, and I told Dani so.

"E, what's your problem? The hottest guy in America wants you, and you blow him off? I can't even believe you." I pictured her shaking her head in annoyance and a pang of homesickness tugged at my heart. It softened me a bit.

"I know, I know. You win. He's hot. But I still don't know what to think of his past. It really bothers me."

"Have you Googled him?"

"Why would I do that? I've seen enough of him in the press. I don't need any more evidence to prove he's a douche bag."

Dani sighed in frustration. "Do you remember the president's interview the night before his reelection?"

"No. But what does that have to do with anything?"

"Just trust me. Watch it."

A half hour later, I sat in front of my computer screen drumming my fingertips next to the mouse pad, contemplating whether or not to watch the video Dani suggested. This was ridiculous. Watch a video to decide whether or not to like a guy? My curiosity finally got the better of me. I pressed play and the president appeared before my eyes.

"How do you feel about being referred to as the most beloved president since Lincoln?" the famous news anchor, Clara Crawford, asked the president during an exclusive interview on the eve of his reelection.

The president shook his head in befuddlement. "I still can't even fathom where that came from. I'm not worthy to be compared to Abraham Lincoln. No one is."

"But you are, sir," Crawford gushed.

"Ah, we'll just have to agree to disagree, Ms. Crawford," the president jested.

Crawford was obviously flustered by the president's quick-wit coupled with his irresistible sex appeal. President Wellington was not admired for his political achievements alone. He was known for being the "Sexiest Man Alive," several times over according to *People Magazine*. His tall, broad physique, thick brunette head of hair, and sky blue eyes could rival the hottest Hollywood actors from any era. Crawford tittered nervously before regaining her composure and moving on to the next question.

15

"But it is a fact, Mr. President, that your approval rating hovered right around a historic 85 percent throughout the first three years of your presidency. What accomplishments do you think the public most approved of?"

"When I made the decision to run for president the country was in a state of gridlock. Some say we may even have been on the fast track to a second civil war. But this civil war would not have been North against South. It would have been Right versus Left. Leading parties were at war with one another and the country was divided. One party had gained all of the power, while members of the other party stood by, helplessly trying to slay the beast that had become so all-encompassing, like a mouse swiping at a dragon.

"As American demographics shifted and our country evolved into the twenty-first century, we began to lose sight of what made our country truly great to begin with. You see, the reason our nation had become a superpower in the first place was due to our checks and balances. Our founding fathers envisioned a country where no one person, or one party, had all the power. America was built upon the foundation of hard work, perseverance, and freedom. Freedom from tyranny, persecution, and discrimination. Freedom from autocracy. Unfortunately, America was becoming the opposite of what our founding fathers had worked so diligently to achieve.

"It was time for a fresh, new perspective. America needed a change. Not just from one party to the other, as in the past, but to a whole new frame of mind. I realized that in order to bring the nation together, we needed a moderate president who wasn't married to either party. Many said it couldn't be done, that an Independent candidate could never take the presidency. I disagreed. Why couldn't a president combine political ideologies from both sides into a newer, stronger vision for America?

"I ran my campaign on this bold new initiative. It turned out to be just the antidote. My administration directed focus away from party politics and toward what was best for the people of this beloved nation. In doing so, the branches of the government were able to come together to rebuild a broken America. America is on the mend, Ms. Crawford, and I think the American people can taste it. I sure can."

"That is true, sir," Crawford praised. "Your bold party-free reformations brought the nation back together and prevented a brewing civil war. But you failed to mention your other accomplishments, such as the improved economy, reduced cost of living, rejuvenation of the health care system, and growing student achievement in our public schools." She flashed a sparkling smile at the president, awaiting his response to her shameless compliment.

"Well now, Ms. Crawford, I can't take all of the credit," the president said with a wink. "Much of that credit belongs to my colleagues in Washington, and the American people themselves."

All of this is interesting, but what does this have to do with Andrew? I skipped over some of the video in search of anything having to do with the first son.

"Mr. President, your approval rating plummeted from that historic 85% average during the first three years of your incumbency to hovering right around the 50th percentile over the past year. You are undoubtedly at risk of losing to your opponent, Philip Jacobsen, tomorrow. What do you attribute this complete 180 to?"

"I think the American people attribute my failure to secure my reelection to my son."

There it is.

"I don't blame my son. I blame myself. My son was just a young boy who lost his mother and freedom all in the same month, and rarely got to see his father for the past four years because he spent too much time raising America out of its doom instead of raising his son. I think the American people have begun to doubt whether I can control an entire country when I can't control my own son. While I can argue that my track record as president is satisfactory, I cannot do the same for my track record as a father.

"I regret that I haven't been there for my son. But why *wasn't* I there for him?" The president looked down as if searching for the answer. After a moment, he answered his own question by explaining, "When I took the oath of presidency, I was no longer the father of one. I became the father of 350 million. How could I sacrifice 350 million for one? Looking back, that one should have been the most important one."

President Wellington paused, trying to clarify his thoughts. "If his mother would have been there..." he trailed off, trying to compose himself. "If his mother would have been there, she would have kept me in line as a father," he finished softly. "But that's not an excuse. I'm a big boy. I failed my son when he needed me most."

The way his remorse resonated through his words was gut wrenching. "I take full responsibility for my son's behavior. He is a casualty of my negligence. I did this to him. It just took the American people to make me see it."

He stopped to wipe away a genuine tear and take a drink of water. "I will not fail him any longer," he began again, stronger with conviction. "I have proven my competency as president. Now I owe it to my son to prove my competency as a father. That will happen regardless of where we live. But I sure hope it will be in the White House."

The video ended and I sat staring at the still of the sorrowful president.

Regret lined his face like a roadmap leading to the hurt inside; hurt usually masked by the handsomeness on the outside. He truly felt responsible for his son's behavior. Why did Dani think this would help? It didn't. All it did was make me more frustrated with Andrew. His behaviors not only almost cost his father the reelection. They scarred the person who loved him the most.

Countdown: 107 Days
August 20, 2021

The next day I awoke to an unexpected eagerness to see Andrew. It gnawed at me, mocking my resistance to his attention. Despite my suspicions there was something about him that intrigued me. I couldn't quite put my finger on it yet, but whatever it was was beginning to transform my opinion of him. Maybe he really wasn't just a party boy any more. He certainly didn't want me to think so. But why? Why did he care so much about what I thought?

As I walked through the front doors, I surprisingly found myself searching through the swarm of people for him, and the longer I didn't see him, the more disappointed I felt. I shook my head, trying to clear it of all things Andrew and trudged toward my locker. When I caught sight of it, I froze in amazement.

Andrew stood leaning on one shoulder against my locker, with one leg casually crossed over the other, thumbs moving swiftly on his phone. His beauty was unfathomable. Every time I saw him, he took my breath away, no matter how unwelcome the sensation was. The cowlick at the front of his brunette head of hair stood up slightly, adding to his intentionally messy look, and his long, dark eyelashes fluttered on the tops of his prominently chiseled cheekbones in concentration on his phone. Today he was wearing khaki shorts, which highlighted his perfectly sculpted calf muscles, and a slightly fitted, blue collared shirt that accented his bulging upper body. I wasn't his only admirer. Every girl passing by shamelessly checked him out. My heart fluttered uncontrollably as I realized this much-sought-after boy was waiting for *me* by *my* locker.

I attempted nonchalance as I strolled up to my locker. "Excuse me," I said, waiting for him to move.

"Good morning, Oxygen," he said, smiling.

"Good morning, Andrew. Can you please move so I can get into my locker?"

He moved exaggeratingly slow and bowed, gesturing to my locker.

I couldn't help but giggle a little before catching myself and scowling at him. "Why are you lurking in front of my locker?"

"I was? Oh, I'm sorry," he said, feigning innocence. "My locker is just a couple down from yours. I didn't realize this was your locker."

I wasn't falling for his little act. "Your locker is across the hall from mine, Andrew," I said, smiling against my will.

"So you know where my locker is, huh?" he smugly pointed out.

I threw him a dirty look.

"Okay, okay. I wanted to walk with you to class," he admitted, shrugging.

My stomach fluttered. "You're not going to take no for an answer, are you?"

"I'll always take no for an answer, Eden," he said, suddenly serious, eyes gleaming. "But I hope you *won't* say no."

"Fine." I sighed, attempting to look annoyed.

He broke into a grin and waited for me to unload my backpack.

As we walked to class, the inevitable gaggle of students gawked at us and whispered in surprise as we passed by. I suddenly felt very self-conscious.

"Andrew, how come every time you're standing with me, or talking to me, or walking with me," I gestured to our little powwow, "everyone looks so shocked?"

"I don't know. I guess I'm usually a loner. I don't usually hang out with girls at school."

"Why not?"

"Because most of the time, girls just want to be around me because I'm the president's son, not because they like me as a person."

"What about guys? Do you have any close guy friends?" I asked, curiosity piqued.

"I have friends I hang out with on weekends and stuff, but I wouldn't consider any of them close friends. I just don't let them get too close, because…well…let's just say girls aren't the only ones who use me for the whole White House thing." At the look of sadness on my face he shrugged and added, "I did have some close friends back home, but I lost touch with them when I moved to D.C."

How sad, I couldn't help thinking as I slid into my seat in class.

Chemistry went by pretty quickly. I was unfalteringly cognizant of Andrew's presence behind me, and got the feeling he was purposely encouraging this phenomenon by "accidentally" bumping against me or grazing

20

my back as he repositioned himself throughout the duration of class. If that was his goal, he was successful, but I wasn't about to let on that I noticed.

After class, Katie joined me to walk to our next class. Andrew looked disappointed for a second, but recovered quickly. "See you in FACS, Oxygen."

"My favorite class," I grumbled. "Can't wait."

"Me either. Turns out, I have a hot little kitchen mate." He winked and turned the opposite direction, prompting his agents to follow him. I couldn't be sure, but I thought one of them flashed me a tiny smile.

"Dude, Andrew likes you," Katie said in awe.

"No he doesn't," I protested.

"Um, yes he does. He has never given a girl even an iota of the attention he's giving you."

"But I can't stand him," I lied, just as much to myself as to Katie.

"Maybe that's why he likes you," she pointed out slyly.

As we continued down the hall chatting, I spotted that strangely familiar girl, Ava, from my FACS and Government classes standing by her locker watching me. No, not watching me. *Glaring* at me. Apparently she was still pissed off at me about Andrew's little request in FACS yesterday. As we passed her, I smiled in an attempt to break the ice, but received nothing but cold rejection in return.

"Who the hell *is* that Ava girl?" I asked Katie. "She looks so familiar."

"Uh…Ava Jacobsen?" she said, as though it were so obvious she couldn't even believe she had to tell me. "You don't recognize her?"

I shook my head in confusion. "Just from class."

"Her dad ran against President Wellington in the last election…" she hinted, shaking her head in astonishment of my ignorance.

"*That's* Phillip Jacobsen's daughter? Duh! I can't believe I didn't recognize her!"

Katie nodded in approval of my tardy deduction.

"But what's her problem? Why is she glaring at me?"

"Because she's a mega-bitch."

I busted out laughing. "I knew I liked you, Katie!"

"Good. Then maybe you'll want to go to the football game tonight with Sam and me and some other people. It'll be a great way for you to get to know everyone."

"That depends." Katie's face dropped at my unexpected stipulation, but brightened back up when I added, "Will Ava be joining us?"

"Definitely not."

"Then I would love to," I said as Katie's face relaxed in relief.

"Great! Let's meet at my house. We can get ready together." As Katie rambled on in excitement and texted me her address, I made the conscious decision to leave all thoughts of Andrew at school, far away from wreaking havoc on my emotions.

This proved to be much trickier than anticipated. As much as I hated to admit it, I was surprisingly disappointed when Andrew didn't show up at the football game. I spent a good deal of the night searching the football players and crowds of people for him, until Sam and Katie informed me that the president had pulled Andrew from the team after he suffered a concussion in the opening game last season. Andrew hadn't been seen at a game since. Evidently the president was not about to risk Andrew's safety after losing his wife only a few short years before. While it made sense in an over-protective kind of way, it made me sad for Andrew.

But why did I care? My bipolar opinion of Andrew Wellington was exhausting me. Perhaps it was time to admit to myself that I liked him. Why I liked him continued to allude me. I certainly didn't approve of his lifestyle, and didn't want any part of it. So what was it that drew me to him? Sure, he was hot, but it was more than that. His no-nonsense demeanor was alluring. He didn't play games. He made it clear that he liked me and wanted to prove he had changed. How he could like someone who was so mean to him was beyond me. But why was I mean to him? Was it because of his past? I didn't even know him then. It wasn't like me to judge someone based on gossip. I resolved to be nicer to him. If he even wanted to talk to me anymore after the way I treated him.

Apparently he did. On Monday morning, he was posed in his usual spot in front of my locker, dazzling as always, typing away on his phone. I took a moment to drink in his magnificence. His perfection was intimidating. No one should be that flawless. It wasn't fair. I couldn't even fathom what he saw in me. I smoothed my pink tank top, like that would help, and strolled up to my locker. When he looked up, he smiled brilliantly in greeting. "What's up, Oxygen?"

"You're pretty predictable, you know that?"

"Yep. Like a reliable old dog."

"Can I look forward to this every morning?"

He cocked his head playfully, trying to suppress a smile. "You look forward to seeing me, do you?"

Crap. Andrew had an annoying talent for picking up on my subliminal compliments. But he was right. I *did* look forward to seeing him.

"Maybe," I said, smiling demurely. "Or maybe not," I added. I could admit to myself that I liked him, but I wasn't ready to let him know yet.

He shrugged and smiled devilishly. "I'll just have to work on turning that 'maybe' into a 'definitely'."

We walked to Chemistry chatting easily about class, complaining about the pile of homework assigned so early in the year, and giggling at the ogling passersby.

"You make it really difficult to dislike you, you know that?" I reprimanded, taking my usual seat in front of Andrew.

"I told you that was my mission."

We smiled at one another unabashedly until Mr. Yang called the class to order.

* * * *

Later that day I exited Independent Studies to find Andrew waiting outside the door.

"Are you stalking me?" I teased.

"Maybe just a little bit." He held up his pointer finger and thumb to emphasize the word "little," and wrinkled up his nose in concession.

I shook my head in disbelief. "At least you're honest."

"Always." He grinned and fell into step beside me. "Ready to make some pancakes?"

"Ready to *burn* some pancakes, you mean," I pouted, much to Andrew's delight.

"Don't worry, Oxygen. I've got you covered. I can make pancakes in my sleep."

A half hour later, we stood in our kitchenette with me standing over the stove frowning and Andrew desperately attempting to hold back the laughter threatening to explode out of him at any moment. "What am I doing wrong?" I asked sadly, scowling at my smoking black pancakes.

"There's a fine line between ready to flip and burnt. It's easy to burn pancakes. Let me show you how it's done." Andrew quickly dumped our pancakes, if you could call them that, down the drain and cleaned out the pan. He poured in some fresh vegetable oil and put the pan back on the burner. "The trick is to have really thin batter and a super-hot pan. Pancakes should only take a minute to cook on each side. You can't turn away for a second." He dropped a tiny drip of batter onto the pan and watched it. "I like to test the pan before pouring the batter in. See how it sizzles and cooks instantly?" he asked, pointing to the drip. I nodded. He smiled at the intensity of my concentration. "That means the pan is ready," he continued. He poured four circles of batter onto the pan. "Now watch for the insides to bubble and the edges to dry out."

I watched carefully, fully aware that Andrew was watching me rather than the pancakes.

"There! It's doing just what you said it would!" I exclaimed.

"Yep. Time to flip." He flipped all four pancakes expertly as I looked on in awe at the perfectly even, golden color. "Now pay attention, because the second side doesn't take as long." We waited. "Now grab a plate!" he ordered. I followed his instructions and held a plate close to the pan. He scooped the cakes off the pan and flipped them onto the plate.

"Andrew, they're perfect!" He beamed with pride. "How does the first son know how to cook pancakes? Can't you just order whatever you want from the White House kitchen?"

"My mom liked to cook. She taught me everything I know." I was surprised by the casual reference to his late mother. But as the sentiment hit home, his face fell and he turned away for a moment to collect himself, pretending to straighten the counter. When he turned back around, he had recovered his usual relaxed countenance and said, "Plus, I haven't always lived in the White House."

I smiled up at him, emboldened by his moment of transparency and touched that he had let his guard down with me. He returned the smile and handed me the "pancake turner," as Ms. Martin told us it was called, not a spatula. "Your turn."

Andrew watched me critically as I followed in his footsteps perfectly, producing beautiful pancakes for the first time in my life. "Let's see how I did." I buttered the pancakes and drenched them in syrup, then cut off a bite with the side of my fork and held it up for Andrew. He leaned forward and accepted the bite. He closed his eyes and chewed in bliss. "Mmmmm…"

Oh my goodness.

Andrew opened his eyes and flashed me a smoldering look. My entire body felt hot. He grabbed a fork and prepared a bite for me. I accepted it and chewed in silence, eyes locked on Andrew's.

A loud crash forced us out of our little moment. I jumped up and searched for the source of the noise. It was Ava. Surprise, surprise. And by the smug look on her face at the success of her little ploy, it was easy to deduce that it wasn't an accident. Andrew turned away from her in disgust, gathering dishes to take to the sink to be cleaned.

"We better get washing these dishes," he said, filling the sink with water. "How about I wash and you dry?"

We washed in electrically charged silence. Any time our hands made contact, a tiny shiver of excitement ran through my body. After finishing the last dish, Andrew smiled and turned to wipe off the counters, while I finished putting the dishes away. "We make a good team," he said, meeting my eyes once again.

"Yes, we do," I agreed.

Countdown: 101 Days
August 26, 2021

I sat in Perspectives on American Government, daydreaming about Andrew. He continued to frustrate me, and intrigue me, simultaneously. One moment I was loathing him and the next I was enamored by him. If I didn't have any preconceived notions of what he used to be like, I would thank my lucky stars that he liked me and that would be the end of it. Or hopefully the beginning of it. But I did know what he used to be like, and his past bothered me. It gnawed away at the back of my mind like Chinese water torture. No matter what he said or did, he could never take back his past decisions. Drugs, girls, alcohol, partying…it says a lot about a person. What if he was changed for now, won me over, and then regressed back to his old ways? I didn't want any part of his past. But there was something about him that drew me in.

"Eden?" Mr. Polk called.

The sound of my name jerked me back to class. Unfortunately it was too late to know what Mr. Polk was expecting me to answer.

"I'm sorry, Mr. Polk…what was the question?" The class snickered a little, making me squirm in my seat.

"I was just wondering what your thoughts were on the matter."

"Ummm…what matter?" I asked apologetically. More snickers.

"Okay, Eden. I'll let you off the hook this time. But try to stay focused on instruction next time, okay?" Polk chastised light-heartedly.

"Yes, sir," I answered, turning bright red. Out of the corner of my eye I could see Ava eating up my humiliation. Nice.

"I was wondering what your thoughts were on the 9409 Apollo conspiracy theory."

Thanks for the clarification.

"I'm not quite sure what you mean, sir."

First Sun

"Eden, please come see me after class," Polk said, disappointment evident on his face. Ava and a few of her disciples laughed again. I glared at them, not caring what they thought.

For the rest of class, I sat there mad at the world. This was not like me. I was not a ditz and that's how I came across in class. I took pride in school and didn't want to send the message that I didn't. What a great first impression to make. I knew what I needed to do. I grabbed my phone and typed "9409 Apollo" into my notes app.

After class, I sheepishly approached Mr. Polk and apologized profusely for my lack of dedication in class today. He seemed receptive to my groveling and let me off with a warning. What I didn't tell him was that this wasn't the end. I would find a way to prove to Polk how committed I was to his class.

* * * *

"Hey, Oxygen," Andrew called, trying to catch up with me on the way to FACS.

"I'm a little mad at you," I said, with a hint of a smile.

"You're mad at me? I'll take that as good news. You had to have been thinking about me to be mad at me." He raised his eyebrows hopefully.

"That's just the problem. I shouldn't be thinking about you."

His face dropped. "I'm lost."

"I was spacing off in Gov today trying to figure you out and got in trouble."

"What were you trying to figure out? Maybe I can help." He smirked, as though I had just told him I had fallen in love with him. I was unintentionally feeding his ego. What I was trying to do was be honest.

"I'm trying to decide if you really have changed," I confessed.

"Ah. I have. I'm just trying to make you believe me."

"That's the problem. I'm not sure if I believe you yet."

"I'll take that 'yet' as a smidgeon of hope." He grinned and grabbed my arm, pulling me to a stop and swinging me around to face him. His hand on my arm brought waves of heat pulsing over my body. I liked his touch a little too much. "Brian's having a few people over Saturday night for a bonfire. Do you want to come?"

"Oh gee, let me think." I put my finger on my lips in exaggerated consideration. "A bunch of people getting drunk or high at a bonfire...sounds fun," I said sarcastically. "I'd rather keep my scholarship, thank you." I tore away from him and picked up my pace, trying to give him the message that I would rather walk alone. Apparently he missed the memo.

Andrew quickly caught up and walked briskly beside me. "It's not that kind of get together. I promise." He made the sign of the cross over his heart with an enticing grin. "Please come," he begged.

I sighed and studied him in contemplation. His flawless face crinkled up in anticipation as he waited for me to make a decision. Despite his beauty and fame, he stood there completely vulnerable, as though his very happiness depended on my answer. It was distracting and softened my resolve. He did keep assuring me he had changed. Should I take a chance?

"Okay."

Andrew's face broke into endearing elation.

I put up my hand and added, "I'll think about it."

His face fell a little. "Well, that's better than a no."

We closed in on FACS and I took my usual seat, waiting for Andrew to do the same. But instead he leaned over and gently brushed my hair away from my ear, into which he whispered, "I'll email you the address. I really hope you come." His fingers brushed the top of my back as he crossed the aisle to his own seat, leaving a trail of heat in their place.

* * * *

That night at home, I flipped open my laptop, woke up my iPad and typed "9409 Apollo" into the Google search. I sifted through the search choices and decided to begin with Wikipedia. As I read the article, a jolt of recognition crossed through my consciousness.

Duh—The asteroid scare!

9409 Apollo was the name of a six-mile wide asteroid discovered a few years back by an American from Oklahoma with a private telescope. The man, Robert Moore, claimed that the asteroid was on course to collide with Earth in the near future, prompting a global uproar. NASA and the government immediately quelled the public's fear by discrediting Moore's claim. They argued that Moore was not a trained astrophysicist and could not possibly predict an asteroid's course without advanced astronomic equipment and computer programming. NASA assured the public that while 9409 Apollo would come the closest to Earth since near Earth objects were first monitored, it was not on course to collide with Earth. This information seemed to pacify global concern, until conspiracy theorists began digging. What they found raised some red flags.

Shortly after Moore's discovery, government-funded space programs confiscated hundreds of observatories and private telescopes around the globe. After only three years of on-air time, the new James Webb space telescope live video streaming was cut off and replaced by recorded snippets of video. And to top it all off, Robert Moore was killed in a car accident less than a month after his discovery.

While I never considered myself a conspiracy theorist, this was looking a bit shady. I decided the next line of action would be to find how the government was responding to these claims. I typed "Wellington response to 9409 Apollo conspiracy" into Google and came across a video clip of the president being interviewed on the topic shortly after the government seized control of the observatories and private telescopes. I hit play and got comfortable with my iPad at the ready to take notes.

A pretty, blond, female news reporter I didn't recognize asked, "Mr. President, four years ago, shortly after you took office, an ordinary American citizen claimed to have spotted a large asteroid on course to hit Earth in the foreseeable future with a private telescope. NASA and your administration claimed this to be false. Can you elaborate on this?"

"I can certainly try. I have never claimed to be a scientist, so I will do my best to explain the issue as I understand it." He brandished a dazzling smile and continued. "It is true that a citizen located a large asteroid using his private telescope. The asteroid does exist. There is a department at NASA with the sole purpose of monitoring our space neighborhood for asteroids or other space debris, such as comets and meteors that could cause potential harm to our home. These are called Near Earth Objects, or NEOs for short. There are currently close to 10,000 NEOs discovered and documented. Approximately 1000 of these could approach Earth and have a diameter of more than one kilometer. Or, in other words, could cause significant damage to our planet. The NEO program monitors these objects closely and communicates with NASA and the public of any findings. If there were an asteroid headed toward Earth, we would know about it and act accordingly. The NEO program confirmed the existence of the asteroid discovered by this citizen, now known as 9409 Apollo, as one of the thousand they have been monitoring for quite some time. The difference between the NEO program and the citizen is that the astrophysicists running NEO are trained professionals with additional equipment used to study the trajectory course of the asteroid, as well as its composition, exact size, etc. The citizen was an amateur hobbyist using equipment he was never trained to use, nor did he have the additional equipment and computer programs NEO has to confirm or deny his findings. In short, I can assure the American public that NEO is monitoring 9409 Apollo, and it is not on course to collide with Earth."

"Sir, the same citizen who discovered the asteroid also claimed, *before his death*," the reporter added pointedly, "that his telescope was confiscated shortly after sharing his findings. Other telescope owners around the globe have made similar claims. Conspiracy theorists are proposing that the telescopes were apprehended because the government was trying to hide the severity of the asteroid threat from the public. What would you say to them?"

"I would tell them that when you put advanced equipment into the hands of amateurs, you are sure to get amateur findings. That is exactly what happened in the case of 9409 Apollo. The citizen caused an uproar over something he knew little about. We couldn't risk panicking the public again over a misconception. With powerful equipment comes great responsibility. If one doesn't possess the knowledge to back up the results of one's equipment, one has no business using the equipment. Of course, soon you won't need advanced technology to spot Apollo 9409. It will come so close to Earth you'll be able to see it with the naked eye as it streaks by. But rest assured, other than providing entertainment for a few nights, it won't affect us."

The video clip ended, but my mind continued to run a mile a minute. President Wellington's explanation seemed logical, but there was something off about his demeanor. He was his usual confident self, and clearly candid as always. But what was it? He almost came across as defensive. This realization made my skin crawl. Was he hiding something? Could Moore's findings actually be accurate? If so, what kind of damage would a 6-mile wide asteroid make? I delved into the computer even further to find out. It wasn't long before I wished I hadn't.

According to multiple sources, an asteroid of that size would cause massive global destruction. The initial impact itself would instantly incinerate anything within 1800 kilometers of the impact site, not to mention the obliteration of anything within 4000 kilometers in just minutes. The impact would trigger global earthquakes, volcanic eruptions and tsunamis, causing additional damage of their own accord.

The long-term effects would be just as devastating as the initial impact. Debris from the impact would be ejected into the sky and rain back down in a global firestorm within hours. The fire toxins would poison the air and generate years of global acid rain, making all water inconsumable. Global destruction of the ozone layer would expose all living things to deadly UV rays for years. Dark skies would turn day to night for months, ceasing photosynthesis and creating freezing conditions, thus killing off all plant life on land and water, and as a result of food shortage, animals as well. Once the sky cleared, excess carbon dioxide and water in the air would produce decades of greenhouse heating. Earth would become inhospitable to all life forms. Goosebumps erupted up and down my arms at this revelation.

Suddenly I had lots of thoughts on the matter of the 9409 Apollo conspiracy theory. I opened up a Word document and began to type.

* * * *

First Sun

The next day, I walked into Perspectives on American Government and slapped a five-page paper on Mr. Polk's desk.

"Eden, I haven't assigned any papers yet," Polk said in confusion.

"I know, sir. I wrote this paper of my own accord. I felt bad about not listening in class yesterday, so I went home and researched the 9409 conspiracy theory. And let's just say that I *did* have some thoughts on the matter."

Mr. Polk smiled and flipped through my work. "You went home and wrote a five-page paper because you wanted to?" He shook his head in amazement. "I really don't think I've ever had a student like you, Eden."

"That's what I wanted to show you, sir. School is important to me. I don't know what got into me yesterday. I promise it won't happen again."

"I'm sure it won't. I appreciate the gesture." Polk shook his head again, beaming. "Can you give me a little preview as to what your thoughts are on the matter?"

"Well, I'm still a little undecided. I have to admit that the signs do point to a government cover-up. But I trust President Wellington. He's always been forthright and honest. I just can't believe that he would cover up something so big. So the jury's still out."

"Interesting thoughts, Eden. I'm excited to read your paper." He smiled.

"What do *you* think, sir?" I probed.

"I think it's our job as American citizens to question the government and keep it on its toes. We're lucky to live in a country that allows us to do so."

"I agree." I began to head to my seat, but as an afterthought, turned back around and said, "And sir? Let's just hope the president *is* telling the truth."

Countdown: 99 Days
August 28, 2021

"Katie, I don't know about this," I said as I pulled up to the curb down the street from the house where we were supposed to meet Andrew.

"Eden, Andrew Wellington invites you to hang out at a friend's house, and you don't want to go? What's the matter with you?" The astonishment on her face was almost comical.

"You're the one who warned me not to become another flavor of the week."

"I was warning you because I thought you should know how he is. But for some reason, I get the sense that this is not a flavor of the week kind of thing. I think he really likes you."

"No he doesn't. He's just not used to being challenged. It's discombobulating to him, that's all. He's intrigued because he thinks I'm 'The Forbidden Fruit'." I stuck my finger in my throat in a fake gag. Katie's infectious laughter rang through the car until she had me in a fit of giggles as well. "Oh, Katie, thank God I found you!"

She gave me a quick hug and said, "Let's go find your man!"

As we got closer to the house, we could hear the bass pounding and voices from what sounded like a heck of a lot more than a small group of friends. They were lucky this house was so far from any neighbors or the cops would've been called long ago.

"Some small group get-together he's got going on here," I muttered to Katie.

"Yeah. Looks like a full swinging party to me," she agreed. A kid running out the front door and turning into the bushes to vomit confirmed our suspicions.

"Classy," I said through clenched teeth. "Katie, I'm sorry, but if there's drinking or drugs here, I'm going to have to leave. I can't risk losing my scholarship."

"That's okay," she said sadly. "Just come check it out with me for a minute. Sam said he'd be here…" She trailed off, not wanting to reveal her blatantly obvious crush on a guy who clearly reciprocated her amorous feelings.

"Okay, but just for a minute." I was beginning to get pretty ticked off. Andrew invited me to a bonfire with a small group of friends. He promised me it wouldn't be this kind of party. Instead, he was probably inside getting drunk, preparing to make me his flavor of the week. Perhaps my initial impression of Andrew Wellington wasn't so off base. I should trust my instincts a bit more.

We walked through the front door and were instantly greeted by a group of kids from school, most of whom I didn't recognize. I did recognize Sam and Ava. Yuck, Ava. She was wasted. She was so drunk she could hardly stand up and staggered over to me as soon as we locked eyes.

"Hey, Ava. How's it going?" I said in the nicest voice I could muster.

"It was better before you got here." Her nasty voice was filled with such hate.

What did I ever do to her?

"I'm sorry, Ava, did I offend you or something?" I asked sincerely. I really wanted to know where her animosity came from.

"No. Well, yes. You offend me just by existing, Even. Eden," she drunkenly snarled as she lifted her hand. To do what, slap me?

I didn't think anyone else had even noticed this little exchange, because Katie had wandered off with Sam and the others. But out of nowhere, Andrew stepped between us and grabbed Ava's wrist mid-swing. The room fell silent as all eyes turned to the scene unfolding before them. Still holding her wrist, Andrew firmly said, "Ava, just leave her alone. She never did anything to you. You don't even know her. I'm sorry it didn't work out with you and me, but you can't treat someone like this just because I like her."

"That's fine, Andrew. I get it. A relationship with a poor girl to build your reputation is probably just what your daddy ordered," Ava spat back venomously.

All of the blood drained from my face and the room started to get fuzzy. *This cannot be happening to me. I have to get out of here. Now.*

"Katie, I'm leaving. Are you cool?" I called in as even a tone as I could manage.

"I'll come with you."

She headed over to me, but I shook my head and said, "That's okay. Sam, can you give Katie a ride home?"

"Of course, Eden."

"Have you been drinking?"

"No, I'm D.D. tonight."

I nodded and pushed through the front door as quickly as I could. The August heat engulfed me like a warm hug as I sullenly walked to my car. What the hell was that? What did I ever do to her? Talk to Andrew? Well, I wouldn't make that mistake again. Not after he lied to get me to come to a party he knew I wouldn't want any part of.

But an irritating voice in the back of my head excitedly said, *He likes me? He told Ava he does.* I suppressed the voice and picked up speed.

"Eden!" Andrew grabbed my hand to stop me from walking so briskly. I wrenched my hand out of his grip and walked faster.

"Leave me alone!" I shouted over my shoulder.

"Eden, will you just stop?" he pleaded.

I abruptly stopped, causing Andrew to ram into my back. "What?" I demanded, whirling around with one hand on my hip and gesturing wildly with the other as I continued. "What could you possibly want from me, Andrew? You invited me to a *small* get together with a *few* friends. So I come, despite every ounce of me screaming, 'Don't do it! Don't do it!' And what do I find when I get here? A big drunken party with a bunch of people I don't know, including your ex-girlfriend with a vendetta against me for no apparent reason. Thanks for the invite. Now I'm going home." I turned on my heel and continued toward my car. My old, rusty, poor girl car.

"Eden!" Andrew yelled after me.

I finally reached my car, threw the door open and slumped down into the front seat. I rested my head on the steering wheel for a moment, and then began to hit it with all my might. How could I have been so stupid? Andrew Wellington was a charmer. I knew that, yet I fell for it. The passenger door of the car opened and Andrew slid smoothly into the seat and shut the door. "Are you done?"

"Get out of my car," I said quietly.

"Nope."

"What? What, what, what, what, *what*?" I shouted at him. "What do you want from me?"

"I want to apologize." His calmness was really irritating.

"For what? For your ex-girlfriend going all ape-shit on me, or for inviting me to a party with alcohol under false pretenses, putting my scholarship at risk?" I asked. "Which one, Andrew?"

"Um...both?" he responded with one of his famous smirks. Damn it. Why did he have to look so damn hot all the time? "And in my defense, I didn't know it was going to be a party. People just kept showing up."

"You smell like beer. How much have you had to drink?" I asked.

"Only one and a half, Eden. Don't worry, Daddy gave my secret service friends strict executive orders to apprehend me and bring me home if I ever have more than two beers." He gestured absentmindedly to the two men standing just outside the car. "I've been in the press a few times for public intoxication and nearly cost him his reelection. Remember? I'm sure you've seen it in the papers, on the news, perhaps the Internet? This is Dad's way of keeping me on a short leash, while still giving me some freedom."

"Well, good for you," I said sarcastically. "Unfortunately, we're not all rich enough to go to Sidwell on Daddy's money. Some of us have to work for it. Some of us have to be careful not to be caught drinking anything at all, let alone be anywhere near underage drinking so as not to lose our scholarships. Enjoy the second half of your beer. Now get out of my car."

"Nope. I'm not thirsty."

"Ahhhhh! You are so frustrating!"

"I'm not getting out of this car until you see me for who I am."

"Oh, I see you for who you are, Andrew. You're a spoiled rotten brat who was handed a rough hand in life when your mom died. Instead of mourning her loss and moving on to become the decent young man she would've wanted you to become, you turned to drinking, drugs, and girls to self-medicate, never thinking about the effect it would have on your father's career or your country. Pretty much nailed it, huh?"

"I've never done drugs," he said softly, "but otherwise, I guess you did nail it. At least the old me. The one who almost lost my dad's presidency and ruined both of our lives." He turned to me with urgency in his eyes. "But you see, that's not the end of the story, Eden. That was the old me. I'm not like that anymore. I'm making changes."

"Ah. I see. You're making changes like, oh, I don't know, instead of getting completely wasted at a party and ending up on YouTube, you only have two beers so your secret service agents won't make you go home. Good job, Andrew. Now *get out*!"

"Nope."

"Seriously. How much do I have to insult you before you get the hint?"

"A lot more than this. I've developed pretty thick skin over the past year. Plus, you haven't said anything that's not true, except about the drugs. I've never done drugs."

"Why not?"

"I promised my mom I wouldn't. Plus, I'm not into that. It really ruins lives. I mean, more than, well…you know."

"More than drinking to excess and getting it on with a different girl every weekend?" I offered helpfully.

"Well, yeah."

"I guess that's true."

"Now you're agreeing with me. See? We're making progress."

For some reason, I found this extremely funny and began to laugh uncontrollably, almost crazily. "Oh, Andrew, you're killing me here." I wiped tears of laughter from my eyes and turned to look at him. "Why do you care so much what I think, anyway?"

"Because I like you."

"You like me."

"Yes."

"All I've done since we've met is be rude to you and insult you. And you like me? Oh, Andrew, you've got to heighten your standards."

He looked at me softly, raised the back of his hand to my cheek and gently rubbed his knuckles against it. I knew I should resist, but I couldn't move. It felt so good. "Oh, I think my standards are pretty high, Eden. You call it like it is. No bullshit. You don't settle for anything but the best. I can tell after only a couple weeks of school that you're a freaking genius and you are the most beautiful person I've ever seen, inside and out. I don't think there are standards high enough for the likes of you."

We sat in silence for a while. He was making it really difficult to hate him. I'd give him some reasons not to like me. "Trust me, I'm no picnic. I'm terrible at sports. I can't even do a somersault. Never could. Can't dance or sing. And to top it all off, I can't cook."

"So? I'm good at sports. I don't need a girl who plays sports; I need a girl to cheer me on. I'll teach you to do a somersault if you want to learn, it's really easy. I can't dance or sing either, so we can look ridiculous together. And I can cook, so we won't starve. Any other reasons why you think I shouldn't like you? Because those suck."

"I plan on being a virgin on my wedding night," I blurted out before I lost my nerve. There. I said it. If he was just interested in making me the next flavor of the week, he was fighting a losing battle. And he needed to know. I sat staring straight ahead in an attempt to feign confidence, when in reality I was more humiliated than I'd ever been before.

"Eden, I would be honored to marry a virgin," he said as seriously as he could, desperately trying to suppress his amusement.

"Now we're getting married?" I asked, exasperated.

"You brought it up," he said, shrugging innocently.

"It doesn't bother you?"

"Why would it bother me? It's just more proof that you're the honorable girl I thought you were. It only makes me like you more."

"Why would it bother you? Oh, I don't know, maybe because you're 'Playboy of the Year' and get with a different girl every weekend."

"*Used* to get with a different girl every weekend. And just because I made out with them, that doesn't mean we actually..." He trailed off in embarrassment. I was surprisingly not embarrassed any more. I was going to get to the bottom of this.

"So you're a virgin."

"Well...I didn't say that."

"Aha! I knew it!" I turned away from him in disgust.

"It was only one," he clarified defensively.

"Ava," I whispered, sure of my inference.

He nodded his head in shame and squirmed a little in his seat.

"How long were you together?"

"We weren't really together. It was a big drunken mistake," he admitted. "One I won't make again," he added quietly.

I looked up at him and thawed a little at his obvious remorse. "Okay, fine. You're the one who's so hell bent on changing my mind about you. So why should *I* like *you*?"

"Hmmm...let's see." He squinted his eyes and tapped his fingertips together in a steeple, deep in thought. "I'm very loyal, to a fault, even if someone hurts me. Kind of like a puppy. Ooh!" His eyes lit up in an irresistible childlike delight. "I love dogs. I would have one right now if I could. I take school seriously and always do my homework, so we could be study buddies."

I sat in silent thought as Andrew waited patiently. Finally I said, "Those *are* pretty good reasons. But I want more. How about I ask you some questions and you say the first thing that comes to your mind."

"Okay! This sounds like a fun game. Shoot."

"What's your favorite TV show?"

"Anything on the History Channel."

"Me too!" I smiled excitedly. This *was* a fun game. "I thought I was the only teenager in the world who was a big enough loser to watch that channel!"

"Are you calling me a loser?" He squinted his eyes in playful interrogation.

"Yes. But I'm calling myself a loser too," I admitted through a flirty smile.

He laughed. "All right. Then we can be losers together."

"What's your favorite kind of music?"

"Hip hop, rap, classic rock."

"Ooh, that could be a problem. Classic rock I can work with, but hip hop? Rap?"

"What do you like?"

"Country."

"That could be a slight point of contention, but nothing we can't work through."

I scowled at him. "Favorite classic movie?"

"*Forrest Gump*. Yours?"

"*Gone With the Wind*. But this is my game, not yours."

"Sorry," he said, suppressing a grin.

"Favorite food?"

"Doritos."

I narrowed my eyes in contemplation. "Cool Ranch or Nacho?"

"Nacho. Cool Ranch aren't real Doritos." I nodded in agreement.

"Favorite color?"

"Red."

"What do you want to be when you grow up?"

"When I grow up?" he asked pointedly.

I lifted my eyebrows at him in mock impatience.

"President of the United States," he said. "Just kidding!" He laughed as he dodged my faux punch. "I want to be a political analyst on a news channel, like Fox News, or CNN. Ideally, I'd like my own show some day."

"What sports do you play?"

"I've played football, baseball, and basketball, but I've narrowed it down to basketball. That's the only sport I play for Sidwell." His voice faltered a bit, revealing a twinge of resentment that would have gone unnoticed had Katie and Sam not told me the reason behind his short-lived football career.

I cocked my head a bit in empathy, but sensed this was not the time to breach the subject. "What do you like to do in your free time?" I continued. "Besides drink two beers at a lame high school party."

"I like to run, read—yes, read—don't look so surprised," he interrupted himself at the look of doubt on my face, "watch movies, and spend time with my dad. Well, when he has time."

"Favorite book?"

"*Catcher in the Rye*. Despite your previously conceived opinions of me, I like the idea of preserving youth."

I rolled my eyes in agitation of his little lecture. "Where do you see yourself five years from now?"

An emotion I couldn't quite pinpoint flashed across his face in response to this question. After a moment of thought, he recovered and leaned in to gently tuck my hair behind my ear. "With you," he murmured hopefully. My stomach did a flip-flop. He hesitantly leaned forward and put his hand on my knee. "Can

I kiss you?"

"Yes," I breathed, unable to move. He leaned forward slowly and brushed his lips against mine. I moved into the kiss to give him the permission he needed to deepen it. He opened my mouth with his tongue and I surrendered myself to the sensations of his mouth. We continued to kiss as his hand traveled slowly from my knee to mid-thigh and his other hand held my face to his under the hair at the nape of my neck.

He stopped for a moment and rested his forehead against mine, searching my eyes. Searching for what? My reaction to his kiss? Evidence that I was finally allowing myself to reciprocate his feelings? He kissed me one more time softly on the lips and pulled away. "Let me take you out on a real date," he said, taking one of my hands in both of his.

He must of noticed the uncertainty in my eyes, because he raised my hand to his lips and kissed it gently, before putting it back in my lap and whispering, "Please."

I simply nodded, because I didn't trust my voice at the moment. An ear-splitting grin spread over his face and he eagerly said, "Next Saturday night?"

I nodded again.

He continued to smile at me while I just sat there, probably looking like an idiot. "Can I have your phone number so I can call you with the details? Or any other reason," he amended shyly. "I could have my secret service friends find it for me, but that would look stalkerish. I don't want to scare you away when I may have just finally made some progress here," he teased with that alluring smirk.

"I guess," I said, trying to recover from the kiss enough to sound coherent. "Give me your phone and I'll put it in."

He handed it over and after about three tries, I was finally able to get my number into his phone with trembling fingers. He didn't make any smart-Aleck remarks to tease me, but rather watched me with delight. "So you're a little affected by our kiss too, huh?"

"Maybe a little," I reluctantly admitted.

"Good, because I'm having a little trouble trying to catch my breath over here myself." He leaned over, kissed me on the cheek, and whispered, "I'll call you," into my ear, unleashing the butterflies all over again.

Countdown: 98 Days
August 29, 2021

The next day, I woke up smiling. *Oh my god, I have a date with Andrew Wellington!* I foolishly picked up my pillow, smooshed it into my face and screamed. The pillow must not have muffled my screech as much as I thought it would, because Mom came running in all disheveled from being abruptly awakened, hastily asking, "Eden, what's the matter?"

I lowered the pillow from my face, and Mom immediately relaxed upon sight of the big, dopey grin on my face. She snatched the pillow from me and hit me on the head with it. "You little snot, you scared the crap out of me!" she admonished with a smile. "Why are you screaming at 7:30 on a Sunday morning?"

"Because I have a date with Andrew Wellington next Saturday night."

Her face fell a little and she studied my face carefully. "Andrew Wellington? Party boy, Andrew Wellington? First son?"

I nodded, unable to hide my excitement. "Mom, he's changed. I saw him last night at a party. This bitchy girl tried to give me some crap, and he let her have it. Then he desperately tried to make me see how much he's grown up. He's trying to clean up his reputation. He feels bad for the way he's acted in the past." Mom didn't look convinced. "Mom, seriously. Think about it. When's the last time you remember seeing anything negative about him in the press?"

She tilted her head and squinted her eyes in thought.

"Yeah, that's what I thought. You can't think of a time." I crossed my arms in triumph.

Mom sighed in defeat. "Okay, okay. You win. I trust your judgment. He is pretty cute…"

"Cute? That's the understatement of the year. He is absolutely gorgeous. Girls melt in his presence he's so hot." I smiled dreamily as I remembered our

40

kiss from last night and blushed.

"What?" My blush did not go unnoticed by my intuitive mother.

"He may or may not have kissed me last night," I admitted.

"Oh, my…good?" she asked with a knowing smile.

"*Very* good." I blushed some more.

My phone suddenly chimed alerting me of a text message. I retrieved it from my bedside table and smiled when I saw Dani's name. She was going to die when I told her what happened last night. But the nature of her message was distracting.

Dani: *Have you seen it?*

What did she mean?

Me: *Seen what?*

Dani: *The video of you running away from the hottest guy on the planet.*

I sat staring at my phone in shock as it continued to chime away, prompted by an impatient Dani whom I pictured scowling at her phone in frustration as she awaited my explanation for the video. She would just have to wait until I *had* an explanation.

There's a video from last night? I opened up my phone's internet browser and frantically typed "Andrew Wellington" into the search box. Much to my horror the video was not difficult to find.

"What the…?" I yelled at my phone's screen.

"What's the matter?" Mom asked nervously.

"There's a freaking video on YouTube from last night!"

Mom came over and tensely sat beside me to watch.

I hit play and held my breath. It was a video of Andrew chasing me to my car yelling, "Eden!" and me telling him to leave me alone. Who the hell took this video? Ava?

"Um, Eden? It may just be me, but it doesn't seem as though you're too interested in Andrew in this video. In fact, it appears as though you can't stand him."

"That was before our little talk…" I managed to stammer out despite my shock.

"But boy is he pursuing you. That's my girl." Her proud grin was almost contagious. Almost.

"Yeah. That's because that stupid girl had just bullied me for no apparent reason other than jealousy over Andrew and all I wanted to do was get out of there. Plus, there was drinking and I didn't want to risk my scholarship."

"Good girl." She beamed with pride. Mom trusted me. She had no reason not to. We talked about everything. I never kept secrets from her. "How long did he date this girl?"

"According to Andrew, they didn't really date." I hesitated for a moment, and then became firm in my resolve. I would test out Andrew's little confession. I typed "Andrew Wellington and Ava Jacobsen" into Google with Mom hovering over my shoulder, and held my breath as I waited for the results.

"Ava *Jacobsen*? Senator Jacobsen's daughter? The daughter of President Wellington's challenger in the last election? He dated his father's challenger's daughter?" Mom's tone indicated that she was less than impressed by this bit of information.

I ignored her judgmental attitude and swiped through the images. Picture after gorgeous picture of Andrew, some of Ava at events with her parents during her father's campaign, but none of the two of them together.

"Do you think she was just one of his many weekend party conquests?"

"Mom!"

"I'm sorry, honey, but let's face it. Mr. Wellington has quite a reputation. And dating Ava *Jacobsen*?"

"I told you they didn't really date." Her knowing smile irritated me, so I lashed out. "Mom, you're being really unfair. I saw a different side of him last night. He's not just a party boy like the media has made him out to be. He was very honest, and from what I can see, he *has* changed." I folded my arms defensively and glared at my mom.

"Okay, okay. Maybe he has changed. He seems respectable in class. Plus, I trust your judgment. But you know as well as I do that there have been many girls, evidently including Ava Jacobsen. Maybe she really cared about him and sees that he has real feelings for you. That would be hard for any girl, Eden."

"Maybe," I admitted.

"Are you excited for your date?"

"Yes."

"Then so am I." She kissed me on the top of my head and left my room.

Once alone, the memory of the kiss I shared with Andrew came rushing back in full force. My face flushed and my skin tingled in response to the memory. I got out of bed and rushed over to open my window to cool down. I closed my eyes and breathed in the cool, fresh air. Morning was my favorite part of the day. The first rays of sun warmed my face, and a cool breeze embraced me like a breath from God. I stood there in contented bliss thinking about Andrew. I believed him. He really had changed. I conjured his face into the black void of my closed eyes and sighed in ecstasy. My phone chimed again, jarring me out of my little daydream. I sighed and picked up my phone expecting to see Dani's name with another frantic message about the video. Instead, I found a number I didn't recognize. But the text could only have come from one person.

202-265-1107: *Hey, Oxygen. Just making sure you didn't fake number me.*

Me: *I would've if I would've known I would wake up to a YouTube video from last night on the Internet.*

202-265-1107: *Crap. I was hoping you wouldn't see it. Secret service is working on removing it.*

Me: *Oh. Well. That's a relief.*

202-265-1107: *Sarcasm?*

Me: *Ding, ding, ding!*

202-265-1107: *I'm really sorry. We don't know who took the video. Dad was pissed. He must have been really close to get that video and secret service didn't catch him.*

Me: *Or her?*

202-265-1107: *The thought crossed my mind too.*

202-265-1107: *Are you mad?*

Me: *Kind of.*

Me: *But not at you.*

202-265-1107: *Will you still let me take you out Saturday night?*

Me: *That depends. Will I end up on YouTube the next day?*

202-265-1107: *I wish I could tell you it won't happen again. I can't make that promise. But I like you and I want to take you out.*

I sat staring at my phone.

202-265-1107: *Are you going to make me beg?*

Me: *Yes.*

202-265-1107: *Please, please, pretty please with a cherry on top, will you go out with me Saturday night?*

Me: *Fine. But if I end up on YouTube again, you're dead meat.*

202-265-1107: *Threatening the president's son? I could have you arrested for that, little lady.*

Me: *Would you be the one to handcuff me?*

202-265-1107: *A guy can only dream, Oxygen.*

Me: *Speaking of dreaming, why are you up so early?*

202-265-1107: *I'm on the way to a super fun charity event with my dad.*

Me: *Sarcasm?*

202-265-1107: *Ding, ding, ding!*

202-265-1107: *Why are you up so early?*

Me: *I like morning. It's my favorite part of the day. I like the feel of the first sun.*

202-265-1107: *The feel of the first sun or the feel of the first son?*

Me: *Ha ha.*

202-265-1107: *I wish I could see you today. I'd like another kiss.*
My heart beat faster. How should I respond?

202-265-1107: *You still there? Or did I scare you away?*

Me: *Just thinking about how to respond.*

202-265-1107: *How about the truth?*

Me: *Okay. I wish I could see you too.*

202-265-1107: *And?*

Me: *And the kiss was pretty incredible.*

202-265-1107: *I thought so too. I can't stop thinking about it.*

Me: *Me either.*

202-265-1107: *I have to go. Dad gets mad if I text at events and we're almost there.*

Me: *Understandable.*

202-265-1107: *I'll be thinking about you.* My heart stopped.

Me: *And I, you.*

First Sun

202-265-1107: *Later, Oxygen.*

I set my phone down and fell back on my bed. The first son. I was dating the first son. Holy crap!

Countdown: 97 Days
August 30, 2021

That Monday Katie grilled me as we walked from Chemistry to AP Statistics. "Okay. Fill me in on what happened after you left Saturday night. All I know is that that stupid bitch, Ava, ragged on you for no apparent reason other than she's evil, you leave, Andrew Wellington runs after you, and we don't see either one of you the rest of the night. Spill."

I filled her in, telling her every little detail.

"Wow, Eden. That's huge. Andrew doesn't do dates. He does making out on a couch at a party. He must really like you." The astonishment on her face said it all.

I smiled dopily. But my face hardened as I remembered my encounter with Ava. "Katie, do you think I have anything to worry about with Ava?"

"Other than the fact that she's a skeething bitch and everyone should watch their back around her? Nope."

When I didn't look convinced, she continued. "I know what you're talking about. But no, you really don't need to worry. It's pretty obvious Andrew can't stand her. I wouldn't worry about Ava Jacobsen."

I decided to take Katie's advice. She was right. Andrew clearly couldn't stand Ava. I resolved to ignore her. And that's exactly what I did in both Gov and FACS. It was a little more difficult in FACS. Like any bird of prey, Ava quickly picked up on her target's weakness, taunting me throughout class with belittling looks. She even attempted to lock eyes with Andrew, flashing one patronizing look after another, but he never noticed. He was all eyes for me.

Even without Ava's little show, I was less-than-enthused at the idea of making muffins from scratch after my pancake-making disaster the week before. But Andrew was the perfect teacher yet again, and I naturally fell into the roll of sous-chef, attempting to perfectly execute his bidding. In reality, I just barely managed to produce satisfactory results. Despite my involvement, our blueberry muffins somehow managed to turn out and Andrew praised my efforts, much to Ava's annoyance. I took the high road and ignored her, trying to enjoy my time with Andrew.

As we walked back to our lockers after class, Andrew said, "Hey, Oxygen, want to help me study for the Chem quiz tomorrow?"

"You honestly still want to hang out with me after cooking with me?" I asked in astonishment.

"Even more so," he said, trying not to laugh.

"So a girl's complete and utter lack of culinary skills gets your blood pumping, huh?"

"No, *you* get my blood pumping." He stopped and tilted his head to the side. "I told you the other night I don't need a girl who cooks." His reference to the night of the party when he kissed me brought an instant flush to my face, so I looked away to hide it. He stopped and pulled on my arm so I would turn toward him. "Really, Eden. Kitchen expertise is not at the top of the list of characteristics I look for in a girl," he said softly with a smile. "It's not 1952."

I returned his smile, still red in the face. We continued walking, and when we reached my locker, Andrew said, "You never answered my question."

"What question?"

"If you would help me study for tomorrow's Chem quiz."

"Tonight?" I asked rhetorically.

"Well, we could study tomorrow night, but that probably wouldn't help us much on the quiz," he teased.

"Where?"

"Your place?"

"I guess that would be okay."

Andrew Wellington studying with me at my house?

"Cool. Do you want a ride home? I have some people who could drive us," he said, waving his arm behind him at his entourage.

"No, I have my car. You can follow me home."

* * * *

Fifteen minutes later, Andrew's Town Car pulled up to the curb behind my junker and I showed him into my house. I was a little nervous he would be underwhelmed. After all, he was used to having rich friends with mansions and living in the White House, the mansion of *all* mansions.

"This is great!" he gushed as he crossed the threshold into my living room. "I love these historical row houses. This is the kind of place I want to live in someday." The strange thing was, I really believed him. It made me like him a little more.

"Do you want something to drink? I'm going to grab a Mountain Dew."

"A Mountain Dew sounds good."

I came back a minute later with a couple cans of pop and found Andrew studying the picture frames on the mantle. He must have noticed there were no pictures of my father, because he carefully asked, "Are your parents divorced?"

"No, my father died before I was born."

"Oh my God, I'm sorry. I didn't mean to…"

"No, no. It's fine. I don't mind talking about him, because I never knew him. It's just been my mom and me my whole life."

"Your mom never remarried?" he asked, curiosity piqued.

I tilted my head in thought.

"I'm sorry. I'm being really rude. I didn't mean to pry." He turned to his backpack and unloaded it in embarrassment.

"That's okay. I'm not upset. I was just thinking about how to answer, that's all." I smiled at him and he looked relieved. "No, my mom has never remarried. She's dated a couple guys, but I don't think she's ever found someone she was sure she could trust."

Andrew tilted his head questioningly.

"Let's just say my dad was not exactly father of the year." At Andrew's continued look of confusion, I clarified. "My mom and dad were high school sweethearts. Apparently 'Daddy' got a full ride to the University of Iowa to play football. Mom followed him there, but when he became Mr. Big-Man-on-Campus, it went to his head. He started partying a lot and cheated on my mom. By the time she found out, she was pregnant."

Andrew had worked his way nearer to me as he listened. "I can see why she would have a hard time trusting someone after that." He shook his head in disgust. I liked the way he stuck up for my mom. "How did he die?" he asked.

"Drunk driving accident. He kept promising Mom that he would change. You know, for the baby." I shrugged. "He didn't. He went out one night, got really drunk, and drove his truck into a tree."

Andrew reached out and took my hand in support. I looked up at him blankly as the realization of why I had been so cautious with Andrew from the start hit me like a bolt of lightning straight to the heart. The drinking, the partying, the "fame"…

He's just like my father.

My hand went limp upon my epiphany, and I turned away in an attempt to break free from Andrew's grasp. I would not make the same mistake my mother had made. He tightened his grip on my hand and pulled my arm gently so I would face him again. "Eden," he said, searching my defeated face until his eyes locked on mine. "I'm not like that anymore. I really have changed." Was I that transparent? Or did Andrew have an innate ability to read my soul?

I studied his face, contemplating whether or not to believe him. My father had made the same promise to my mother, and all he did was break promise after promise, until the shards of his lies finally cut the ultimate ties—his life. Was Andrew different? As he looked down upon me with determination glinting in his eyes and the strong set of his jaw affixed in conviction, I knew he meant what he said. He *had* changed, and for the first time I truly believed him without any reservations.

"We'll see…" I teased, squinting my eyes in faux scrutiny to lighten the mood.

"I told you it was my mission to prove it to you," he said, breaking into a relieved grin.

I gave his hand a reassuring little squeeze before releasing it and crossing the living room to unload my backpack so we could get to work.

Andrew wasn't kidding the other night when he said he took school seriously and would make a good study buddy. An hour and a half later I knew the periodic table like I knew the back of my hand. Perhaps even better.

"I need a break. I'm starving," I announced, throwing down my pencil when I couldn't look at the elements for one more second. "Want to go to McDonald's?"

"McDonald's?" he repeated, all smiles.

"Well, yeah. I could cook something, but we both know what happens when I try to do that. Plus, McDonald's is my fave."

He shook his head a little and looked at me in amazement. "Do you know how few girls our age will eat at McDonald's?"

"Yes, I do. Try talking one of them into going."

He scooted over closer to me on the couch and brushed a piece of hair carefully out of my face. "You amaze me." He leaned forward slowly. So slowly the anticipation was killing me. My stomach fluttered in excitement and I closed the gap, bringing my lips to his. He chuckled a little, loosening his lips just enough to say, "And I was worried you wouldn't want to kiss me." He pressed against my lips again and deepened the kiss, drawing me closer with one hand on my back and the other on my waist. The spots where his hands touched my body burned with desire and I longed to touch him with mine. I decided to go for it and put a hand on his thigh. He let out a soft noise, almost just a breath, but a little more. It sent a tremor of pleasure down my spine knowing that my touch excited him. It gave me the courage to place my other hand around his waist. He made the noise again and moved his entire body closer. We continued to kiss for a few more minutes before Andrew reluctantly pulled away and breathed, "We really should go to McDonald's."

I laughed softly and agreed.

As we packed up our backpacks, Andrew's phone chimed. He sighed and fished it out of his pocket. He frowned as he read it and shook his head.

"What's the matter?"

"Nothing. It's just that my dad wants me to come home for supper tonight. He hasn't been home all week, and the one night I actually have plans, he's home. I'll just text him back and tell him I can't." He unlocked his phone and began to text.

I grabbed his arm and said, "No, don't. It's okay. Go home and eat with your dad. You probably don't get to see him as much as you'd like to."

"I'd really rather eat with you."

"I'll take a rain check."

Andrew sighed and texted something back to the president. He placed his phone back in his pocket and took my hands. "Okay. I'll go home to eat. But only if you promise we'll do McDonald's some other time."

"Well, nobody said *I* wasn't still going to go to McDonald's," I joked. "But I promise I'll go with you sometime too. My treat."

He smiled and brushed his lips against mine. "It's a date."

I walked him to the door and gasped when I opened it to find a crowd of people in front of my house. "Oh no," Andrew said. "Eden, I'm so sorry. I should've known better. A Town Car and secret service agents outside your house are a dead giveaway." He turned to me with worry written on his face. "I'll be more careful next time. If there is a next time after this," he mumbled uncertainly, looking at the floor.

I took his hand in mine. "Of course there's a next time, Andrew. You promised me a date this Saturday, remember?"

His shoulders relaxed and he replied, "Yeah, and we'll always have McDonald's." He shut the door enough to give me one more swift kiss and was gone. I watched out the small door window as he walked smoothly toward the Town Car waving to the crowd.

What am I getting myself into?

Countdown: 92 Days
September 4, 2021

Saturday morning I woke up panicking over what to wear on my date with Andrew. I had a whole closet full of nothing to wear. I called Katie for advice and she suggested we go to the mall. A couple hours later, she pulled up in front of my house to take me shopping. I climbed into her yellow Hummer and said, "You drive *this* and you've been letting me drive you around in my junker?"

She laughed and genuinely said, "I don't care about that stuff, Eden. Plus, this isn't technically my car. It's one of my dad's." *One* of my dad's. How many cars did he have? I was out of my league with these Sidwell kids.

A couple hours of shopping and quite a few bags later, we sat down to eat some lunch and began to talk about the wonder that is Andrew Wellington.

"You've gone to school with him for a while, Katie. Do you think he truly has changed?"

"I don't know. Andrew has always been kind of a mystery. He came to parties, got drunk, made out with a girl, and then the secret service would drag him out. Nobody really knew him. But he was always invited to the parties because he, well, I guess because he was *Andrew Wellington*. It didn't matter that no one really *knew* him."

"So the secret service never called the cops on an underage party? They just let him drink and break the law?" I asked.

"It wasn't their job to be the police. It was their job to keep Andrew safe. When they thought he'd had his limit, they would drag him out. They didn't care what the other kids were doing. Their services were strictly for Andrew's benefit."

I contemplated this new information for a bit.

"He told me the night of the 'small get together'," I said with air quotes, prompting laughter from Katie, "that his dad only allowed him two beers at a party anymore and that if he had more than that, 'his secret service friends'," Katie smiled again, "would take him home. Why didn't his dad make that rule sooner? Maybe Andrew wouldn't have gotten so out of control."

"Your guess is as good as mine. Maybe he was just letting Andrew deal with stuff his own way and hoped he'd come out of it on his own. Maybe he was too busy being president to be Dad. But my theory is that he didn't realize how big of a problem it was until he almost lost his election from it."

"Good point," I said, sipping the last of my pop.

We dumped our trays in the food court trashcans and walked back down the center of the mall.

"What time is Andrew picking you up?"

"7:30," I answered, nerves taking over and making my stomach churn.

She grabbed me by the arm and said, "Good. We have enough time to get you a blowout."

"A what?" I asked in confusion.

"Oh, Iowa, you have some learnin' to do!" She grabbed my arm and dragged me away to teach me.

* * * *

It turns out a "blowout" is a salon service that washes, dries, and straightens or curls your hair for you. I would have never thought of it in a million years, but I had to admit, it was pretty cool and my hair looked amazing. My mom even noticed when I walked in the door. After I explained it to her, she looked as though I had just told her I had found the fountain of youth. I had a feeling Mom would be getting a blowout soon.

I took a quick bath, did my makeup, and put on my new clothes and shoes. Katie and I had chosen white skinny jeans, a purple silk halter-top, and strappy silver sandals. When I walked out of the bathroom, my mom gasped. I must have done okay.

When the doorbell rang my heart jumped into my throat. How did I go from despising this boy to falling for him so quickly? He was good. Too good. The nagging knowledge of his playboy past lurked just below the surface, waiting to jump out and say, "I told you so!" It was really kind of a downer. I tried to suppress the beast and let myself be excited for a date with an amazing guy.

I took a deep breath and opened the door. It was a good thing I was holding onto the doorknob, because I may have swooned. He was breathtakingly beautiful. His bright blue eyes sparkled, enhanced by his sky blue, slightly fitted t-shirt and dark jeans. Andrew and his father were known for their dark hair and baby blue eyes, and tonight those features shined. When he saw me, he smiled from ear to ear, shook his head and said, "Eden, you look so good."

"You look pretty handsome yourself, Andrew."

"You ready?" he asked, taking my hand. The contact made the already present butterflies in my stomach flutter.

"Have fun, kids!" Mom called, strolling toward the door.

"We will, Dr. Warren. But don't worry, I've already finished my reading for class on Monday," Andrew said quickly.

My mom laughed. "Don't worry Andrew, I'm not grading you at the moment. But I'm glad to hear you finished your reading. That's more than I can say for Miss Eden here," she teased.

"Don't worry, ma'am," Andrew assured her, "I'll get her in line for you."

"Thank you, Andrew." She turned to me. "I like this one, Eden."

I rolled my eyes at her. "Goodbye, Mother."

Andrew shook Mom's hand in his normal gentlemanly manner and ushered me toward a chauffeured Town Car waiting on the road in front of my house. When we reached the car, he opened the door for me and whispered suggestively in my ear. "I didn't tell her *how* I'd get you in line…"

"And how is that?" I asked, flashing him a wicked smile as I climbed into the Town Car.

"Use your imagination," he teased, closing my door behind me.

Once settled into the car, I turned to Andrew and asked, "So what are we going to do?"

"Well, I figured since you're still pretty new to D.C., maybe you haven't done all the touristy stuff yet. So I thought we could go to one of my favorite places in the city. The Smithsonian," he said with a smile.

"Ooh! You read my mind! I've been meaning to go there since we moved here, but just haven't gotten around to it yet. Which one are we going to?" I silently wished for the Museum of American History.

"Which one do you want to go to?" he prompted.

Oh no. What if I said the wrong one? But I really wanted to go to the American History one the most, so I took a chance and truthfully answered, "Well, I really want to see them all, so whichever one we're going to would be fine. But the one at the top of my list would be the Museum of American History."

Andrew broke into a grin. Apparently I said the right one. "I was hoping you would say that. After our talk last week when you told me you love to watch the History Channel like me, I thought the Museum of American History would be a great first date," he explained.

First date? That meant he thought there would be more dates. The revelation made me beam. But a thought occurred to me.

"What time do they close? It's already 7:45. How can we possibly see anything, if they're even open at all?" I asked. The proud look on Andrew's face was telling. "What did you do?"

"The museum technically closes at 7:30, but I have some connections. We've been given special permission to come after closing."

I shook my head at him. "You are unbelievable. You're making a bunch of poor museum employees stay after hours just for us? Absolutely not." I crossed my arms and sat back in disgust.

"Boy, you don't let me get away with anything, do you, Oxygen?" Andrew said, shaking his head in good-natured amazement. "I promise you, nobody has to stay past their hours, and no tax money is being spent purely for our benefit." Upon this news, I uncrossed my arms, but kept my eyes squinted at him in interrogation. He shook his head again and smiled. "My father is a regular donor to the museum and he's friends with the director. She stays past closing almost every night, because it's quiet and she can get a lot of work done. There will be custodians cleaning, so lights have to be on anyway. Well, some of the lights," he added provocatively.

My heart sped up a bit.

"She trusts me to be respectful of the museum, and she understands that after closing time is easiest for my security. It's okay, really."

"Okay, you win. I guess it would be pretty cool having the museum to ourselves," I admitted.

The rest of the way there, Andrew filled me in on some of his favorite artifacts and exhibits of the museum. He assured me we would see my wish list as well, including the ruby slippers from *The Wizard of Oz*, Abraham Lincoln's famous top hat, and Thomas Edison's light bulb. His unbridled excitement was endearing. I could tell he loved history as much as I did. It was adorable.

When we pulled up to the museum, I didn't wait for Andrew to come around and open my door. Instead, I jumped out on my own in anticipation. I couldn't believe I was finally about to be in the presence of so much American history. Andrew beamed at my display of uncontained excitement as I ran around the car to meet up with him. He casually took my hand and led me to the front door. Of course there was someone waiting at the door to let us in. Was there ever anything Andrew wasn't prepared for? A uniformed, middle-aged man let us in and Andrew shook his hand.

"Mr. Wellington," he said formally.

"Sir," Andrew courteously replied.

54

First Sun

I was pretty sure some cash was exchanged in this little greeting, but they were discreet. I was still so naïve to the world of the wealthy. Andrew was a pro. But for some reason, it didn't bother me as much as I thought it would. He never flaunted his wealth. In fact, this was the first time I even noticed it.

With business attended to, Andrew turned his attention back to me, took a step back, raised his arms in the air and asked, "Where to first?"

I stepped forward, put my hands on his shoulders and answered, "Everywhere!" I took off, leaving Andrew to follow me, chuckling as he tried to keep up.

* * * *

We strolled through the entire first floor hand-in-hand, drinking in everything the museum had to offer. We had so much fun, taking turns reading the plaques, and ogling at the priceless artifacts. After visiting Julia Child's kitchen, Andrew stopped and turned toward me with uncertainty painted on his lovely face.

"Eden?" he asked. "Will you do something with me?" He swallowed audibly. I could tell whatever it was he wanted me to do with him was not going to be easy.

"Of course." I took both of his hands to comfort him and looked deeply into his eyes.

"I would like you to come upstairs with me to see my mother's inaugural gown in the *First Ladies* exhibit." He spoke the words quickly, as though he might change his mind if he didn't get them out right away.

I took a deep breath and softly answered, "I would love to see your mother's gown, Andrew."

Tears began to collect in his eyes, and I could tell he was desperately trying not to cry. I squeezed his hands and asked, "Have you ever seen the display before?"

"No," he whispered. "I haven't been able to go see it...It was too hard..." He trailed off in despair. "I didn't think I'd ever want to see it." He paused. "But with you here...I want to see it with you."

"Okay," I whispered back.

He released one hand so we could walk, but clung tightly to the other as we walked in silence. He led me to the stairwell and slowly up the stairs. He paused in front of the door and turned back to look at me for reassurance.

"Are you sure you want to do this?" I asked.

Stubborn determination replaced the apprehension in his eyes as he nodded. I nodded back. He took a deep breath and opened the door. We slowly worked our way forward with Andrew holding onto my hand as if it were his

55

lifeline. I knew the instant he caught sight of the dress because his entire body tensed and he held his breath. I moved a step closer to his side and entwined my arm around his. He gratefully squeezed my hand in response.

I followed Andrew's eyes to locate the dress. It was in a large freestanding glass case in the center of the display. I recognized it at once. When the first lady passed, news channels played glowing video tributes of the sensational lady in all of her finest moments in memoriam. My favorite featured the first lady, clad in the dress before me, dancing with the president at the Inaugural Ball. The dress was truly amazing. The full-length, lavender, one-shouldered silk gown adorned with thousands of Swarovski crystals shimmered in the subtle after-hours lighting. It took my breath away.

When I was finally able to tear my eyes away from it and refocus my attention on Andrew, my heart broke for him. He stared at the gown as if his mother would appear inside of it as silent tears streaked his beautiful face; the face mirrored in the photos of his mother surrounding the gown.

Andrew dropped my hand and briskly walked back out the door we had just entered. I followed behind him, and when I reached him, I put both of my arms around his waist and rested my head on his back. He turned into my embrace and silently shuddered as his tears continued to fall. I pressed him to me as he let out his anguish. I didn't shush him. I wanted him to know it was okay to cry with me. I didn't tell him it was okay. It wasn't okay for him to lose his mother so early in life. I just held him.

"I'm sorry, Eden," he eventually said through his tears. "You must think I'm such a baby. You've lost your father too and here I am—" He broke off, desperately trying to mop up his tears with the palms of this hands.

"You are not a baby, Andrew. I never even met my father, so it's completely different." I took his hand away from his face to stop him from wiping away his tears. "Don't ever be sorry for crying for your mom," I warned. "You have every right to mourn her. She was remarkable."

"She was," he said with a smile breaking through the tears, hands on my hips. "She was the glue that held our family together." He took a deep breath before continuing. "She insisted on the three of us sitting down to dinner together every night we could, even when we moved into the White House. If Dad couldn't be there, which was a lot, it was just the two of us. But we were used to it since Dad had always been gone a lot for the military. It was always just Mom and me. I took it for granted at the time, you know? Having such a great mom. I thought she'd always be there..." He paused for a moment, but I didn't think he had any tears left. "The morning of the accident, we ate breakfast together. Mom refused to let the kitchen staff cook me breakfast if she was home. She always said a mother should cook breakfast for her own child.

First Sun

That morning she made me pancakes. When she went to the cupboard to get the syrup and realized there wasn't any, she cursed out loud, then clapped her hand over her mouth. She hated swearing in front of me." He smiled at the memory. "She said we would just have to make do with what we had. All we could find was grape jelly. So there we sat, eating pancakes with grape jelly on them…" He trailed off and after a little while whispered, "They were the best pancakes I ever had." I slowly stroked his arm with my fingertips, and gazed into his eyes.

"I've never told anyone that. Not even my father," he said, as though surprised himself.

I smiled up at him tenderly, and he leaned down to kiss me. As his mouth met mine, the world disappeared. It was only Andrew and me. As he deepened the kiss, I could feel the moisture on his cheeks and taste the salt of his tears. I could actually taste his sorrow. The intimacy of it overwhelmed me and I teared up myself. The feeling of my hot tears on his cheeks sparked the return of Andrew's tears, which mingled with mine between our kiss. Andrew must have felt the connection as well, because he began to kiss me almost frantically, as though I might pull away and the connection would be broken. I matched his urgency to reassure him. He pushed me up against the wall and pressed against me in angst.

"Eden," he breathed, as he pulled his mouth away to kiss my neck, my bare shoulders, under my ears, everywhere he could find. Every time his mouth connected to my skin, he left tears behind. The pleasure of the sensation was almost unbearable. I pressed into him and explored his upper body with my fingers. Up and down his muscular arms, into his hair, down his back to the top of his jeans. He moaned. "Eden," he repeated, letting his hands roam down my sides to my hips, returning his mouth to mine, consuming me. His hands stopped abruptly on my hips and he stepped back, pushing gently away from me. "I'm so sorry," he said, still trying to catch his breath.

"What are you sorry for?" I asked, consciously aware that my heart was about to beat out of my chest.

"I'm sorry I let that go so far," he said sadly, shaking his head.

"Andrew, I'm a big girl. I could've stopped it too. But I didn't, because I didn't want to. That was…" I said, trailing off at the realization that there weren't words sufficient enough to describe the sensation.

"Freaking amazing?" he said seductively. Oh that face…standing there still tear-stained…lips swollen from the intensity of our kiss…he had never looked sexier.

"Oh yeah," I answered, nodding my head in agreement.

He came back to me, took me in his arms and held me to him. "Oh, Eden. I've never felt this way before." He held my head to his chest with one hand,

and softly stroked my back with his other hand. Neither one of us could let go. We just wanted to be near one another. I listened to Andrew's heartbeat and after a while, it began to slow.

He stepped back and looked into my eyes. "These tears..." he began as he attempted to clean them up by brushing his thumbs under my eyes, "are they for me, or am I missing something?" He sat down on the floor with his back against the wall and pulled me down in front of him between his legs so my back rested on his chest.

"A little bit of both," I answered. "I was crying because I felt your pain. It was surprisingly difficult for me to feel your sadness. I couldn't help but think how we just met and I shouldn't feel this way so soon. It took me by surprise."

"Yeah. I know exactly what you mean. Eden, I never thought I would come here at all, let alone tell someone about such a private moment I had with my mom. I did both with you. Even though we just technically met a few weeks ago, I feel like I've known you my whole life. It felt right standing here with you, telling you my most private thoughts. Crying with you," he added quietly.

I grabbed his hands and wrapped them around my waist as tightly as I could. I felt him take a deep breath and let it out through his mouth with his chin resting on the top of my head.

"Andrew, I'm really sorry I never got to meet your mom."

He tugged on me so I would turn around. When I did, he tucked my hair behind my ear and said, "Me too. She would have really liked you." Then his face lit up and he said, "You know what? Come meet my mother." He stood up, took me by the hand, and led me back through the doors.

"Andrew, are you sure you want to go back?"

"Yes. I'm okay now," he said. "Thanks to you." He leaned over and kissed me lightly on the lips before leading me down to the beginning of his mother's exhibit. It was set up like a timeline, beginning with a picture of her as a baby. I could already see the resemblance to Andrew in her baby blues and said so.

"Just wait until some of the later pictures. She's kind of like me with long hair." His favorite portion of the timeline was obviously the part he shared with her. I couldn't help but gush over his baby pictures. He was the cutest kid I had ever seen. As he took me down memory lane, Andrew's sorrow disappeared and he glowed with love, the same love shining through his mother's smile in any picture she shared with Andrew. It was endearing to see him so alight with passion for his mother. It made me adore him even more.

As we made our way to the end of the timeline, I wondered if Andrew would talk about the accident. I didn't have to wait long to find out.

"Do you know the story of my mother's death?" he asked, surprisingly calm.

"Only what they reported on TV and in the news."

"That's pretty much the gist of it. You know, I used to be so mad at her. She knew better than to take a car out on her own. She was the first lady. She had no business driving a car alone. But my mom loved cars. She loved driving. But most of all, she loved normalcy. Her biggest worry was that she would lose touch with herself if she gave in to all of the rules of the presidency. Of course, when she wanted a cappuccino—you know, the kind at the gas station that comes out of a machine?"

"Yes—I'm a fan myself."

He smiled sadly and continued. "Well, when she wanted a cappuccino, she didn't want anyone to go get it for her. She didn't want anyone to drive her. She just wanted to drive to the gas station on her own and get one. Her secret service agents did everything they could to talk her out of it. She wouldn't have it. So they let her drive, but insisted on having a car in front of and behind hers.

"I begged her to let me come, but she wouldn't let me. She said she'd get me a treat. Looking back, I think she knew it was wrong. That's why she wouldn't let me come. If I would've gone with her…" I took his hand in mine again and we slid down to the floor, sitting cross-legged, facing one another, but holding hands.

"As she traveled down 16th, she must have gotten frustrated that she couldn't find a gas station. The police concluded…" He stopped to swallow hard.

"That she looked down at the dash to adjust the navigation, ran a stoplight, and was broadsided by a speeding car," I finished for him.

He nodded. "The doctors said she died instantly, that she didn't feel a thing." He stood up and walked over to the pictures showing the totaled car. "Will you walk with me?"

I jumped up in answer and went to his side. We walked down the rest of the timeline depicting the death and funeral of Angela Wellington, hand-in-hand. He didn't cry again, but studied everything intensely. I had seen all of the pictures in the display, yet they somehow had different meaning now. These were not just pictures of the beloved first lady's tragic death anymore. These were pictures of Andrew's mom's death.

When we approached the end of the exhibit, we stopped one more time in front of the inaugural gown. I noticed for the first time that next to the dress was a small, clear stand, holding the jewelry Angela Wellington had worn to the Inaugural Ball. The rose gold and tear-dropped shaped diamond earrings and necklace were stunning. But it was the ring between the two earrings that really caught my attention.

"Andrew, is that your mother's…" I couldn't finish my question in fear of bringing more heartache to Andrew.

"Yes, it's my mother's wedding ring. When the Smithsonian called to ask to put Mom's Inaugural gown on display, my dad came to me to ask my opinion. I told him it didn't matter to me, as long as I never had to see the thing again. He told me he was thinking about giving her wedding ring to the museum as well. He didn't know what to do with it, and thought that the public may want to see it in memory of her. I again told him I didn't care. I didn't even want to think about her, what did I care about some stupid dress or ring? Dad told me I might feel different about it someday. He said he would give them the ring on the condition that when I met someone I wanted to marry, I could have it back to give to her. I didn't think I would ever need to worry about that." He turned to me. "Maybe I was wrong," he said, almost to himself. "Come on, let's get out of here." He kissed his fingers and gently touched the glass box holding his mother's gown, then took my hand and led me through the doors of the *First Ladies* exhibit, moving on to the next chunk of history.

Even though Andrew returned to his usual charming self for the remainder of the night, I could sense an ache for his mother deep in his soul, brought closer to the surface by his encounter with her exhibit. Perhaps it moved him one step closer to healing his broken heart.

Countdown: 91 Days
September 5, 2021

That night in bed, I tossed and turned. I couldn't stop thinking about Andrew. Everything made more sense now. He truly was a good person; he just didn't know how to handle the sudden fame that came with his father's presidency and the sorrow of his mother's unexpected death. Either would be hard enough to deal with on its own, let alone both at the same time. And God, was he amazing. He was not just a pretty face. There was so much more there, and I couldn't help but think that I had only seen the tip of the iceberg.

And mmm...that kiss.

I turned over yet again and stared at the ceiling. My stomach still turned somersaults every time I thought of it. I wished I could hear his voice right then. As if summoned by my longing, my phone chimed. A text? I looked at the clock. At 1:15 in the morning? I retrieved my phone from my bedside table and flushed at the sight of Andrew's name and the words, "Are you up?" next to it.

I immediately woke up my phone and texted him back, fingers flying.

Me: *How did you know?*

Andrew: *Cause I can't stop thinking about you long enough to go to sleep and was hoping you were having the same problem.* My heart sped up.

Me: *Me either. Tonight was amazing.*

Andrew: *YOU are amazing.*

Me: *You're making me blush.*

Andrew: *Good. You look hot when you blush.*

61

Andrew: *Correction—You look hot all the time. I just like it when you blush because it makes me think you like me.*

Me: *I do like you.*

Andrew: *I like you too. A lot.*

Me: ☺

Andrew: *Did you just give me a smiley face???? LOL*

Me: *I was speechless. That doesn't happen often. LOL???*

Andrew: *LMFAO* ☺

Me: *Now I really am laughing out loud.*

Andrew: *Good. It's better than making you cry like I did earlier tonight.*

Me: *I'm glad you let me share that with you.*

Andrew: *Me too. I miss you.*

Me: *I miss you too.*

Andrew: *Can I come over?*

Me: *I doubt it. The White House is probably pretty difficult to escape from unnoticed.*

Andrew: *It is. Damn it. I want to kiss you good night.*

Me: *You did a pretty thorough job of that earlier tonight.*

Me: *Not that I'm complaining. I could take some more goodnighting.*

Andrew: *I don't think I'll ever get enough of you, Eden.*

Me: *You're not helping to calm me down for sleeping.*

Andrew: *Sorry. I think the only way I'd be able to sleep tonight is if you were in my arms. And if you were in my arms, I wouldn't be able to sleep for other reasons.*

Me: *Very true. I would love to not sleep with you, Andrew.*

Andrew: *Now I'm coming over. There are not enough secret service agents in the world to keep me away now.*

Me: *Good night, Andrew. Sweet dreams.*

Andrew: *Good night, baby. I'll miss you.* His use of the endearment, baby, got my heart pumping again. I liked it. I liked it a lot.

Andrew: *Can I see you tomorrow?*

Me: *Yes, please.*

Andrew: *I'll call you tomorrow. Or should I say later today?*

Me: *Talk to you tomorrow (later today).*

I drummed my fingers on my bedside table. He's not going to text back? That was really it? I stared at my phone, willing it to chime with a new message. Instead, it rang. "Hello?" I said breathlessly.

"I couldn't go to sleep without hearing your voice one more time."

"You read my mind."

"Good night, baby." He paused as if thinking, then said, "I wish I could kiss you."

"Me too." Silence. "Andrew?"

"Yes?"

"Just seeing if you were still there."

"I'm having a hard time saying goodbye."

"Me too."

He hesitated. "I'll hang up now, but I'll call you later, okay?"

"Okay. Bye, Andrew."

"Bye, baby. Sweet dreams."

With that, we both finally hung up. *Oh my gosh.* What was happening? If I would've heard anyone have a conversation like that a few weeks ago, I would've thrown up in disgust. Now I sat holding my phone, struggling against every ounce of my body not to call him back again. It was pathetic. I groaned, flopped back on my bed, and covered my face with my pillow, willing myself to go to sleep.

* * * *

The next morning, I woke up still thinking about Andrew. I remembered our texts and quick conversation from the night before and snatched my phone from my bedside table. I frowned in disappointment that there was nothing new. This was crazy. I could not get him out of my head. I never thought I'd be one of those girls who would fall head over heels over a guy. But I was certainly headed down that road.

It was only 7:00 in the morning. It would be hours before he'd call. I had to do something to get my mind off of him. I wanted to go for a run, but I needed to eat breakfast first. I headed down the stairs to find a note from Mom telling me she went to the gym and then was going to run some errands. She left a list of chores for me to do before I left the house for any reason. I sighed. So much for my run.

I poured myself a bowl of cereal and sat at the breakfast bar eating and thinking. What did Andrew see in me? He seemed to reciprocate my feelings, so he obviously saw *something*. But what? He was rich, smart, witty, and absolutely gorgeous. I mean, girls swooned when he walked by. All of these attributes alone would be enough to put him out of my league. But to top it all off, his father was the President of the United States. He was famous. Everyone in the country, probably everyone in the world, knew who he was. Girls fantasized about him and guys wanted to be him. And he chose me? It was just too inconceivable. Soon he would figure all of this out on his own and it would be over. The thought truly scared me. To reassure myself, I picked up my phone and reread through our texts from last night. They did not fail to reassure me. Wow. If you didn't know this was Andrew Wellington, son-of-the-president, you would think this boy was head over heels for me. Why couldn't he be? Why was I so self-deprecating? Ahhh! I shook my head as I took my empty bowl to the sink.

Okay, Eden. Chill out. Do your chores and stop thinking about Andrew Wellington.

I was able to quickly dust and vacuum the downstairs before heading back to my room to clean it. It really wasn't too bad due to the fact that I was a neat freak, but it wasn't up to my standards. I made my bed, straightened my dresser and bedside table, and decided to vacuum. I put in my ear buds and cranked up my iPod to some old school Garth Brooks and jammed out while I vacuumed. Garth Brooks was my absolute favorite. I listened to all country, mostly modern country, but I grew up listening to Garth Brooks. My mom was a fan and listened to him my whole childhood. I knew every one of his songs by heart. I sang *Friends in Low Places* at the top of my lungs, pushing and pulling the vacuum cleaner as though it were a dance partner.

I've got friends in low places
Where the whiskey drowns
And the beer chases my blues away
And I'll be okay

I swung the vacuum around to do the hallway and stopped dead in my tracks. My mouth must have been hanging open, because Andrew got up off the chair in the corner of my room, walked over to me, and put his finger under my chin to push it closed.

He then took my ear buds out so they fell to the floor, put his arms around my waist, and said, "Hey, Oxygen," with a gigantic grin on his face. It wasn't even a smirk. It was a huge, slaphappy grin.

"Ummm...Andrew...how long have you been here?" I asked in utter horror, face burning.

"Long enough to see the cutest thing I've seen in my entire life," he muttered into my neck and began to laugh so hard that his entire body shook and I felt the puffs of air come out of his mouth onto my neck, giving me goose bumps all over. "Oh. My. God. Eden, you are the sexiest girl I've ever met in my life," he said between breaths.

I swatted at him in fury. "Quit making fun of me! Some people actually call someone before coming to her house. Especially at 8:00 in the morning! I'm still in my pajamas, you big fat jerk!"

"I am not making fun of you. I have never been more serious." He picked me up, threw me over his shoulder with ease while I swatted at his butt, and gently lowered me onto my bed. He crawled up next to me, took me into his arms, and continued to laugh. I swatted at him some more and struggled to free myself from his hold.

"Okay, okay, I'm sorry. I'll stop." He pressed his lips together as hard as he could to keep from laughing until he couldn't contain it any longer and let it all out, convulsing in laughter yet again. I finally struggled out of his hold, grabbed my pillow from under his head and proceeded to hit him over the head with it repeatedly, laughing right along with him without abandon. He finally stopped laughing and his face turned serious in an instant. I froze mid-hit. Andrew grasped my wrists gently and pulled me onto the bed beside him again.

He leaned over me, pressing the bottom half of my body down with his, and whispered, "Eden, I'm serious. You have no idea how turned on I am right now. You are so unbelievably sexy and you don't even know it." He stroked my face so lightly he was barely touching it. "Why do you ever wear makeup? You are flawless." He kissed me gently, first on my eyelids, then down the edge of the plane of my face, working his way back to my lips, kissing them once again before murmuring, "I'm sorry. I really didn't mean to eavesdrop—"

"Peeping Tom would be a better name for it," I scolded.

He ignored me, continuing. "But if you would've known I was there, I would have missed out on seeing your little performance." I swatted at him again. "And it was a treat. I felt like I got a glimpse of the real Eden. What was really cool was that I felt like the real Eden wasn't so different from my Eden." He looked into my eyes, searching. "You're pretty real with me, aren't you?"

"What would be the point if I wasn't?"

"Very true." He looked deep in thought.

"What are you thinking about?"

"I'm thinking about how I want you to be my girlfriend, but I'm not quite sure how to ask you without it sounding like a line you'd hear on the Disney channel."

My heart skipped a beat. "Why?" I asked, dumbfounded. "Why would *you* want *me* to be your girlfriend?"

"Because you are the most amazing person I've ever met. You're not afraid to be who you are. You're comfortable in your own skin. You sing one hell of a Garth Brooks song." I smacked him. "You're beautiful." He smoothed my unruly hair and tucked it behind my ear. "You don't take my shit. That's my favorite one," he added with a smile. "You're brilliant, you're not materialistic, you love history…how many more reasons do you need, because I could go on for a pretty long time…from what I can tell you actually eat, even McDonald's, I can cry in front of you without feeling like a loser, you're an amazing kisser—"

"Okay, okay, okay. I surrender!" I conceded. "I surrender to you whole-heartedly," I whispered and kissed him.

"I'll take that as a yes," he murmured into my lips. We melted into the kiss and as Andrew's hands wandered down my back, I remembered I wasn't wearing a bra. I felt the intensity of his kiss deepen as he slipped his hand under the back of my tank top and rubbed my bare back. Oh my gosh, his hand felt so good. My entire body was in tune to Andrew's and I just wanted to lose myself in him. He pulled away, chuckling, and rested his forehead on mine. "Eden, we have to get out of your bed," he said huskily.

"I know," I said, reconnecting with his lips and exploring his muscular back.

Andrew reluctantly pulled away and sat up. "Eden, I'm going to get up now, because this is not a good idea. I'm going to leave this room and you are going to get dressed, because if I have to look at you in your pajamas one more second, I will seriously explode. Okay?"

I nodded. I didn't trust myself to speak or I would have told him he was not going to leave, he was going to stay right here and continue what we started.

"We can go do whatever you want, okay?"

I nodded again.

"Okay. I'll be on the other side of this door, wishing I were on this side." He stood up, turned to walk out of the room, stopped, and turned back. He looked at me and groaned with his hands on the sides of his head, as though at war with himself. He swiftly came back to me, kissed me on the lips, kissed me on my neck, moved aside my tank top strap and kissed me on the shoulder, put my strap back, then tilted my head up with his finger and kissed me on the lips one more time before quickly walking out the door and closing it behind him.

I couldn't move.

"Eden?"

"Yeah?"

"Have you moved?"

"No."

I heard him chuckle. "Are you going to make me wait out here all day?"

"You can come back in if you want."

"I'm not walking back in that room, Eden."

"All right. I'm moving," I grumbled before getting up and quickly getting dressed for running.

When I opened the door, Andrew sat leaning against the opposite wall, messing with his phone. He looked up and smiled brightly. "What are we going to do?"

"Go for a run."

"Great idea. I need a run, too. I'll need to change though. How about we go running on the track at my house?"

"At *your* house? You mean the White House?" I asked, astonished.

"Yeah. I'd have a heck of a time talking my agents into letting me run in an unsecured location. President Clinton used to jog near the White House on the road and caused traffic problems, so he had a track put around the South Lawn. It's only a quarter of a mile, but it gets the job done. It's nice and spongy, so it's better for your legs than running on concrete. I run on it all the time."

"You're just a walking White House encyclopedia, aren't you?" I teased.

"It's interesting to me." He shrugged his shoulders. "Sometimes I wonder why I got so lucky to live there. There's so much history. It's humbling. My dad and I are just specks of dust in the history of the White House," he said modestly.

"Andrew, your father is referred to as one of the most beloved presidents of all time. And you are his son. The two of you are not just a speck of dust. You are history in the making." As I spoke the words, the reality of them shook me to the core. The enormity of Andrew's fame all came crashing down around me at that moment. I felt like I was suffocating. I needed air. Immediately. "If anyone is just a speck of dust, it's me," I murmured, looking away from his greatness as though I were not worthy.

I ran down the stairs and out the front door, only to freeze at the sight of Andrew's Town Car and secret service agents standing guard at the door. This just reinforced my insecurities. I turned right around and slammed through the door back into the house.

Andrew had followed me down the stairs and watched me in confusion as

I paced around the living room. "What just happened, Eden?" he asked, eyebrows crinkled together in worry.

"Andrew, don't you see it? You are the son of the frickin' president! And not just any president. One of the most successful and beloved presidents of all time. I'm a nobody. A *nobody*, damn it! You and your father are currently making history. Your names will be in the history books of tomorrow. I'm just another civilian, living a boring civilian life. I'm not *worthy* of you."

Andrew blanched as though I had physically struck him. "*Whoa!* You stop right there, Eden. So my dad and I are famous. So what? How does that have anything to do with you and me?"

I ignored his question and resumed pacing.

"Eden, fame doesn't matter," he continued, getting more and more heated with each word. "It's just an illusion created by the public who desperately need a distraction from the monotony of everyday life. So they put people on a pedestal. The only reason I'm on that stupid pedestal is because my dad just happens to be President of the United States. But does that really make me any different from anyone else?" He paused, clearly waiting for me to answer. When I didn't, he grabbed my arm to stop me from pacing. "Does it?" he asked, pulling me around to face him.

"I guess not," I admitted.

He gently traced the outline of my face with a finger, mollifying my insecurity with his touch. "That's right. It doesn't. I'm just a person like anyone else." He took me into his arms and pulled me close. When he continued speaking, he sounded almost sad. "What does fame do for anyone anyway? It doesn't make you superhuman. It doesn't make you invincible…"

I stood face to face with one of the most famous people in the world. Only he was right; I didn't think of him as famous anymore. He was my Andrew. My *boyfriend*. I sighed in concession. "Okay, you win. You're just a regular person."

"Thank you," Andrew whispered.

"Just a regular, gorgeous person with a president for a father," I clarified to Andrew's scowl. "But that's the problem. Just when I'm able to forget about the whole son-of-the-president thing, something happens that reminds me and it freaks me out."

He pointed to himself with that smirk I love so much lighting up his face and said, "Regular person, Eden. Just a really famous house."

I smacked him on the shoulder in jest and he picked me up and twirled me around in a circle before kissing me tenderly. "Now let's go do something very normal, like run," he said, taking my hand.

"At the White House," I added and we walked out of the house laughing at

First Sun

the irony.

Countdown: 91 Days
September 5, 2021

I sat quietly in the car with Andrew's hand on my knee, looking out the window as the Town Car turned from Pennsylvania Avenue into the White House grounds. Andrew could sense my apprehension and stroked my knee with his thumb, letting me take it all in. The car drove right up to the North Portico and stopped in front of the president's front door. This was the White House, and I was about to go in, not as a tourist, but as a guest.

Andrew turned to me and asked, "Is this a little weird for you?"

"A *little* weird?" I repeated, staring at him through wide eyes.

He chuckled and climbed out the door opened for him by someone I couldn't see. When I looked back to my door, it was already opened as well.

A man in a fancy uniform offered me his hand and said, "Miss?" I shyly took his hand and stepped out onto the drive. I blushed at the state of my appearance while accepting this formal gesture. I was in my running clothes. I hadn't showered for crying out loud!

As if Andrew could sense my feelings of inadequacy, he stepped to my side, put an arm around my waist and whispered into my ear, "You look adorable in running shorts."

"Hmph! I can't believe I let you talk me into this! I don't look fit to visit the White House for the first time!" I hissed.

"Eden, you're just stopping into your boyfriend's house so he can change into running clothes. We're not attending a state dinner." As we walked through the North Portico Entrance holding hands, he nonchalantly added, "Yet."

"Welcome to my home," Andrew said then in mock modesty as I stepped onto the pink and white marble tile of the Entrance Hall. I dropped his hand and took a few more tentative steps forward, as though I could break the historic

70

house with my normal stride. I slowly turned in a circle, taking in the enormity of the space. There was little furniture, only a few red-upholstered Queen Ann style chairs evenly spaced around the perimeter of the room against the marble-paneled walls. Six immensely tall columns seemed to hold up the decoratively molded ceiling beams that separated the Entrance Hall from the red-carpeted Cross Hall. Layers upon layers of intricate plaster molding around the ceiling drew my eyes directly to the grandest chandelier I had ever seen. Straight ahead open doors led into the famous Green, Blue and Red Rooms.

"You okay?" Andrew asked, trying to act casual.

"Yes. I'm just taking it all in." I smiled at him in reassurance. "Andrew, this is a dream come true. I'm trying really hard to act like I see this every day, but I don't, so I can't. I'm sorry."

"Oh, Oxygen. Don't be sorry. I knew this would be weird for you. But the fact that you love history so much and I can give you this experience means a lot to me. Take your time. I want you to enjoy yourself and not feel rushed." He paused. "But remember, this is only the beginning. You'll be here a lot from now on," he said thickly, almost in embarrassment.

"I can only hope so, Andrew. But not because it means I'll get to come back to the White House a lot. Because I get to be with you."

He turned to me and took both of my hands in his. We hungrily looked into one another's eyes and then kissed gently. Andrew pulled away, smiled, and said, "Are you ready for your tour?"

"Ooh! I get a tour?"

"Of course. It is your first time here, after all. But since this place is ginormous, we'll start small. You've seen the Entrance Hall. Come upstairs with me and I'll show you around the family residence. You know, the stuff they don't show on the public tours."

He pulled on my arm and led me to the left toward the red-carpeted Grand Staircase. The bottom of the stairs was a strange shape, beginning in a U-shape, then straightening out for the main part of the stairs. While we ascended the iron and gold-banistered stairs, Andrew comically pointed out the different portraits, "Gerald Ford, FDR, yada yada yada..." as I giggled.

When we reached the top of the stairs, I stopped again to get a good look. The yellow-painted walls were adorned with three-tiered wall sconces, and white molding accented the bottom half of the walls. "So what am I looking at?" I asked.

"Let's see, straight ahead is the Treaty Room." Gasp from me, smile from Andrew. "Down that hall to the left is the East Sitting Hall, and those doors on either side of the hall are the Lincoln Bedroom and Queen Bedroom." More gasps and smiles. "And to the right..." Andrew busted out laughing. "I'm sorry, you are just too frickin' cute right now. You should see your face. You're like a kid in a candy store." I punched him lightly on the arm. "Ouch! Okay, okay…to the right is the Center Hall leading to the First Family Residence." He nodded his head to illustrate the end of his little show and tell. "Where to first, little lady?" He offered me his elbow like we were in an old western movie or something, but I was too stunned by my surroundings to make fun of him.

"Lincoln Bedroom," I said definitively.

"Good choice," Andrew agreed.

We walked down the hall to the left a short distance. Andrew opened the door to the legendary room and I reverently stepped in. The opulence of the room was overwhelming. It was decorated in a gold, purple, and green color palette and the diamond patterned wallpaper and floral carpet that would clash under any other circumstance just added to the majesty. But it was the famous bed that stood out the most. Luscious purple fabric and lace hung from an oval-shaped, gold-gilded tester, framing the ornately carved wooden headboard. I crossed directly to the bed and sat tentatively on the edge, brushing my fingers against the ivory silk linens.

"Did you know that Lincoln probably never even slept in that bed?"

"Really?" I asked, disappointedly rising from the bed.

"Yeah. He didn't sleep in this room at all. It was his office. But a lot of the other furniture in here was used by Lincoln."

"Did he use this couch?" I asked, approaching a gold, damask silk upholstered couch trimmed in dark wood.

"Almost certainly. Are you a Lincoln fan?"

"He's my favorite president," I said automatically without thinking. When I realized what I had just done I tried to quickly correct the mistake by adding, "Until your father of course."

"Eden, you can't even compare my father to Lincoln. He can be your favorite. It's all right." He smiled sincerely and I knew it really was okay. "Look at this." He pulled me over to a desk in the corner. On it stood a framed copy of the Gettysburg Address. "It's written in Lincoln's own hand. It's one of only five in existence." I went to pick it up and stopped myself. "It's okay, go ahead," Andrew prompted, amused.

I picked it up gingerly, as if it could disintegrate in my hands. I couldn't believe I was holding a document written by Abraham Lincoln, in his actual handwriting. The emotional tears that welled in my eyes took me by surprise, but I was able to stop them before they spilled over.

"This really does mean a lot to you, doesn't it?" Andrew asked in amazement.

"Yes," I whispered as I carefully set the Gettysburg Address back on the desk.

"In that case, follow me. There's something really special I want to show you," he said excitedly.

I followed him out of the Lincoln Bedroom and down the Center Hall to the second door past the staircase we had just climbed. The door was open, so Andrew pushed past it, through a tinny, bare room about the size of a closet, through another door into another closet-sized room with a window at the end. "Come here," he said, his eyes alight with anticipation. I obeyed and he put his hands on my hips to position me in front of the window at the end of the tiny room.

The view out the window was outstanding. In the center of the North Lawn stood a nondescript fountain surrounded by bed flowers. The perfectly green manicured lawn met up to the street separating the White House grounds from a public park.

"What do you think?" he asked, clearly expecting a certain response.

I shook my head in confusion. "I don't understand. Besides the great view, what's so special about this spot?" I asked, gesturing to the underwhelming room.

"This," Andrew murmured into my ear, "is where Abraham Lincoln gave many of his speeches. In fact, this is the very spot he stood on to give his last public address." My mouth dropped open and I grabbed onto the windowsill as goose bumps erupted all over my body. Andrew must have felt them, because he rubbed my arms.

I turned into Andrew and hugged him, resting my head on his chest. "Thank you, Andrew." He rubbed my back in response and kissed the top of my head. I stood there, happily listening to Andrew's heartbeat, standing in the spot that Abraham Lincoln himself stood years ago.

"Do you want to see my room?" Andrew asked shyly, releasing me. "I need to change."

I smiled and nodded, excitement filling my stomach. He led me through the first little door, but not out into the hall. Instead, he went through a door to the side into what had to be his room.

"Well that wasn't very far."

He laughed and walked around his room kicking clothes out of the way in search of something. "Yeah, that little hall used to be closets. Now it's just basically a hall, so they named it the Closet Hall."

"Creative name," I mused.

"Ha. We should put you in charge of naming the rooms from now on."

"I'm up to the task," I said distractedly, looking around in amazement. This was not just Andrew's room. This room had belonged to a number of presidential offspring over the past two centuries. "So who's slept in this room in the past? Surely other first kids."

"Yeah, lots of them. But my two favorites are Willie Lincoln and John Kennedy Jr."

"You have got to be freaking kidding me...and now Andrew Wellington."

"Normal guy, remember?" he smirked. "A normal guy who can't find his damn shoes..." He continued to hunt through his room until he located them and said, "I'm no Willie Lincoln or JFK Jr."

"Nope. You're Andrew. *My* favorite first son."

He smiled charmingly and headed over to a dresser against the wall. He rummaged through the drawers a bit before selecting a white and red Ohio State t-shirt and black shorts.

"Ohio State? Really?" I shook my head at him in mock disappointment.

"Hey now, don't be a hater, Oxygen. I grew up in Ohio." He thumped his chest twice in pride and I laughed at his little display of testosterone.

"Now what about you?" He narrowed his eyes in contemplation. "You're dad played for Iowa and you lived in Cedar Rapids...must be a Hawkeye fan."

"Born and bred."

He wrinkled his nose in distaste. "At least it's a Big Ten school. And since you're dad played for them, I suppose I can forgive you."

"But I haven't forgiven you yet, have I?"

Andrew's eyes lit up in surprise and he swatted my butt with his Ohio State shirt.

"I have some t-shirts of my own," I said, laughing. "There's one in particular that you might like." I smiled at the thought of Andrew's face when I showed up at school donning the shirt I wore to the OSU versus Iowa game last season that read, "OS*Who*?"

"Oh yeah? You're lucky you're hot. I don't care what you're wearing. Even if it is an Iowa shirt." I blushed at the compliment as he pulled me close and slid a hand from my cheek into my hair making my entire body tingle in excitement. "I looked your dad up. He was a legend at Iowa. The entire campus basically shut down for a week when he died."

I nodded indifferently. I knew the story. I just didn't feel connected to it. I couldn't feel sad over losing someone I never knew.

Andrew stroked my cheek with his thumb. "I'm sorry he never got to meet you. He would've been really proud." I smiled up at him and he leaned in to give me a quick kiss. "I'll be right back. I'm going to go into the bathroom to change. Into my Ohio shirt." I playfully grabbed for his shirt as he bolted toward the bathroom.

Chuckling to myself, I took advantage of Andrew's absence to explore his

74

room. I wandered around the room still marveling at the fact that this was his room in the *White House*. It was pretty fancy for a teenaged boy. The white walls had the signature White House molding on the bottom half and detailed crown molding around the ceiling. Two arches, one around built-in shelves, and the other around a door flanked a white marble fireplace on the west wall. Most of the wooden floor was covered with a gold, blue and green colored oriental-looking rug. My eyes were drawn to Andrew's bed. It had an antique carved wooden headboard and green and gold plaid bedding. My legs carried me over to his bed of their own accord and I shyly ran my hand over his pillow. This was where Andrew slept. Last night, he texted me from here. It made my heart beat faster and I could feel my face turn bright red.

I turned away from his bed to collect myself and noticed a Sidwell basketball poster from last year hung on the wall. Its newness stood out like a sore thumb against the historic walls. But it reinforced Andrew's argument that he was just a normal person living in a historic house. I smiled and ran my finger over the poster to find Andrew. It wasn't difficult. There he was, looking just as gorgeous as ever next to all of the other ordinary boys. It really wasn't even fair to compare him to anyone else. I could not think of one other person you could place next to Andrew and have him even come close to Andrew's beauty. And he chose me. I shook my head before I could start thinking about how I wasn't worthy of him. I already got in trouble for that once today.

As I continued to look around the room, a silver picture frame on the shelf caught my eye. I walked over and picked it up to get a closer look. It was a close-up of Andrew and his mother laughing together. The picture should have evoked joy, but instead, it made me incredibly sad. The pure maternal love pouring out of Angela Wellington's eyes conflicted with the haunting notion that soon she would become nothing but a faded memory. Andrew came up behind me, put his arms around my waist and rested his chin on my shoulder.

"Andrew, I'm sorry...I..." I said, frantically trying to put the picture back where I found it.

"No, no...it's okay," he said encouragingly. He removed a hand from around me to stop me from setting the frame down, before placing it back on my stomach. "That's my favorite picture of my mom and me. It's from my 12th birthday party, right after dad's inauguration." *And right before her death.* The unsaid words hung in the air between us.

"Andrew, it's so beautiful. She was so happy. You were so happy together." I gently put the picture down in its spot and turned around in Andrew's arms. "Are you okay?" I asked, cocking my head to the side.

"Yes. With you, I'm okay." He looked so sincere. He kissed my forehead, picked me up by the waist and threw me over his shoulder for the second time that day. He sure knew how to lighten the mood.

"Andrew!" I said, giggling. "Put me down!"

"Fine." He swatted my butt. "But you owe me a run."

* * * *

"This path is a dream to run on," I said to Andrew, sprightly jogging next to him. "You were right. It's very spongy!"

Andrew laughed at my enthusiasm and said, "You're the only person I know who is this happy while running."

"It makes me feel good!" I sprinted ahead of him and called back, "What's the matter? Can't keep up?"

"Oh, I can keep up," he panted, "but maybe I don't want to..." he said suggestively.

"Why wouldn't you want to keep up?" I asked, confused.

"Because the view back here is amazing!" He looked me up and down in appraisal and shook his head. "Yep. I could run back here forever."

I giggled and purposely exaggerated my long gait and wiggled my bottom.

"Mmmm...yes...that is very motivating!" he said, grinning.

"My turn," I said, slowing down to let him pass me. "I see what you mean," I shouted.

Andrew hammed it up just as I had, only he actually tore off his shirt and threw it to the side of the track. I gasped audibly, and could almost see his smile from the back of his head. I slowed for a moment in shock of his beauty. It was the first time I had seen him shirtless, and it was a sight to behold. I had never seen a more sculpted, perfect back. I'd always known he was muscular. I could tell even when he was fully clothed. But seeing it out in the open like this was something entirely different. His tan back glistened with sweat and his running shorts hung just a little bit too low on his hips, revealing the waistband of his Under Armor compression underwear. The way his calf muscles flexed and extended with his even gait made my heart palpitate. I stopped running and bent over, putting my hands on my knees to catch my breath.

Somehow Andrew sensed my absence and turned around. He yelled, "Eden!" and was by my side in a millisecond. "Are you okay? Is this too much for you? We can cool down." The worry in his voice was evident.

"I'm okay," I panted. I looked up and came face to face with his chest. *Oh my God.* "Andrew," I attempted to say. "You're going to have to put your shirt back on."

He broke into a gigantic Cheshire cat grin. "Why?" he asked rhetorically with a glimmer in his eye.

"Because if you don't, I'm going to jump you right in the middle of the

South Lawn," I managed to get out.

"Then I'm definitely not putting my shirt back on," he said throatily and took me into his arms, kissing me passionately. We forgot where we were for a moment and hands were everywhere. He picked me up into the air and pulled my legs around him, backing me up to the nearest tree. He kissed me everywhere there was skin and breathed, "You taste so good, Eden."

"So do you," I breathed between my own kisses. Oh, the taste of his sweat, the feel of his bare back, his heart beating against mine, it was all so good. "Andrew…" I said with my lips still against his. "We have to stop."

"Mm hmm."

"Andrew, we really have to stop," I murmured against his lips unconvincingly. "We're on the South Lawn."

"I don't care," he said against my neck, sending tingles all down my body.

But the sound of the presidential helicopter, commonly referred to as Marine One, approaching in the sky froze us.

"Yeah, but your dad might."

"Oh, crap," he groaned, still holding me suspended around him. "This is one hell of a compromising position to be caught in." He rested his forehead against mine, both of us laughing breathlessly.

"Do you really think he can see us?"

"Probably not. But trust me. He knows." Andrew kissed my nose and set me down gently. We entwined arms and he threaded his fingers through mine as we waited to greet his father. Despite my nerves at our impending doom, I couldn't help but watch in awe. Marine One was not alone in the sky. Two additional choppers escorted it, one flanking each side. I wondered if their purpose was to act as decoys or to provide additional security. Perhaps both? The two decoys didn't land, but rather hovered above while Marine One landed. While the chopper slowly descended, I took a moment to look around at the ground level. Secret service agents were scattered about and police corralled the people gathering in the distance to watch the pomp and circumstance of the landing.

How long had they all been there? I thought, horrified.

When the chopper finally came to a stop, two Marines dressed in full uniform marched over to the helicopter and helped lower the stairs to the ground. They stood at the bottom of the stairs facing one another at the ready. A man whom I guessed was a secret service agent exited the copter first. President Wellington followed. He descended the stairs with a dashing smile and saluted the Marines who saluted him back. He marched directly over to Andrew's shirt, picked it up, and strode purposefully toward us. He handed the shirt to Andrew and said through a clench-toothed smile, "Diplomatic Room.

Now." He turned, gave the audience a wave and one of his famous heart-melting smiles, and headed straight toward the White House, leaving Andrew and me behind.

Andrew quickly threw on his shirt, took my hand and said, "Okay, Eden. I need you to do something for me. In a moment, we are going to turn and wave to the crowd. They've already seen us together, so there's no hiding now. It's better to acknowledge them than act like we have something to hide. Are you comfortable with that?" he asked, squeezing my hand.

"Nope. But let's do it anyway." I winked at him, and we turned to the people and waved. Then we followed his father into the White House through the legendary green South Portico doors.

* * * *

As the door shut behind us, I let out the breath I had been holding for what felt like a year and leaned back against the wall with my eyes closed. I could not believe what had just happened.

"Are you okay?" Andrew asked.

"Yes. I'm with you. That's all that matters," I reassured him with my eyes still closed.

"My thoughts exactly." He kissed me quickly on the lips.

I opened my eyes and gasped. "Andrew, this little room is stunning."

"I know. It's the Vestibule to the Diplomatic Reception Room. Look at the wall murals. Jackie Kennedy commissioned them based on the American scenery most admired by the Europeans. These are just a preview of what's in the Diplomatic Room."

It was amazing to me how much care was taken to make such a tiny little entryway so breathtaking.

The president interrupted my reverie by appearing in the doorway. "Andrew, Miss Warren," he said, gesturing for us to join him in the next room. He turned around and disappeared into the depths of the Diplomatic Room, expecting us to follow.

I took a deep breath and let it out slowly. *The president knows my name.*

Andrew turned toward me and took my other hand. "Are you ready to go deal with my father?" he asked with a nervous smile that didn't quite reach his eyes. It was disarming.

"And what am I supposed to say? Nice to meet you, Mr. President. I'm sorry I had my tongue in your half-naked son's mouth for all of the world to see on the South Lawn?" I nervously joked.

"The truth shall set you free," Andrew answered and we walked through the doors of the Vestibule into the Diplomatic Reception Room.

First Sun

Despite the fact that I was entering the room under less than ideal circumstances, I couldn't help but react to the beauty surrounding me. I tried to quickly recover from my moment of awe out of respect for the president and the seriousness of the visit, but I was surprised at the tenderness in the president's eyes when I met them.

"Beautiful, isn't it?" the president said with a twinkle in his eye. His resemblance to Andrew was unnerving. He walked over to me and held out his hand. I took it in stunned silence and we shook. Before letting go, he closed his other hand over our shake and squeezed gently. "It's so nice to meet you, Miss Warren. Apparently my son is quite fond of you."

I looked into his eyes, trying to gauge his mood. He didn't look mad at all. In fact, he looked rather amused. This revelation made me blush profusely and I responded in the steadiest voice I could manage. "It's a pleasure to meet you, sir."

He squeezed my hand one more time and let go. "I couldn't help but notice your admiration of the room. Have you ever been in the White House?" he asked.

"Not before today, sir. When I first arrived, Andrew briefly took me up to your main residence. I'm trying to take it all in, but I'm afraid I'm a little distracted by my surroundings at the moment. And perhaps a little star struck as well," I admitted. Andrew snickered. I gave him a dirty look, much to his father's delight.

"You give him hell, Eden," the president whispered with a conspiratorial wink. This made me giggle and I was thankful for the unexpected light mood. "You have no reason to be star struck from me. I assure you I'm not as cool as everyone thinks I am."

More snickers from Andrew.

"But as for being unnerved by your surroundings, that I can understand. I often feel that way myself. These walls have been graced by some of the greatest characters in the story of American History. I think it's important to acknowledge that and keep it in the forefront of my mind."

"Well said, Mr. President." I genuinely agreed.

He beamed warmly at me. "Come look a little closer at the mural and I'll tell you what you're seeing." He led me around the room pointing out the different scenes of the Kennedy mural including a Virginia bridge, Niagara Falls, New York Bay, West Point, and Boston Harbor. I was in awe of their beauty, and in awe of President Wellington's warm reception of me, especially under the circumstances. At the end of his tour, he led us to a group of chairs in front of an ornate fireplace with a painting of George Washington hanging above it. Andrew and I sat on a little yellow settee, careful to leave a couple of inches between us, and President Wellington sat in a yellow wingchair facing us.

"Okay, time to address the elephant in the room," he said with a smile. I squirmed. "I understand the two of you are pretty fond of one another. I get that. I've been in love before." He paused as he appraised our reaction. Andrew reached over for my hand and entwined his fingers between mine, giving me butterflies like his touch always did. The president smiled understandingly at his son. "I am just asking you to employ a bit more discretion."

"Like not making out on the South Lawn?" Andrew clarified with a smirk.

His father cleared his throat and his face turned bright red. "That would be a good start, son."

The irony of the situation was too much. Here I sat in the historic Diplomatic Reception Room of the White House, designed by Jackie Kennedy herself, discussing making out with the president's son. Much to my chagrin, I busted out laughing uncontrollably. The president and his son looked at me in surprise, but then joined me in laughter.

Our laughter eventually died down and the president wiped away tears of amusement. "Oh, kids. Thank you. I needed that." He took a deep breath. "But on a more serious note, we have some damage control to take care of." He turned to me. "Eden, you understand that there will likely be pictures, possibly videos, of this little rendezvous on the Internet, in the papers, and on the covers of tabloids?" His face conveyed the worry he felt for me.

"I didn't, no. But I do now, sir," I said, looking down.

"The Secret Service Department will shut down what they can, but it won't be everything."

I nodded.

"I think you should also understand that this is only the beginning. I take it you wish to continue your relationship with my son?" Andrew took in a sharp breath and held it, waiting for my response.

I nodded again and heard Andrew let out his breath in relief.

"That's what I thought. Then I must prepare you for what you can expect in the immediate future. The press is going to swarm you. They will camp out on your lawn to get a picture of you at a compromising time. You will be in the newspapers, tabloids, magazines, and on the Internet. You will be talked about on TV. Comedians will make jokes about you and your relationship with my son."

I continued to look down.

"Dad," Andrew warned.

"Andrew, she needs to know what to expect if she plans on having any kind of relationship with you," he replied. Andrew reluctantly nodded and I could feel his eyes watching me for my reaction. "In other words, Miss Warren, you will need to develop some pretty thick skin. Is this something you are ready to get yourself into?" he finished.

The tension in the room was tangible as Andrew and his father waited for my response. I got up and paced back and forth, trying to collect my thoughts. Was this something I was willing to do? Basically give up my freedom? My anonymity? I realized that once I went down this road, there was no going back. I tried for a moment to picture my life without Andrew. I did it for almost eighteen years and I had been perfectly happy. But could I be happy now without Andrew? In just a few weeks, he had changed me. How was that even possible? Was I falling in love with him? Perhaps I already *was* in love with him. The realization made my head spin. There was no way. No one fell in love that fast, did they? As if in answer to my own question, moments from the past few weeks began to flash through my mind like a movie. I had never felt so alive. Andrew had become more than just a boy. He had become as necessary to me as air or water. He was *my* oxygen. I couldn't imagine cutting him out of my life. The thought scared me, but excited me at the same time. As I made my decision, my entire body relaxed. I confidently went to stand behind Andrew and placed my hands on his shoulders.

"Mr. President, I won't lie to you and tell you that all of this doesn't scare me." Andrew raised a hand and placed it on mine. "But I like your son. And if all of this comes with him, I'll take it." I lowered my voice and said, "I'll take all of him."

The president's face wilted minutely and for the first time in his presence I detected a trace of discordance. Had he been hoping I would say no? Had he been trying to scare me away? But he recovered in a flash. Perhaps I had just imagined it. I really needed to file away my insecurities.

"All right," the president said. "Now that you have made your decision there is one more thing to attend to."

Andrew and I raised our eyebrows at him in question.

"I will put secret service detail at your house as an added precaution," he said.

"Oh, I don't think that's necessary, Mr. President," I assured him. "You don't have to do that."

"Yes, he does, Eden. I'm sorry," Andrew said sadly.

"Okay, whatever you need to do is fine, sir," I quickly revised, trying to sound nonchalant.

"All right. I will give you two kids some privacy." He got up to leave us, but stopped after only a few steps. "Eden, my schedule has unexpectedly cleared for next Saturday night. Andrew and I would love it if you and your mother could join us for dinner."

"We would be honored, sir."

"Wonderful. I will send a car to pick you up at 6:00 on Saturday then?"

"Sounds good, sir."

He walked back over, shook my hand one more time, and said, "It's been a pleasure to meet you, Miss Warren."

"Likewise, sir," I said with a smile. The president clapped his son on the shoulder once before leaving and took his exit.

* * * *

I anxiously walked in the front door of my town house and called for my mom.

"I'm in the kitchen, honey," she called.

"Can you come out to the living room?"

She came out of the kitchen, drying her hands on a dishtowel. "What's up, E?" she asked, concerned.

"Well, kind of a lot," I admitted apprehensively.

She pointed to the couch and said, "Sit."

I followed her order and sat down, waiting for her to get comfortable as well.

"Now, shoot."

"Okay. Andrew and I kind of got caught making out on the South Lawn of the White House. There were people everywhere because President Wellington was landing in his chopper attracting the public. There are probably pictures and videos of us on the Internet, so now the president thinks I need secret service detail. My two new agents will be here any minute to meet us." I blurted all of this out as quickly as I could and then waited for my mother's reaction.

"You were at the White House?" Mom asked in awe.

"*That's* what you got from all of that?" I asked. She looked at me, waiting for my answer. "Yes. Andrew took me on a tour of the residence, and the president talked to us in the Diplomatic Room."

"Ahhhhhh!" she screamed. "You are so lucky!"

"Mom? Did you hear anything else I said?" I asked her, quickly becoming annoyed.

"I'm sorry, honey." She shook her head, trying to clear it. "Okay. I assume the president already talked to you about how making out with his son on the White House grounds for anyone to see is probably not a good idea?"

"Yes."

"Was he mad?"

First Sun

"Surprisingly no."

"Did you think I would be mad?"

"Yes. Are you?"

"No. I'm not mad at you." I studied my mom to see if I believed her. I did.

"Mom, I *really* like him," I said, blushing.

"I know, honey. I'm happy for you. I really am. But you do understand that you are now going to be open game for the press, right? This relationship is really going to change your life," she lectured.

"I do, Mom. But I don't care. Andrew's worth it."

"Then let's see what the damage is." She reached over to the coffee table and grabbed her laptop.

As she booted it up, I thought I'd tell her about dinner. This was going to be great. She was going to die. "Do you have any plans next Saturday night, Mom?"

"Hmmm, let's see. I have my normal Saturday night date with some Chinese takeout and a bottle of Moscato. I'm pretty busy," she joked.

"Bummer, cause the president invited us to the White House for dinner. I guess I'll just have to call him and tell him we can't come." I pretended to reach for my phone, waiting for the news to sink in.

"*What?* We're going to dinner at the White House? *The* White House? With the President of the United States?" she blubbered.

"Yep, that's the one. And the president's son," I added.

She reached down, grabbed my hands to pull me up, and we jumped up and down in excitement as my mom screeched.

After she finally calmed down, panic crossed over her face. "What am I going to wear? What are you going to wear? We need to go shopping!"

"Okay, Mom, slow down. We've got a whole week to worry about what we're going to wear." I reached for Mom's computer on the coffee table and opened it up. "First let's watch some YouTube videos of me making out with the president's son and meet my new secret service agents, okay?" We both froze as the reality of my words began to sink in. "Well, that's something I never thought I'd say."

We stared at one another through wide eyes until the ding of mom's computer waking up woke us up out of our dreamlike moment. Only it wasn't a dream. The videos proved that much. They weren't that bad. They were from pretty far away. You couldn't even really tell they were of me. But there was no mistaking Andrew. He took my breath away in the videos just like he did this morning in the flesh. And what sexy flesh that was. The photographs were a little more disarming. Someone had a pretty high-resolution camera with one heck of a lens, because there were some pretty clear pictures of shirtless

Andrew and me with the president when he had just exited Marine One. There were also clear pictures of us waving to the crowd with the question, "Who's the first son's latest conquest?" as a heading. Anyone with half a brain could deduce that the girl in the clear pictures was wearing the same clothes as the girl in the grainy videos of her kissing the first son with her legs wrapped around his waist, and therefore must be the same girl. I slammed the computer shut in frustration.

"Eden, you said you were prepared for this," Mom reminded me, pointing to the computer.

"I know. But that doesn't make it any easier to see."

"You'll just have to take this as a lesson to be more careful next time."

"Thank you, Mom," I said.

"For what?" she asked, confused.

"For not being like most moms and freaking out seeing those pictures."

"You're a big girl and I trust you. And you know you can talk to me about anything, right?"

"I do. But there is nothing to talk about yet."

"Okay." She kissed me on the cheek. "I'm going to go put on a pot of coffee in case your secret service agents need some refreshment." She got up and started to the kitchen just as the doorbell rang.

"Too late, Mom."

We nervously walked to the door together, and looked at one another before Mom opened the door.

"Hello, ma'am. Miss," a large, youngish black man said politely. "My name is Jarvis, and this is John." He pointed to an older, thin, but fit white man. "We're the detail sent by President Wellington to serve Miss Eden Warren, AKA Sapphire."

"Sapphire?" I asked, raising my eyebrows.

Jarvis smiled. "Sapphire is your code name. All detailees have them." At my look of continued confusion he continued. "We use it over radio when referring to you with other security personnel. It used to be a necessity before communications could be encrypted. Now it's just mostly for formality purposes and tradition."

"Huh." I was learning more and more about this foreign world that was my government every day. "Sapphire...I like it," I said with a smile, shaking his hand. Mom invited the two men in and motioned for them to sit on the couch.

"So how does this work?" I asked, businesslike.

"Basically, you just go about your normal routine, and we'll be in the background, doing what we do."

"So you've literally 'got my back'?" I said with a smile.

The two agents smiled, despite themselves, and nodded in agreement. They were men of few words.

"When do you get breaks? You can't be with me every moment of every day."

"No, miss. We are just part of your detail, primarily during the daytime. You will notice others relieve us at night. But we're the ones you'll see the most."

"Okay. Well…welcome. Please let us know if you ever need anything."

An awkward silence followed until the men stood up and excused themselves. I got the feeling they didn't wish to nourish a personal relationship. They just wanted to be left alone to do their job.

"Oh, excuse me. Ummm…if we want to go somewhere, what do we do?" I asked, feeling stupid.

Jarvis answered, "You simply go, miss." He smiled kindly and exited the house with John. I realized that John never said one word. Weird.

"Well, that was bizarre," I said to my mom.

"Yeah. Not conversationalists, huh?" she said with a smile.

"I'll ask Andrew for some more details on how to act, what to expect, all that kind of stuff."

"Ahhhhh!" Mom screamed.

Jarvis immediately slammed through the door with his gun raised, ready to pounce whatever was threatening us.

"It's okay, Jarvis," I said hastily. "It's just my crazy mother." Jarvis nodded his head, holstered his gun and retreated to where he had come from.

"Mom! The agents are going to think we're nuts!"

"I'm sorry, honey. I'm just a little jittery about next Saturday."

"Geesh! This is going to be a long week. I've never seen you like this. You're like a giddy little school girl," I said, shaking my head in amusement.

"I know. But it's James Wellington. The man who single-handedly saved the nation from a one-party dystopian society...and People's 'Sexiest Man Alive'," she gushed. "He's legendary..."

"My date, Mom. Not yours," I teased, but with a little bit of an edge to my voice. She picked up on my subliminal message and tried to reign in her excitement.

Countdown: 85 Days
September 5, 2021

The Saturday pre-White-House shopping extravaganza Mom insisted on proved to be successful. Mom picked out a modest little black dress and black stilettos. I chose a floral, strapless dress, and high-heeled strappy blue sandals that I knew would drive Andrew wild. Mom treated us to a mani pedi and a blowout before heading home to put on our new clothes and makeup to complete the look. I had to admit, we looked pretty fabulous.

At 6:00 on the dot, a Town Car pulled up in front of our row house, and a man in a black suit stepped out of the front seat and opened the back door. Andrew stepped out of the car and my heart skipped a beat. He was impeccably dressed in a formal black suit, white shirt and royal blue tie.

I ran out the door without even telling my mom he was there and straight into his arms, like a magnet to a steel Andrew. He hugged me tightly before pushing me at arm's length.

"Hey now, let me see you, Oxygen." He looked me up and down and made a funny little noise of approval deep in his throat. He twirled me around in a circle, then drew me to him with one arm around my waist and the other behind my neck. "Eden, you are...you look...oh my God, you're beautiful," he finally stammered out.

"I was just thinking the same thing about you. You literally took my breath away when you stepped out of that car." Even with high heels, I had to strain my neck to kiss him. "I didn't know you were coming. I thought your dad was just sending a car."

"Like I was going to let that happen. I wasn't going to send someone on an errand to pick up my girl," he said, rubbing my arms with the palms of his hands.

First Sun

"You are too good to me," I said, shaking my head and smiling.

"You deserve it," he answered, rubbing his nose against mine. "Should we find your mother and head on over to my place?"

* * * *

When we drove up to the North Portico, a formally dressed man again opened my door for me and I accepted his hand with ease this time and gracefully exited the car. Andrew came around and met me at the door. "You're getting good at that, Oxygen," he said with a wink.

"It's a little easier when I'm dressed for the occasion," I reproved light-heartedly.

We waited for my mom, and when she joined us Andrew held out both arms to escort us into the Entrance Hall. As we each took an arm, Andrew playfully said, "I am one lucky man," and we all giggled our way into the mansion. I was proud of my mom. She was handling the situation with grace, although I could tell her barely controlled giddiness could boil over at any moment.

A man dressed like a butler (I supposed he actually could be a butler) approached us and told us the president awaited our company in the Red Room. Andrew led us through the Entrance Hall and across the Cross Hall into the Red Room, still holding our arms. As we crossed the threshold into the Red Room, the president discreetly slid his cell phone into his pocket, rose and walked toward us shaking his head in awe. "Son, you are one lucky man," he said in good humor. The three of us looked at one another and resumed our laughter. The president kept a smile on his face, but looked a bit self-conscious.

"I'm sorry, sir," I said, trying to regain control. "It's just that Andrew said the exact same thing a couple minutes ago."

The president's smile relaxed and he said, "Like father, like son." He shrugged his shoulders in defeat and we all continued to laugh, the president included. "You must be the lovely Eden's lovely mother," the president said as he offered his hand. "Like mother, like daughter," he witted. His eyes wandered up and down, drinking in my mother from head to toe. Clearly, he liked what he saw. Sometimes I forgot how hot my mom was. Her light brown hair caught the light just so, and her hazel eyes twinkled in excitement. But it was the little black dress caressing her thin, womanly curves and the black stiletto pumps accenting her perfectly sculpted legs that would make any man weak in the knees. The president was no exception.

My mom blushed, but shook the president's hand, trying desperately to look at ease.

"I thought we would eat up in the residence this evening. It's a little less

87

formal and intimidating. Is that all right with everyone?" The president's smile was so endearing. He was just as good-looking as his son, but in a distinguished, grown-up way. I could see why my mom and every other woman in the United States was so gaga over him. "Please, follow me."

The president explained to my mom what we were seeing as we progressed up the Grand Staircase. "Would you like the five cent tour?" he asked my mother and me.

"Andrew showed me around a bit last weekend, but of course my mother hasn't seen any of the house yet," I said.

"Well then. Most people like to start at the Lincoln Bedroom." Mom gasped in excitement. "I'll take that as a yes." The president beamed. Andrew and his father were so much alike. I didn't even know if they realized it.

After a thorough tour of the Family Residence, including the Lincoln Bedroom, Treaty Room, East Sitting Hall, Queen's Bedroom, Yellow Oval Room, and the Living Room Andrew and his father spent time in together, we retired to the Dining Room. "This is where Drew and I eat when we are actually able to sit down together. Unfortunately, that doesn't happen as much as I'd like it to," he said with an air of genuine sadness. He clapped his son on the back tenderly. Andrew put his arm around his dad's shoulder and gave him a little squeeze. It was so refreshing to see them interact in such a normal father-son way. They were adorable.

As Andrew pulled out my chair I whispered, "Your dad calls you Drew?" with a smile.

"Yeah. My parents have always called me Drew. At least in informal settings."

"Which do you prefer?" I asked, self-consciously realizing that I may have been calling him by the wrong name all this time.

"Either is fine. But I kind of like hearing you call me Andrew," he admitted, a little red in the face. We smiled at one another coyly as Andrew sat in the chair beside me.

The table was set for a formal dinner, despite the president's earlier suggestion of the Family Dining Room being "less formal" than the State Dining Room. I was glad Mom and I were attired for such an event. Almost immediately after we were all seated, four servers appeared out of nowhere and simultaneously placed a bowl of light yellow, creamy-looking soup in front of each of us. I looked at Andrew and as though he could read my mind, he whispered, "Lobster bisque." I nodded and tentatively sipped a spoonful. It was awful. I hated seafood.

"Thank you so much for coming to dinner tonight on such short notice, Dr. Warren," the president said to my mom.

First Sun

"Of course, sir. It's an honor," my mom replied.

"How are things going at Sidwell? Are you all settled in?"

"I am. The staff is great. They've been so welcoming."

"I've heard great things about you, Dr. Warren. Drew's lucky to have such a legendary, educational guru for a teacher."

Mom flushed at the compliment and modestly responded, "Ha! I'm nothing of the sort. Just an enthusiast who took her interest to the level of an obsession."

"Well, that makes two of us then, Doctor," the president said, raising his wine glass to my mother. They clinked glasses in camaraderie.

"So I take it you've met your secret service detail?" the president asked, turning his attention to me.

"Yes, sir. It was a little…surreal." I stopped, hesitating for a moment, then decided to proceed with my questioning. "I'm just not sure of the etiquette, sir."

Andrew and his dad looked at one another and laughed.

"Hey!" I said, my face turning red as the lobster that was chopped up and cooked into the soup I was forcing down.

"No, Eden, it's just that we remember when we received detail for the first time too. We had no idea what to do. We were offering them beer, narrating every action we were about to do, including them in conversations," Andrew explained through his laughter. "There's no right or wrong. You just go about your business. They take your lead. If you want to talk to them, talk to them. If you want to ignore them, ignore them. If you want them to check under your bed for ghosts…" he broke back into laughter, his father joining him.

"You had them check under your bed for ghosts?" I asked, looking in adoration at Andrew.

"Of course. I had heard there were ghost sightings in the Lincoln Bedroom, which is just down the hall from my room. I was scared to death the first night I slept in the White House. Remember, I had just turned twelve years old. Old enough to want to act all tough and grown up, but young enough to truly worry about things like ghosts. Mom and Dad were gone that night at the Inaugural Ball, so it was just my agents and me. I asked them to look in my closet, bathroom, and under my bed for ghosts. They were so great and acted like I had asked them to sweep the place for terrorists." We all laughed, and I placed my hand on Andrew's knee under the table. This story was so cute I couldn't help but touch him. He placed his hand on top of mine and lifted it to his mouth to kiss it before replacing it on his knee. It was so casual and so innocent, but it made my entire body sing.

As though they were watching, the four servers came out of hiding the moment everyone had set down their spoons and snatched our bowls and plates out from under us.

"I can't imagine what it must have been like to be twelve years old and move into the White House," Mom said with a smile.

"Yeah, it was a little overwhelming. I made my fair share of trouble," Andrew admitted.

"'Fair share' would be putting it mildly, son." The president looked at me and said, "Let's just say that your boyfriend here thought it a good idea to tool around on his skateboard everywhere in the White House. One day, he came soaring down the West Wing Colonnade on that Godforsaken thing and as Harry, my chief of staff, opened the door to leave the Oval Office, Drew zipped right through the door and crashed into the Resolute Desk, taking a chunk out of the side." He smiled at the memory and shook his head. "I was horrified. I had been president for all of ten minutes and my son was permanently maiming priceless historical artifacts. Boy did I let him have it." Father and son beamed at one another. "I felt so bad that later that night, I took him out to the path on the South Lawn and let him instruct me on how to ride it." He shook his head. "Such fond memories of this place..." he trailed off in despair, as if it were almost over.

"And over three more years of new memories to make...and hundreds more historical artifacts to maim," I pointed out in jest. Andrew locked eyes with his father, clearly communicating something somber before chuckling politely. A wave of heat crept up my face in horror. Andrew squeezed my knee under the table in an attempt at reassurance, but it just made me more embarrassed. Obviously he thought I had made a mistake and needed to be reassured. *What just happened?*

"To making memories," the president said, raising his wine glass in an attempt to quell my obvious embarrassment.

We all followed his lead, Andrew and I with water glasses, and repeated, "To making memories!"

The president's little ploy proved successful in putting me at ease, and the rest of dinner went well, unless you considered the fact that the next two courses had some kind of seafood involved; Caesar salad with sardines for the salad course and garlic butter scallops over a bed of wild rice for the main course. I did the best I could to make it appear as though I enjoyed the food, but I noticed Andrew studying my plate knowingly throughout the meal. The best part of the meal was dessert. I had never had crème brulee before, but it lived up to its fanciful reputation. I polished mine off in no time, and when no one was looking, Andrew casually switched his full ramekin with my empty one. I glanced at him shyly, as though I had been caught with my hand in the cookie jar, but he just nodded toward the full custard cup with bright eyes and put his

First Sun

arm around the back of my chair, waiting for me to eat it. I hesitated for only a moment, and then dug in happily. When I finished, I smiled at him gratefully in thanks and he stroked my bare back with his thumb in response.

After dinner, the president had a conference call to attend to, so he regretfully said his farewells and saw my mother down to a car waiting to see her home. They gave Andrew and I permission to retreat to the Truman Balcony for a short period of time before Andrew would accompany me home in another car.

We stepped out of the Yellow Oval Room onto the glossy red floor of the Truman Balcony and I marveled at the way the door was almost hidden. It would look like another window from a distance.

"Come here, baby," Andrew said and put an arm around my waist to guide me to a specific spot on the balcony. "You're freezing," he said, removing his jacket and draping it around my shoulders. He moved me in front of him and pointed southeast. "Look," he whispered in my ear. I drew in a deep breath at the sight before me. The Washington Monument stood tall and proud and to its right was the Jefferson Memorial, not quite as grandiose, but eloquent in its simplicity.

Andrew pulled a small white wicker chair with a blue-upholstered cushion over to the railing and drew me down into his lap on the chair. I gazed into his hypnotic blue eyes and he kissed me, sending a blissful shiver down my body.

"You don't like seafood," he said out of the blue.

"No, I don't. Apparently I'm not as good an actor as I thought," I said, embarrassed. "I didn't want to hurt your father's feelings."

"He doesn't care. But he did notice. When you were saying goodbye to your mom, he told me to remind him not to try to feed you seafood again," he revealed, smirking.

"Oh no!" I said, hiding in his neck. He chuckled softly and rubbed my back.

"What *do* you like to eat?"

"If it's bad for you, I like to eat it."

"You're skin and bones!" he said, attempting unsuccessfully to pinch some fat around my waist. "How is that possible?"

"Good metabolism?" I shrugged my shoulders.

"Seriously, what's your favorite meal? Besides McDonald's."

"Chicken strips and French fries. With lots of ketchup."

He smiled a gigantic, toothy grin and kissed me, mumbling against my lips, "Then chicken strips and French fries it is next time, Oxygen."

He lifted my chin to gaze into my eyes, and seizing the moment, kissed me hard, first on the lips, then all over my neck. "You. Drive. Me. Wild." He let

91

out each word in between kisses, driving *me* wild.

After a while, I stopped kissing him and scooted back on his knees a little so I could get a good look at him. He looked so sexy. His hair was messy from me running my hands through it, and his lips were red from kissing. But it was the look in his eyes that spoke to my soul.

"Oh my God, Eden," he said in wonder. "What are you doing to me?" He shook his head in amazement. "I can't stop thinking about you. I can't stand being apart. Every moment I'm not with you, I'm counting down the minutes until I get to see you again…" He broke off. "I never thought it was possible to feel this way about someone so fast…"

I leaned forward and lightly kissed his lips in response.

"Tell me you feel the same way," he begged.

"I do. Oh, Andrew, I do," I breathed.

Instead of kissing me again, he pulled me close to him, and I rested my cheek on his chest, watching the Washington Monument blink along to the beat of Andrew's heart.

Countdown: 83 Days
September 13, 2021

A couple days later, I awoke to birds chirping outside my window. I rolled over in my bed and stretched. My phone chimed, announcing a text message. I looked at my clock and was surprised to see that it was only 6:00. Are you freaking kidding me? The first chime must have been what woke me up. My phone chirped, not birds. I fumbled around on my bedside table, trying to locate my phone as my stomach flip-flopped. I grinned when I read the message displayed on my phone.

Andrew: *Good morning, Oxygen.*

Me: *You better have a good reason for waking me up.*

Andrew: *It's nice to talk to you too.*

Me: *I need my beauty sleep.*

Andrew: *No you don't.*

Me: *Compliments will get you nowhere at the moment. I'm too tired.*

Andrew: *I can't wait any longer for an answer.*

Me: *An answer to what?*

Andrew: *To my invitation.*

Me: *What invitation?*

Andrew: *It didn't come?*

Me: *What didn't come?*

Andrew: *Go check your mail. I'll wait.*

Me: *All right. I'm going downstairs right now.*

What could Andrew possibly be sending me in the mail? Excitement built with each step I took. I was about to head to the front door to go to the mailbox, but an official-looking envelope propped up against the fruit bowl on the counter caught my attention. I picked it up carefully, as if touching it would mar its beauty and turned it over in my hands, inspecting it. The fine classic linen envelope was addressed to "Miss Eden Warren" in handwritten calligraphy. On the back was a gold stamp of the Presidential Seal.

I opened the mail drawer under the counter and located the letter opener that I always made fun of mom for keeping. Apparently there were some uses for it. I didn't want to risk tearing the beautiful envelope. I stuck the letter opener in a small hole in the seal and gently tugged, releasing the folded paper. Inside was another envelope, this time made of clear vellum. On the front was my name once again, "Miss Eden Warren." Inside the vellum was the most beautiful work of art I had ever had the privilege of holding. The top of the metallic gold card was embossed with the Presidential Seal and black handwritten calligraphy scrawled across the card in effortless beauty. As I read the words, my heart beat uncontrollably.

President Wellington
requests the pleasure of the company of
Miss Eden Warren
at a dinner in honor of
Sir Henry Wright, Prime Minister of the United Kingdom
and
Mrs. Margaret Wright
to be held at
The White House
on Thursday, September 24, 2021
at seven o'clock
Black Tie   *East Entrance*

I held the invitation in stunned silence. President Wellington requests the pleasure of *my* company...I couldn't believe it. I felt like Cinderella being invited to the prince's ball. I set the invitation down on the counter, desperately trying not to smudge it. My phone chimed, sending me into the air in surprise. I glanced at it in detached curiosity. It was Andrew.

Andrew: *Do you accept?*
I was still too shocked to move. My phone chimed again.
Andrew: *Please?*
I picked up my phone with shaking hands and somehow managed to reply.
Me: *I don't have anything to wear.*
Andrew: *I'll take you shopping today after school.*
Me: *You want to go shopping?*
Andrew: *Watch my smokin' hot girlfriend try on dresses all night? Sounds like torture.*
Me: *You win. I accept.*

     I set down my phone and continued to stare at the invitation as though it could disappear and become a figment of my imagination.
     "Crazy, huh?" I jumped at the sound of my mom's voice. "Who would've ever thought the Warrens would take the White House by storm?" she joked.
     "You got one too?" I forced out, despite my lingering shock.
     She just nodded in amazement.
     "Holy crap." The softness of my voice didn't match the intensity of the expression. We both laughed nervously, for lack of knowing what else to do.

* * * *

     Later that day, after making a quick pit stop by our lockers for the last time that week, we walked out to the parking lot and got into the waiting Town Car.
     "So where are we going to shop?" I asked.
     "You'll see."
     We rode in silence for a while as I nervously considered where Andrew could be taking me. I had a feeling it wouldn't be Gap. What did people wear to state dinners anyway? Designer gowns. My heart fluttered in excitement at the thought. Trying on designer gowns with my first son boyfriend...quite a metamorphosis from how I spent my Friday nights in Cedar Rapids.
     The car came to a stop and Andrew got out. He started to come around to let me out of the door, but I beat him to it. He smirked at me and led me into the store holding my hand.
     I glanced at the sign on the storefront. Neiman Marcus? "Andrew, I'm

pretty sure Neiman Marcus is out of my league," I hinted, a little self-conscious.

"Just trust me, okay?"

I nodded hesitantly in consent.

"Good. Because they're expecting us," he said, taking my hand and pulling me into the store.

"You called ahead?"

"Of course I did. This way, they'll have stuff already pulled for you in your size. Don't look at me like that! I called your mom."

"How embarrassing!" I smacked him.

"I wouldn't say a size 4 is anything to be embarrassed about, Oxygen. Especially someone who eats like you. You should be hella-proud of that."

I giggled, partly out of embarrassment, and partly from the term, "hella-proud."

As we continued to stroll through the store hand-in-hand, our secret service trailing a respectable distance back, a crowd began to collect behind us.

"Um, Andrew?" I whispered.

"Mm hmm?"

"We're being followed."

"Yes, we are."

"And this doesn't surprise you?"

"Nope."

"Does this happen to you often?"

"When I'm out in public, which isn't very often. We should probably acknowledge them." He smiled at me, then turned around and walked back to the gathering crowd, shaking hands and bantering graciously. He even signed a couple of autographs. I smiled at him as he played the part he was born to play. And he didn't even know it yet. He may think he wants to be a political analyst, but he was born to lead.

When Andrew was able to peel himself away politely, he led me to a woman waiting unassumingly by a door behind a customer service desk. "I think we're ready," he said, putting his arms around me.

The lady held out her hand and said, "Miss Warren, it's a pleasure to meet you." She smiled and shook my hand vigorously between both of hers, before turning to Andrew. "Mr. Wellington," she said as she shook his hand. "My name is Vickie and I'll be helping you out today." Her smile was contagious and I instantly felt comfortable with her.

I couldn't help but notice how well put together she was. Her black suit was cut to perfection for her petite shape and her jet-black, sharp-angled bob accented her cheekbones. She was beautiful in an exotic way. She opened the door behind her and led us into a little dressing room suite. Straight ahead of me stood a rack holding gown after magnificent gown.

I froze in anticipation, and felt Andrew's chin rest on the top of my head. "Ready, Oxygen?"

"Where do I even begin?" I asked, wide-eyed.

Andrew and Vickie laughed. I walked tentatively over to the rack and put out my hand to touch them, but caught sight of a price tag. $1,150? *Holy crap! I can't touch these dresses!* I looked inconspicuously at my hands to make sure they were clean before touching a green silk dress that caught my eye.

"You like that one?" Vickie asked, suddenly grabbing the dress and hanging it on another empty rack. "What else?"

I just stood there, awkwardly glancing back and forth between Vickie and the dresses for a moment before turning around and walking back to Andrew in defeat.

"What's wrong, Oxygen? You don't like the dresses? I'm sure they have others…" He glanced at Vickie who moved toward the door, but froze when I put up my hand to signal her to stop.

"No, no, it's not that. They're beautiful. It's just that I…well, Andrew…I can't afford them." I sat down on the small settee pushed up against the wall for shopping companions and hid my face in my hands in horrified humiliation.

"Eden, I told you to trust me," Andrew said in amusement. He sat next to me and attempted to pry my hands away from my face. I couldn't face him. I didn't want him to know money was a concern. But it was.

"Actually, Miss Warren," Vickie interjected, nervously clearing her throat, "I pulled dresses from designers who would love for you to wear their gowns to the state dinner free of charge. As long as you mention them, of course."

At this, I peeked out of my hands to find both Andrew and Vickie waiting in relaxed silence for me to come around.

"Why would they do that?" I asked in a small voice.

"Because believe it or not, Miss Warren, you're the new 'It Girl'," Vickie explained. "Designers would die for you to wear their gown to the state dinner."

I looked incredulously at Andrew, who sat there beaming at me. A small, relieved smile finally crept its way onto my face. Not because I was the new "It Girl" (*Yikes!*), but because it meant I could actually wear one of these amazing dresses to the state dinner with Andrew. With new determination, I stood back up, rubbed my hands together and said, "Well in that case, let's do it!" to the delight of both Andrew and Vickie.

I swept through the rest of the dresses, and every time I stopped at one for a moment, Vickie grabbed it and moved it to the other rack as if she could read my mind. After sorting the dresses, she expertly wheeled my choices behind another door I hadn't even noticed. "This is where we'll change you into the dresses. Then you can come show Mr. Wellington," she explained.

"You're going to help me?" I asked, blushing a deep crimson color. All I could think about was how I hadn't chosen the best underwear for the occasion. I didn't know someone was going to actually dress me. I was horrified.

"In the dressing room you'll find a little corset number to put on underneath. It holds everything in all the right places," she whispered with a wink to ease my mind. It worked. "You go ahead and put it on and then open the door a crack when you're ready for me."

I took a deep breath to calm myself and stepped into the dressing room. Hanging on a hook against the wall was the "little corset number." I slithered into it, feeling way too nerdy and unsexy for the likes of it. But when I turned around and looked in the mirror, I was blown away. Whoa, was it hot! It was lacy and black and, as Vickie said, hugged all of the right places.

If Andrew only knew what I was wearing right now.

I smiled and cracked the door, just enough so Vickie would know I was ready and Andrew could "accidentally" catch a glimpse. Then I stepped behind the door so I could see out but he couldn't see in and chuckled as his face turned red and he repositioned himself in his chair, clearing his throat.

Vickie sauntered in giggling and pointed her finger at me. "Tsk, tsk, you little vixen! I like you. We're going to get along just fine." I joined her in giggling and she grabbed the first dress on the rack. It was a backless red sweetheart gown with a full skirt. It was beautiful.

"Oh, no fair," Vickie said. "You're one of those girls who looks good in anything." I blushed at the compliment. "Let's see what your man thinks."

I stepped out of the room and Andrew took in a breath. "Wow, Eden..." He moved to stand up, but I put my hand out.

"No way, Andrew. You are not going to manhandle these dresses!" I reprimanded him. Vickie laughed out loud and Andrew pouted, sitting back down.

"But I want to touch you," he said, like a little boy who just had his favorite toy stolen from him. Perhaps he had.

"We'll never get anywhere if you do that, Andrew." I smiled wickedly. "Stay put."

"Fine." He crossed his arms, but couldn't help but smile. "You drive me crazy, you know that?"

"Yep. That's my goal."

"This is only dress one. We have quite a few others," Vickie pointed out. "Time to change, Miss Warren."

"Please, call me Eden," I corrected.

"Okay, Eden. You lead." She smiled warmly, holding the door open for me.

"Feel free to crack the door for Vickie again," he called after us.

"That boy is head over heels, Eden," Vickie cooed.

I beamed in response.

We went through several dresses, all beautiful, and all eliciting the same response from Andrew. I was beginning to think it didn't matter what dress I chose. I liked them all the same.

"How am I ever going to choose?" I asked Vickie as I put on dress number seven.

"You'll know."

"How?"

"Mr. Wellington's response."

"But he seems to like them all."

"Trust me. You'll know."

She zipped dress number seven and I turned to look in the mirror. My hand went automatically to my mouth as I gasped at what I saw.

"I know. It's a Dina Bar-el. She's an amazing designer. She dresses celebrities of all walks of life. Actresses, singers, models...you name it. This dress is called the Brigette. Look at how the asymmetric drop shoulders accentuate your bosom. The crisscross cut of the fabric cinches in your narrow waist...my God, what I wouldn't give to have that tiny waist. And don't even get me started on what that emerald green color does for your skin and eyes." She shook her head in envy.

I blushed, uncomfortable with compliments as always.

"Let's see what Mr. Wellington thinks of this one." She opened the door and I stepped into the light before Andrew. I watched for his reaction, hoping this was the one.

Andrew's mouth opened in awe and his eyes filled with an emotion I couldn't quite place. He stood up and slowly approached me. Without looking away, he whispered, "Vickie, could you please excuse us?"

Vickie silently slipped through the door leading to the main store. Andrew ran his hands softly down my sides, grazing the delicate green silk.

"Eden..." he whispered. "I have never seen anything so beautiful." He looked into my eyes and I recognized the emotion in them. It was love. It had to be. And it was the same way I felt. We could both feel the words on the tips of our tongues, but were too chicken to say it.

"Eden, I have something I want you to wear with this dress for the state dinner." Andrew put his hand in his pocket and drew something out in a closed fist. He walked around to the back of me, grazing his empty hand around my waist. I tingled in pleasure. "Close your eyes," he whispered in my ear. I did as I was told. He drew back my hair and kissed my neck. I took a deep, longing breath. He dropped my hair over my shoulder and I felt cold metal settle onto my neck and collar bone. His trembling hands struggled with the clasp before securing it into place. He kissed my skin just below the clasp and drew my hair back over my shoulder, letting it slip through his fingers onto my back. He stepped forward and pulled me tight to his body. I could feel his heart beating rapidly against my back and longed to turn around to kiss him.

"Okay, open your eyes."

I took a breath and opened my eyes. My hand automatically went to the stunning teardrop diamond encircling my neck. I recognized it as the necklace displayed with the late first lady's inaugural gown at the Museum of American History.

"Andrew, I can't…"

"Yes, you can. Please. This was my mother's and I want you to have it."

"But your father…"

"I already cleared it with him. He liked the idea of you having it." He stopped for a moment, then finished with, "My mom would want me to give it to you instead of letting it…" A dark cloud passed over Andrew's face for an instant and he stopped himself from saying whatever it was he was going to say.

Instead of letting it what?

"It belongs with you," he finished, his face softening as he retrained his eyes on my reflection.

I stood completely still, basking in the unspoken love pulsing between us. "Andrew, it's…I can't believe…" I didn't have the words to express what I was feeling, except for the three words I wouldn't say. I turned around and kissed him instead. "Thank you," I murmured against his lips.

"You're welcome." He put his hand in his other pocket, continuing to kiss me as he took one of my hands, opened it and dropped more cool metal into it. "The matching earrings," he explained, and closed my hand over them into a fist. I couldn't help it. I began to laugh. I felt his mouth curve into a smile against mine before breaking contact and laughing with me.

"What?" he asked innocently, mid-chuckle.

"As if a million carats of diamonds wasn't already enough. Let's add," I opened my palm and looked down at the beauty it unveiled, "ten more." I shook my head at him in defeat and put them on, ever so delicately. "I've never been a big jewelry person," I admitted carefully, so as not to hurt his feelings.

"I know. I've noticed. I'm not asking you to wear them every day. Just special occasions like the state dinner."

Andrew stepped to the side to give me a clearer view in the mirror. I took one final look, barely recognizing the girl staring back. The reflection girl glowed almost as brightly as the diamonds encircling her neck and dangling from her ears. But it wasn't the dress or the diamonds. It was love.

Countdown: 81 Days
September 15, 2021

Later that week at school, I trudged down the hall toward Perspectives on American Government. I was really tired. I had been up late the night before yet again at the White House with Andrew. I loved being with him and wanted to spend every waking second with him. But boy was I exhausted. I supposed there would be plenty of time to catch up on sleep this weekend since Andrew would be accompanying his father on some kind of diplomatic trip to London. A twinge of regret pulled on my heartstrings at the thought of not seeing Andrew for a few days. But it sure was enjoyable saying goodbye the night before. I smiled to myself in blissful memory and pushed through the restroom door to make a pit stop before heading to Gov.

The door closed behind me to the sound of retching in one of the stalls. Someone was sick. *Very* sick. I was just about to call into the stall to see if whomever it was needed me to get the nurse, when the toilet flushed and out came Ava. She was dewy with sweat and ghostly white. Despite my general dislike for the girl, I asked in genuine concern, "Are you okay, Ava?"

She rolled her eyes at me nastily and went to the sink to tidy up. "Geez, can't a girl throw up her breakfast without you sticking your nose where it doesn't belong?"

Oh, so that was it. Bulimia. I felt sick to my stomach in pity. "Why do you think you have to do that, Ava? You're so beautiful. It isn't worth it."

"That's what you think this is? Bulimia?" She snorted in twisted amusement. "Of course that's what you'd think. It couldn't just be a hangover, could it? But I guess you wouldn't know anything about that, would you? As perfect as you are…"

I shook my head in defeat, heading toward the nearest stall, but froze in

102

response to her next words. "Or maybe I'm pregnant." A malicious spark glinted in her eye, as if savoring her moment of genius. "Hmm…how long has it been since that memorable night with Andrew?"

My stomach dropped at her insinuation and she waited patiently for me to do the math, arms crossed in defiance. Could it be? That would have been over two months ago. I shook my head vehemently. No, she was just bluffing.

"That was over two months ago, Ava. You would've known by now," I argued.

"Would I have?" She placed a perfectly manicured fingernail to her lips, as if deep in thought, then wrinkled her nose and nodded in fake concession. "You're right. I'm probably not pregnant. Phew! That would have been messy for you, huh?" She winked and turned in a satisfied flourish, leaving me in silent fury.

As soon as she was gone, I closed myself into the nearest stall and collapsed against the door in outrage. I drew in a few deep breaths to calm myself enough to digest what just happened.

She's not pregnant. She's just a vindictive masochist on a mission to torture me.

Of course this would happen when Andrew was away on a trip. Should I call him? No. This was not something I wanted to discuss with him over the phone. I didn't want to freak him out when he was thousands of miles away and there was no way she was actually pregnant anyway…was there? *She's lying.* I saw the idea light up in her eyes. Hell, I could practically see the light bulb suspended over her head. Satisfied with my conclusion, I pulled myself together and freshened up a bit before heading to class.

I snuck into Government a little tardy thanks to my less-than-pleasant encounter with Ava, but Mr. Polk was immersed in a conversation with another student and didn't seem to notice. Ava did. She smiled wickedly and raised her hand as I slid quietly into my desk.

She's not pregnant. She's just trying to get under my skin.

"Yes, Ava?" Mr. Polk asked politely. Teachers loved Ava. They couldn't see through her sugary sweet persona down to the nastiness beneath.

"Well, I was doing some research last night on the Internet for my paper on government-related myths and stumbled upon something interesting. I thought perhaps you would have some insight."

Mr. Polk took the bait and rubbed his hands together in anticipation. "Alright, bring it on." Mr. Polk was a fantastic teacher, but he was known to be easily distracted when a student dangled a topic of interest in front of him. I didn't know what today's lesson was supposed to be about, but I wasn't surprised when he was so easily segued into a new topic to suit Ava's evil plot.

Tara Tolly

I knew full well that Ava didn't need Polk's input. She just wanted to use him as an excuse to expose me to whatever vendetta she had planned at the moment. Her evil smile told me as much. She was on a role today.

"Well, it's called 'The Curse of Tippecanoe'," she began. "It was something about how every president who was elected or reelected in a year evenly divided by twenty would meet his death in office. It interested me because the current president was reelected in 2020. *Barely* reelected, but reelected none-the-less," she pointed out childishly. Everyone in the class turned directly to me, gauging my reaction. I just sat even-faced staring at Mr. Polk. Polk looked over at me as well, worry in his eyes.

I smiled at him and said, "It's okay, Mr. Polk, this sounds interesting. Perhaps I can warn James when he gets back from Europe." The class snickered in response and Ava gave me a dirty look at my obvious use of President Wellington's first name to aggravate her. What she didn't know was that I would never even consider calling him by his first name to his face. But she didn't need to know that.

Mr. Polk smiled warmly and said, "Good point, Eden. We wouldn't want the president to go unwarned, would we now?"

I continued to smile.

Mr. Polk cleared his throat and began, "Yes. 'The Curse of Tippecanoe' can also be called 'Tecumseh's Curse', the 'Twenty Year Curse', and probably several other nomenclatures. But 'The Curse of Tippecanoe' is probably the most commonly used name. According to believers of the curse, any president elected in a year evenly divisible by 20 will die during that term. Let's see…" He pulled his computer over to his podium and began to type. He hit a button and projected Wikipedia for the class to see. "Yes, this webpage has the names and years of the presidents who supposedly died under this curse. Let's look at the origin of the curse." He read from the webpage as all of his students leaned forward on their elbows in fascination.

The name "Curse of Tippecanoe" derives from the **1811 battle.** As governor of the Indiana Territory, William Harrison used questionable tactics in the negotiation of the 1809 **Treaty of Fort Wayne** with Native Americans, in which they **ceded** large tracts of land to the U.S. government.**[2]** The treaty further angered the **Shawnee** leader **Tecumseh,** and brought government soldiers and Native Americans to the brink of war in a period known as Tecumseh's War. Tecumseh and his brother organized a **group of Indian tribes** designed to resist the westward expansion of the United States. In 1811, Tecumseh's forces, led by his brother, attacked Harrison's army in the **Battle of Tippecanoe,**

104

earning Harrison fame and the nickname "Old Tippecanoe".[2] Harrison strengthened his reputation even more by defeating the British at the **Battle of the Thames** during the **War of 1812.[2]** In an account of the aftermath of the battle, Tecumseh's brother **Tenskwatawa,** known as the Prophet, supposedly set a curse against Harrison and future White House occupants who became president during years with the same end number as Harrison. This is the basis of the curse legend.[3]

"So you see, this rumor comes from actual historic circumstances. Whether you believe in curses or not is up to you. It's just a claim. Now it's our job to find evidence to prove or disprove the claim. I'm going to give you all some time to look through the evidence on your own and do just that. But don't just use Wikipedia. Corroborate your source. Let's see what you can find out…" He clicked his mouse a few times and said, "There. I've sent you all this link. Dive in." He rubbed his hands together and dove into his own computer. I recognized the look on his face; it was the look a teacher gets when he or she was given the gift of mental fodder. He was more excited to find out more about this curse than anyone else, except for maybe Ava. I glanced over at her and she met my eyes, rubbing her stomach gently. Seriously. She was un-frickin'-believable. I shook all thoughts of "Ava's pregnancy" out of my head and turned my attention to my computer. I brought up my email to get the link and scrolled down the page to the timeline of presidents who were elected or reelected in a year divisible by twenty. I would disprove this claim and knock Ava off her pedestal.

But as I read through the timeline of presidents, I realized I had my work cut out for me. Harrison, Lincoln, Garfield, McKinley, Harding, FDR, JFK…all elected or reelected in a year divisible by 20 and all died in office. *Holy crap.* Goose bumps emerged from my skin and the blood drained from my face.

The next two presidents on the timeline were Ronald Reagan and George W. Bush. Both were elected in a year divisible by 20, but neither died in office. That was encouraging. After reading further, I found that both had assassination attempts made on them. Reagan was hit by gunfire, but made a full recovery, while Bush was never actually shot. The last two presidents under the "curse" had survived.

The bell rang, so I shut down my computer and packed up my stuff. I would have to corroborate with some other sources, but at least the last two presidents survived the curse. Perhaps my president would too.

* * * *

The weekend dragged on with Ava's lie buzzing around in my brain like an annoying little gnat I couldn't swat away. While I knew deep down she wasn't pregnant, I couldn't shake the inevitable apprehension that comes from the minute possibility of truth. And it didn't help that I couldn't talk to Andrew about it. I tried to pass the time by staying busy. I went to a movie with Sam and Katie, shopped with my mom, worked on my Gov paper on the Curse of Tippecanoe...anything to keep my mind off of Ava Jacobsen.

On Sunday night, Katie came over to work on our AP Statistics homework together, but we were railroaded off track by a news clip on *Entertainment Tonight*, starring none other than Ava Jacobsen. A split screen image appeared on the television—Ava on the left and Andrew and me on the right (I didn't even know when the picture was taken since being photographed was unfortunately becoming the new norm)—followed by a news clip narrated by the weekend news anchor. Katie jumped up and adjusted the volume to not miss a word. I just sat in stupefied silence.

"Has the first son moved on from his controversial relationship with the president's former opponent's daughter, Ava Jacobsen, to Sidwell Friends schoolmate, Eden Warren?" Picture after picture of Andrew and me flashed on the screen. Holy crap! People were watching *all* the time. Even when I didn't know they were. My stomach turned in revulsion. The reporter continued, "I'm sorry to break it to you, ladies. It appears to be love. But as rumors of a Jacobsen pregnancy surface, will there be trouble in paradise?"

I gasped in horror.

Katie turned to me, cringing. "Oh, my God..."

When the reporter had finished pouring salt on my still fresh wound, she segued seamlessly to the next snippet of news. "After the break, Jordan Lawman, host of The Science Channel's *Cosmic Phenomena*, gives his two cents on the 9409 Apollo conspiracy as the asteroid hurls ominously close to Earth. Could it veer off its projected trajectory course? Stay tuned to—" I pointed the remote at the television and switched it off. If only it could switch Ava Jacobsen out of my head as easily as it switched her off the TV.

"Eden, she's not pregnant. We already decided that," Katie reminded me logically.

"I know, but—" My response was interrupted by a pounding at the door.

"Who could that be?" I opened the door flippantly, knowing that if whoever was there were a danger, he or she wouldn't have made it as far as the door. Jarvis and John would make sure of that.

"Andrew! What are you doing here? I thought I wouldn't see you until—" I stopped midsentence, distracted by the medicinal stench of alcohol wafting off of him. "Ew, did someone spill a drink on you?" I asked, ushering him in the door with a raised nose.

"Yep. *I* did," he said through a sarcastic smile, stumbling against the door and grabbing onto me in a clumsy attempt at righting himself. He was drunk. Stumbling stinking drunk.

I wrenched my arm out of his grasp in disgust. "You're drunk," I accused.

"Bingo," he said, pushing past me and dropping something in the process.

I leaned over and picked up the discarded item. "Oh, my God," I breathed. A bashful Ava stared up at me from the cover of a tabloid, her hand on a slightly rounded stomach as though she were the mother of the year. Her wicked little smile sickened me. My eyes skimmed over the heading "First Baby? The jilted mother of Andrew Wellington's baby speaks out" and my heart skipped a beat.

Andrew caught sight of a wide-eyed Katie watching his little performance from the couch and grinned. "Katie—how the hell ya doin'?" He plopped next to her on the couch and patted her familiarly on the shoulder, missing once or twice but not noticing. "Much better than me, I'm guessing." He abruptly sat up straighter and bluntly asked, "You're not knocked up are ya?"

Katie shook her head in astonishment.

"Then you are *definitely* better than me." He folded his arms over himself and fell back against the couch in a huff.

Katie rose and said, "I'm going to take off. It sounds like you two have some things to hash out."

"Don't leave on my account. I should be the one leaving. Apparently, it's what I do best," Andrew mumbled.

Katie flashed a half smile, half grimace and signaled that she would call me later before escaping out the front door.

I approached Andrew with the tabloid in hand, anger building by the second. "This sucks, Andrew," I said, holding up the magazine. "I get that. But this is how you choose to deal with it? I thought you had changed," I accused.

"Me too. But this—" He snatched the tabloid out of my hand and threw it down on the coffee table, stabbing at the picture of Ava with his finger. "This is proof that I haven't. This guy—the guy in this article—he's the kind of guy who knocks a girl up and moves on to someone else. So guess what? This—" he said, gesturing from his head to his feet, "is the way 'that' guy deals with it."

"That's what this is? Some stupid self-fulfilling prophesy? Jesus, Andrew! So some disreputable rag prints garbage about you that they most likely got from a lying bitch making a last ditch effort to get you back. So what? Do you really think this is the last time a tabloid is going to print bullshit about you?"

"How do you know it's bullshit?"

"Because this picture is clearly photoshopped. There's no way someone who's just over two months pregnant would have a belly this big. Plus, I saw it in her eyes the other day when she cooked up her brilliant little plan."

"She *told* you she was pregnant?" he shouted, jumping up on unstable legs. He closed his eyes momentarily to catch his balance, but teetered a little none-the-less. "Why didn't you tell me?" he asked in fury.

"Because it happened Friday after you had already left for London. Did you really want me to tell you something like that over the phone?" He didn't answer. He just stared at me through blank, bloodshot eyes. "Plus, I wasn't too worried about it."

"You weren't *worried* about it?" he roared.

I sighed in frustration at his short fuse, which temporarily superseded his normally patient countenance thanks to the effects of alcohol. "Andrew, she was *lying*. I could tell."

He fell back onto the couch and whispered, "You don't know that for sure. It could be true..."

"What do you mean it could be true? Please tell me you were at least smart enough to use a condom." The thought sickened me.

He nodded. But his questioning look told me he knew as well as I did that they didn't always work. "What am I going to do if it's true?"

"I don't know, Andrew. You tell me."

He sat in silence for a maddeningly long amount of time before answering, "I'll have to do the right thing. I'll have to...I guess I'll...be a...a...father." He shook his head as though he could rid it of the notion.

"And where would that leave me?" I hated the way my voice sounded. It sounded weak and small. I *felt* weak and small.

"I was going to take you with me..." His head snapped up in hope, his eyes glistening in earnest. "Will you still come with me?"

"Come with you where? To the state dinner?" I asked, shaking my head in confusion. "Who the hell cares about a frickin' state dinner right now?"

As though talking to himself he added, "It was supposed to be just you and me. Now I'll have to bring the baby..."

"To where, Andrew? What are you talking about?" I prompted in irritation.

"I want to tell you. I want to tell you so bad...they won't let me...I can't."

"You can't tell me where you want to take me?"

"No, no..." He shook his head vigorously and jumped up from the couch. "I want to tell you...I can't..." He grabbed me urgently and pulled me roughly to him. "I can't tell you! I'm sorry!" He planted a hard, clumsy kiss on my lips and tightened his hold on me.

I pushed against his chest with all my might to free myself from his unintentionally harsh grasp. "Andrew...let go." He didn't move. "Let go, dammit!" I growled, pushing harder. My little push was enough to knock him off balance in his drunken state. He lost his grip and stumbled backward a couple of steps. "Andrew, I want you to leave," I said, staring at him through steely cold eyes as though he were a stranger. This wasn't the Andrew I had fallen for. This was the Andrew Wellington I had despised from afar, the one who drowned his sorrows in alcohol instead of dealing with them head on.

"Now you hate me," Andrew said, despair replacing the urgency from moments before. He sat on the couch and leaned forward, putting his head in his hands.

"I don't hate you. I just don't know who you are anymore. At least I don't know who *this* Andrew is," I said, pointing to his inebriated state. "I've made it clear from the start that I didn't want anything to do with this Andrew. You worked so hard to prove to me that he was gone. And I believed you. I was stupid, but I believed you. Now you can just go home and bask in the glory of his return."

He reached out and wrapped his arms around my legs, pulling me to him. He rested his cheek against my thighs and begged, "Please don't leave me, Oxygen. I'm sorry. I promise I won't do this again."

I backed away from him as the tears I had been desperately holding back finally overflowed. "I don't believe you."

As Andrew looked up at me, the little boy mourning the loss of his mother in the pictures I saw of the first lady's funeral on our first date peeked out from behind the toughened mask that was now his crutch—his defense against facing the affliction of pain. He curled up in a ball on the couch and closed his eyes as a single tear fell down the side of his face. "I love you, Oxygen," he drunkenly murmured.

So *that* was what he wanted to tell me.

"Even if there really is a baby...even if you never speak to me again...I'll love you till the end of the...till the end of time." And he passed out, unable to fight the effects of the alcohol a moment longer.

* * * *

That night was a long one. After crying to Dani for a couple hours on the phone and enduring her myriad reasons for forgiving Andrew, I finally succumbed to a fitful slumber. When I woke up the next morning I trudged through the house, getting ready for school in a zombie-like state to the questioning looks of my mother. She knew better than to ask what was wrong before I was ready to talk. I didn't know if I'd ever be ready.

As I approached my locker that morning, I found a pale, disheveled Andrew camped out on the floor in front of my locker. His arms encircled his legs and he rested his head on his knees with his eyes closed, clearly miserable. *Good. Serves him right.* I ignored him and entered my combination, yanking on the door despite its hungover obstacle.

Andrew stood up gingerly and put a hand on the locker door to prevent me from opening it. "Eden, you know we need to talk," he said gently.

"I don't know who you are any more. My mom always told me not to talk to strangers."

"I'll take that little joke as a good sign," he said hopefully.

I sighed in frustration. "Andrew, I have nothing to say to you. Please leave me alone." I decided I didn't need anything in my locker after all and turned to leave. Andrew grabbed my hand to stop me, but I recoiled in disgust. "Don't touch me."

Andrew flinched as though I had slapped him. I shook my head in mourning, regarding the boy I thought I had known so well. But the hungover boy standing in front of me was not *my* Andrew. He was the damaged first son I had detested from the press of the past.

I sullenly retreated down the hallway, leaving Andrew behind to wallow in his self-created misery. As the distance between us grew, Andrew desperately called out, "Eden! I promise I'll make this right…please don't go!" not caring about the vast audience of awestruck students surrounding us. Tears streaked down my cheeks in response to Andrew's public display of anguish. The sorrow in his voice tore me apart. I wanted to run back to him and hold him. But I couldn't. He wasn't who I thought he was.

* * * *

The day drug on, the longest parts being the two classes I had with Andrew. I spent much of Chemistry and FACS at war with myself, torn between the animalistic need to take a groveling Andrew into my arms and seething in unbridled anger at his relapse into his old ways. I made a pointed effort to ignore him, which hurt me just as much as it punished him.

But the day took a major turn when I stepped foot in Gov and caught sight of Ava, AKA Mommy-to-be. My eyes automatically wandered down to her stomach, half expecting to find the unmistakable baby bump highlighted in the tabloid, but all I found was the same old perfectly flat midsection she so proudly flaunted on a daily basis. Today was not an exception. The skintight t-shirt she had painted on this morning was not the best wardrobe choice for a girl trying to sustain a pregnancy ruse.

I was right. She's not pregnant. I knew it all along, but the sight of her flat stomach proved my suspicions that the baby bump in the tabloid was photoshopped. But if she wasn't really pregnant, then what was this all about?

110

First Sun

A way to torture me? One last attempt to win Andrew back? A publicity stint? I didn't know. And I didn't care. All I cared about was putting an end to her little game. I knew just what I needed to do. And I needed to get her to my house to do it.

When Mr. Polk dismissed the class, I took a deep breath and walked confidently up to Ava, despite the fact that she was surrounded by a small group of cronies. "Ava? Can I talk to you for a second?"

She set her bag back down on her desk and folded her arms defensively. Her friends trickled away, throwing curious glances over their shoulders on the way out of the room. Ava cocked her head to the side in obvious mistrust, waiting for me to reveal the catalyst of the interaction.

"I'd really like to talk to you about…your problem," I said, gesturing to her flat stomach.

"Why would I want to talk to you about anything?"

"Because I think I could help you."

"You think *you* could help *me*," she said, clearly doubting my sincerity.

"Yes. I think I can get Andrew to discuss all of this. My mom's speaking at a night class tonight, so you could come over after school. I'll make sure Andrew's there."

"Why would you want to do that?" she asked, truly befuddled.

"Because despite what you think of me, I'm not a home wrecker." The words were so difficult to spit out I almost choked on them. "Look—I never would have started anything with Andrew if I would've known." That much was true.

"Little Miss Perfect strikes again." She shook her head and laughed condescendingly. "I'm not interested in your help." She continued to laugh as she walked away. "But thanks for the laugh."

I slumped over in defeat, wracking my brain for a way to get her to reconsider. It turned out I didn't need to. After only a few steps, she stopped abruptly and twirled back around to face me, smiling suspiciously. "You know what? On second thought, I think I will come over. Say 5:00?" Not waiting for an answer, she continued down the hall with a bit more pep in her step.

* * * *

A few hours later, Andrew and I pulled up to the curb in front of my house, ending an excruciatingly silent ride home from school. Andrew knew he was treading thin ice and intuitively kept his mouth shut to prevent further incriminating himself. But as I put the car into park I ended the silence, speaking more to myself than to Andrew. "Why are there so many people here?" In fact, there were so many people that Jarvis and John had to corral

111

them to clear a path for us to get inside.

Andrew shook his head. "This has Ava written all over it."

"So *this* is why it was so easy to get her here. That attention-seeking little—"

"I'm sorry," Andrew said so quietly I could barely hear him. "I'm sorry for showing up drunk last night...I'm sorry that I ever slept with Ava...I'm sorry you have to live in a fishbowl to be with me..." He shook his head in shame. "But most of all, I'm sorry that I'm too selfish to let you go, even though you would probably be better off without me. If you even still *want* to be with me."

I turned to him and put my hand on his thigh. A spark of hope flickered in his eyes at the conciliatory gesture.

"Is my Andrew still in there?" I asked, searching his soul through the portal of his eyes.

He nodded earnestly.

"Good. Because *he's* worth it."

He leaned over and kissed me lightly, then rested his forehead on mine and said through closed eyes, "Let's get this over with."

We walked hand-in-hand up the walk to my house, ignoring the paparazzi. Ava would give them plenty of what they sought.

"Don't even ask what I had to go through to get this," Jarvis said, slipping the handle of a small bag into my hand as I passed him on the porch.

I smiled at him in thanks. "Send her right in when she gets here."

We didn't have to wait long. At precisely 5:00, Ava sauntered up the walk, hand on her belly, waving and smiling brightly for the cameras. The moment she was through the door and out of the limelight, the smile dropped from her face and her usual sneer replaced it like an old friend. "What do you two want?"

"We want you to prove you're pregnant," I said matter-of-factly, holding up a pregnancy test stick.

"I need to know for sure," Andrew said.

"You do, do you?" Ava asked. "Are you ready to be a daddy?"

"Well, if that test is positive, I'll help in any way I can. We can discuss our options—" Andrew answered diplomatically.

"You mean you'll try to talk me into having an abortion so you can be rid of this little *inconvenience*," she hissed.

"No...I don't believe in abortion. At least not in situations like this. I just mean...if you decide to keep this baby—and you prove it's mine," he stressed, much to Ava's annoyance, "then, yes. I guess I'll be a father." As hope lit up Ava's face, he added, "But no matter what that test says...I'm with Eden." His face fell a little as he amended, "If she'll still have me." He reached over and took my hand in his.

"Uh! Andrew! What happened to you? You used to be fun. Now you're just whipped over this…this…nun." She folded her arms in satisfaction. I just rolled my eyes at the poetic justice of her attempted insult.

"I grew up. Life is too short to waste on manipulative attention-seeking people like you. Now piss on the damn stick, Ava." Apparently Andrew was through playing Mr. Nice Guy.

"No thanks. I'm not taking some stupid pregnancy test just because the president's son wants me to. This is none of your business." She stomped off toward the door.

"Wrong. You made it my business the second you claimed I got you pregnant."

She ignored him and threw the door open, only to find Jarvis standing guard. "Hello, Miss Jacobsen."

"Get out of my way. You might be paid to babysit these two, but I'm free to do what I want."

"That's exactly right, miss. I follow Eden's orders, not yours."

"It's okay, Jarvis. Let her go. I'll just follow right behind her and fill 'her guests' in on her refusal to take the pregnancy test. That ought to be newsworthy," I said, knowing media disgrace was her Achilles heel.

"Yes, miss," Jarvis said, stepping out of the way.

"So what? I'll just tell them I don't need to take a pregnancy test. I already know I'm pregnant," she challenged.

"You could tell them that. But eventually they're going to want proof too. Especially if Andrew and I tell them you're lying. Thanks for inviting them. It'll make it so much easier to get that accomplished."

Ava sighed in defeat, pausing for a moment to take inventory of her options. She threw her arms up in surrender. "Fine! I'm not pregnant, okay? Now just let me go home."

"I'm afraid we'll need you to prove it, Ava," Andrew said.

I held out the test stick patiently, waiting for Ava to succumb to her fate. She glanced out the window at the gaggle of journalists, then looked at me. "If I do it, will you let me leave without talking to the press?"

I nodded. I wanted to say, *Yes, Ava, I will let you leave without talking to the press, even though you throw me to the wolves every chance* you *get*, but I needed her to take that test.

She huffed across the room, yanked the stick out of my hand and closed herself into the bathroom.

"How do we know it'll be accurate?" Andrew whispered nervously.

"Because the only way you get a false negative is if it's too early. If she were pregnant, it would definitely show up by now. It's been over two months since…" I trailed off, not wanting to verbalize the rest of my thought.

Andrew looked down in shame. "Can you get a false positive?"

I shook my head.

"How do you know all of this?"

I shrugged. "I did my research."

Ava swept out of the restroom and slammed the lidded test stick on the coffee table. "There. Happy now?" She sat heavily in an armchair and brought her legs up in subconscious defense.

"Thank you, Ava," I said, genuinely grateful for her cooperation, reluctant as it may have been.

"How long does it take?" Andrew asked, fidgeting with a pen he had found on the table.

"Just a couple minutes," I answered, sitting on the arm of the couch, my nerves running rampant. We sat in awkward silence, the fate of our futures hanging on a plastic wand.

When I couldn't take it a moment longer, I took a chance and picked up the test as though it were a ticking time bomb. I closed my eyes momentarily, bracing myself for the results. At that moment, time stood still. I knew no matter what the results were, I would stick by Andrew. I loved him. And last night, whether he remembered it or not, he told me he loved me.

I opened my eyes and all of the tension in my body released upon sight of the words "Not Pregnant" in the results window. I handed the stick to Andrew and he exhaled loudly in relief. He set the wand on the sofa table and bent over, running his fingers through his hair and pressing the palms of his hands into his temples.

"Can I go now?" Ava whispered with her eyes trained down in humiliation. In that split second Ava's armored exterior lifted, revealing the lonely desolation she worked so hard to conceal. She looked so small and alone. It weakened my animosity toward her. Now all I felt was pity.

I crouched down in front of her and put a hand on her arm. "Are you okay?"

At my words her armor clanked back into place, hardening her expression. "Okay? I've never been better." She yanked her arm away and jumped up. "Like I want to have your boyfriend's bastard baby." She threw the insult over her shoulder like a grenade in an attempt to shield her vulnerability as she strutted to the door.

"Ava…wait," Andrew said, quickly meeting her at the door. Ava froze in surprise. "I'm really sorry. About everything. I really do want you to be happy."

First Sun

Ava's eyes squinted in hatred as they flitted from Andrew to me, and then back to Andrew again. "Go to hell, Andrew," she said, full of vitriol, and she slammed the door behind her. We watched through the door window as she scurried through the press pool, dodging questions as though they were bullets. How ironic that it was she who invited them to the frontline in the first place.

Two hands tentatively came around me and rested on my hips, not quite knowing yet if they had the permission to be there. I scooted back into him and he slid his hands onto my stomach, testing his boundaries. The desire and tension between us was palpable in equal parts. I wanted the tension gone. I wanted it gone right then. I whipped around and met his lips, kissing him fiercely. He pushed me up against the wall, pressing into me in angst-ridden hunger as he spoke to me. He spoke with so much passion behind his words that I knew they came straight from the heart beating in succession with mine. "I never thought about having babies before, but for a moment today when she was in that bathroom taking that test, I wished it were you. For a moment I saw our future..." He trailed off, deep in thought. "The way our future will be if...if..." A certain kind of sorrow took hold of him, rendering him unable to continue.

If what? Was he still worried that I didn't want to be with him after his relapse last night?

"Andrew, I'm not going anywhere," I murmured into his ear in reassurance. "I know who you are. One mistake isn't going to change that."

A sad smile lit a resolve in his eyes, and he spoke with more authority— almost aggressively, as if challenging someone or some force to disagree. "One day it'll be just you and me taking one of those tests. And we won't be hoping for a negative."

* * * *

A couple days later, I sat admiring the final copy of my Governmental Myths paper. It was truly a work of art, and I was quite proud of it. I looked over at Ava in appreciation for sparking my interest in the topic, and fueling the fire to disprove her claim. Having to disprove Ava's claims was becoming a necessary evil of late. She eyed me as though she could feel my stare and smiled her nasty little fake smile.

She raised her hand, glaring at me, and when Mr. Polk acknowledged her, went into all of the fascinating evidence she found proving The Curse of Tippecanoe. Mr. Polk nervously looked my way, but I just smiled at him innocently. He returned my smile and asked, "Eden, did you get a chance to 'warn'"—he put up silly little air quotes at the word, "warn," earning him brownie points in my book—"the president of his impending doom?" More

115

brownie points for his sarcastic tone.

"I sure did, Mr. Polk," I answered, turning my look to Ava. She picked the wrong day to challenge me. I was still on fire from her little pregnancy fiasco. I was not going to be pushed around today.

"And?"

"And he reacted just the way I thought he would. He already knew about the curse, of course, because James is so all-knowing," I joked, as Ava's face turned sour at my continued use of the president's first name, "and he just laughed it off. He said that while the deaths of all of those presidents elected in years divisible by twenty is 'eerily coincidental'"—I mimicked Polk's air quotes—"he attributes those deaths to (a) a lack of modern medical care, (b) a president's unavoidability of causing political unrest for approximately 50% of the American population alone, due to differences in opinions between parties, not to mention a percentage of the world population, and (c) the fact that advances in technology have provided more recent presidents with better and more timely intelligence. He thinks 'c' is the main reason why the last two presidents under the 'curse'," more air quotes, "have survived it." I nodded my head in satisfied disproval of the claim.

What I failed to mention was how although the president had pretended to laugh the curse off, his smiles didn't quite reach his eyes. Instead, a look of dread hid beneath the forced nonchalance, as though he was scared of something. But what? Did he really believe in the curse? Did he have a reason to think he could fall prey to it?

"That's just what the president tells himself to make himself feel better," Ava said, picking at her fingernail polish as if bored to death by my little monologue.

"No, James's claims are actually backed up in several sources I found. Perhaps you would've found that too if you had taken the time to research both sides," I lectured her. "And if you had access to a primary source as I did," I made sure to add smugly. "Feel free to read my paper when Mr. Polk is finished with it. Or I'd be happy to share the doc with you if you'd like."

The term "if looks could kill" reverberated in my head as Ava's glare threw darts straight into my soul.

"Sounds like you have both invested a great deal in your claims and evidence. I look forward to reading both papers," Mr. Polk said to draw the argument to a close. And while he did draw the argument to a close between Ava and me, he couldn't quite repress that nagging little memory of the look of doubt on the president's face when asked about the Curse of Tippecanoe.

Countdown: 73 Days
September 23, 2021

"Are you ready for this, Mom?" I asked, nervously looking out the window of the Town Car at the throng of people waiting to enter the White House for the state dinner.

"Ready as I'll ever be."

Our doors opened simultaneously and we stepped out of the car. Flashes immediately blinded us as people called out, "It's Eden!"

I smiled and waved, waiting for my mom to exit the car. As soon as she was by my side, I grabbed onto her elbow for some much-needed support. I wished Andrew were there to get me through this, but he had to be by his father's side in the presidential receiving line. He had never seemed so far away. I took a deep breath, smiled at my mom, and led her up to the line. While we waited, I took the opportunity to glance around at my surroundings. Every person in attendance was exquisitely dressed. Tuxedos and ball gowns were abundant and the aroma of hundreds of different colognes and perfumes mingled together, creating a unique bouquet of scents.

The line to the Southeast Gate continued to move and before I knew it we were standing before a White House uniformed guard. I didn't recognize him, but he smiled as if he knew me and said, "Welcome, Miss Warren, Dr. Warren. How're you doing so far?"

"Well…" I attempted to answer nervously.

"You're doing just fine, miss." He smiled and squeezed my hand. I returned his smile, grateful for the reassurance. He didn't even look at the invitations and photo IDs my mom and I had tried to hand him, following state dinner protocol. Evidently, I was even more recognized than I had anticipated. The secret service agent next to the guard nodded us through, indicating he didn't need to look at our invitations either. It was a little unnerving realizing that people I didn't know knew who I was.

Tara Tolly

Mom and I worked our way through the Lobby, Garden Room, and East Colonnade. Even though I hadn't been in the East Wing yet, I was too preoccupied with the formality of the event to truly appreciate what I was seeing. I made a mental note to ask Andrew for a more private tour in the future.

A queue formed at the door separating the East Colonnade from the Visitor's Foyer. I watched in fascination as each guest or couple spoke into the ear of a uniformed Marine standing in the doorway. The Marine would then clearly announce the name of the guest before he or she entered the Visitor's Foyer, where the press waited, cameras and recorders at the ready. Some guests were whisked through in a flurry, while others were stopped by a question or two from the press before continuing on into the Center Hall. The couple before us, whom neither my mom nor I recognized, was lucky enough to be whisked through, no questions asked. The Marine studied me with interest and extended his hand. "It's a pleasure to meet you, Miss Warren." I shook his hand and he grinned. Without asking my first name, he announced, "Miss Eden Warren," to the excited murmurs of the press pool.

I walked through the doors into the spotlight, concentrating profusely on not stumbling in the gold Christian Louboutin stilettos Andrew had surprised me with at Vickie's suggestion. I attempted a natural smile (which I prayed didn't come across as insincere), and was immediately stopped by a frenzy of questions as a sea of flashes attacked me. I froze in panic for a moment before recovering enough to politely say in embarrassment, "I'm sorry, but I can't understand any of you."

They let out a collective chuckle and a short, middle-aged man stepped slightly forward. "How are you feeling, Miss Warren?"

"A little overwhelmed," I answered honestly. "I usually have Andrew to get me through this stuff."

More chuckles. I seemed to be winning them over.

"What do you have to say about all the pregnancy rumors flying around about Ava Jacobsen?" Now that was a question I hadn't expected. I stood there in silence, numbly staring at the sharks before me who stood at the ready, prepared to strip me bare at the first sign of weakness. They would just have to go hungry.

I straightened my stance and confidently said, "Ava *who*?"

It worked. They laughed and moved on to the next line of questioning.

"Who are you wearing?"

Now this question I had prepared for a million times with Mom, Dani, Katie, and anyone else who would listen. "Dina Bar-el," I said, smoothing my hands over the soft silk of my waist. "And the shoes are Christian Louboutin," I added, lifting the hem of my dress to show off my stilettos in reverence.

The crowd loved it.

"How about the jewels?"

I automatically drew my hand up to lovingly caress the diamond necklace hanging over my heart. "Andrew's mother's," I said quietly. The press pool fell silent. I tried to lighten the mood back up by saying, "Well, I'll get out of your hair so you can meet the next guest. I hear she's pretty phenomenal." I winked and scurried out of the Visitor's Foyer and into the Center Hall, slumping against the wall in relief for a nanosecond. I didn't think anyone noticed, but as I straightened up, one of the uniformed Marines lining the walls of the Center Hall turned up one side of his mouth and winked. By the time the gesture registered in my brain, he had resumed his indifferent façade, looking straight ahead at nothing in particular, making me wonder if I had imagined the little exchange. I smiled and stood in the hall waiting for my mom. Unlike me, my mother had always loved the limelight and sauntered through the Center Hall doors beaming.

"What did they ask you?"

"They wanted to know how it felt having my daughter date the first son," she answered, smirking.

"What did you say?" I demanded.

She just shrugged her shoulders innocently and pretended to zip her lips.

"You suck. You seriously suck." We laughed at the irony of my inappropriate comment at such a formal event.

The parade continued up the Center Hall stairs to the first floor of the residence and down the Cross Hall. The line of people curved into the Blue Room, but I couldn't yet see into the room. As we approached the door, a White House aide handed us each a card. She, like all the others, recognized me and greeted us warmly. She asked us to write our names on the card, but clarified, "For formality purposes, of course," as if we may think it unnecessary.

"It's okay, ma'am. It surprises me every time someone knows who I am."

We smiled at one another at my private sentiment. She patted my arm and moved onto the next guest. As I walked through the door to the Blue Room, I locked eyes with Andrew.

The sight of him in his traditional bowtie tuxedo sent waves of pleasure to every nerve end in my body. I could tell by the look on Andrew's face that he was experiencing a similar sensation. Despite a hand being offered to him by a guest in the receiving line, Andrew was unconsciously drawn to me, and in a few large steps was able to take me in his arms. "You are breathtaking," he whispered, looking down on me in pure adoration. The group of people in the

Blue Room laughed softly at Andrew's obvious pleasure upon sight of me. He took me by the hand and led me to his spot next to the president and held his hand out to the gentleman he had abandoned. The man accepted his handshake and Andrew apologized. "I'm sorry, sir. But I saw my girl and had to greet her."

The man smiled knowingly and said, "I completely understand, Mr. Wellington. Beauty before age, am I right?" Everyone laughed.

The president turned to me and with eyes alight with fatherly affection said, "Welcome, Eden. You look radiant."

I blushed and looked down, smiling at the compliment. As my mom worked her way through the line, a Marine announced her name yet again. "Dr. Ann Warren."

"Ann, you look incredible. The two of you make quite the pair."

She blushed and said, "Mr. President, thank you for the invitation. This is...amazing," she admitted, looking around her.

"It's our pleasure to have you here."

I released Andrew's hand and made to walk away with my mother, but Andrew clasped my hand, tighter this time, and said, "Stay with me. Please?"

I looked at the president and he nodded his approval. Andrew beamed. I shrugged my shoulders at my mom in apology. She kissed me on the cheek and whispered, "You're doing great, honey." Then as an afterthought added, "Work it." We giggled quietly and she confidently took her leave, following the line ahead of her. I wasn't worried about her in the least. She could strike up a conversation with a mute.

I glanced back over at Andrew and caught him staring me up and down. I tried to scowl at him, but instead ended up smiling.

"What?" he asked, feigning innocence.

I grinned at him and we refocused our attention on the task at hand. Together, we shook hands and welcomed everyone with a smile. Andrew blew me away. He was a natural. The thing that impressed me the most was that it wasn't fake. He was genuinely glad to meet and greet each person. This was his calling.

After the line trickled down the president excused himself to prep for the speech he was scheduled to give in just minutes. When his father was gone, Andrew turned to me hungrily and brushed his fingers down the inside of my arm until his hand met mine, prompting my body to yearn for his. He hastily pulled me out of the Blue Room, through the Entrance Hall, and into some kind of little office.

As soon as the door shut behind us, Andrew pushed me up against the wall with the entire length of his body. "You. Are. So. Freaking. Hot." After each word, he kissed me on my neck, my shoulder, my collarbone…

"Mmm, Andrew," I breathed, my entire body on fire.

We kissed passionately for a few moments, pressing against one another in want. But our little moment of bliss was interrupted when a server came bustling through the door. "John, we need another…Uh, Mr. Wellington…I'm so sorry…I was just looking for…" The bumbling server's face turned a comical shade of red as his eyes darted desperately around the tiny room for a way to escape this horrific little encounter.

Andrew and I bolted out the open door and into the nearly empty Entrance Hall in hysterics. When we calmed enough to catch our breath, Andrew's laughter turned to tender amusement. He kissed me softly on my lips and brushed the back of his hand against my temple. We stood in the Cross Hall dangerously close to one another with the drone of the president's speech in the background, wishing we were still alone. "We should get into the Dining Room. We're missing Dad's speech, and people will start to notice we're gone."

I nodded and squeezed his hand in agreement. We quietly entered the room hand-in-hand and snuck up to our table as inconspicuously as bulls in a China shop, taking our seats next to my mom. As the president finished up his speech I took a moment to take in the grandiose Dining Room. It was stunning. The room was lit solely by candles, which produced a cozy, warm ambience. In the center of each round table stood a floating, five-tiered candelabra, wreathed in a bouquet of lilac roses, blue hydrangeas, and white wax flowers. The most complicated place setting I had ever seen was placed with careful precision over a silk cerulean tablecloth in front of each chair. The gold embossed charger in the middle was festooned with an indigo linen napkin folded to do double-duty as a menu cardholder. Three forks laid to the left of the charger, three different knives to the right, with a spoon and fork at the top. Four glasses of varying sizes and shapes sat to the upper right hand side of the place setting. *Four* glasses. *What do I need* four *glasses for?* I guessed none of them were for Mountain Dew.

The content of the president's next words jolted me out of the analysis of my surroundings and redirected my attention to the speech. "When I talked my favorite musician into gracing us with his presence tonight, I thought, 'What better way to depict my message than with one of my favorite songs?' This song has touched me since the first time I heard it three hundred years ago. Sorry, Garth," he said to a rumble of laughter.

I shot a look of shock at Andrew, who shrugged innocently and whispered, "Surprise," through an ear-splitting grin. I shook my head in disbelief and grabbed my equally shocked mom's hand. She couldn't contain her glee and practically squealed in delight.

"This song, *We Shall Be Free*, has stood the test of time for a reason. The message reminds us that while we may be fortunate to live in the land of the free, the world is far from free, and it is my mission, along with the help of the prime minister, to get as close to that ideal as possible. Please help me in welcoming Mr. Garth Brooks." The room broke out into eager applause and even a couple of catcalls and whistles.

Garth stepped onto a platform set up in the corner of the room where his guitar waited for him. He leaned into the microphone and said, "Hello, everyone. Imagine my surprise when my phone rings one day and I hear the voice of the president pleading me to come sing a little song at his state dinner. What he didn't know was that he didn't have to plead at all. All he would've had to do was mention the words, 'Kobe Beef Wellington' and I would've been on the first plane here." The audience laughed. "I am touched that the president finds the message of our song so powerful. We're proud of it and still stand by the message it sends. With that said, I will let the song speak for itself, and for the president."

Garth strummed the first chord on his guitar and a slideshow appeared behind him as if by magic.

> *When the last child cries for a crust of bread*
> *And the last man dies for just words that he said*
> *When there's shelter over the poorest head*
> *We shall be free*

Both beautiful and disturbing images of historical world events flashed before us in perfect synchronization to Garth's words. The marriage of visual and auditory sensations was almost overwhelming, but the poignancy of the message was so beautiful it brought tears to my eyes. Andrew brought my hand to his lips and kissed it, moved by my emotional response to the moment.

When the song came to an end the entire room of people jumped to their feet in a standing ovation, applauding emotionally. There were few dry eyes in the room.

"Join me in the East Room after dinner for some more songs," Garth announced before exiting the stage and heading back to his table to join his wife and other eager tablemates.

Shortly after Garth had settled into his seat, a lavish spread of four courses was served over a long stretch of time. The kitchen did not disappoint. The courses consisted of grilled halibut with kale (not my favorite dish, but raved about by the entire table), a White House garden salad, Kobe Beef Wellington with wax beans and herb butter (a play on the president's name and a traditional British entrée), and for dessert, apple cobbler with vanilla bean ice cream.

When I couldn't possibly force down another bite of food, I happily rested my chin on my hands to take in the merriment surrounding me, marveling at the improbability of an ordinary Iowa teenager sitting in the White House State Dining Room as the guest of the president's son at a state dinner.

My eyes inadvertently made their way to Andrew and covertly watched him deep in conversation with the man sitting on his other side. I wasn't listening to what he was saying. I didn't need to. It was enough just to watch the way his smile lit up his face, crinkling the skin at the corners of his eyes and softening the hard lines of his chiseled jaw. I could watch him forever. He must have felt my stare, because he looked over at me, cocked his head to the side a bit, and smiled softly.

I love him. I know I do.

My private sentiment surprised me and made my face flush in embarrassment, as though Andrew could hear them. Luckily, he didn't seem to notice because his attention had turned back to his conversation.

Before long the president returned to the podium to invite his guests to retreat to the East Room for some more entertainment via Garth Brooks. I jumped to my feet in excitement before anyone else, prompting the room to break out in enchanted laughter. Embarrassment washed over me for a moment, but quickly vanished when Garth closed the gap between our tables, tucked my arm in his and led me out of the room toward the East Room, calling, "You snooze, you lose, Andrew," over his shoulder to the delight of the crowd.

Andrew came hustling down the hall after us, amidst a swarm of guests and laughing good-naturedly. When he finally worked his way through the crowd in the East Room and to my side, he shamelessly pulled me to him and planted a big kiss on my lips. Garth broke into the song, *Shameless*, to the amused laughter of his recently gathered audience. Andrew took me to the center of the room and pulled me close to dance. I smiled up at him in adulation as couples surrounded us on the dance floor.

When Garth sang the words,

I've never lost anything I ever missed,
But I've never been in love like this.
It's out of my hands.
I'm shameless.

Andrew stopped moving and looked into my eyes with an intensity I had never seen before. He put a hand on both sides of my face and whispered,

"Eden, I love you. I love you so much."

At that moment, the world stopped moving. The room went silent and it was just Andrew and me. We weren't in the White House. He wasn't the president's son. He was just the boy I loved. I looked into his eyes and said, "Oh Andrew, I love you too." He let out a breath I didn't even know he was holding and pulled me closer. We danced the night away, basking in the glow of our newly professed love.

Countdown: 64 Days
October 2, 2021

"Do you want to see the Oval Office? It's really close to here."

My heart skipped a beat. "Are you serious? I thought that room was off limits."

"My dad's gone somewhere in the chopper and said he won't be back until tomorrow."

"I don't know, Andrew. I don't want to make your dad mad."

"He won't care. I go in there all the time. We'll just go in, look around quickly and move on. I promise my dad won't be mad at you. He loves you."

"Well, it *is* tempting…"

"Ha! I knew you wanted to see it." With a wink and a smile, he pulled me into a brisk walk. We had been taking a walk out on the White House grounds, enjoying the cool early fall day. We came to the edge of the Rose Garden, went up some shallow steps, took a left onto some kind of outdoor hallway and walked past a couple of windows. Andrew swept me through a door and we were standing in the Oval Office.

"Oh. My. God." It did not disappoint. I dropped Andrew's hand and took a few more steps forward to fully immerse myself in history. I wanted to remember everything about it. The smell, the color of the carpet, the masculine monochromatic stripes of the couches, the intricate design on the hidden door of the resolute desk. The resolute desk…

I must have taken a few timid steps toward it without realizing, because Andrew softly coaxed, "Go ahead, you can touch it." I quickly looked at him, and the look on his face was priceless. It was like a dad watching his daughter take her first steps. I threw him a quick smile of appreciation and turned my attention back to the desk. *The* desk.

I closed the gap with a couple more big steps and reverently brushed my fingers over the smooth surface in awe. I stooped over, looking for the gouge his skateboard had taken out of the side. When I located it, I smiled and touched it gently, looking at Andrew. He smiled back. I moved to the front of the desk and gently tugged on a tiny metal latch to open the door on the front panel put there during the FDR administration to hide the president's wheelchair. When it clicked, I pulled it ever so carefully and marveled at the ingenuity of the design as it creaked forward. It was so simple, yet effective. The picture of JFK Jr. peeking out of this door while his father worked flashed through my mind, making the hairs on my arms stand straight up in response. I couldn't believe I was touching the resolute desk.

I walked around to the back and gingerly sat in President Wellington's desk chair, placing my hands on the desk and looking forward at what every president would've seen since the West Wing was rebuilt after a fire during the Hoover Administration (minus a few cosmetic alterations made from time to time). My breath caught a little at the realization that I would remember this moment for the rest of my life. Andrew came up behind me and placed his hands on my shoulders. I stood up and turned into him, hugging him tightly. He buried his head in my hair and whispered, "Is it everything you ever hoped it would be?"

"Even more." And I knew we weren't talking about the Oval Office.

His arms tightened around me in response and lifted me up so I was sitting on the desk and he was standing between my legs. Placing one hand on each side of my face, he gazed into my eyes, and seizing the moment, kissed me without abandon. When I finally came up for air, I huskily teased, "Oh boy, Andrew. Is this how you get all the girls? Bring them to the Oval Office and make out with them on the resolute desk?"

"Nope. You're the only girl I've ever brought to the White House, let alone into the Oval Office. You are the only one." He brought his fingers to my face, lightly tracing the curves and whispered, "Always."

A nearby door slamming shut shook us out of our little moment, reminding us that even though the president may be gone, we were certainly not alone. Andrew lifted me off the desk and smoothly set me down on the floor. "Do you want to continue the West Wing tour?"

"Where else would we go?"

"To the Situation Room," he said casually.

"The Situation Room? Isn't that some kind of terrorist act, bringing a civilian into the Situation Room?"

"Who's telling?"

"But won't there be an army of your father's minions solving the world's problems?"

"My father and his minions aren't here at the moment. It's Saturday. Even the world's leaders need a rest every now and then. Last I knew, the world's problems were status quo for the moment. There's minimal staff, and the ones there won't mind if we sneak past them."

He stood there, smirking. Darn it. I couldn't be mad at him with that mischievous smirk painted on his face. I reluctantly accompanied him hand-in-hand down some nearby stairs, and through a couple of doors.

On the way to the Presidential Emergency Operations Center, Andrew briefed me with the short history of the Situation Room, located in the basement of the West Wing. Apparently, most of the pivotal presidential decision-making since the Kennedy administration had been made there, not in the Oval Office. That surprised me. The Situation Room has all of the latest technology available for the president to use at his beck and call. It was also the most secure place for the president to communicate with world leaders and run his armed forces. It was unbreachable, except from Andrew Wellington, presidential offspring extraordinaire.

As we rounded the corner and spotted an eccentrically dressed young woman with short, spiky red hair, Andrew sang out, "Suzanna! How are you doing? How's the new boyfriend?"

"Andrew! What's happening? Oh, you know, same old, same old."

As this exchange continued, I let my eyes wander and take in what I was seeing. "Minimal staff," as Andrew called it, still consisted of about five people, all in front of their own computer with multiple screens. I couldn't tell what they were doing, but they were all pretty engaged in their tasks and barely glanced up at us.

"I just wanted to introduce you to my girlfriend, Eden. I was giving her a tour of the West Wing."

"Eden, it's so nice to finally meet you." She extended her hand warmly and smiled. "Any friend of Andrew's is a friend of mine."

"Thank you. It's nice to meet you too. You'll have to pardon my nervousness, I'm a little overwhelmed at the moment."

"Understandable. I'm so immersed in all of this that I sometimes forget how special it really is." Suzanna was an easy person to like.

"Eden, I'll show you to the bathroom," Andrew interjected with a smirk. "Just a quick stop at the loo for this one, and we'll be out of your hair."

"Of course, Andrew. Eden, come back to visit again soon."

As soon as we were out of sight, I hissed at Andrew, "Does your shame know no bounds? Preying on that poor, defenseless, young woman. Tsk, tsk, tsk."

"That poor, defenseless, young woman knows my charms all too well, Oxygen. She knows what I'm up to. She also must know there's nothing important going on at the moment, or she would've never let us out of her sight."

"I suppose that's true…"

"Of course it is. Are you ready to see the main conference room?"

"Oh, all right. But if we get in trouble for this, I'll throw you under the bus so fast…"

"Deal!" He kissed me on the forehead, grabbed me around the waist, and playfully opened a door behind my back, pushing me backward with each step he took into a room. He turned me around, flicked a light switch, and the Situation Room appeared around me.

It was surprisingly underwhelming. It was actually a pretty boring room. Cream, suede-covered panels lined the upper walls with dark wood paneling on the lower half; a drop ceiling, and large common-looking conference table with common-looking chairs around it did not scream Presidential Situation Room. The only clues that gave away the nature of the room were the high-tech television screens hanging on the walls and numerous digital clocks indicating times around the world, including one showing what time it was wherever the president happened to be at the moment. Apparently, he wasn't far.

As usual, I must have been sporting my thoughts on my face because Andrew said, "A little anti-climactic, huh?"

"A little bit. But I guess this room wasn't built with the intentions of impressing dignitaries and foreign ambassadors like the state floor. It was built to get information. And it looks like it functions well for that purpose."

"I guess that's true. Should we move on to something more exciting? Or should we take advantage of the unbreachable security?" he said, gathering me into his arms. He leaned in, preparing to continue what we started in the Oval Office, but suddenly stopped as his eyes met mine. "Unbreachable security," he whispered, an intensity settling into his blue eyes.

"Andrew, what—?"

His face hardened as determination set in. "Eden, there's something I need to tell you." The intensity in his voice was alarming. Whatever it was that he wanted to tell me was serious. He made to close the door, but froze in the middle of his stride.

"What's wrong?"

"Shhhh," he said, moving closer to the door and listening through the opening.

"Is that your dad?" I whispered.

"It can't be. That's impossible. He's…" He stopped to listen some more.

"Shit! He's here! He will kill me if he catches us in here!"

"Andrew, you told me it was fine for you to be in here," I hissed.

"I lied!" he snapped. He frantically looked around the room for a way out. His eyes rested on a refreshment table up against the far wall. It was laid out for coffee and was luckily draped with a white floor-length tablecloth creating the perfect hiding place. "Get under that table."

I couldn't move. I was too terrified. The voices came closer.

"Now!" He urgently pulled me into a neat army roll that placed us under the table in one swift motion. He held me close to him, face to face. The terror etched into his face suggested just how much trouble he would be in if we were caught.

"What the hell do you *mean* he let it slip?" the president bellowed, storming into the room with some poor man trailing behind him. I had never heard him like this. He was furious. It was scary. "You don't tell something to someone by accident! You open your fucking mouth, and the words come out! If you don't want to tell someone something, you simply don't fucking tell them!"

President Wellington yelling swear words at someone? This must be some kind of mistake. What happened?

"Mr. President, I know this seems like a big deal right now…"

"*Seems* like a big deal? Why stop at telling his immediate family? He may as well alert the media!"

"Mr. President, they have signed a Confidential Disclosure Agreement. They know it's classified information and understand the ramifications of telling—"

"Do you think they're going to give a flying fuck about a CDA? The end of the world is coming in two months! What do they care about a stupid sheet of signed paper? What's that piece of paper going to mean two months from now? That's right. It won't mean a God-damned thing!"

I was frozen in shock. Surely he couldn't mean the end of the world. That couldn't happen. The "end of the world" could be an exaggeration for all sorts of things. Or did he mean the actual end of the world? No way. He must mean hypothetically. But what could be happening in two months that would be bad enough to be referred to as the "end of the world"?

The room went silent as we watched the president's feet pace back and forth, until finally collapsing into a conference chair. "Where are they now?" he asked in a tired, defeated tone.

"They are still in their home, sir. We sent a car immediately with detail to ensure they don't leave until the situation is under control."

"Under control," the president said sadly. "Great. You find a way to prevent the world from ending in two months. You find a way to stop a six-mile-wide asteroid from hurtling toward direct impact with Earth. When you accomplish what every nation and space program on Earth has been trying to accomplish for the last four years…when you do that, Harry, the situation will be under control."

Fear pulsed through my body as I made the connection, manifesting in waves of nausea. 9409 Apollo. It was true. I clapped a hand over my mouth in terror. Blood pulsed in my head as I realized the levity of what I just heard. The world was ending in two months. Andrew pulled me even closer, as if he could protect me from what we just heard, as if he could protect me from the end of the world.

After a long pause, Harry said, "What do you want to do, sir?"

"Bring them here. I need to talk to them."

"Yes, sir." The chief of staff's footsteps tapered off as he exited.

A long stretch of silence was interrupted when the president resumed his pacing. He stopped right in front of the coffee table for a moment, then continued to pace. Suddenly, something crashed into the wall directly above us, eliciting an uncontrollable gasp from me, and I watched a shard of coffee mug with the presidential logo fall as if in slow motion to the ground behind Andrew.

The tablecloth hiding us from view and the reality of our new knowledge was abruptly swept away, scattering what remained on the table to the ground with a crash. "Get up!" the president snarled.

I couldn't move. My body was frozen in fear.

This cannot be happening. It's not possible.

"Get up," the president repeated, this time eerily calm.

Andrew made to move, but I held him tight. "Please don't go, Andrew. I can't face this. It's not possible…"

"Eden, I promise I'm not going anywhere. I won't leave you. Please just get up with me."

Somehow I found the will to robotically move my body enough to come out from under the table. Andrew pulled me down into his lap on a conference table chair and put a hand on either side of my face. The warmth of his hands felt good against my ice-cold face.

Focus on Andrew's touch.

"Eden? Are you okay? Your face is ghostly white and you're shaking. Please look at me."

"Andrew, what the *hell* are you two doing in here?" the president bellowed. "This is a classified area and you know it—"

A heated argument droned on around me but didn't reach my

consciousness. The only sensation I was aware of was the emptiness within my body. Everything I thought I'd ever known, anything I ever *had* known, everything that could be in the future—none of it mattered now. It had all been swept away from me in the blink of an eye. I blankly watched Andrew and his father yell at one another. I just couldn't grasp the implications of this information. The knowledge of the end of the world was too much.

The end of the world...

Snippets of information gleaned from my 9409 Apollo research on the fallout of an asteroid collision with Earth reverberated through my head with each pulse of dread. The asteroid the president told the public would not hit Earth.

"It's true," I said, the sound of my own voice startling me.

The fight brewing between Andrew and his father ceased and they snapped their heads around to look at me.

"9409 Apollo...it's true...it's going to hit...we're going to die..." I managed to stutter out between bouts of uncontrollable shakes.

Andrew knelt in front of me, taking my hands in his. "Eden, I know it's a lot to take in..." he said calmly in an attempt at pacifying me. Too calmly. Why wasn't he as shocked as me?

I looked deep into Andrew's eyes, searching for evidence of surprise. There was none. All I found was reluctant resignation and uneasy anticipation—almost as if bracing himself for my reaction. But not surprise. Upon this epiphany, my world fell out from under me, sending me into a frenzied spiral of dismay.

He knew all this time...

"You knew," I whispered in horror. I gingerly stood up, not sure my legs would hold me and looked at Andrew as if for the first time. "You knew," I repeated a little louder.

"Eden, I—"

I backed away from him.

"Eden..." Andrew said, standing up and tentatively stepping toward me. I took another step back. "I wanted to tell you. They wouldn't let me...But I was going to tell you anyway. Just now—right before we heard my dad." The desperation in his voice was palpable.

"You were going to tell her?" his dad roared in the background, as if he were thousands of miles away.

I shook my head, staring at the boy before me. His beautiful melancholy face was distorted in pain; pain orchestrated from his own deceit. This couldn't be happening. The world couldn't be ending and the boy I thought I loved couldn't have been deceiving me the entire time we were together. It was too much. Claustrophobia set in. I needed to get out of there. I didn't belong there any more. Perhaps I never did. I threw open the door to the Situation Room and ran.

"Eden!" Andrew yelled in pursuit. The sound of his desolate voice tore at my heart and a single cry of despair escaped my lips as I clumsily combed my way through the Presidential Emergency Operations Center to the confused looks of the president's staff.

"Drew, let her go," the president's calm voice said in the distance.

"Let go!" Andrew cried, audibly struggling against a force I couldn't see.

When I had cleared the door out of the dungeon from which I had fled, I collapsed onto the stairs and sobbed. My thoughts ran rampant, plaguing me with my new reality. *The end of the world...Andrew knew...I am going to die...Everyone I had ever known is going to die...*I hiccupped to get air.

The door from the Presidential Emergency Operations Center opened and closed quietly behind me. "Miss?"

"Jarvis...I-just-want-to-go-home."

I tried to stand up, but my legs failed me and I clung to the railing, attempting to get a hold of myself to no avail. Jarvis scooped me up into his arms and gently said, "Yes, miss." The gesture I would have considered demeaning under normal circumstances comforted me and I burrowed my face in his neck, continuing to shed tears in mourning of my old life; the life I left behind with each step Jarvis took.

Part Two

Countdown: 64 Days
October 2, 2021

"Let go, you son of a bitch!" Andrew yelled, struggling against the secret service agent preventing him from running after Eden.

"Andrew, he'll let you go if you stop fighting him," the president said. "She's gone, son. She wants to be alone. Give her some time."

Andrew went limp and the agent let him go. The president nodded at the agent, dismissing him. Then he fished his cell phone out of his pocket and spoke into it like a walky-talky. "Jarvis, escort Sapphire home. Confiscate her cell and make sure she doesn't talk to anyone. She is privy to classified information she shouldn't know. Her mother doesn't return until this evening. I'll be in contact before then."

"Copy, sir," Jarvis replied.

The president set his cell phone on the conference table and rested his weary head in his hands.

Andrew stood staring at his father in silent fury, contemplating his next move. "Dad, please tell me there's a spot for Eden in the safe house," he finally said, a sense of overwhelming fear replacing the anger. "Please tell me she's not going to die."

The president took a deep breath and met Andrew's eyes. "Drew, you know it's not that easy."

Andrew glared at his father. "Yes, it is. Is there or is there not a place for Eden?"

"Drew, I can't just give some girl a spot in the safe house because you happen to be dating her for the moment."

"She's not just *some girl*, dammit! I love her!"

135

The president blanched. "That's what I was afraid of." He closed his eyes and pinched the bridge of his nose between his thumb and forefinger in distress. Andrew's relationship with Eden had popped up unexpectedly, causing a glitch in the perfectly orchestrated planning of the safe house. "Drew, how many people do you know have loved ones in danger of dying from the disaster?"

"Everyone I know."

"Yes. And how many people in the world have loved ones they would do anything to save?"

"All seven billion of them," Andrew answered impatiently. He knew where this line of reasoning was headed.

"Precisely. Do you see why my job has been so difficult? How do I choose who goes into the safe house and who doesn't? Everyone has a reason for going in or has someone they want to save. There's just not enough room for them all. God knows I wish there was."

"I'm not asking you to save everyone. I've never asked you to find a spot for anyone. I'm not asking for a thousand people. I'm asking for one. I'm asking you to save Eden's life."

"Andrew, I can't just—"

"You're the President of the God-damned United States! Doesn't that count for something?"

"Exactly, Andrew! I *am* the President. But the difference between any other president and me is that I'm not just governing to improve the economy or reform education. This is governing to save mankind, for Christ's sake! This isn't about protecting some teenaged puppy love!"

Andrew froze as if the president had slapped him across the face. He may as well have. "I'm sorry you think this is *puppy love*," Andrew spat out venomously. "I'm sorry you are so jaded by Mom's death that you don't remember what it feels like to love someone so much you can't imagine living without her. I'm sorry you *had* to live without her. I don't have to live without the girl I love. So I won't. You already lost the love of your life. I'm not about to lose mine." Andrew headed to the door, hell-bent on finding Eden and begging her forgiveness, but stopped right before the door and turned back to face the president. "And if you think I'm going to step foot in that safe house without her, you are sadly mistaken."

"Andrew you *will* go into that safe house. With or without Eden. I'll make sure of that."

Andrew took three swift steps back to his father and stood nose-to-nose with him. "You're wrong, *Mr. President*. If you don't find a spot for Eden, I will leave this house and never come back. I will spend my last two months with Eden and her mother and die in the arms of the girl I love. I will happily move on with her to the next place, where Mom will be waiting with open arms, and I won't shed a single tear for you." He lowered his voice and quietly but ominously added, "And if you try to take me by force, you might as well have let me die, because *you* will be dead to *me*."

Andrew stormed out the door, leaving his father amidst tears of regret.

Countdown: 64 Days
October 2, 2021

I stumbled in my front door behind Jarvis and made it as far as the living room before crumbling onto the couch in a ball. I pulled the fleece throw blanket Dani had made me all the way up to my neck in an attempt to find comfort, but all it did was remind me that another person I loved was going to die. She didn't know. And I couldn't tell her. I couldn't even tell my mom. How was I supposed to keep this from her? All she needed to do was take one look at me to know something was seriously wrong.

Tears flowed down my cheeks at the thought of how worried Mom would be about me. Would breaking up with Andrew be a good enough excuse for my state of mind? No. I would have to tell her. But did I want her to know? Did I want her to feel this way? No. I wanted to protect her. Is that why Andrew didn't tell me? Had he been trying to protect *me*? Suddenly I wanted him. Really bad. But he had lied to me. Could I ever trust him again? Did it really even matter? There was only two months left. Could I live out my last two months without him? The thought chilled me to the bone. The thought of leaving Andrew, of never seeing him again hurt physically. It actually hurt more than the knowledge that the world was ending. Without Andrew, my world was ending anyway.

Oh my God, the world is ending.

Bile rose up into my throat and I ran to the kitchen, making it to the sink just in time. My stomach voided its contents into the sink, but it couldn't void the knowledge that the world was ending. I slid down to the floor and sobbed uncontrollably, my whole body heaving.

"Miss?" Jarvis came running in, worry evident on his face. He grabbed the towel off the oven handle and wet it in the sink, not even flinching at the vomit

138

as he washed it down the drain. He knelt down and wiped my sweaty forehead with the cool cloth.

"Jarvis, it can't be true...it can't..." I wrapped my arms around my legs and rocked, halting his attempts at calming me.

"What can I do, miss?"

What *could* he do? His job was to protect me from danger. But the biggest threat of all was one he couldn't protect me from. "There's nothing you can do. There's nothing anyone can do." Except for Andrew. I needed him. God, how I needed him. Hysteria set in again and I gasped for air. But air wasn't what I needed.

Jarvis swiveled around, stood up, and retrieved something from the refrigerator. He handed me a cold Mountain Dew and sat on the floor beside me, leaning against the cupboard. "Drink that. It'll help."

I looked at the can of pop in my hand. Its normalcy threw me. My cans of pop were numbered. The thought made me shiver. I popped the tab and took a sip. I closed my eyes as the ice-cold pop spread down my throat into my equally cold body. The monotony of a ritual I had performed thousands of times soothed the fear of the unknown. Jarvis was right. It did help.

"Do you know?" I asked, my voice hoarse from crying.

He nodded minutely.

"How are you able to just go on living like the world isn't ending?"

We sat in silence as he considered my question. "I'm not," he finally answered, so quietly I could barely hear him. He stood up to leave, but I grabbed his arm to stop him.

"Please, don't go. I don't want to be alone right now."

He nodded and lowered himself back down to the floor. We sat side by side in silence staring ahead at nothing in particular.

I finally broke the silence. "Should I forgive him?"

He raised his eyebrows.

"For not telling me."

"Why *didn't* he tell you?"

"All he said is that they wouldn't let him. That he was going to tell me just before, but I don't know if I believe him. And I don't know how he could have kept something that big from me for so long." Tears attempted to form in my eyes again at the thought of Andrew's betrayal, but I was all cried out.

"So you think he should've blabbed classified information known by only the smallest group of international leaders to a girl he just met?"

"I wasn't always just 'a girl he just met.' I thought what we had was more than that."

"Then don't you think he would've told you if he could've? Don't you think it was killing him wondering how you would react when you found out?"

"Maybe…"

"He finds himself falling in love with a girl and he has no idea what's going to happen to her—or him—when…" He trailed off in despair. I got the feeling he wasn't talking about Andrew anymore. He turned to me with urgency in his eyes. "Eden, that boy would do anything for you. He didn't tell you because he couldn't. He loves you. Don't give up on him now. You need each other now more than ever."

I studied Jarvis's sad face. It was strange to see emotion from him. He was always so impassive. "Who is she?"

He shook his head dismissively and answered, "Just someone who got tired of my secrets. It was an occupational hazard she couldn't accept."

I placed my hand on his shoulder and said, "I'm sorry, Jarvis."

He shrugged. "I guess it doesn't matter now…"

I acted on impulse and hugged my protector. "Thanks for being here, Jarvis."

He returned the hug and said, "Remember, I've got your back." As an afterthought he added, "Until the end," eliciting more tears I didn't even know I still had in me. "Come on. You need to go rest." He pulled me to my feet and mental exhaustion finally took over. I just needed to go to sleep. If I were asleep, I wouldn't have to think about anything. I numbly trudged up the stairs and into my room. Despite the fact that it was only early afternoon, I crawled into bed and instantly succumbed to sleep.

I was startled awake by the feel of a hand on my brow, but relaxed immediately when I met Andrew's troubled eyes. Neither of us said a word. He kicked off his shoes and climbed into bed with me, pressing the entire length of his body against mine. We lay in one another's arms for a while before Andrew's sad voice finally whispered into my neck, his words melding into my soul. "Eden, I'm so sorry. I wanted to tell you the whole time. You have no idea how much I wanted to tell you. It was killing me."

"I know. I understand why you didn't." Tears squeezed out of my closed eyes and I whispered, "Just please tell me everything else was real."

He loosened his grip on me enough to look into my eyes and ran his fingers through my hair. "It was. Oh, Eden, it was." He kissed me gently on the lips and looked into my eyes once again. "When you left today, I was so scared. I was worried you'd never forgive me…I love you, Oxygen." His voice broke on the word "Oxygen," serving as a reminder to both of us that no matter what happened from this point forward we needed one another. I was his oxygen and he was mine. We kissed softly, comforted just to be together.

"What are we going to do?" I whispered.

First Sun

He wrapped his arms around me as tightly as he could. "I'm going to fight to keep you safe."

"How are you going to keep me safe? How can anyone be safe?"

"Eden, there's something I need to tell you."

I pulled away in surprise.

"No more secrets." His eyes glistened in earnest.

I nodded. "No more secrets."

"There's an underground safe house built by the U.S. and some of its ally nations. Its purpose is to protect people who can help rebuild life after the asteroid, until it's safe to resurface."

I bolted upright in shock.

"I'm supposed to go."

A mixture of shock and relief gripped me. *Andrew is going to live.*

"But I'm not going."

My heart stopped, fear wrenching it once again. "What do you mean you're not going?"

"I'm not going without you."

I sprang out of bed and glared at Andrew. "Yes. You. Are."

"No, I'm not. I'm not going without you." His calmness was irritating.

"Andrew I won't let you do that—"

"You don't have a choice."

"I don't have a choice?"

"No. I'm not leaving you."

My thoughts ran a mile a minute. He has to go into that safe house. He has to live. "What if *I* left *you*?" I suggested in desperation.

"Left me?"

"If I broke up with you, you wouldn't have any reason *not* to go into the safe house."

Andrew scoffed in amusement, turning my determination into anger.

"Oh, you don't think I would break up with you, huh? You are such a...a...pompous ass!" I finished with satisfaction, punchy from the myriad of emotions I had experienced over the past few hours.

"'Pompous ass'?" he mocked with a smirk.

"Yes! A 'pompous ass' is someone so arrogant he thinks there's no way in hell someone would break up with him."

Andrew's smirk was replaced in an instant with intense conviction. "That's where you're wrong, Oxygen. I thank my lucky stars every day that you want to be with me. But what you don't realize is that it doesn't matter if you break up with me. I still wouldn't go into that safe house without you. You are my world. If the asteroid takes out my world, it'll have to take me too." He

141

rose out of my bed and strode over to me, taking me in his arms. "It's you and me until the end of the world, baby. Whether you like it or not." With that, he pushed me up against the wall and kissed me hard, his hands wrapping around my bottom and pressing me into his arousal. We devoured one another without abandon. After all, what was the point of restraint now? Soon we would be dead. Did I want to die without experiencing Andrew to the fullest extent possible? Suddenly I knew I had to have him. I would not die without becoming one with my soul mate. I threw Andrew's shirt off and he gasped in longing, biting my lower lip. Our sorrow mixed with passion manifested in a desire that was almost violent in its intensity. We just wanted to escape the reality of the end of the world; we could escape it through indulging in one another.

But we were startled out of our moment of passion by a quick rap on the door.

"Y-yes?" I stammered, unable to speak clearly as Andrew kissed the hollow at the base of my neck.

"The president is requesting you at the White House," Jarvis stated through the closed door.

We froze.

"I'm not leaving Eden," Andrew answered matter-of-factly.

"He's requested both of you."

Andrew shook his head vehemently, but I put a hand on either side of his face, forcing him to look me in the eyes. "We need to talk to him. He's your father." When Andrew's hard expression held steadfast, I added, "Do you really want to die on bad terms with your father?" This clearly hit a chord and he shook his head solemnly.

I kissed Andrew gently and he pulled me close so my cheek rested against the warm flushed skin of his chest. When our breathing slowed and Jarvis let out an impatient sigh on the other side of the door, I released my hold on Andrew and retrieved his shirt from the floor. He smiled sadly in thanks and pulled it back on. I took his hand in mine and led him through the door to face what we had been trying to escape. There was no escaping it. The world was ending. But with Andrew, I could face it head on.

* * * *

Andrew and I walked hand-in-hand into the Situation Room, a unified front prepared for battle. But what we found on the other side of the door was not what we had anticipated. The wilted man that sat slumped over the conference table was not the confident, put-together presidential persona portrayed for public eyes. It was a broken man. When he caught sight of us out of the corner of his eye, he cautiously stood up, trying to gauge Andrew's reception of him. Andrew gripped my hand tighter and straightened his stance, making it clear to his father where he stood. The president nodded his head sadly in response and turned his attention to me.

Tears glistened in his eyes as he took two awkward steps toward me. He hesitated for a brief moment before wrapping his arms around me in a warm, fatherly hug. "I am going to keep you and your mother safe, Eden. I promise you that."

"Dad?" Andrew prompted hopefully.

The president turned to his son with a smile washing over his exhausted face. "I have found a spot for Eden and her mother."

Andrew took a deep breath, closed his eyes, and turned his face up as if in silent prayer. "Thank you, Dad," he barely forced out, taking me into his arms from behind and squeezing so tightly I could barely breathe. He buried his face in my hair and whispered, "It's okay. You're going to be okay." I turned around in his arms to meet his eyes, and an unspoken wave of serenity flashed between us. Then Andrew went to his father and enveloped him into a heartfelt embrace of thanks. When they clapped one another on the back drawing the hug to a conclusion, Andrew asked, "How did you do it, Dad?"

The president casually perched on the edge of the conference table, visibly lighter upon shedding his news. "I had actually been gunning for Eden's mother for a while." He turned to me. "A candidate had been selected for the United States History expert shortly before you moved to D.C., Eden. After Andrew set his sights on you, and your mother just happened to be a history expert with more than adequate credentials for the job, I nominated your mother as the alternate candidate in case the primary candidate didn't pan out. Since experts are allowed to bring their immediate family members, both you and your mother would be taken care of."

"So what happened to the primary candidate?" I asked, not quite sure I actually wanted to know.

"I received word this morning that he didn't pass the medical examination. He was diagnosed with pancreatic cancer," the President revealed.

Light-headedness set in as the pieces began to fit together. "Did the primary candidate have any immediate family members?"

"Yes. Two—a wife and a son," the president answered.

I sat down heavily in a conference chair. "No."

"Eden...what do you mean, 'no'?" Andrew asked, fear creeping into his voice.

"I mean I'm not taking the place of someone else who was supposed to be in that safe house. I won't do it. It's not right."

143

Andrew fell to his knees in front of me, studying me pleadingly. I wouldn't meet his eyes. I couldn't. If I did, I knew I would lose some of my resolve. He gently took my head in his hands, positioning it so we were face to face. "Please, Eden…" he whispered.

I shook my head adamantly. "I'm sorry, Andrew. But I can't."

Andrew kissed me on the lips and nodded resolutely. "Okay. Then neither will I."

"No! Andrew! That's not what I meant. You always *had* a spot. You're not taking anyone else's spot. You have to go—"

"Eden, we already discussed this. If you don't go, I don't go." A new determination had awakened in his eyes. Andrew was at peace with his decision. But I was not. A new determination awakened in me too. I would not let him die. I would find a way to get him in that safe house without me.

The president put a hand on Andrew's shoulder. "Andrew, will you please excuse us? I would like to speak with Eden in private."

"Dad, I don't think—"

"Andrew," the president warned.

"It's okay, Andrew," I said. He nodded and kissed me on the cheek before stepping out of the Situation Room and closing the door behind him.

"Sir, I know what you're going to try to do. And it's not going to work. I'm not taking someone else's spot." I stubbornly folded my arms and sat back in my chair.

"Eden, even if you don't accept the spot, it won't be filled by the primary candidate's family. They have been rejected through the protocol agreed upon by a group of international leaders. No matter what you do, they will not be granted amnesty."

"So what you're saying is he gets diagnosed with cancer and now his entire family is going to die?"

My accusatory tone did not go unnoticed by the intuitive president. He recoiled in response to my harsh words and fell into a chair. "I suppose that's the way it looks, doesn't it?" He shook his head sadly. "It's just not that simple. The whole purpose of the safe house is to ensure humanity's survival—to save mankind and rebuild life as we know it. In order to do that, we need the healthiest participants possible. The primary candidate just didn't fit the bill. If it's his family you're concerned about…well…there are about seven billion other people on this Earth with family members too. I can't save them all. Damn it, Eden, I wish I could! I would put every soul on Earth in that safe house. But I can't. It's just not feasible."

The president stood up and paced around the Situation Room, just as he had earlier that day as Andrew and I hid under the coffee table. That seemed like a million years ago. "You know, ever since I learned of this disaster I've questioned my faith. Why would God do this? What is his master plan? And why am I part of it? I still don't know the answer. But I do know that you and your mother are the answer to my prayers."

I shook my head in confusion.

"I've experienced what it's like to have a soul mate," he continued. "To love someone so much you can't imagine having to live a moment without her. It kills me to think of sending my son, a product of that rare kind of love, to help rebuild humanity like some kind of…of…stud," he spat out in detest. "I've always wanted him to experience true love and have children out of that love like his mother and I did; not from some forced initiative to preserve the human race. I've prayed and prayed for a solution to this fear."

He stopped abruptly in front of me and met my eyes before continuing. "Do you think it's purely a coincidence that brought a United States history expert literally to my front door with a daughter my son just happens to fall in love with right as my United States history expert gets diagnosed with cancer and rejected from the initiative? I don't think so, my dear Eden. You and your mother were brought here for a reason. You are part of a greater plan."

"So you think God wants my mother and me to be part of this initiative?"

"I know it can't just be a coincidence."

I shook my head in frustration and rested my forehead on the table. The cool wood soothed my flushed face.

"I know this is messy, Eden. But let's look at your two options. If you accept this spot in the safe house, your mother and Andrew will both go with you and all three of you will survive to help rebuild humanity. If you don't accept your spot, no matter how much you try to convince them, Andrew and your mother will not accept theirs. All three of you will die in the aftermath of the asteroid collision. And the original inhabitant still doesn't get a spot."

"Whom would the spots go to?"

"Your mother's spot would go to another alternate candidate. One that is less qualified, I may add. Yours would go to the alternate candidate's immediate family member." His voice cracked as he added, "And Andrew's…" He couldn't continue. He didn't need to continue. I couldn't let Andrew and my mom die if I had the ability to save them.

I took a deep breath. "Sir, I'll go. I'll go to save Andrew, and I'll go to save my mom."

The president closed his eyes in relief, letting a single tear fall down his cheek. He gathered me into his arms and whispered, "Thank you."

I melted into his reassuring embrace and through my own tears managed to force out, "Sir, you promised to keep my mom safe. I will keep your son safe."

My words of encouragement were all that were needed to tip him over the edge of despair. All of his fears and frustrations came to a head as sobs shook his entire body and the President of the United States crumbled in my arms.

* * * *

"Eden?" Mom said timidly as she was ushered into the Situation Room. As soon as she saw my white face and look of absolute horror, she dropped her purse and ran to me. "Eden, what's the matter?" She scooped me into a hug and her familiar touch and smell brought all of my fears and anxiety back out in a flourish of sobs. I cried into the shoulder of her shirt as she soothingly uttered, "Shhh, it's okay, honey, I'm here. Shhh…" After a couple of minutes, my sobs began to subside and she broke the embrace to look me in the eye. "What happened?"

President Wellington took a step forward, cleared his throat to make his presence known and said in his recovered presidential poise, "Dr. Warren, thank you for coming. Under the circumstances, we felt it best not to tell you anything until you got here. It was not safe to give you classified information over a cell phone."

"Classified? What does anything 'classified' have to do with my Eden?"

"Well, the information I'm about to give you will scare you. You can tell by the state of the kids that it's difficult to grasp. It's on a need-to-know basis, but since Eden has fallen upon this information by accident, she felt it was best for you to know. We cannot expect her to keep this information from you."

Mom's look of concern was all the president needed to continue. He took a deep breath and disclosed the information as casually as if he were giving a weather report. "A 6-mile wide asteroid is on course to collide with Earth in two months time. The collision will be a complete devastation. It will be the end of the world, as we know it. Not a soul on Earth will survive."

Mom put her hand to her mouth and slumped down into the nearest chair in shock. President Wellington took a couple of steps toward her and reassuringly added, "Dr. Warren, please look at me."

Mom raised her ghost-white face and looked at the president through glassy, detached eyes.

"There is an underground safe house built with the purpose of rebuilding humanity post-disaster. You and Eden have been granted a spot. You will both be safe."

Mom's face didn't register this news.

"Dr. Warren, did you hear me?" the president asked.

Mom nodded solemnly. "Eden will be safe?" she whispered.

"Yes."

As this realization hit home, the tears began to flow. I walked over to my mom and put my hand on her shoulder. She lifted her tear-streaked face and looked at me with eyes full of questions. Her lost look alarmed me. Mom had always been so strong and self-sufficient. She's always had the answers. But nobody had the answers now. "Mom," I said, squeezing her shoulder. "We're going to be okay." She nodded and gathered me into a reassuring hug.

The president cleared his throat. "I know this is a lot to process, Doctor. Would you like some privacy for a while?"

Mom shook her head vehemently. "No. I need to know what we're dealing with here."

"Understandable. Now that you know, you deserve the full disclosure."

Mom nodded her head, mopping at her face the best she could with the palms of her hands.

Andrew pulled out the chair nearest my mom and pulled me into his lap. I nestled into him, not caring that both our parents were near.

"Okay, listen. I'm going to let my presidency take a back seat for this conversation. I will divulge any information I gleaned as president, but for the most part, I am just a father talking to his son, his son's girlfriend, and his girlfriend's mother. I will speak candidly, in a manner I would not speak to the public. I also want to ask for your discretion. Please do not repeat anything said in this room until I give you the word that you may. Do we all understand?"

We all nodded our assent.

"Good. Now that that is out of the way, I will begin by describing exactly what this asteroid means to life on Earth." He took a deep breath and let it out slowly before continuing. "An asteroid over six miles in diameter will hit Earth. It is just over the size of the asteroid that caused the mass extinction of dinosaurs 65 million years ago, called the KT Extinction. The impact event will hit Earth with a force about a billion times stronger than the nuclear bomb dropped on Hiroshima. But the actual impact event itself is just the beginning of the end. Debris will be ejected into and through the atmosphere and heat up upon return, creating an infernal oven of astronomical temperatures, baking everything on Earth. Once the heat recedes, the residue left in the atmosphere will create a nuclear winter, killing off anything that may have survived. The sun is essential to life on this planet, and if it is blocked for years..."

"Where is it going to hit?" Mom asked with an ashen face.

"Asia," the president answered matter-of-factly.

"Sir, is there a chance some on the surface can survive?" I asked, already knowing the answer.

"No one on the surface of Earth will be safe. Those who are not killed by the initial impact will die from exposure to fire, contamination of water sources

147

from acid rain, lack of food, and deadly UV rays from the destruction of the ozone layer. Asteroid impacts can also trigger major earthquakes and volcanic eruptions. The super volcano under Yellowstone alone would cause catastrophic global conditions. And it's right in our backyard."

I shivered as the details of the paper I had written on the effects of 9409 Apollo came crashing back down on me in painstaking detail. The asteroid the president told the public would not hit Earth. This realization lit a fire of anger within, momentarily replacing fear. "9409 Apollo," I whispered.

Everyone's attention switched to me. My attempts to control the seething anger upon this recollection failed. I glared at the president and accused, "You went on national television and assured the world that 9409 Apollo would not hit Earth. You lied. You lied to the news reporter, you lied to me, and you lied to the American public. Sir, I want an explanation. I deserve an explanation."

"Eden!" my mom chastised. "Do not speak to the president that way."

"It's okay. She's right. She does deserve an explanation," the president conceded quietly. "That lie has haunted me since the moment it passed my lips. I owe you all an apology. I owe the entire world an apology. They will get it. But in due time." He turned to me urgently. "Eden, what would happen if I went on TV right this moment and revealed to the world that an asteroid was on course to demolish our Earth and all life on it in two months?"

I closed my eyes in consideration of his question. A movie played in my head. President Wellington solemnly addresses the public, alerting them of the looming disaster. People sit in stunned fear until yielding to their instinctual fight or flight response and resort to screaming, fighting, looting...killing. The last two months of life on Earth would be chaos. Hell on Earth. I opened my eyes and shuddered in answer to the president's question.

"Do you see, Eden, why the public can't know until the very last possible moment? While it hurt me more than you'll ever know, more than anyone will ever know, I had no choice but to lie to the public, to the citizens of the country I love more than anything." He looked down at his hands in shame.

I climbed off Andrew's lap and sat next to the president, putting my hand over his. "Mr. President, I think you are the most courageous, heroic person I have ever had the pleasure of knowing," I said, sincerity pouring out of my mouth with the words.

The president's glistening eyes met mine, and he closed his other hand over mine. "Thank you, Eden. That means the world to me."

We all sat in emotionally charged silence for a few minutes, before I resumed my position in the chair with Andrew and the president began to speak again.

"I wish this were the part where I reveal the plan to destroy the asteroid before it hits Earth, saving mankind. Unfortunately, it's not. NASA, along with every major space program in the world, has worked tirelessly for the last four years to devise a plan. Nothing has worked. We can't blow it up, because we didn't see it in time. If we broke it into pieces, the pieces would still hit Earth, causing the same amount of damage. Possibly more, because the impact site would not be limited to one place, but rather scattered across the globe. There were attempts to deflect the asteroid using light, others to disrupt the gravitational pull of the asteroid to nudge it into an alternate trajectory course..." The president paused and shook his head in frustration. "I could go through the laundry list of everything tried, but it wouldn't change the outcome. Nothing worked. The asteroid is just too big. All options have been exhausted. The asteroid will hit." With every word, the president looked more and more tired. Lines I had never noticed creased his face, making him appear older. He was exhausted. How he managed to uphold his public persona was beyond me.

"Which is why the underground living was conceived," Mom concluded.

"Yes. The *only* option for survival is to go underground. During the KT Extinction, not all species went extinct. Smaller species that could live underground survived the disaster. We have been working for the last four years on the creation of a safe house; an underground haven to collect and house everything needed to reestablish life as we know it when it is safe once again to resurface. This includes human, capital, and natural resources, as well as plant and animal species. It's not just a United States initiative, but rather a collaboration with allied countries from around the world. That means we will share the safe house with people, artifacts, animals and plants from all over the world.

"For our human resources, we needed to select the best of the best in every trade from all over the world; electricians, doctors, farmers, historians, physicists, mathematicians—you name it. Another consideration was age and health. No one above the age of 60 will be allowed. Every safe house nominee will undergo the full gamut of testing. General health, psychiatric health, intelligence, fertility, genetics...you get the idea."

"Fertility? Meaning you want to make sure they can procreate." I blushed.

"Yes. At least those of childbearing age. We need to begin the repopulation of the entire planet," the president answered.

Andrew rested his chin on my shoulder and brushed his fingers against my side. The implications of our contribution to this initiative did not go unnoticed.

Andrew changed the subject. "Dad, you never did tell me where the safe house is located."

"I suppose I didn't. This was a project of gigantic proportions. We needed a location large enough to house an underground city and secretive enough for such a massive construction project to go unnoticed with unbridled security. A place no one was allowed near. A place where no aircraft could fly over..." He looked at Andrew, waiting for him to catch on.

"Area 51," Andrew commented, sure of his deduction.

"Yes. Known as Area 51 to the layman, Groom Lake was the perfect location. No other place on the planet is more secure."

"Area 51? As in the place conspiracy theorists claim the government has hidden evidence of alien life forms?" I clarified skeptically.

"Yes. You see, Eden," the President began, "Area 51 has never had anything to do with alien life forms. There are many contributing factors to the rumors surrounding Area 51. But the rumors began because Groom Lake has been used as the building and testing site for classified military aircrafts and weaponry. When the aircrafts were taken on test flights at night, people thought they were UFOs because the general public had never seen anything like them before. Plus, since the security surrounding Groom Lake was so tight, people thought we must be hiding aliens from the UFOs so frequently sighted around the area."

I stared at the president blankly, attempting to digest what he was saying, but I was too distracted to fully appreciate this little nugget of information.

"How do Eden and I fit into all of this?" Mom asked, shaking her head in confusion.

"I was hoping you would agree to be our United States History expert," the president said.

"What would I do?"

"Catalog and organize books, articles, and photographs of historical artifacts in a computer database, consolidate information on the history of the other trades, things like that."

"Are any historical artifacts being taken into the safe house?" Mom asked.

"No. As much as it kills me, we can't have artifacts taking space that could be occupied by another soul."

We all nodded in understanding.

"We are, however, preserving some artifacts, only the most important, in other underground locations across the globe to be recovered when possible. We don't know how safe they will be, but it was the best we could do. You would assist with the retrieval and documentation of hidden United States artifacts upon resurfacing, if, of course, they can be safely reclaimed." He paused to let my mom take in the information. "Does this sound like something you would be willing to do, Dr. Warren?" the president probed.

Silence closed in as Mom pondered this proposal. The president and I locked eyes, silently agreeing not to tell my mother she wasn't the primary candidate. I would not give her the opportunity to react the way I did and turn him down. I had to keep her alive. In order to do that, she needed to accept the president's offer.

"And Eden would get to come with me," she reiterated from earlier.

"Yes."

She nodded her acceptance.

Everyone visibly relaxed. It was agreed. Andrew, my mother, and I would all be safe. We would all live.

Countdown: 63 Days
October 3, 2021

Andrew and I traipsed into my bedroom in the dark, not bothering to switch on the lights. I stumbled numbly to my bed and crawled under the covers, fully dressed. My head pounded from crying and my eyes were so swollen they could barely stay open. Andrew lifted the covers and climbed in next to me. He wrapped his arms around me and pulled me tightly to him. We lay together in silence, comforted by one another's touch. "Andrew, please don't leave."

"Not for a while. I promised both our parents that I would just stay until you were asleep." He kissed my head and rubbed my back.

"Fine. I just won't go to sleep then," I mumbled, already halfway there.

Andrew chuckled a little, and that tiny bit of normalcy was enough to lull me into a deep, but fitful slumber.

I woke up in the dark of my room, looking for Andrew. He was gone. I slumped back onto my pillow and looked at the clock. It was only 4:00 in the morning. I turned back over in my bed, but knew the attempt at sleep was futile. Thoughts raced through my mind a mile a minute. I tried to remember what I had done the day before. If I could just remember what I had done, perhaps the memory of the Situation Room was only a dream. But I knew it wasn't.

I got up, grabbed a hooded sweatshirt from the hook in my closet, and tiptoed out of my room, down the stairs, and into the chilly night air of my backyard. It was tiny, but it had a paved patio and nice-sized patch of grass. I looked into the night sky and frantically searched for an asteroid. When I was satisfied that it was not in the direct vicinity, I stepped off the patio into the dewy grass. It's cold embrace of my bare feet comforted me. I stood there for a while, wiggling my toes into the earth. Suddenly such an ordinary motion took on a whole new meaning. How many more times would I feel the moist grass tickle my toes?

"Ahem."

I jumped around in fear, only to calm instantly at the sight of Jarvis.

"Sorry, miss. I just wanted to make my presence known so I wouldn't scare you. Apparently I was unsuccessful."

"That's okay, Jarvis. And please, call me Eden."

"Why are you up so early?"

"My thoughts were running too wild for me to sleep."

I walked over to the swing and patted the seat next to me so he would join me. Surprise flitted across his face, but he obliged. We sat and swung slowly for a couple of minutes.

"Jarvis, what do you think the meaning of all this is?"

"What do you mean?"

"Do you believe in God?"

He looked at me in confusion, but answered, "I do," without hesitation.

"I thought I did, too. But I don't understand why, if there really is a God, He would choose to destroy Earth and kill so many innocent people."

Jarvis sat in silence for a moment before answering. He always chose his words carefully, if he spoke at all. "I don't suppose He *chose* to do anything."

"But if He is all powerful, why would He allow an asteroid to hit Earth? I didn't think God was in the business of destroying billions of innocent lives."

"It depends on what you believe. Billions of people believe in God, but there are many different beliefs on how He operates. If you think He's a puppet master and controls everything that happens every second, I could understand your frustration with Him."

"You don't think He's a puppet master?"

"No, I don't."

"Why not?"

"Because there's too much suffering in the world. I truly believe that if God were a puppet master, there would be no suffering. He wouldn't allow that as the force of all good."

"So what *do* you believe then?"

"I believe that God was the Creator. He put us all here, but gave us free will. After we were created, we were allowed to do as we wished."

"But if that's true, what's His job now then? To just sit around and watch us all make mistakes and suffer? Why would people pray then?"

"I don't pray for God to change anything for me. I pray for the strength to handle what happens to me."

I sat thinking. I had never thought about it that way. I always thought of

God as a puppet master. But if what Jarvis was saying was true, Armageddon made a lot more sense.

"So according to your beliefs, God created the universe, therefore, he also created Earth and asteroids. Since asteroids and Earth both share the same universe, it's inevitable for them to collide every now and then?"

After a long pause he answered. "Yes."

"And you're okay with that?" I asked, exasperated.

"Permission to speak candidly, miss?" At my scowl, he revised. "Permission to speak candidly, Eden?"

"Of course, Jarvis. Consider this an all-time permission."

"Hell, no, I'm not okay with that. I'm scared shitless." I looked at his enormous physique and couldn't help but laugh at the idea that someone his size would be afraid of anything. He smiled at my laughter. We sat in companionable silence for a while, both searching the night sky for answers.

"Hey, Oxygen."

"Andrew!" I ran to him and fell into his open arms. "You came back." I nuzzled into his chest and breathed in his familiar aroma of soap and deodorant. Jarvis stood up and hastily took his leave, nodding at Andrew on his way through the sliding doors to the kitchen.

"I didn't know the two of you made it a habit of staying up all night chatting," Andrew said, trying to make it sound like a joke, but I could sense the jealousy through his faux relaxed façade.

"Andrew, we *don't* make it a habit," I said, rolling my eyes at him. "This was actually one of the first real conversations I've had with him." Andrew's face retained its terse look.

"Are you jealous?" I asked, incredulous. "Of Jarvis?"

"Of course I am. I talk my agents into driving me over here pretty much in the middle of the night to find you in a deep conversation with another man." He shook his head in frustration. He let go of me and stormed off to the edge of the yard.

I stood there with my mouth open wide in shock. He was actually mad at me. I stormed right after him and said, "Fine. You go ahead and be jealous of the secret service agents I have to have because of you. That's really fair, Andrew."

He turned around, malice in his eyes for the first time since I've known him. And it was directed at me. "I'm sorry my lifestyle is so inconvenient to you. It seems as though it's worked out for you and Jarvis after all though, hasn't it?"

I took a step back in shock. "Andrew, Jarvis is nothing more than a secret service agent, assigned to me by your father. I happened to talk to him tonight because he was the only person available. I love you, and only you. I will always love only you. But right now, you're acting like a jealous teenager, and it's so far from the normal Andrew that it's scaring me. And right now, I have enough to be scared of." I stormed off and plopped down on the swing in a huff. I was so mad at him I didn't even cry. I just sat there seething in anger.

He stood looking out of the yard for a couple of minutes, then walked over to me with new determination, sat down, and took me into his arms. "Eden, I am so sorry." He pulled away so he could look into my eyes. "You are my world. Tonight I was lying in my bed and all I could think about was how I didn't want to be separated from you for a second. The world is ending soon and there I was, four miles from you instead of in your arms. It seemed ridiculous to be wasting even a moment of our time together. So I hunted someone down to bring me here, which wasn't easy, and I find you not in your bed, but on this swing with a good looking young guy with a badass body, deep in conversation. It killed me."

I softened at his confession and stood up. I positioned myself between his legs and pulled his face to mine. He kissed me and murmured, "I love you," against my lips.

I kissed him again and then traced his jawline with my lips, kissing until I reached his ear and whispered, "I love *you*, Andrew. Not Jarvis." He chuckled against my neck and kissed everywhere he could find.

He stood up and lifted me with him. I thought perhaps he would take me to my bed, or wished he would take me to my bed, but instead he carried me over to the hammock strung up between two trees at the edge of the yard. He positioned us as securely as he could, pulled the blanket left there by my mother over us, and we laid in the hammock, kissing and touching, until I felt the first sunlight of the day cradling us in a halo of warmth. I pulled my lips from Andrew's and let out a small moan of contentment, resting my head against his chest. He was breathing hard and his heart's rapid beat pulsed rhythmically against my cheek. I kissed his chest, realizing that I had pulled his shirt off in my excitement and my face blushed against his skin.

"Why did you stop?" he whispered between breaths. He put a hand under the back of my shirt and rubbed tenderly.

"Because I felt the first rays of sun shine down on us and wanted to focus on the sensation. This is the first time I've spent my favorite part of the day with you."

I felt him nod and luxuriated in his continued attention to my back. I ran my hands over his biceps and let out a small giggle.

"What?" Andrew asked, suddenly self-conscious.

"It's just pretty funny to me that you, of all people, was jealous of someone else's 'badass body.' Have you seen yourself?"

"Yes I have, and I'm no Jarvis."

"Um, Andrew?"

"Yeah?"

"You're pretty close. Besides, Jarvis is too big. He looks like he takes steroids. You," I said seductively, positioning myself to kiss his arms, "are perfect. You're still hella-huge," he smiled at my use of his favorite phrase, "but in a non-steroids kind of way." I kissed his arms all over to drive home my point. He lay still until he couldn't take it any more and flipped me over, pinning me beneath him. I giggled therapeutically, and Andrew kissed the base of my neck. "Please don't lose that carefree, fun-loving girl I love so much. We'll get through this together, okay?"

My face went solemn and I nodded. I pulled him down to lie beside me and we gazed up into the lightening sky.

"What were you talking to Jarvis about?"

I frowned at him.

"I'm not asking because I'm still jealous. I'm asking because I'm curious and because I want to know what's going through your mind after everything that happened yesterday."

"We were talking about God."

"God?"

"Yeah. I was wondering how God could let the world end and kill off billions of people."

Andrew nodded his head and said, "Yeah, I've struggled with that ever since I found out too."

"And?"

"And I still don't know. I have a couple of theories."

"What are they?"

"One theory is that God works in mysterious ways. This won't be the first time He made a huge overhaul of Earth. I mean, when the K2 asteroid killed off dinosaurs, it was for a reason. If dinosaurs would've continued to live, humans would have probably never evolved into what we are now. Dinosaurs and humans could never coexist. So maybe God wanted to give humans a chance to live, but had to get rid of the dinosaurs to make it happen. I wouldn't be lying in this hammock with you today if the asteroid hadn't killed off the dinosaurs."

I contemplated this theory for a while. He made a good point. But I didn't think the dinosaurs would think it was a good point. "So if your theory is correct, then we're the dinosaurs, getting killed off so some superior race can evolve over millions of years?"

"I guess so."

"That's comforting. What did we ever do to deserve it?" As soon as the words left my mouth, I knew the answer. I shivered.

"What?" Andrew asked.

"I guess we do deserve it. Humans are, overall, a pretty nasty species. Just look at what we've done. Modern humans have only existed for about 200,000 years, and look at all the pain and destruction we have caused. If this asteroid doesn't destroy Earth, humans would in a matter of time. We're a disgusting species."

"No, I don't think so, Eden. Sure, some humans are evil and destructive, but most humans are innately good. Do you really think you can group people like Mother Theresa, Abraham Lincoln, Martin Luther King Jr., Benjamin Franklin—"

"Andrew Wellington," I shyly added.

He shrugged and kissed my cheek. "You think you can call those people part of your 'disgusting race'?"

"I guess not," I said. "But this could be a survival of the fittest type of scenario. Maybe God hopes that only the best will survive, and the rest will be naturally weeded out. Isn't that what your father and the other ally nations are doing? Selecting the best in each field?"

"You think my father is playing God?" he asked defensively.

"No, that's not what I think. I don't think your dad would ever play God. He's too good. I think he's doing what he can to save the human race. I wouldn't want the job." Poor President Wellington. He has had to make some big decisions in the last four years. Bigger than any other leader in history. "I don't know if I like that theory. What's your other theory?"

"God created us, but doesn't control us or anything else He created. Once we were brought into existence, we were left to our own devices."

"That's what Jarvis thinks," I said.

"What do you think?"

"I honestly don't know. But what I do know is that this asteroid is making me rethink everything I thought I ever knew."

"Me too." We lay in one another's arms, looking up at the sunrise. The shades of pink and blue mixed together, painting the sky in an awe-inspiring purple ombre. "What I do know is that whoever or whatever created this magnificent place would never purposely destroy it."

Countdown: 60 Days
October 6, 2021

A couple nights later, I sat on my bed with my laptop, procrastinating getting started on my homework. After all, what was the point of homework now? Going to school post "full disclosure" was just for show. If Andrew and I all of the sudden stopped going to school and Mom quit her teaching job, the public would begin to suspect something. The public watched our every move. People continued to congregate outside my row house, waiting for me to make a mistake or catch me in a compromising position, just as the president said they would. But I also had a sneaking suspicion they were hoping to catch a glimpse of Andrew on one of his many visits.

I got up and pushed my curtains aside a sliver to look out my window. Yep, there they were. But the sight of them didn't irritate me the way it usually did. Instead, I pitied them. There they were, worrying about something as menial as catching a glimpse of the famous first son, when little did they know that in less than two months the world was ending. And when that time came, the first son would be the last thing on their minds.

What would happen to them? Would they die of exposure to the inhospitable environment the asteroid would create? Would they starve to death? Would they be killed in a frenzy of chaos as people fought for the diminishing necessities of life? I violently pulled the curtain closed and paced around my room, looking for an escape from this line of thought. But there was no escape. There was no escape for billions of people.

I ran down the stairs to find Mom typing away on her computer. I lay next to her on the couch and rested my head in her lap as tears began to fall. She didn't ask me what was wrong. She knew what was wrong. Instead, she played with my hair like she did when I was little and let me cry.

"Mom?" I sniffled.

"Mm hmm?"

"How are we supposed to just go on living like everything is fine?"

"I don't know, E. I just know that if we don't and people find out...well...you know what would happen."

"I know. But I can't sit and write a stupid paper for Government class. What's the point? I can't focus on anything right now, let alone school just for appearances sake."

"Trust me, I know how difficult it is. I'm sitting here planning for pointless lessons that won't mean a thing in two months. But you know what else it's doing? It's keeping my mind off of Armageddon. If I don't follow my normal routine, I'll go crazy. I used to think that if I knew when I was dying—"

I glared at my mother.

"You know what I mean. I know I'm not going to die. Well, if the whole safe house thing works..."

We both shuddered.

"I used to think if I knew when the end would be I would quit my job, travel, check items off my bucket list...but now all I want is normalcy. I want to sit here and plan lessons that I used to complain about and pretend like the end of the world is not coming."

"I know what you mean."

"Can you think of a way to write your paper so it will help you?"

I shrugged.

"What is the biggest thing you're struggling with right now?"

"Duh."

"No, I mean, what part of this new knowledge are you struggling with?"

"Faith."

"Okay, so make your paper focus on something to do with faith. What was the assignment?"

"Societal threats." An idea began to take form in my mind. "Mom, you're a genius! I know exactly what I'm going to do. Thank you."

I kissed her on the cheek and jumped up to get started.

"Eden?"

"Yeah?"

"I'm struggling with faith right now too. Let me know what you come up with, okay?"

I smiled. "Okay, Mom. In the meantime, talk to Jarvis. He helped me a little."

Once I was settled back on my bed with my laptop I Googled, "end of the world prophecies." Let's face it. The end of the world was definitely a societal threat. And I didn't think Mr. Polk would be suspicious of my topic based on the previous paper I had written on 9409 Apollo. I shivered as I remembered how scary the idea was when it was purely hypothetical. It wasn't hypothetical anymore.

As I scrolled through the articles Google handpicked for me, I wasn't surprised to see December 21, 2012 referenced numerous times. Hmph! Conspiracy theorists had a heyday with that one. According to numerous ancient civilizations such as the Egyptians, Chinese, Hindus, Hopi, Aztecs, Incas, and most notably, the Mayans, the winter solstice of 2012 was the end of something. Nobody knew what, so people began to predict that it was the end of the world. When December 21, 2012 came and went in one of history's most anticlimactic notable dates, the conspiracy theorists desperately attempted to explain why the world hadn't ended. They claimed that the prophecies were "misunderstood." They began to point more toward the positive prophecies claiming that 2012 was actually the end of a desolate era and the beginning of an "age of enlightenment." It was all a bunch of BS if you asked me. Scientists took a more reasonable approach, claiming that many ancient civilizations understood astronomy and the 2012 winter solstice was the end of a 5,000-year moon cycle or something.

I was ten years old when December 21, 2012 hit. People seriously hid in their homes and self-made doomsday shelters, awaiting the end of the world. Mom and I had made a joke of the whole ordeal, binging on junk food all month because, "It didn't matter, the end of the world was coming anyway." But millions of people around the world genuinely feared the coming of the end of time. Even I was surprisingly relieved when I woke up on the morning of the twenty-second. And the twenty-third, and the twenty-fourth, and every day for a couple of weeks. But the world moved on, and 2012 became the butt of late night talk show hosts' jokes and fodder for cocktail party wit. Scientists continued to warn, however, that the end of the world was always a possibility. We lived in an unstable universe with dangers lurking everywhere. Right they were. How ironic that just when people felt safe on Earth and no longer had to dread a specific doomsday, the universe threw them a curveball proving that we were never safe to begin with.

I refined my search to omit anything having to do with December 21, 2012 and studied the new results. Two prophets were listed over and over. Michel de Nostradamus and the Bible. Nostradamus didn't surprise me. I was pretty familiar with his prophecies from back in 2012. But the Bible? I decided to delve into the Biblical prophecies a bit further and clicked into some of the websites to see what the Bible had to say about the end of days. It turns out it had a lot to say. I copied and pasted some of the most profound and eerily close to home Bible quotes. But the Bible passage that chilled me to the bone was from the book of Isaiah. The blood drained from my face and I broke into a cold sweat as I read the ominous words.

Wail, for the day of the LORD is near! It will come as destruction from the Almighty. Therefore, all hands will fall limp, and every man's heart will melt. They will be terrified, pains and anguish will take hold. They will writhe like a woman in labor, they will look at one another in astonishment, their faces aflame. Behold, the day of the LORD is coming, cruel, with fury and burning anger, to make the land a desolation; and He will exterminate its sinners from it.

For the stars of heaven and their constellations will not flash forth their light; the sun will be dark when it rises and the moon will not shed its light. Thus I will punish the world for its evil and the wicked for their iniquity; I will also put an end to the arrogance of the proud and abase the haughtiness of the ruthless. I will make mortal man scarcer than pure gold and mankind than the gold of Ophir. Therefore I will make the heavens tremble, and the earth will be shaken from its place as the fury of the LORD of hosts in the day of His burning anger. (Isaiah 13:6-13)

"Hey, Oxygen."

I jumped a foot into the air. "Andrew! You scared the crap out of me!"

"Geesh. A little jumpy?" he asked, smiling and leaning over to kiss me on the cheek. "What are you doing that has you so freaked out? You look like you've seen a ghost."

"I'm reading Bible passages."

"Bible passages? Yeah, those can be pretty scary," he mocked.

"I just found out that they actually can be. Read this."

He sat next to me on my bed, put an arm around my waist, and rested his chin on my shoulder to read what I pointed to on my screen. I watched his face the best I could out of my peripheral vision. It was frustratingly unreadable.

"Hmm," he finally said. "I can see why this freaked you out." He wasn't making fun of me anymore. He took my laptop from me and placed it on my bedside table, then pulled me back so we were leaning against my headboard. We sat in silence, both trying to make sense of what we had just read.

Andrew finally broke the silence by saying, "Do you take the Bible's words as figurative or literal?"

"I don't know. My mom and I have never been super religious. Whenever

Tara Tolly

I would ask Mom about religion and why we didn't go to church, she would tell me that she believed in God, but didn't think you needed to be a member of an organized religion to have faith. She has always told me that as long as I was a good person that was what mattered. But when I was in second grade, a bunch of my friends would talk about Sunday school and their churches, so I asked my mom if I could go. I went to Sunday school for two years before I grew out of that phase."

"You *asked* to go to Sunday school?" he teased.

"Don't make fun of me."

"I'm not. I think it's adorable." He kissed me, chuckling.

"In Sunday school, they taught the Bible as though it was literal. But I always thought that was a little weird. If the Bible was literal, then Harry Potter could be too."

Andrew began to laugh uncontrollably. "Oxygen," he said when he had calmed down enough to do so, "Promise me you won't say that out loud to anyone else ever again."

I laughed too and agreed. "But seriously, Andrew. The Bible is full of magic. Could it actually be literal?"

"It depends on who you ask. There are millions, if not billions, of people who think it *is* literal."

"What do you think?"

"I've always thought it was more figurative myself. Because of the whole 'magic' thing," he added with a smirk. "I guess I just thought it was a vehicle for teaching moral lessons."

"That would make sense."

I sat there thinking for a while, trying to figure out how to put what I was feeling into words. "I guess the reason that passage bothers me so much is because I always thought of God as the epitome of good; a peaceful, forgiving, and unconditionally loving being. That passage makes Him sound like a vengeful, controlling, evil power. It scares me."

"Only if you think it's literal."

"But that's just the thing. It hits a little too close to home to *not* be literal."

"It is eerily coincidental." He shook his head. "But I don't think God is that vengeful either. Remember the other night on the hammock when we talked about God?"

I nodded.

"I've been thinking a lot about that. And I think God was the Creator and He created the universe. In the universe are planets and asteroids. They are bound to collide every now and then. I don't think it's because God is punishing anyone. He's too forgiving and all-loving."

"That's what I thought too before I read that," I said, motioning to the computer screen.

"Then think about it as figurative, as a story someone wrote long ago to warn people to be good."

I still wasn't convinced.

"Did God write the Bible?" Andrew challenged.

"No. But according to theological history, Jesus's apostles did. And Jesus was the Son of the Lord."

"So it's hearsay, right?"

"Well…"

"And do you think that the hearsay ever got exaggerated or embellished along the way?"

"Maybe…"

"So we have three possibilities here. One: the Bible is a literal work based on facts. Two: the Bible is hearsay written long after the primary events, opening up the possibility for exaggerations and embellishments. And three: the Bible is a collection of stories fabricated by religious leaders to teach moral lessons. Which seems most plausible?"

I sat thinking.

"Don't overthink it. Which seems most plausible?"

"Two or three."

He nodded in agreement.

"Andrew, how did you get so smart?"

"I'm not. I'm just trying to figure it all out, just like you. And it's not easy."

"No, it's not."

"You know what's getting me through all this?" he asked softly.

"What?"

"You. Eden, what we have, this kind of love, was created by God. I really think that. It's too powerful. It's too pure. The same God who created love and all the other amazing things in the universe couldn't destroy it all in a vengeful rage. That God," he continued, gesturing to my computer, "was fabricated by man. This," he said, kissing me gently, "was created by God."

Countdown: 50 Days
October 16, 2021

"Happy birthday, Oxygen." Andrew gathered me in his arms and swung me in a circle, lifting me off the ground.

"It is now," I said as I nuzzled into his neck. Mmmm...he smelled so good.

"You look amazing," he whispered as he bent over to kiss me. Then he pushed me at arm's length and looked me up and down. "Oh my," he breathed as he twirled me in a circle drinking me in. I had chosen a simple, long-sleeved, loose-fitting, but extremely short cobalt blue dress. He pulled me back to him so our entire bodies were pressed against one another and kissed me long and hard. When we finally broke apart, he murmured, "Let yourself have fun today, Oxygen. You deserve it." Then his face broke into his trademark smirk. "Actually, you just try *not* to have fun with what I have planned," he added cryptically.

"What *do* you have planned?" I grilled.

"It's a surprise." The twinkle in his eye was contagious, and I felt a sense of excitement build in my stomach. He led me to the Town Car parked in front of my house, opened the door for me to get in, then walked around to the other side and got in himself. In this new world of uncertainties, one certainty I could count on was Andrew being a perfect gentleman. And today I let him be one.

I watched out the window in curiosity and tried to guess where we were going, but unfortunately, my knowledge of the D.C. geography was still pretty limited, and I was lost almost immediately. The only thing I knew was that we were leaving the city and heading into Maryland. I really had no idea what could be in store for me today.

Finally, we approached an elaborate and highly guarded entry gate with a sign that read, "Andrews AFB, Main Gate."

"Andrews AFB? What's that mean?" I asked.

"Andrews Air Force Base."

"Andrew! I didn't know you had your very own Air Force Base!" I joked.

"Ha ha ha."

"No, seriously, what are we doing at an Air Force Base? I really don't have any aspirations for joining the armed forces."

"You don't? Crap. You're not going to like my surprise much then," he teased.

What could we possibly be doing? As the car slowed, a giant airplane on the tarmac came into view. On the side it said, "United States of America." Air Force One.

"Are we meeting your dad here?"

"Nope."

"Then what are we—Oh my God—" I interrupted myself, "We're going on Air Force One?" I exclaimed in astonishment.

"Yep. Well, technically if the president isn't actually on the plane, it's not called Air Force One. But this is one of two planes used as Air Force One to transport the president. It's going to take us to Cedar Rapids. I thought with everything going on, you might need a little bit of home." He smiled waiting for my reaction.

I clapped my hands in glee and planted a kiss on Andrew's cheek. "Cedar Rapids? Oh my gosh! I need to call Dani! When are we coming back? I need to call my mom, she'll worry…" I babbled as my mind ran a mile a minute.

He took my phone out of my purse and handed it to me. "There should be a message from your mom on your voicemail."

I grabbed my phone and punched at it to find my mom's message. There it was. I hit play and put it to my ear.

"Hi, honey! Happy Birthday. I love you so much. I can't believe my little girl is now officially an adult. Eighteen years goes by in the blink of an eye. I could not be prouder of all you have become, and I know that despite everything going on, you are bound for bigger and better things. Your life will mean something. No asteroid can stop your shooting star." She paused, and I visualized her wiping away a tear. I did the same. "I gave Andrew permission to take you in Air Force One to Cedar Rapids. You have quite the boyfriend. He's been planning this all week. He really loves you, Eden. I don't want to give anything away and ruin his surprise, but you're in for an eventful day. Try to forget your troubles and have a blast. I'll see you tomorrow! Love you!"

I set down my phone and sat still for a while, only moving to wipe an occasional tear from my cheek. Andrew got out of the Town Car, came around to my side and opened the door. I climbed out of the car, took his hand, and let him lead me up the lowered staircase and onto the plane. We stepped onto Air Force One (or whatever it's called when the president is not on it), and through a door on the immediate left into the nose of the plane. It didn't look like an airplane; it looked more like an upscale hotel suite. Ahead of me, there were a few doors leading into different rooms. I craned my neck, trying to see into some of the rooms.

"You like?" Andrew asked with raised eyebrows, smiling at my obvious approval.

"How could I not? It's amazing!"

"Over there is the bedroom, which I would *love* to take you into," he said, pulling me close to his side with an evil grin as my eyes lit up, "but I won't," he added, smiling and kissing me on the cheek when my face transformed into an exaggerated pout. "There's a bathroom if you need it during the flight," he continued, pointing, "and here," he said, pulling my waist and leading me into a room, "is the office. I think we'll spend the flight here, if that's okay with you."

"Gee, I don't know, Andrew. I'm not sure if the Presidential Office aboard Air Force One is good enough travel conditions for me…"

"Ah, that's my girl. High maintenance as always," he joked ironically. "Come sit down with me."

We snuggled into a leather-upholstered couch against the far wall of the office that mimicked the odd, dogleg shape of the presidential desk. The room was surprisingly plain, but its lavish finishes were chosen for comfort.

My eyes gravitated toward a decorative box sitting on the side table next to the couch. It was the size of a picture box covered in a black and white striped pattern. On the top of the box was an oversized red gift bow.

Andrew followed my gaze to the box and said, "Go ahead, it's for you. Open it," with a smile.

I smiled back at him shyly. But he had piqued my curiosity, so I carefully picked up the box and took the lid off. Andrew put an arm around me and stroked my upper thigh with his thumb as I rummaged through the box trying to make sense of its contents. The moment I realized what the items had in common, my eyes deceived me and conjured up tears I didn't even know I had for the subject matter. Inside the box were medals, pictures, and newspaper clippings featuring my father. I gingerly picked up a laminated article showcasing my father, AKA Robby Reemer, mid-sack in a game against Michigan State. The headline read, "Can Reemer Ream the Big Ten Sack Record?" I took a deep breath and tried to swallow the lump that had formed in my throat. I dropped the newspaper article back in the box and flipped through several others, all depicting my father as the football hero that he was in both

First Sun

high school and college.

Besides newspaper articles, there was also a collection of photographs of my father as a child growing up with my grandma and grandpa and pictures of him later with my mother. I was particularly drawn to a professional picture of my mom and dad at prom. Mom was stunning in her blue, floor-length, form-fitting gown, and my dad's muscles filled in his tuxedo quite nicely. He could've given even Jarvis a run for his money. But the picture that rocked me to my core was the one of my parents beaming at one another, my father's hands possessively placed over her slightly protruding baby bump. My father's green eyes sparkled with love for my mother and their unborn child. His eyes sparkled with love for *me*. I held the picture to my heart and through closed eyes whispered, "Andrew, this is..." I couldn't finish. Tears for my father streamed down my face, tears that proved I cared more for him than I ever realized. "Thank you."

"You're welcome." He put a finger under my chin and gently tugged my head around to face him. "You're always so interested in everyone else's history. I just wanted to make sure you had a piece of your own history before it's too late; before it's all gone."

"I love it." I brushed my lips against his. "How did you get all of this stuff?"

"With a little help from your mom and your grandma."

"My grandma?" Now the tears fell even more freely. My father's parents had remained in contact with me throughout my entire life, even though my father was gone. Now they were going to be gone too. They were just two more people I loved who were going to die.

Andrew carefully returned the photograph of my mom and dad back to the box, replaced the lid, and set the box back on the side table. He wiped my cheeks with his thumbs and said, "I'm sorry. I didn't mean to make this harder on you. I just—I know what it's like to be judged based on a few bad decisions. I wanted you to see that your dad wasn't all bad. He loved your mother and he loved you."

I closed my eyes and shook my head in awe of Andrew's thoughtfulness. "Andrew, I can't even tell you how much this means to me. I couldn't think of a more perfect—"

"Mr. Wellington, are you ready for takeoff?" a voice boomed into the cabin, making me jump a mile into the air and abruptly drawing our conversation to a close.

Andrew chuckled and answered, "Ready when you are."

"Don't we have to get buckled in or something?" I asked, nervously looking around for a seatbelt.

167

Tara Tolly

"On a commercial flight, maybe. But not on this plane. Have you flown before?"

"Yes, but only in coach. With a seatbelt," I added stubbornly.

"Come here, Oxygen. You don't need no stinkin' seatbelt," he joked. "I'll keep you safe." He pulled me down onto the couch so I was lying on my back and he positioned himself lying on his side, holding me in his arms. He whispered in my ear, "I'll always keep you safe." And I knew we weren't talking about airplanes anymore.

Taking off in Andrew's arms was the most wonderful sensation I had experienced in my life. The plane began to taxi down the runway as Andrew kissed my neck. As the belly of the plane lifted into the air, Andrew moved onto my collarbone. And as the plane ascended into the air, Andrew rolled on top of me and plunged his tongue deep into my mouth. I moaned in pleasure and we explored each other for the remainder of the flight.

* * * *

A couple hours later, the pilot came over the loud speaker alerting us of our descent. I looked out the window and broke into a huge smile as I saw the Cedar Rapids skyline. It was a small skyline, but it was *my* skyline. Andrew leaned over and asked what we were looking at. I excitedly pointed out all of the landmarks I could make out as we descended.

As we stepped out onto the Eastern Iowa Airport tarmac, I took a deep breath. I never realized it before I moved, but cities have distinct smells. D.C. just doesn't smell right. Not bad, just not right. This air smelled like home. And it instantly lifted my spirits. I took a couple of large steps forward, turned to Andrew with my hands raised in the air and with a gigantic smile on my face shouted, "Welcome to Cedar Rapids, Iowa!"

"Happy to be here, Oxygen. I'm happy to be anywhere with you." He swept me back into an embrace and kissed me in my hometown, then grabbed my hand and led me to a Town Car waiting near the plane. How did he do that? How did he have a Town Car waiting everywhere we go? I realized I didn't really care at the moment. I was just glad it was there.

As we got into the car, I asked, "What's the plan?"

"You'll just have to wait and see." The car took off and as we drove to wherever we were going, I acted as the tour guide, giving details of my early life prompted by the sight of different places along the way. "Do you see the word 'PRAIRIE' spelled out on that hill in cement? That's where I used to go to school," and "I went there on a field trip in third grade." Andrew couldn't have been more attentive. He actually acted like he cared. And I think he actually did.

168

First Sun

As we sped down I-380 North, I opened my window and stuck my head out of the car to catch a whiff of my favorite smell in the world. When I caught the smell of Quaker Oatmeal, I closed my eyes and breathed it in as deeply as I could. The smell was therapeutic, and for a moment the world wasn't ending.

I retreated back into the Town Car to a smirking Andrew. "I didn't know you were part dog."

I ignored his comment. "Can you smell it?"

He nodded enthusiastically. "Yeah. It smells like..." He took a couple deep breaths, "like..." I nodded encouragingly while he processed the smell and searched his schema. I knew the second he placed the smell, because his eyes lit up. "It smells like Crunch Berries!" he exclaimed.

I laughed and nodded. "It's the Quaker Oatmeal factory. Is that the best smell ever or what?"

"It is! It smells so good!"

"I can't believe our luck! Usually it smells like oatmeal, which is still good, but Crunch Berry day has always been my favorite!"

I put my face back out the window and soaked in my hometown. As we continued on our road trip, I realized where we might be going. We moved out of Cedar Rapids and into Marion, a quaint suburb of Cedar Rapids.

"Andrew, are we going to dinner?" I asked hopefully.

"Yes."

I closed my eyes and crossed my fingers and when the car came to a stop, my wishes came true. We were in front of Zoey's Pizzeria in Marion. It was my favorite restaurant. "How did you know?" I exclaimed. "Andrew, you are in for a treat. This is by far the best pizza you will ever eat." The unspoken words, "or one of the last pizzas you will ever eat," sat between us like a brick wall. We both felt it.

Andrew lifted my chin so I would look into his eyes and said, "Forget about that. Let's enjoy the best pizza ever." He smiled and ushered me out of the car and into a horde of people and news cameras that had collected in response to word that we would be making a visit. Andrew and I turned on the charm for the crowd and posed for pictures and shook hands.

When we were finally able to break away from the crowd, Andrew held the door open for me, and as I walked through it, a bunch of familiar smiling faces shouted, "Surprise!"

I stood there in shock for a moment, then turned to Andrew and buried my face in his shoulder. "Thank you," I said foolishly to his shoulder, but he heard me and kissed the top of my head. I came out of hiding, looked around, and tears of happiness sprung into my eyes. My eyes locked on Dani, and the tears came flowing. I ran to her and threw my arms around her. "Oh, Dani! I've

169

missed you so much!"

She returned the hug and tears and said, "Welcome home, Eden."

I pulled away to look at her. Had she changed at all? Long full head of wavy brunette hair, olive-toned skin, big brown eyes…nope, she was still my Dani.

"Um, Eden? Holy crap is he hot," she muttered in awe as we watched Andrew shake hands with my friends. "I mean, I've always known he was hot from the press, but wow! Pictures don't do him justice, do they?"

"No, they don't," I said dreamily as he caught my eye and flashed a heart-stopping grin.

"Can I lick him?" she asked, equally dreamily.

I busted out laughing. "Oh Dani, I've missed your inappropriateness! No one else gets it. But no, you may not lick him. I might later, though," I said raising and lowering my eyebrows suggestively. We could not stop laughing. We just got each other.

"What are you two laughing about?" Andrew asked as he joined us.

"Dani wants to lick you," I admitted as Dani slapped my butt in horror.

"Okay, well…maybe later." He grinned raising and lowering his own eyebrows, unknowingly mimicking my actions from only moments before.

This got us going again and Andrew joined in the laughter. I thought they'd get along just fine. As much as I hated to leave Dani's side, I left her with Andrew so they could get better acquainted while I acknowledged the rest of my guests, knowing full well Dani would tell him every humiliating story about me that she could think of before I returned. They were given strict directions to order a New York-style taco pizza with no onions or black olives, and another Chicago-style pizza with just pepperoni. Andrew raised his eyebrows at the mention of taco pizza, but I left Dani to fill him in. What is it with New Englanders and their ignorance of taco pizza? They didn't know what they were missing.

I made the rounds happily catching up with high school and family friends. All of them ogled over Andrew. Even the guys were in awe. I sometimes forgot that he was famous. To me he's just my Andrew, not Andrew Wellington, son of the President of the United States.

At one point during dinner, I looked around at all of my friends and the realization that this would be the last time I would see them struck me like a bolt of lightning. In two months they would all be dead. A giant lump formed in my throat and I couldn't eat. I set down my fork, and excused myself to the restroom. As soon as I shut the door, I relented to the sobs as my despair consumed me.

Eventually, someone knocked gently on the door. "Eden? Are you okay?"

First Sun

Andrew softly questioned through the door.

I threw open the door, pulled him in and slammed the door shut. I paced back and forth, sobbing. "How can I do this? How can I sit and eat dinner with my friends knowing this is the last time I will ever see them? That in two months they will all be...be..." I couldn't say it out loud. If I said it out loud, it would be true.

Andrew pulled me into a tight embrace and rationally said, "Because if you don't spend this time with them, you will regret it. If you waste another second of this precious time in the bathroom crying, you will regret it for the rest of your life. Because you love them and you are glad they don't know. Because if they knew, they would not be out there eating pizza and laughing and talking about Homecoming. Because if they knew, they would be somewhere panicking, scared out of their wits, living their final months in terror. You want them to live their last two months in happy ignorance of their impending doom. You love them and you need this closure. You deserve it." I continued to sob into Andrew's shoulder as he rubbed my back, letting what he said sink in.

I realized at that moment how President Wellington was able to act so normal for all this time around the public even with the burden of the inevitable end of the world on his shoulders. The public could live happily, as though the world wasn't ending, because to them, it wasn't. Ignorance truly was bliss.

I pulled away from Andrew and said, "You're right. I don't want them to know. I don't want *me* to know." We smiled ironically at this realization and hugged. "Oh my gosh, how am I going to go back out there now? I'm a mess."

"You're beautiful. You always are."

"You're a good liar," I said through a reluctant smile. "Will you go grab my purse so I can try to put on a better face?"

"Okay, but there is no better face." He swiped his thumbs under my eyes to wipe away what remained of my tears, gave me a quick kiss, and went to retrieve my purse.

When I finally exited the restroom, ready to face my reality, the entire room broke into "Happy Birthday." On each table was two Zookies, the best dessert on the face of the planet. It's a giant chocolate chip cookie cooked to order in a cast iron skillet, served fresh out of the oven with scoops of ice cream and topped off with whipped cream and drizzles of hot fudge. It is heaven on a plate, or rather in a skillet. I smiled and curtsied for my audience and said, "Andrew, step away from the Zookie. That one's all mine!" Everyone laughed as he pushed it in front of my seat, raising his hands in surrender.

* * * *

Later that night, after reassuring Dani's mom a million times that everything was adequate in her basement for Andrew to sleep, I was at last alone with him for a moment. He pulled me down onto the couch on his lap and kissed me. "I have been waiting to do that all night," he said with a deep sigh, still holding on tight. "And I've been waiting to do this all night..." He shifted enough to reach into the inside pocket of his jacket and came out with a small box. "Happy birthday, Oxygen," he said shyly as he handed it to me.

"*Another* present? Andrew, you've already done enough. You didn't have to do this," I said, shaking my head at him.

"The other one was just part of your present. This is the rest of it."

I shook my head in reproach, but couldn't help but smile. I moved to open the little box, but Andrew stopped me.

"Hang on. I want to explain something before you open it. I think you can tell by the box that it's a ring. It's not an engagement ring. I want it to be. So badly. I can see now why people married so young long ago. They didn't live as long. They wanted as much time with the person they loved as they could get. That's how I feel now. Every moment with you is precious. I would marry you right this minute if I could. But first of all, I'm not eighteen yet. I won't be for three months. That's after..." I stopped him from having to say it by kissing him tenderly. He reluctantly pulled away after a moment and said, "Let me finish. Second, a month and a half from now, we don't know for sure what's going to happen. I mean, we know what's going to happen. But we don't know what the full fallout will be. We may be in a safe house, or we may be in heaven. But wherever we are, we will be there together." He paused to wipe away another one of my darn tears. "Are you okay? Am I scaring you? I can stop," he said, worry wrinkling his forehead.

"No, I'm fine. Surprisingly, these are happy tears. Please continue," I whispered.

He nodded. "I always thought promise rings were stupid. I always thought, why not just wait for the real thing? Why do you need a stupid ring to prove how you feel about someone? But now I get it. Especially with an asteroid heading straight toward us. This ring," he opened up the box and I gasped at its beauty, "is my promise to you, not only that I will marry you someday, because I will, but that despite what happens in the next couple of months, we'll be together." With that, he slipped the ring on my right hand.

* * * *

"Holy crap!" Dani exclaimed as she examined my hand. "That ring is un-frickin-believable!" It really was. It was a Cartier platinum and diamond ring.

172

Each diamond was encircled in platinum and they were all connected to make it look as though they were simply pushed together in a row encircling my finger. The effect was breathtaking.

"I'm sorry, but I can't stop smiling," I said, grinning like an idiot.

"Ya think? Geesh, Mr. Hot-Pants-Son-of-the-President is hopelessly in love with you and just put a freakin' pound of diamonds on your hand. Smile away." Then she squealed with delight and pulled me up on my feet to jump up and down with her.

"Oh, Dani. I miss you so much!" I said and hugged her tight.

"Okay, it's my turn to give you a present! It's no diamond ring, but I think it's pretty cool."

I excitedly tore open the package to find a memory book, the kind you can make online with personal pictures but ends up looking like a real book. "Ooh!" I clapped my hands in excitement. "You made me a photo book!"

"I did. Now let's crack it open and take a walk down memory lane."

For the next hour, Dani and I reminisced about each picture, laughing so hard we cried. The book was phenomenal. It started with pictures of us together as babies, simply lying there on the floor with our moms nearby chatting about anything and everything, to pictures of us playing in a backyard pool as toddlers, to those awkward elementary school years, all the way up to more recent pictures of us in cowboy hats at a country concert and all trussed up for the Christmas dance at school. She made sure to highlight every important moment of our lives together growing up and include everyone from home whom I hold near and dear to my heart. It was a work of art.

But the page that touched my heart the most was the final one. The heading at the top said, "Roots and Wings." Under the word "Roots" was a picture of Dani and me posing in front of Cedar Rapids' Five Seasons statue on the Fourth of July. Under the word "Wings" was a picture of Andrew and me that my mom took of us in the White House the night of the State Dinner. I gently brushed over both pictures with my fingers and looked at Dani. She was watching me carefully.

"Dani, this book…" I began to cry. Really cry. I grabbed her into a hug and sobbed into her shoulder. She had no idea how perfect this gift was. My friend, my best friend in the world…how could I say goodbye? How could this be it?

Dani patted my back. She's never been good at hugs. Tough. "Hey, it's okay, Eden. You see, that's what this book is for. To show you that nothing is over, it's only just begun. Cedar Rapids is your roots. Washington, D.C. is your wings. You can have both. We will always be here when you need us, and I know you will always be there for me even as you move on with your life."

I continued to cry until I didn't have any tears left. Poor Dani just sat there hugging me and rubbing my back. When I finally calmed down, Dani said, "Okay, this is totally not just an 'I miss you' kind of cry. What's up, E?"

I sighed, trying to think of a way to tell her what was bothering me without telling her too much according to President Wellington. "Andrew and I overhead his dad, the president," Dani rolled her eyes at my clarification, "talking to the chief of staff about something super classified that I can't tell anybody about and it's killing me because I feel like I'm lying to the people I love."

"Oooooh…is it that he's secretly a vampire and Andrew is his vampire offspring? Because that would explain a lot," Dani asked, wide-eyed with hope.

"Sorry to disappoint you, Dani. But thanks for the smile. I really needed that."

"It was worth a shot." She shrugged her shoulders innocently. "Okay, it's super-secret. So what? Will the public find out eventually?"

"Definitely." I nodded my head vigorously to stress the truth of my agreement.

"So then it's not lying, right? It's just delaying. I promise I won't be mad at you, no matter what it is. Okay?"

The funny thing was I believed her. She won't be mad at me. She will understand and be there for me. She will be about to die, but she'll want to tell me something silly like be sure to have lots of mini Andrews because not only would that rebuild the population, but it would also be the beginnings of a superior race. That was why she was my best friend.

I hugged her one last time and said, "Thank you. Thank you for being you. I honestly think you are the only person in the world who could make me feel better at this moment in time."

"You're welcome. Now can we go to bed? I need to get my beauty sleep so I don't look like hell tomorrow morning in front of Mr. Wonderful. You might look like hell, though. Your eyes *are* going to be pretty puffy. I may be able to steal him right out from under you!"

"Touché, Dani, touché."

We had finally settled down and I was just about to fall asleep when Dani cried out, "Holy crap! Andrew Wellington is asleep in my basement!" We both giggled as I took my pillow and beat it repeatedly over her head. God, I have missed my friend.

As Dani lightly snored through the night, I lay awake, absorbing every last moment with the girl who was like a sister to me. I resisted sleep, knowing it was the last time I would ever see her. Tears fell onto my pillow as I watched her peaceful slumber, unaware that her days were numbered.

First Sun

How do I say goodbye?

Knowing I couldn't say the kind of goodbye I wanted to without giving away the reason for my despair, I said my goodbye in silence under the blanket of night. By the time morning came, I was able to fake my way through a more generic goodbye knowing I would still be able to talk to Dani on the phone over the next couple of months. In this way I could trick myself into believing it was not actually goodbye. If I allowed myself to think about the alternative—the reality that my best friend was going to die a horrific death—I wouldn't be able to go on living. But would it really be living? Hidden away like a cockroach refusing to be squashed while the rest of the souls on Earth suffered to their inevitable end? No. I wouldn't allow myself to go down that road. Instead, I would do what I needed to do to cope, even if it meant lying to myself. The reality was too terrible to face.

Countdown: 32 Days
November 3, 2021

I couldn't breathe. A burning inferno of heat enveloped me, threatening to suffocate me. Fire rained down from a blood red sky, hungrily igniting anything it touched. People and animals frantically ran engulfed in a shroud of fire trying to escape their destiny. I frantically searched for a safe haven, somewhere to hide. A door appeared out of nowhere and swung open, wafting a cool wave of oxygen-rich air in my direction. I ran through it, greedy for serenity. I turned around to close out the heat, the pain, the suffering. But as I pulled the door shut, I realized the fire people looked familiar. They ran to me, fires blazing, fed by the breeze of their haste. As they closed in, I caught sight of their blistering faces, the faces of the people I loved, immersed in a sea of fire. I had to save them. I looked through the door at the tranquility awaiting me, then back at the people I loved in distress. I closed the door and stepped back into hell. As the door latched shut and disappeared, a burning hand closed upon my wrist. I looked to see who it was and screamed at the sight of Andrew, burning in a ring of fire. Another burning hand clasped over my mouth. I turned my head to meet the anguished eyes of my mother, red with fire.

I woke with a start soaking in sweat, wrapped in the covers of my bed. I was momentarily relieved by my surroundings, until I realized there really was a hand clasped over my mouth. But it wasn't my mother. It was a stranger cloaked in black with a black hood covering his face, with holes cut only for eyes. Eyes scorching with hatred.

"Mom!" I tried to call out, but found I couldn't. A cloth was stuck way back in my throat, threatening to choke me.

"If you scream, I will kill your mom, you little bitch," an accented voice spoke harshly into my ear. I recoiled at the feel of a knife on my neck. Was I still dreaming?

You have to keep Mom safe, my subconscious told me. *Don't scream.*

Someone picked me up and threw me over his shoulder, knocking the wind out of me. He walked across my room and threw me through a hole in the wall where my dresser should have been into the neighboring row house. I landed on the ground with a thud. It hurt. I instinctually put my hand on my shoulder where it struck the ground and groaned.

"Shut up, you little bitch, or your mom will pay for your lack of self control."

I shut up. *Whatever you do, Eden, don't risk Mom's life.*

I was thrown over someone's shoulder again and lugged through the row house and out into the backyard. All I could hear was crickets. My captor walked as quickly as he could with me as a burden through a couple of yards and dropped me into the trunk of a car. He slammed the trunk into place and I was immersed in darkness.

Claustrophobia set in and I panicked, kicking and hitting anything I could get at and screamed as loud as I could despite the rag in my mouth, over and over until my voice went hoarse, and then I screamed some more. The trunk reopened and a hooded man said in his mid-Eastern accent, "Shut up, bitch." He swung his hand back and struck me with all the force he had, knocking me unconscious.

* * * *

I opened my aching eyes slowly. My head felt like it was going to explode. It pulsed with pain, as if someone was taking a hammer and pounding it against my temple in a regular beat. My first instinct was to try to spit out the gag tied around my head and almost choking me from being shoved so far into my mouth. It was too tight. I was so thirsty, and I couldn't even swallow my own saliva to alleviate it. I tried to take a quick inventory over the rest of my body. It hurt. Every square inch hurt. I attempted to move my legs and arms to see if they were broken, only to find they were tied to the chair I was slumped in. This renewed my panic and I struggled against the ropes until my wrists and ankles were raw. They didn't budge. I finally slumped over in exhaustion.

Where the hell was I? I looked around at my surroundings to try to catch my bearings. I was in some kind of garage. It was huge and looked fairly new. Nearby was a large, flat panel TV and several computers crudely set up on collapsible tables facing away from me. Two men stood heatedly talking across the room near some kind of overhead doors. They were both holding huge guns, which looked like they could be automatic. *Oh my God.* What did they want from me? It had to be about Andrew or his father. I knew it did. It was the

177

only explanation.

Andrew...my beautiful Andrew...I would never see him again. This was it. This was how I was going to die. For the past month, I had been dreading the end of the world. The thought never occurred to me that I wouldn't make it to the end of the world.

Another wave of panic washed over me as I desperately attempted to swallow. I was suffocating. My nose was so clogged that little air made it through when I breathed in. I had to get this gag out of my mouth. I thrashed around some more in a vain attempt to loosen something...anything. I fell over sideways with a crash, chair and all.

The noise startled the men across the room, who briskly walked over to me. I grunted foolishly as if they could understand that I wanted them to remove my gag, as if they would care. I continued to jerk around, trying to move my chair back and as far away from these men as I could get. They both laughed at me.

"Save your energy, bitch," one of them sneered. "You may need it later." More laughter. The two men were about the same height and Middle-Eastern in appearance. They were clean-cut and dressed well.

The other man roughly upturned my chair, jarring my fresh injuries and causing me to grunt in pain. He yanked my gag out of my mouth and shook his hand in disgust at the wet, grimy feeling. I immediately inhaled as deeply as I could and felt my head clear slightly. That little bit of air strengthened my resolve and kindled the fire of fight or flight. Since flight wasn't a possibility at the moment, I was fully prepared to fight. I closed my eyes for a moment and Andrew's face appeared in my mind, clear as if he were standing in front of me.

Andrew, I will come home to you. I love you.

I opened my eyes and glared at these men. The men who took me away from the people I loved.

"What do you want from me?" I spat.

"We want to know where the president is building the safe house," the first man said, eerily calm, as if he knew he'd get the information he needed one way or another.

I did the best I could to feign confusion. "A safe house?"

"Oh, so it's gonna be like that, huh?" the first man taunted. "Okay, have it your way." He backhanded me with all the strength he had right across the face. My eye felt as though it exploded on the spot. I gasped, but did not yell out.

"Now, let's try this again, darling. Where is the president building the safe house?" he asked, more forcefully this time.

"I don't know what you're talking about!" I cried, exasperated. "In case you forgot, it's not the president I'm dating." Another slap. "You can't slap something out of me that isn't there!" I yelled into the face of the first man.

The second man stepped over to me, pushing the other man out of the way. "Sweetheart, we really don't want to hurt you. You have such a beautiful face," he said, sickeningly sweet. He traced my face lightly with his fingers, kind of how Andrew so often does, but with quite the opposite effect. It made my skin crawl. It was such an intimate action from such a disgusting person. "I can see what the first son sees in you. So hot, yet so innocent. I would truly hate to mess up this face permanently." He dropped his hand, crouched down and looked into my eyes. "You don't want that either, do you, sweetheart?"

I stayed still as a statue.

"Let's see if you do," he said, pulling a knife out of his pant pocket. "You know where the president is building the safe house. We've been watching you since your first date with that pretty boy. So you can quit the ignorant act. We'll ask you one more time, and if you don't give us an answer we like, we will scar up your pretty face. Do you understand?" he asked with a smile, as though he had just asked me if I wanted to go for ice cream.

I would wipe that smile off his hideous face. I hocked a loogy and spit it forcefully in his eye. It was the only defense I had at the moment, with my arms and legs tied up.

He yelled, "You stupid bitch!" as the other man laughed hysterically. It was an ugly, evil laugh. "Shut up, you son of a bitch, or I'll shut you up myself!"

The other man kept laughing, but said, "Fine. You keep working on her and I'll go check with our doormen about the status of our clearance." He continued to snigger as he stalked off toward the door.

"So, like I said, sweetheart, I'm going to ask you a question one more time, and I will get a straight answer, or your face will suffer. And do you think your precious boyfriend will still want you and your scarred face when he could have any girl in the world?"

He struck a chord and he knew it. I tried not to let my face show my doubt, but as always, it must have betrayed me. "That's right, sweetheart. That's a good girl. You just tell me what I want to know, and you get to keep your pretty face." He leaned forward and kissed me straight on the lips. As soon as he pulled away, I leaned forward and threw up. The man jumped out of the way right before my vomit hit the floor, saving his pants and shoes. "I didn't think I was that bad of a kisser," he tittered disapprovingly. He pulled my chair roughly away from the fresh pile of vomit and positioned himself yet again in front of me.

"Let's try this question again." He lifted up the knife so I would see it clearly and ran his finger along the blade in warning. "Where is the president building the safe house?" He poked the tip of the knife into the skin just under my ear to remind me of the consequences of not telling the truth.

I took a deep breath and said as confidently as I could, "I'll tell you as soon as you get me a drink of water."

"Ah, a negotiator. I like it. Okay, we'll do it your way." He pressed the knife down just a little, leaving a small, deep cut, before removing it from my skin and replacing it in his pant pocket. "Oops," he said with a smile as he walked away to get some water.

Okay, that bought me less than a minute to think. What could I tell them? Of course I couldn't tell them the truth, but I had to make them think I was telling the truth. The actual site was under Area 51. What about under a mountain? That was where I thought it would've been before finding out the actual location. What mountain range should I say? If I said the Himalayas, they probably wouldn't believe me, because that would be the first mountain range anyone would think of. What other mountain ranges did I know? The Rockies, but I didn't want to say anywhere in the United States. That was too close to the actual sight. Where else? I once watched a show on the Discovery Channel about the tallest mountain peaks in the world, and for some reason Mount Huascaran of the Andes Mountains stood out. I think it was due in part to my fascination with volcanoes and Huascaran was an extinct volcano. It was located in Peru, so I could use geography and the warm climate as being key deciding factors in choosing the location for the safe house. Huascaran it was. It was time to put on the show of a lifetime.

The first man finally came back with a glass of water. He dangled the glass in front of my face and said, "Now remember, sweetheart, I rub your back, you rub mine. If I give you this here water and you don't tell me what you told me you would tell me, the damage will be double. And like I said before, Andrew Wellington isn't going to be caught dead with a deformed girl," he said, watching for my reaction.

I didn't disappoint. While I was genuinely concerned about Andrew's reaction to my face being permanently altered, I needed this man to think it was the key to getting me to tell the truth. I needed him to believe me.

"Andrew wouldn't leave me just because some psycho cut up my face," I said fiercely with just a hint of uncertainty.

"Oh? Have you ever seen any of the girls your boyfriend has been with? All lookers. Not one with a deformity. Why would he? He could have anyone." He gesticulated so vividly that the water sloshed over the sides of the glass he held.

I squirmed for effect. "He doesn't want just anyone. He wants me," I replied, this time not having to act so much as I still struggled with how someone of Andrew's beauty could possibly choose me.

"Okay, have it your way," he said moving toward me, purposely pouring the remainder of the water into a puddle on the floor with a sick, sadistic smile. When he reached my side, he retrieved his knife yet again from his pocket.

"Wait!" I said as he came within a millimeter of the skin on my nose. I didn't know what he was planning to do, but I didn't want to wait to find out.

"Are you ready to talk, sweetheart?" the man drawled sweetly.

"Why do you need me to tell you? Surely you have other means to find out? A project of this magnitude shouldn't be too difficult to uncover."

"Sweetheart, if I was able to find out any other way, do you think I would be wasting my time with a kid?" he snapped, temporarily abandoning his sugar sweet persona. "It's time to speed this up. Enough stalling." He held the tip of my nose to the side with the knife resting on the bridge, as though to cut the tip right off. My heart began to beat so hard I could feel it pulsing in all of my injuries. "Where is the president building the safe house?" he whispered into my ear, making my skin crawl again.

"It's not just a United States project, but rather a worldwide collaboration. It's not just the president building it. Countries from all over the world are helping."

"Too much information. You're stalling again. Tell me where it is, sweetheart..." He pressed the knife so it slid easily through the skin down to the cartilage.

"*Stop!* It's under Huascaran Peak! It's an extinct volcano in Peru!" I shouted as quickly as I could so he would stop cutting.

"Why there?" he snarled. "Why not under Mount Everest in the Himalayas? It's deeper and would provide more protection," he argued.

"They chose Huascaran because it's located in a better climate and it would be easier to control the interior temperature of the safe house. Plus, it's further away from the impact site," I spat out.

"How do I know you're not lying, you little slut?" he screamed and placed the knife under my jaw, pressing until it broke the skin. Tears of fear rolled down my face, salt stinging my wounds.

"You don't," I sobbed.

A sudden outbreak of yelling and gunshots startled my captor into releasing the knife from my neck. He looked around frantically, scoping out an escape and smiled at something I couldn't see.

He quickly stepped back behind me, replaced his knife under my jaw and muttered into my ear, "If you lied, you little bitch, I will hunt your boyfriend down and slit his pretty little neck." The tender sound of his voice did not match the venom of his words. He kissed me on the mouth again and was gone.

I turned my head to the side to vomit again, but produced nothing more than air. I had nothing left to void. I had nothing left inside.

Suddenly the warehouse was a mess of armed officers.

"Miss!" A middle-aged man with a gun and a vest with the letters "FBI" across the front ran toward me, frantically yelling, "Are there any in here?"

"One just went that way," I managed to squeak out and nodded in the direction I thought he went with my head. The man ran off without responding. He wouldn't find him, my little friend got too much of a head start.

I continued to watch the chaos unfold around me with a detached sense of interest. I couldn't really feel any of my injuries at the moment. I was too numb. All I wanted was Andrew and my mom. I closed my eyes and pictured their faces. I would make it home to them after all. I would make it to the end of the world.

"Eden," a familiar, worried voice called.

"Jarvis!" I said, opening my eyes and beginning to cry. "Jarvis, I…"

"It's okay, Eden. You don't have to say anything. Let's just get you out of here." His face was gentle and kind. My buddy, Jarvis. He spoke into his arm cuff, "I have Sapphire. I repeat, I have Sapphire." Pause. "Yes, sir. She is alive and conscious."

"Andrew—" I croaked, hoping Jarvis would know what I meant.

"He's fine, Eden. Well, physically fine," he said with a smile. "He had to be physically restrained to keep him away, but he's not hurt," he assured me.

"My mom…"

"Everyone's fine, Eden." He began to untie me, hands first. I winced as the reluctant rope was peeled from my skin with a sickening suction sound. When my hands were free, I stretched them a little and rotated my wrists to see how much damage was done. It seemed as though it was just surface damage. The raw skin burned, but nothing seemed to be broken. I felt a twinge of relief when I saw the ring Andrew gave me still sparkling on my right hand. I repeated the inspection process, this time on my ankles. They were okay too, aside from broken skin and bruising.

When I was freed from my bondage, Jarvis knelt in front of me and took my hands. Tears welled in his eyes. "Eden, I'm so sorry. They tricked us…they must have been working in the neighboring row house when we were monitoring you at school…we should've been more careful…this is all our fault…"

"Jarvis, this is not your fault. You have done so much for me." I put my hand on his shoulder and looked into his eyes in reassurance. He finally nodded and wiped away the tears streaming down his face. His emotional response to my abduction was touching. I gave him a hug and put my hands on his shoulders to convey the urgency of what I was about to tell him. "Jarvis, you need to get a message to the president immediately. Can you do that?"

He nodded.

"These men wanted to know where the president was building the safe house. I told them it was being built under the Huascaran Peak in the Andes Mountains in Peru. That's where these men will be headed next."

He nodded his understanding, picked me up off the chair into his arms, and carried me out of hell.

* * * *

Jarvis gently settled me in the car and handed me my phone. "Call Andrew. I'm going to relay your message." He began to walk away, but stopped and turned back to me. "You'll be okay?"

I nodded with tears in my eyes. "Thank you, Jarvis."

"My pleasure, Eden," he said and squeezed my shoulder before closing the car door.

I woke up my phone to find text after text and call after call from Dani and Katie who were desperate to know I was okay. I knew my mom would call them as soon as she knew I was safe. I called Andrew, and when I heard his worried voice say, "Eden, is that you? Are you okay?" I started to sob into the phone. "Eden, please say something so I know you're okay."

The desperation in his voice jerked me back into reality and I cried, "Andrew, I'm okay. I just want you…I need you…"

"I know, baby, I'm already at the hospital waiting for you," he said, trying to sound calmer than he actually was. "Thank God you're okay, Eden. I was so scared…"

"Andrew, I'm okay. I don't need to go to the hospital. I'm fine. Just a little bruised and cut up."

He inhaled sharply. "You're going to the hospital, Eden. You need to be assessed. But I'm already there. I won't leave you. I'll never leave you again," he promised.

For the remainder of my hospital escort, we stayed on the line in silence, too afraid to hang up. When I couldn't take it another second, I cried into the phone, "Andrew, I need to see you, I…"

"I know. I see your car pulling into the ER. Look out your window; I'm standing outside the door."

There he was. He stood in the glow of the ER lights like an angel waiting for me, surrounded by reporters awaiting their prey like vultures circling their target. I ignored the press, focusing on Andrew, and for the first time since my rescuers came, I was able to feel some hope. He briskly walked up to the car and impatiently waited for it to come to a full stop. As soon as it did, he threw the door open, located me, and in one swift motion scooped me up into his arms and held me as close as he could. I buried my head in his neck and, comforted by his touch, finally broke into tears. Andrew's uneven breathing suggested he was holding in his own tears in an effort to stay strong for me. I could hear reporters yelling out questions and saw the flashes of light from their cameras through my closed eyes. I didn't care.

Andrew murmured, "I've got you, Oxygen. I'm here. Let's go inside and have the doctors take a look at you." He ignored the nurse offering a wheelchair and carried me into the Emergency Room.

* * * *

When we reached the room I would be examined in, my mom came running in in hysterics. "Eden!" she cried, hugging me tight. I once again broke into tears in my mom's arms. It was so comforting to feel Andrew sitting beside me and my mom holding me; the two people I loved most in the world. My rocks. I realized at that moment I didn't care if the world collapsed around me as long as Andrew and Mom were holding me when it happened. The thought strangely comforted me and lightened my spirits a little.

After a couple hours of neurological exams, CT scans, and a bit of skin glue, I was given the all clear to go home with strict instructions to rest for the next day or two. As I was being released, the president came into my room to check on me. I didn't even know he was there. He came directly to me and hugged me warmly, but gently. "Thank God you're okay, Eden. I'm so sorry this happened. It won't happen again, I can assure you of that. We'll do whatever we can to bring the men who did this to justice." He turned to the doctors and nurses (suddenly there were a lot more present) and shook all of their hands and put on the James Wellington charm to thank them for the excellent care of his son's girl. They all gushed and displayed their best impress-the-president behavior.

The president turned his attention back to me and spoke softly so only Andrew and I would hear. "Eden, I've spoken to your mother, and we think it's best for the two of you to stay at the White House for a while to keep you safe." Then he cryptically added, "Until we can secure your safety at another location," for the benefit of any prying ears. I understood what he meant. And I was not going to argue against being taken to the White House, considering the last time I was home I was kidnapped from my bed. I just wanted to be with Andrew. If I was with him, I was safe.

I nodded my consent and both Wellingtons let out a breath of relief at my lack of resistance. The president thanked the crowd of doctors and nurses one final time and left the room to finalize the details of our pilgrimage to the White House.

When a nurse offered me a wheelchair upon my discharge, I shook my head vehemently in protest. "No. Absolutely not. I will *walk* out of here with my head held high. When the reporters ask questions, I will answer them. I am not going to hide. I will not let terrorists get the best of me."

Andrew, my mom, and the ever-growing group of nurses and doctors watched in surprise as I marched, or rather limped, out the door and through the lobby. Andrew ran after me and stopped me by grabbing my waist. I winced in pain and he drew his hand back quickly and screwed up his face in apology.

"I'm not going to break, Andrew," I said, allowing a small smile to form in reassurance. I took his hand and placed it back where he had put it.

"You don't have to do this."

"Yes, I do." The finality of my voice convinced him of my decision.

He took me by the hand and said, "Then let's do it," with a shadow of a smile on his lips.

I nodded and stepped out onto the Emergency Room entrance. The second the doors closed behind us, we were swarmed by reporters trying to capture our moment of exodus. I froze as camera flashes blinded me. I blinked a few times, trying to clear my head. I wanted to answer some of the questions being thrown at me by the herd of people launching words like bullets, but couldn't make out a single word. The effect was overwhelming.

I put my hand up to silence the cacophony. Andrew squeezed my hand and looked at me imploringly. I knew he wanted to save me from these scavengers. But I needed to do this.

"Last night I was abducted from my bed by men who thought they could get what they wanted from the president by kidnapping me and threatening everyone I love in the process. They were wrong. I put up a fight…" I smiled obtusely, gesturing to my injuries and added, "obviously," to the nervous chuckles of my audience, "and was rescued by the FBI and Secret Service. That is the only information I have to give. I am hoping you will now leave me be to rest and recover. Thank you." I turned to Andrew, who pulled me to him and kissed the top of my head before opening the door of the Town Car waiting to whisk us away from the spotlight.

* * * *

The Town Car pulled into the North Portico Entrance of the White House. Andrew, Mom, and I entered into the Entrance Hall. Andrew explained that my mom would stay in the Queen's Bedroom, since it was a full size suite including a sitting room and private bathroom. I would stay in the East

Bedroom, a slightly smaller suite, still with its own bathroom. I remembered that the East and West Bedrooms were separated only by the tiny Closet Hall and my heart sped up involuntarily. Here I was, fresh out of the hospital after being kidnapped, and the thought of sleeping next door to Andrew got me all hot and bothered.

Andrew told my mom that the president had requested her to wait in the Red Room for him so he could talk to her before she retreated to her room, but he would take me up to my room. Mom was a good sport, and although I could tell she didn't want to let me out of sight, she also knew I wanted to be alone with Andrew.

Mom hugged me with tears in her eyes and said, "Oh, Eden. I love you so much. Thank God you're safe." She kissed me on the cheek and said, "I'll talk to you tomorrow, sweetie." She gave Andrew a stern look and added as a warning, "After you've rested." Andrew smiled at her, put his hand on her arm and squeezed it in reassurance. She couldn't help but smile back. She hugged Andrew too and whispered, "Take care of my baby," before strolling into the Red Room to wait for the president.

Andrew took me by the hand and led me up the Grand Staircase and into the East Bedroom. As I stepped into my new room, I looked around in curiosity at my surroundings. Like most rooms in the White House, it was lavishly decorated with precious antiques. But the features that made this room stand out were the lime green silk-covered walls, a mosaic of framed flower paintings arranged in a grid on the wall to look like a single work of art, a luscious canopied bed with gold damask linens, and two arched built-in alcove shelves with a fireplace in between. Upon closer inspection, I was surprised to find that many of the personal items from my room at home had been brought and displayed in my new room. I walked over to the shelves and ran my finger along the edges taking inventory. There was the book Dani had made me, a few of my stuffed animals from when I was little, the box of my father's artifacts, pictures of friends from both Sidwell and Cedar Rapids, my favorite books, and the most recent addition to my collection, a picture of Andrew and me that I had put in a frame and kept on my bedside table.

"What do you think?" Andrew asked nervously.

"It's beautiful. Thank you," I said. "There's just one thing that won't do."

"What's that? We can change anything you don't like, even the walls if you want. It hasn't been redecorated since the Reagan administration when it was used as the first lady's office," Andrew anxiously informed me.

I shook my head and said, "No, nothing like that." I walked over to the alcove, picked up the picture frame displaying the photo of Andrew and me, walked across the room and placed it on the table next to my new bed. "There.

Now it's perfect."

Andrew smiled and walked across the room to join me. He didn't touch me, but stood so close that I could feel the heat from his body warming my soul. "What can I do, Eden?" Worry radiated through his weary eyes.

"You can hold me and never let go," I whispered.

He breathed a sigh of relief and wrapped himself around me. I bashfully backed out of his arms, and added, "After I shower. Andrew, I don't want to let go. I'm scared to let you out of my sight. But I really need a shower."

Andrew chuckled quietly and said, "You don't need to shower for me, but if you need a shower for *you*, I completely understand. You've been through so much over the last 24 hours…" He broke off and brushed a piece of hair behind my ear. "How about this? I'll show you into the bathroom, and then I'll go get you something to eat while you shower. You have to be starving. Does that sound okay?"

I nodded and he led me to my bathroom and showed me where to find everything. Whoever went and got my stuff thought of everything. My shampoo, conditioner, shower gel, shaving cream, and razor were all waiting for me in the shower. A fresh toothbrush and tube of toothpaste had been placed thoughtfully next to the sink. Andrew kissed me quickly on the top of my head and left me to shower.

A shower had never felt so good in my life. It felt like I could wash away my injuries along with the sweat, blood and tears. I shuddered when I thought about my captor kissing me on the lips. I took some soap and rubbed as hard as I could on my lips to try to wash off the offensive kisses. Even though I knew how stupid it was, it made me feel better. My lips were for Andrew, and Andrew only. And that bastard took that away from me. Thank God that's *all* he took from me.

When I stepped out of the shower, I dried off and stood in front of the full-length mirror to assess the damage. I gasped and put my hand to my mouth. I looked like I had been run over by a truck. My wrists and ankles were raw and just beginning to scab over. There were bruises everywhere. Absolutely everywhere. I didn't even remember how most of them got there. But the ones that caught my eye the most were the ones on my face. Both eyes were beginning to bruise, but luckily they didn't look too swollen. The effect was more like I hadn't slept in weeks. There were some cuts under my ear and jaw and a pretty deep cut on the top of my nose. I was embarrassed for Andrew to see me like this. I sighed and put on the robe hanging on the back of the door and brushed my teeth. I felt better, but I wanted pajamas. *My* pajamas. I silently wished that my pajamas had been brought with everything else from my room. I wandered back into my new room and rooted through drawers for underwear and pajamas.

Oh my God! Someone touched my underwear. How embarrassing!

I froze as I remembered that my underwear drawer was where I had kept the first lady's jewelry. I rummaged through the drawer and was surprised to find the box at the bottom of the drawer, just as it had been at home. I hastily took it out and opened it, praying the necklace and earrings would be there. When I saw them glistening in the box, just as they should be, I sighed in relief and slid to the ground in front of the fancy dresser, clutching the box close to my heart.

I found myself praying not to God, but to Andrew's mother.

Mrs. Wellington, please watch over Andrew and keep him safe. Don't let those terrorists find him and take him from me.

I shuddered as the terrorist's final words came flooding back. I would not let them get to him. I would give my own life before I would let them touch a hair on his head. I sighed and replaced the box gingerly in the drawer, covering it back up with my delicates.

I robotically dressed in whatever I found first and was clambering over to the bed when someone knocked softly on my door. I jumped about a foot into the air and timidly peered through a tiny crack to find Andrew standing outside with a tray of food.

"Oh, Oxygen. You're safe here. That's why you're here. I was just knocking because I wanted to make sure you were decent," he assured me. Usually he would have made some comment about how he wished I wasn't decent, but he didn't. It alarmed me. Was he disgusted by how I looked? Maybe my captor was right. Maybe he wouldn't find me attractive anymore. Or maybe he was being careful with me, like I would break. I didn't know which possibility pissed me off more.

I became unglued and snapped at him viciously. "Andrew, what the hell are you doing? Do you think I'm going to break, or are you disgusted by the way I look right now? Because you're acting weird and it's the last thing I need."

He stood in the doorway stunned for a moment before he stepped into the room, set the tray on a table, and shut and locked the door. He picked me up in his arms, went over to the bed, turned down the blankets and sheets one-handed, and laid me down. He kicked off his shoes and climbed into the bed next to me, bringing the blankets up to our waists. He pulled me as close to him as he could, and whispered, "Eden, you are my world. When I found out you had been abducted, I died inside. I didn't even want to think about living my life without you." He shuddered, then continued, "If you had died, I wouldn't have gone into the safe house. I would have happily died with everyone else in the world, because it would've meant I would get to be with you again." He looked into my eyes and said, "You will always be beautiful to me. These cuts, these bruises," he brushed a fingertip over them as he referred to them; "they only make you more beautiful, because they are part of your fight. The fight you had to fight because of me."

I tried to protest, but he put a finger to my lips to stop me.

"Don't tell me it's not true. It is. If I hadn't dragged you into this public life, this fishbowl, this would have never happened to you. This happened to you because whoever did it knows you are what will hurt me, and therefore my father, the most. And you know what? He was right. Eden, I love you more than I ever thought I could love anyone or anything. It's scary. I've never had so much to lose." He brushed back my hair with his hand and pulled me in closer. I didn't even care that it hurt a little. I just wanted to be close to Andrew.

"I was so scared I wouldn't make it home to you. All of this," I gestured to my injuries and Andrew kissed the cut under my jaw, "didn't hurt nearly as much as the thought of not seeing you again. I knew that as long as I could feel pain, I was alive, and that meant I could still make it back to you."

"Eden," Andrew breathed, and kissed me ever so gently, as though he could break me. I moved into the kiss to show him I wouldn't break, but winced in the process, giving away my delicate state. He stiffened in response and his face darkened as the reality of my condition dawned on him. He threw the blanket back to look at me carefully. His face changed from angry to sorrowful in an instant at the sight of my battered body. "I'm so sorry this happened to you, baby," he whispered, full of anguish. "I'm sorry for this," he said, softly kissing under my eyes, "and for this," he said, kissing the cut on the top of my nose, "and this," kissing the cut under my jaw. He continued this ritual until he had kissed every injury that had been inflicted in the last 24 hours. It was so passionate, and so comforting. When he finished, I felt safe once again. "I will never let anyone or anything hurt you again," he whispered in promise, more to himself than to me. "Not even an asteroid." He gathered me into his arms, and we lay there, breathing in tandem for a while.

"Are you asleep?" Andrew whispered.

"No," I whispered back.

"You have to be so tired after all you've been through. You need to go to sleep."

"Will you stay with me?" I pleaded.

"I promised my dad we would be good. For some reason he was concerned about us living in rooms right next to each other," he said innocently. I giggled a little. "That's the Eden I know. I was hoping she was still there," he said, almost to himself. "Part of that promise," he continued, "was I wouldn't spend

189

the night in your room and you wouldn't spend the night in mine."

I pouted.

"But I think since this is your first night here, and after everything you've been through, I could stay with you until you fall asleep."

"Thank you." I smiled sweetly at him.

"I'm going to have to open the door so Dad doesn't freak out," he added. My eyes began to get heavy and I struggled to keep them open as Andrew got up to open the door. "I see my dad's light on. I'm just going to let him know my plan, and then I'll be right back, okay?"

"Okay," I said through a yawn. He came over, brushed my hair back with his hand, and kissed me once on the lips.

"Mmmm," I murmured in response.

"I love you, Eden."

I was too tired to respond.

Countdown: 30 Days
November 5, 2021

"If you lied, you little bitch, I will hunt your boyfriend down and slit his pretty little neck." I awoke with a start, sweating through my clothes and shivering. I forgot where I was for a moment and panicked, thinking I was still being held captive. I thrashed around trying to free myself from the bed. When I broke free and jumped to my feet, frantically turning to and fro to ground myself, I realized where I was. Andrew!

I hysterically pushed through the Closet Hall and into Andrew's room. He bolted upright, realized it was me, and jumped out of bed. He met me in the middle of the room and took me into his arms. "Eden, I'm here. I've got you." He rubbed my back and pushed my hair out of my face.

"Andrew, they're going to come after you, they said...they're—" I tried to catch my breath through my tears.

"It's okay, Eden, they can't get to me. They can't get to you either. You're safe now. I'll keep you safe," he assured me soothingly.

I nodded into his neck and gave myself in to Andrew's care.

"Come on. Screw what my dad thinks. You're sleeping with me tonight." He pulled me over to his bed, laid me down and climbed in behind me, holding me close to him. "Go to sleep, baby, I won't let anything happen to you. I've got you."

I let myself begin to relax and fell asleep moments later, safe in Andrew's arms.

Several hours later I awoke in Andrew's bed, calmer. I stretched, but stopped when the pain struck. I rubbed my eyes and gingerly turned over looking for Andrew, but sunk in disappointment when I found he wasn't there.

"I'm here," said a familiar voice from next to the bed. I looked over to find

Andrew sitting on a wingback chair near the bed with his iPad in his lap. He looked so hot. His hair stuck up in uneven little spikes, and he was wearing running shorts and an old t-shirt that were still wrinkled from sleeping. He cocked his head to the side with a smile and said, "I didn't want to wake you. You looked so peaceful. But I didn't want to leave you either, so I thought I would read for a while." He set his iPad down on the bedside table, came around to my side of the bed and sat on the edge. He leaned over and whispered in my ear, "I could watch you sleep all day. You are so beautiful." He kissed my neck softly, just once. "And you have no idea how badly I want to jump into bed with you right now," he breathed. My skin broke into goose bumps and the butterflies in my stomach flittered rampantly. "But my dad is nearby," he said, resigned. "So I can't." He kissed me on the lips this time, and ran his fingers down my side, before stepping away from the bed. He took a deep breath, ran a hand over his face, and said, "Are you hungry? I'm thinking we could eat a quick breakfast before going down to meet Dad."

"Meet your dad?"

"Yeah. He wants to talk to you about what happened if you're ready," he said, studying my face carefully. "If you're not ready, that's okay. I'll tell him no."

"No. It's okay. I think it's best for me to tell him everything I know as soon as possible. Plus, I have some questions for him, too."

"Okay." He leaned over and kissed me on my forehead. "I'm going to jump in the shower. Why don't you call Katie or Sam while you wait?"

"I need a shower too," I said, smiling hopefully.

"Don't change the subject," he scolded. "They were really worried, Eden. You need to call them. Now that we're going to be 'homeschooled to keep us safe from the predators who abducted you'," he said cheekily with air quotes, "you won't get to see them at school."

"I know, Andrew. But I just can't handle any more goodbyes," I grumbled. "It's too hard."

"So don't say goodbye. Just talk to them like normal."

"I'm not that good of an actor."

"You just got kidnapped, Eden. They're not going to expect you to be jumping for joy," he argued.

He had a point…

When I still didn't concede, he sat beside me on the bed. "I know this sucks. But it's not fair to your friends to just drop off the face of the earth. They don't know what's going on. If you don't talk to them, they won't understand why. They'll just think you're ditching them." He took me into his arms and whispered, "Call your friends," before heading to the restroom for his shower.

First Sun

I heeded Andrew's advice, and after chatting with both Katie and Sam I felt rejuvenated. They really were worried; and just like with Dani, I could convince myself that it was not time to say goodbye just yet. Instead, I found myself reassuring them that even though Andrew and I would not be at school until our safety could be guaranteed, I would stay in touch. And much to my surprise, I found the sincerity pouring out of my mouth with the words. I really did need my friends, regardless of what the future held for each of us.

* * * *

As Andrew and I entered the Situation Room, my stomach automatically dropped. The last time I was in there, I had learned the world was ending. It was quite discomfiting. "Are you okay?" Andrew asked.

"Actually, I am." I wanted to tell the president everything I knew so he could catch the bastards before they got to Andrew. Andrew nodded and pulled out a chair for me to sit in. He sat in a chair next to me and put his hand on my knee. I placed a hand over his and threaded our fingers together. He leaned over and kissed me on the shoulder, sending shivers to every part of my body.

"Are you cold?" Andrew asked, moving to get up.

"No, not at all. Your kiss just felt really good."

He grinned and leaned toward me, but the president interrupted us by walking into the room. "Eden, Drew. Thanks for meeting me here, kids," he said casually. "I know it's not necessarily the most hospitable of environments, but it's the safest place to have this conversation—at least now that the refreshments table is gone."

We nodded our understanding and smiled at his little joke.

"Eden, since what happened to you is a matter of national security, I have invited my national security advisor, secretaries of defense and homeland security, and my chief of staff to listen in on this debriefing. Is that all right with you?"

"Dad, I don't think—" Andrew began.

I cut him off. "That's fine, sir."

The president stepped out of the room for a moment and reentered with his cabinet members in tow. Andrew raised his eyebrows at me and I nodded at him to let him know it really was okay. He shrugged and stood up to greet his father's staff. Andrew introduced me and I shook hands all around before we all made ourselves at home. Although the cabinet members tried not to show their surprise at my battered appearance, the shock (and maybe even a little bit of pity) was evident in their eyes.

President Wellington clapped his hands together informally to call the meeting to order. "Okay. As you can see, our Eden here has had a rough couple of days."

Aww, he called me "our Eden." While the president has always made me feel comfortable in his presence, this comment made me feel accepted. I smiled at him and he smiled back.

"Eden, before you give us an account of your experience, I think it's only fair that we fill you in on the intelligence we have acquired since your return to safety. Your timely message on where to locate the terrorists was received and inquired. It was confirmed and we have tracked them down. We have not apprehended the terrorists yet because we think they're working as part of a larger sleeper cell and we're hoping they'll lead us to other members. But please rest assured that they are being monitored 24/7 and will not be let out of sight until they and their friends are in our custody."

I breathed a sigh of relief and Andrew put his hand on my back, rubbing it reassuringly.

"Can I ask a question, Mr. President?" I asked, strangely confident, despite the company of so many distinguished guests.

"Of course, Eden."

"Is our safe house the only safe house being built in the world?"

"That we are aware of," the president said. "But there could be others. We are not advertising ours, so other coalitions would probably do what they could to keep theirs secret as well."

I nodded. "Why were there only select countries involved in the creation of the safe house? Why wasn't it a worldwide collaboration?"

"I don't think it's a secret, Eden, that some countries do not share the United States' democratic and peaceful ideologies. We didn't want to build a safe house that would not be safe. If certain countries were asked to join the initiative, with their participation may come violence, discrimination, and corruption. Or more simply stated, terrorism."

I nodded again. "That's what I thought. So these men who abducted me were terrorists who were trying to get back at us for not including them in the initiative?"

"We think partly so, yes."

"Are they trying to destroy the safe house or take it over?"

"That's something we're currently trying to figure out through our surveillance, my dear Eden." He smiled at me, proud of my deductions.

"Mr. President, sir, it's too bad you don't have any openings on the cabinet," laughed the Secretary of Defense. "She has a good sense for this kind of thing."

I couldn't tell if she was complimenting me or patronizing me. Regardless, I returned my attention to the president and said, "I saw their desperation, sir.

They want to take it over."

"Thank you, Eden. That helps." He stepped over to me and put a fatherly hand on my shoulder. "Could you please tell us everything you can remember about your abduction?"

Andrew took my hand once again, giving me the strength I needed to tell my story. I told them everything I could remember in a detached, matter-of-fact manner, focusing straight ahead on nothing in particular. The only time my voice faltered was at the end, when I repeated the last words the man said to me before kissing my lips and running. When I finished and fell silent, Andrew dropped my hand, stood up and paced for a minute, trying to calm himself.

He stopped in front of his father and through clenched teeth said, "You find every single one of those mother-fuckers and bring down the weight of the entire United States Armed Forces on their asses."

I gasped in surprise and looked around the room at the shocked faces of the cabinet members as I waited for Andrew's father to put him in his place for his lack of manners.

Instead, President Wellington placed his hands on his son's shoulders and said clearly with resolve, "My thoughts exactly, son." And he hugged his son with all he had in him.

Countdown: 18 Days
November 17, 2021

The days droned on in precious monotony as Earth breathed in and out in perfect sync with the universe, oblivious to her fate. The citizens living off of her bounty peacefully went about their business in ignorance of the terror they would soon face. There were no breaking news stories, no weather anomalies, no conspiracies popping up out of the woodwork. The world was quiet; too quiet. Holed up in the plastic bubble that was the White House, I could almost convince myself that the world wasn't ending, that I was just there temporarily while the president sorted out my safety from terrorists. But Earth wasn't going to remain quiet for long. Little did she know she was resting up for the fight of her life. And I was just waiting it out, playing house with Andrew.

Unfortunately, our parents were making it extremely difficult to play house. Despite the fact that our rooms were separated solely by the tiny Closet Hall, finding private time was not easy. The White House was always bustling with activity; public tours streamed through the Ground and State floors regularly, an over-abundance of custodial staff frequented the second floor (almost as if strategically placed there by the president and my mother), and our secret service agents stationed themselves suspiciously within earshot of us at all times. And of course, to top it all off, our parents made it perfectly clear we were not, under any circumstance, allowed behind closed doors alone.

"Knock, knock," Andrew said, pushing through my door and closing it as far as he could without actually letting it latch. I smiled at his backdoor way of getting around the rule.

He took me in his arms and I rested my head contentedly on his chest.

"Mmm," Andrew mumbled as he buried his face in my hair. "What are you doing?"

First Sun

"I'm downloading all the music and ebooks I can onto my iPad. Since your dad said we would have electricity in the safe house, I thought I'd load up all I could in preparation."

"Well, aren't you smart." He kissed the top of my head and walked over to my bed. He picked up my iPad and scrolled through the music to see what I had bought. "Hmmm," he said critically.

"What?" I demanded.

"It's all country," he said, smirking.

"It's not *all* country," I defended myself. "There's some classic rock and pop too."

He snickered, continuing to scroll through my choices. "Aha," he said, breaking into a huge smile. He selected whatever it was he found, pressed the button to turn on my wireless speaker, and strolled over to me seductively, causing my body to tingle in want of his touch. God, he looked sexy. My heart melted as *She's Every Woman*, by Garth Brooks began to play. It was my favorite song of all time, one of the songs we had danced to the night of the state dinner. I glanced in the direction of the open door, and reading my mind, Andrew said, "It's all clear."

After closing the last couple of steps separating us, Andrew linked his hands in mine, lifted my arms above my head and ran his fingers down the insides of my arms and down my sides until his hands rested on my hips, leaving goose bumps in their wake. His hands went under my shirt and up my sides. Sensing his urgency, I boldly threw my shirt off. He moaned in pleasure and stepped back to take in the view. He took in a sharp breath and stared for what felt like forever, heat sizzling between us.

"Andrew," I said, barely audible. "Touch me."

He smirked and shook his head.

"Andrew," I said, a little more forcefully. "Touch me."

This time he placed his forehead on mine and gazed into my eyes. He gently stroked his thumbs just above the waistline of my jeans. He was driving me crazy. I took a handful of his shirt in each hand and tried to pull him closer. He didn't budge. I whipped his shirt off, almost tearing it, and he took in another sharp breath. We still kept a good three inches between our bodies, but the heat radiating from my body mingled with Andrew's. He moved his hands in toward my stomach and slowly, very slowly, unbuttoned my jeans, all the while maintaining eye contact. He stopped for a moment, silently asking for permission to proceed. I nodded my head minutely and he slid his hands into the sides of my jeans and down my hips. I couldn't breathe. He kept sliding his hands down ever so slowly, until my pants began to slide down with them. He moved his hands down and around, to the curvy part of my bottom. I wriggled

197

my legs slightly so my jeans would fall the rest of the way to the floor. Andrew let out a quiet moan in response. He stepped back again and looked me up and down in appreciation. I thought I would be embarrassed the first time Andrew saw me in my underwear, but instead I felt excited. He seemed to like what he saw. It emboldened me. I moved my hands to his jeans and repeated the motions he had just done to me. As his jeans dropped to the floor and he stood there in his boxers, I felt an overwhelming sense of love pressing down on my heart, threatening to break me. As if he could read my mind, Andrew met my eyes and looked deep into my soul. We finally closed the gap between us from head to toe, and both of us breathed out in pure ecstasy.

"*Andrew!* What the *hell* is going on?" the president's voice bellowed into the room. We froze in shock and turned our heads to the door to find the president glaring at us in horror.

When I realized I was only in my bra and underwear, I frantically ran through the Closet Hall door and slammed the door shut. I rested my forehead against the door in absolute humiliation. "Oh my God, oh my God, oh my God." I stood there listening to the president continue to yell at his son, and for lack of better options, chuckled to myself in humiliation.

When all seemed quiet (and after laughing with Dani on the phone until my side ached about being caught red-handed), I went down to the Family Kitchen to make some chocolate chip cookies to try to earn the president's forgiveness. As I was stirring the chocolate chips into the batter, Andrew walked in smirking at me with his dad and my mom at his heels. The amusement evident on Andrew's face was making it difficult for me to keep a straight face. I turned toward my cookie dough, biting at the inside of my cheek, and pretended to be deep in concentration. My mom came over and put her arm around my waist in camaraderie. I beamed at her in appreciation. She kissed me on the temple and stuck her finger in the cookie dough.

"Mmm…it's been a while since you've made cookies."

Andrew came over and kissed me on the top of my head and stuck his finger in the bowl as well.

"Ahem," the president said.

"What, Dad? A kiss on the top of the head is not the worst you've seen today," he said, trying not to laugh.

"I'm glad you think this is so funny, Drew. Apparently the 'no closed doors' rule means nothing to you. I thought I could trust the two of you. Perhaps I was wrong."

My eyes flashed around the room at my unconventional little "family." Andrew stood his ground, smirking defiantly; Mom uncomfortably averted her eyes, looking anywhere but at the president; and the president angrily glared at his son in disappointment. I just stood there red in the face wishing the ground would swallow me whole. Since it wouldn't, I dropped the metal spoon into the glass bowl with a loud clank and bolted straight to my room. After pacing the room for a while in an attempt to rebuild my fragile ego, I switched on my TV with the intentions of losing myself in some mind-numbing reality television, subconsciously aware that that wouldn't be an option for long. It worked. The hot messes chronicled on TV for my entertainment made it feel as though the president seeing me half naked with his son was completely normal.

A little while later, a soft knock rapped on my door. I figured it was Mom, so I leisurely said, "Come in," stretching and yawning. At least with my mom I knew I wouldn't be lectured. To my surprise, it was President Wellington.

I bolted upright. "Mr. President…I'm—"

He put up a hand to stop me. In his other hand was a plate full of fresh chocolate chip cookies. "Please don't apologize, Eden, or you'll make me feel worse." He stood awkwardly in the doorway, not knowing what to do next. I got up and walked over to the settee on the opposite side of the room and motioned for him to sit on one of the nearby chairs, reversing the roles we had played the day I met him in the Diplomatic Room so long ago.

He came over and set the plate of cookies on the coffee table. "Peace offering," he said, scrunching up his face in apology.

I started laughing. "That's exactly why I started making them in the first place."

He smiled. "I finished them up for you."

"*You* finished them? I figured my mom did."

"She wanted to, but I insisted on doing it. I felt like I owed it to you."

"You felt *you* owed it to *me*?" I asked, astonished.

"Well, yeah. I never meant to insult you, Eden. It was unfair of me and I hope you'll accept my deepest apologies."

"Considering the circumstances, sir, I'm the one who should be apologizing to you. You take my mom and me in to keep us safe and how do I repay you? By…" I couldn't finish. What was I supposed to say? By jumping your son?

"Eden, I'm not going to let you apologize for being in love with my son. And I certainly can't expect the two of you to never kiss or touch." His face turned red. So did mine. "It's just that I'm entering uncharted territory here. Two teenagers in love living under the same roof is not exactly ideal for the parents."

I considered his point for a moment and smiled. "Yeah. I can see how that may be…problematic. But I can assure you, sir, that I have a good head on my shoulders. I'm not going to do anything stupid."

"I can see that now. And despite what I said earlier, I *do* trust you. It's just…" He shifted in his chair, and I could tell he wanted to say something that made him uncomfortable. "It's just that I've come to think of you as kind of a daughter. I care about you and want what's best for you."

I beamed at the president and said, "And you're the father I never knew I wanted until you came into my life. Thank you for that, sir."

The president leaned over and took me into his arms in a warm, fatherly embrace. "No, Eden. Thank you."

He stood up to leave and as he walked toward the door he said, "Oh, and Eden?"

"Yes, sir?"

"I don't know too many daughters who call their father figures 'sir,' or 'Mr. President.' Call me James."

I smiled. "We'll see, sir." He grinned the famous Wellington grin and left me diving into the plate of cookies.

Countdown: 9 Days
November 26, 2021

As the end drew ominously nearer, my itch to escape the confines of the White House walls grew proportionately stronger. After one of my many runs on the South Lawn path, the scent of fallen leaves in the brisk fall air spoke to my senses, prompting a leisurely stroll through the grounds.

It was warm for late November, still in the upper fifties. It was my favorite kind of weather; cool enough to necessitate a sweatshirt or jacket, but warm enough to be comfortable outside for an extended period of time. Peak leaf change had come and gone, but many of the fall bulb flowers survived due to the unseasonably warm weather, wreathing the Rose Garden in color. I made my way to the white wrought iron bench on the east side of the garden and sat down, content to be alone with my thoughts. I closed my eyes and basked in the feeling of the warm sun on my face and the cool breeze lifting the hair off my neck.

When I opened my eyes and they grazed across the beauty before me, my euphoria quickly diminished and I found myself falling down a rabbit hole of despair. Soon this utopian mecca of beauty would be engulfed by a fiery inferno of death. This was one of Earth's last peaceful days. And one of my last chances to breathe in fresh air. Tears streaked down my cheeks at the realization that the end really was near. But the asteroid was not the only thing that scared me. I was suffocating being stuck in the White House, free to walk outside within the grounds. How was I going to survive years, possibly decades, in an underground safe house? I felt like I was being torn in two. Half of me dreaded the isolation and claustrophobic conditions of the safe house, while the other half of me felt guilty for feeling that way when billions of people around the globe didn't even have the luxury of worrying about the conditions of the safe house. How dare I dread the safe house when so many people would give anything to get in?

I was quickly shaken out of my misery by the sight of an ecstatic Andrew exiting the Oval Office and hurrying down the West Wing Colonnade toward the Residence.

What could he possibly be so happy about?

"Andrew?" I called, rising from the bench and making my way toward him.

He looked up at the sound of my voice and when he located me, he broke into a radiant smile of pure elation. He ran to me, took me into his arms, and whispered, "Dani's coming into the safe house with us. She's going to live."

I stood there in shock until relief fell over me, allowing me to let go of the tension that had gripped me like a vice since the day I had learned 9409 Apollo would destroy everything and everyone I had ever known. My muscles relaxed and if it weren't for Andrew's strong arms holding me tight to him, my legs would've fallen out from under me.

"How...?" I managed to force out.

"Does it matter?" Andrew asked, cocking his head in amusement.

I shook my head. It *didn't* matter. The three people I loved most in the world were going to live. My family was safe.

"Your dad?"

Andrew nodded.

I broke free and ran the short distance to the Oval Office, threw the door open and stopped in the doorway just long enough to locate the president. He was perched on the front edge of the resolute desk talking on his cell phone. When he caught sight of me, he grinned and quickly finished up his call. When the president pocketed his phone I flung myself at him, and he accepted me into his arms with a hearty chuckle.

"Thank you, sir," I murmured into his suit coat, dampening it with tears of gratitude. "I don't know how I'll ever repay you."

"You don't need to repay me. This is thanks enough."

"But...sir...why Dani?"

"Because Dani's your family. And you've become part of mine. That makes Dani my family too."

I broke into a gigantic grin and shook my head in amazement. "You're one heck of a guy, Mr. President."

"Don't give me too much credit. You might not like where her spot came from."

My stomach dropped. "What do you mean? Where *did* her spot come from?"

First Sun

"The primary American History candidate had *two* immediate family members. Your mother only has one…"

"So Dani gets to be Mom's other immediate family member?"

He nodded. "I had to fight for it, though, since she's not technically an immediate family member. Let's just say there was some…resistance."

"You fought for Dani?"

The president shrugged modestly.

"And you thought I would be mad?" I asked, shaking my head in disbelief.

"You didn't like the idea of taking somebody else's spot for yourself, so I thought you may not like me pulling strings."

Without hesitation I said, "Sir, you can pull all the strings you want when it comes to saving Dani."

"Phew! That wasn't nearly as difficult as getting you to agree to *your* spot," he joked. The president looked genuinely relieved, prompting me to feel a twinge of remorse. I obviously hadn't expressed my appreciation for his efforts in saving my life.

I hugged him and whispered, "Sir, thank you for saving my best friend, and thank you for saving my mom." And to the president's surprise I added, "And thank you for saving *me*."

The president smiled and placed his hands on my shoulders. "You're welcome, Eden. Thank *you* for saving my son."

I smiled shyly and headed to the door.

"And Eden?"

I froze in the doorway leading back out to the Colonnade and spun around to face the president. "Yes, sir?"

"You're supposed to call me James."

"Yes, sir."

The president shook his head in good-humored defeat and I took my exit, content in the knowledge that my best friend had been saved. The missing piece from the puzzle of my happiness had finally fallen into place. In only days that piece would be pressed alongside all the others, and as long as everything went according to plan, no asteroid could break it up.

Countdown: 3 Days
December 2, 2021

Andrew, Mom and I sat leisurely around the table in the Kitchen feasting on omelets and pancakes one morning when the president came in dressed in full suit and sat down at the table formally.

"Today's the day," he said.

We froze.

"For what, Dad?" Andrew asked rhetorically, as though he didn't really want the answer.

"For you to go to the safe house."

"Oh, my God," I said in disbelief.

"James, are you—" Mom began.

"Yes, Ann."

Mom nodded. I wasn't sure what this private exchange was all about, but I couldn't focus on it at the moment. We were going to the safe house today.

The president turned to us and said, "I think it's best for the three of you to be taken to the safe house before I make the announcement to the public tomorrow. It will be next to impossible to get you there in secret after the public knows. We cannot risk the location being disclosed."

"What about you?" Andrew asked, a twinge of challenge to his voice.

"I can't leave yet, Drew. The people will need me. I can't abandon them," he said, resigned.

"What about me?" Andrew asked venomously as he jumped up, knocking his chair over. "You'll just abandon me?"

"It's not that simple, Drew," his father answered sadly.

"I'm not going without you!"

"You would risk Eden and Ann's lives just to wait for me?" he challenged and promptly received the response he had sought.

"No, of course not," Andrew answered, his voice softening at the realization that his father made a valid point. He put his chair right, sat back down and put his hand on my knee under the table and squeezed.

"What's the plan?" Andrew asked, reconciled to our fate.

"You will be airlifted by chopper to an aircraft carrier. From there, you will wait until nightfall and be taken to the safe house by B-3 Spirits."

Andrew nodded. My mom and I looked at one another in confusion. It didn't go unnoticed.

"A B-3 is a stealth bomber," Andrew clarified, which failed to enlighten us.

The president explained further. "A stealth bomber is a fighter jet that cannot be detected by radar, radio, or laser designators. They are virtually untraceable."

"Virtually?" I questioned.

"There is currently no aircraft that is 100% untraceable. This is the closest we can get. But I can assure you that no B-3 has ever been detected." The president smiled, trying to reassure me, but the smile didn't quite reach his eyes. He was more worried than he was letting on. It was unsettling.

"Dad, you said 'stealth bombers,' in the plural tense," Andrew pointed out.

The president sighed. "I knew you weren't going to like that." He took a deep breath before continuing. "Stealth fighters were not designed as passenger jets. It's going to be hard enough to fit one passenger in. There are three seats, one for the pilot, one for the mission commander, and one small extra seat. There is no way to get two or three passengers in."

"No! Absolutely not. I will not be separated from Eden. You'll have to find another way," Andrew declared stubbornly.

"Drew, there *is* no other way. I knew what your reaction would be. Please trust me when I tell you we have exhausted every other scenario we could think of. This is the safest way. This is the *only* way."

"It's okay, Andrew," I said, putting my hand on his. "It's just a fleeting moment in time. It'll be okay."

"Sure," he said sarcastically, eyes still on his father. "Separate the protagonists on their way to avoiding certain death from Armageddon. What could possibly go wrong?"

"Son, I know it's scary. I'm sorry."

"When are we leaving, sir?" I asked, trying to redirect the conversation.

"In two hours."

"When are all of the other safe house occupants coming?"

"They are all already there."

"Dani?"

"Yes. She's there, safe and sound, waiting for you."

I exhaled in relief. "How did she get there?"

"We have secretly been taking everyone there in all different kinds of vehicles; vehicles not uncommon to be seen entering and departing Groom Lake. Semis, delivery trucks, Hum V's…"

"Why can't we go that way?" Andrew said.

"You are too high profile. We don't know if we're being watched. Leaving from the aircraft carrier is the only way we can ensure you are not being followed."

"When are you addressing the nation?" Andrew asked.

"Tomorrow morning at 0900 eastern standard time. That will give you enough time to get to the safe house before I make the announcement."

We nodded our understanding and sat in silence.

"James, when is the asteroid predicted to strike?" Mom asked, with her fingers steepled, holding up her chin, unsuccessfully attempting to look calm.

"It's going to hit at 0837 Wednesday. Almost exactly three days from now. And it's not a prediction. It will strike at that exact time."

The hairs on my arm stood straight up in response to the president's tone of doom.

"When are you coming, Dad?" Andrew asked.

"Drew—"

"When are you coming, Dad?" Andrew repeated more forcefully.

His father paused, then replied with despondence, "When I can, son."

The truth that he probably wouldn't be coming at all hung in the air.

* * * *

I took one last look around my room at the White House. Did I have everything I would need or want in the safe house? I looked at my standard-sized suitcase—the one that all inhabitants of the safe house were given. Each person could only bring what would fit in the suitcase. I had packed as many clothes as I could fit over top of my keepsakes and brought only the items I couldn't live without. That didn't include much. As long as I had my mom, Dani, and Andrew, I had everything I ever needed. Along with my iPad, the only non-clothing items in my suitcase were the book Dani made me, the box of my father's artifacts, the framed picture of Andrew and me, the First Lady's jewelry, and the stuffed animal I had slept with every night for the first twelve years of my life.

I touched the ring on my right hand with my thumb to ensure it was still there, and walked through the Closet Hall to find Andrew. He stood there, looking around his room, just as I had a moment ago. "Do you have everything you need?"

He looked up in surprise, walked over to me and kissed me. "I do now."

"Andrew, I'm scared," I confessed.

"Me too," he agreed. "But not of the asteroid. Of losing you." He took my hand and brought it to his lips and held it there. "Eden, I don't want to put you on that jet without me," he spoke into my hand with his eyes closed. "I can't do it."

"Yes, you can. Because if you don't, we only have three days. If we go to the safe house, we'll have a lifetime."

He nodded, kissed my hand and pulled me into a hug.

"Eden, Andrew, are you ready?" Mom stood in the doorway, hesitant to interrupt us, but clearly needing reassurance herself.

"Oh, Mom!" I ran to her and held her close. She chuckled through tears and said, "It's not time to say goodbye yet, E," and pulled away to kiss me on the cheek.

Andrew joined us, pulling both my suitcase and his own. Jarvis appeared in the hallway with an agent I recognized as one of Andrew's regulars. "Ready?" he asked us. We nodded and I stalked over to Jarvis and took him into my arms. "Jarvis…" I didn't know what to say. He wasn't just my detail. He was my friend. What would happen to him? "I can't leave you behind to…"

"You're not leaving me behind just yet, Eden." His smug, knowing smile confused me.

"Jarvis volunteered to fly your jet, Eden," Andrew told me with a smile. "He thought you would be more comfortable that way."

A large weight immediately lifted off my shoulders as I broke into a big grin. "You fly, Jarvis?"

"Yes, ma'am. For over ten years now. Before joining the secret service, I was trained in the United States Air Force and served under the president in his Middle East initiative. I am fully qualified to fly you to safety, miss."

"Oh, Jarvis!" I exclaimed and hugged him again, this time out of sheer relief rather than grief.

Jarvis smiled shyly. "Okay, okay. I'll see you in the chopper. I would recommend not eating too much today, because I'm going to take you for one heck of a ride tonight."

He smiled brightly and winked before grabbing two of the suitcases and pulling them toward the elevator. The other agent took the final suitcase and followed Jarvis. I marveled at their state of composure. They were businesslike as usual. It was just another day at the office for them. Except for the fact that they were helping to save us from the same fate they were certain to face in three days. After all, they were trained to take a bullet for their protectees.

Andrew held out his arms like he did the night of our first dinner in the White House, and I took hold of one elbow without hesitation. We looked at Mom, who looked uncertainly at President Wellington.

"Go ahead, kids. We'll follow you in a minute," the president said, not looking at us. His eyes were fixed on my mom's. It gave me an uneasy feeling. Andrew's eyes meaningfully met mine, as if they could read my mind. The ghost of a smile on his lips suggested he suspected something too, but I simply didn't have enough stress to spare at the moment. I would worry about it later.

Andrew and I put our arms around one another and headed toward the Grand Staircase. As we approached the landing, my eyes fell on the open door to the Lincoln Bedroom, awakening an experience tucked neatly into the depths of my memories. "Wait!" I let go of Andrew and ran quickly into the Lincoln Bedroom, grabbed the Gettysburg Address, holding it close to my chest to protect it, and rejoined Andrew at the stairs. "Okay," I said with finality, as though now I was prepared to leave it all behind. And I was, as long as Andrew was with me.

Andrew smiled earnestly and hugged me so hard, the frame pressed into my chest, making it difficult to breathe. I didn't care. He kissed me on the lips, lingering there for a moment, and we descended the Grand Staircase for the final time without looking back.

* * * *

Marine One (*Would it still be called Marine One if the president wasn't on it, kind of like Air Force One?* I wondered pointlessly) slowly rose into the air, two decoys at the ready to accompany us to the aircraft carrier. Andrew held my hand tightly as we watched the White House get smaller, fully aware that this was the last time we would ever see her. Her majestic face smiled in ignorance of her violent future. I searched through the sky for the Washington Monument, easily locating it, standing strong and defiant, pointing up to the asteroid like an arrow, challenging it to a fight. Both the White House and the Washington Monument would meet their demise in just a few days' time. Over 200 years of history was about to be obliterated in an instant. This realization caught my breath without warning and pushed me over the edge. I held my hand up to the window and looked at my past. Then I looked to the front of the chopper and into my future. Only there was no future. Instead, all that stretched before me was an endless void. Its bleakness took hold of me and suffocated me. I put my head down between my legs, trying to catch my breath.

"Eden, look at me," Andrew said. I shook my head frantically between my legs. I couldn't. I could not look back up and see a world full of beauty that was about to be destroyed. "Look at me," he repeated.

I obeyed.

"Don't look back. Don't look forward. Look right here," he coached me, taking my face between his hands, and bringing my eyes to his. "Just be here, in the present with me," he continued soothingly. The sea of blue staring into my soul grounded me. My heart began to slow and my breathing came easier. Andrew rested his forehead against mine, not breaking eye contact. "That's right," he whispered. "We're okay. You and I—we're going to be fine."

"But...the White House..." I stammered helplessly, heart pounding once again.

"It's going away," he said matter-of-factly. "It's all going away. But it's just stuff, just piles of bricks and wood."

I shook my head vehemently. "It's not just bricks and wood! It's flesh and blood! There are people inside those piles of bricks of wood—"

"But you and I—we're going to be fine." When I failed to calm, he added the only thing he knew would serve as an anecdote to my fear. "And Dani, and your mother—they're going to be fine, too."

My head snapped up and I searched the cabin for my mom. When I located her safely tucked into her seat, her brow crinkled in worry at my state of panic, I caught her eye and attempted a reassuring smile. She returned the gesture, just as half-heartedly. But it was enough to calm me and pacify my mom.

I turned back to Andrew and looked into his eyes. He stroked my cheek gently with his thumb and touched his lips to mine. It was brief, out of respect for those in our presence, but it was enough to remind me that while some beauty would be wiped off the face of the Earth, the beauty of love would endure.

* * * *

When we stepped off the last step of the helicopter onto the aircraft carrier, I looked around in awe of my surroundings. A small group of Navy pilots stood on the flight deck waiting to welcome us. I wondered if they knew what this mission was all about. Surely they knew they were transporting the first son, his girlfriend, and his girlfriend's mom, but did they know about the asteroid? About the end of the world? That they would soon die?

Andrew stood close behind me, one arm around my waist, the other extended to shake hands with our new acquaintances.

"Mr. Wellington, sir? Captain Dodge. It's a pleasure to meet you."

Andrew shook the short, middle-aged man's hand politely. "This is my girlfriend, Eden."

"So you're the famous girl who snagged the first son," he said playfully and shook my hand.

"I sure did," I answered with as much enthusiasm as I could muster. He clearly did not know of the dire circumstances. Lucky him.

"It's so nice to meet you, miss," he said, smiling.

"This is my mother, Ann," I said, gesturing to my mother.

"Thank you so much for helping us out today, sir," she said, genuinely grateful, and shook his hand.

"You are most welcome. It's our pleasure to fulfill the president's bidding. It's a pretty quiet day on board. Strangely so," he added, looking at us quizzically. "Please, come with me and I'll show you to a more comfortable place to hang out in until takeoff."

As we walked he explained how the aircraft carrier was run, but I was too distracted to really absorb anything he was saying. The gist I got was that the B-3s would remain in the hangar until dark. At that time, they would be lifted by the hydraulic elevators and brought to the flight deck where they would be prepared for takeoff. My mom piqued my attention when she asked the question I had been pondering since I saw the size of the runway.

"How do the planes take off on such a short runway?"

"Amazing, isn't it?" The captain shook his head as if it still amazed him after all these years. "They used to be catapulted by steam-powered pistons, which produced enough air pressure to propel a plane from 0 to 165 in two seconds." We gasped. "Now we use more modern technology called EMALS. That stands for Electromagnetic Aircraft Launch System. It's a linear launch system that uses electricity to create an electromagnetic field, which propels the plane to about the same speed as the old-fashioned steam-powered pistons. It's pretty remarkable technology. It's much more reliable and cost-effective, takes up less space, and doesn't require as much manpower to run. Rest assured, ma'am, EMALS will get you in the air with no problem."

Captain Dodge took us down to one of the mess halls to ensure we didn't leave hungry. The entire time we were below deck, Andrew did his father proud, walking around the hall, shaking hands, patting people on their backs, joking with them and thanking them for their service to our country. As I watched him, I realized he didn't do this for the publicity or the pomp and circumstance of it. He did this out of guilt. None of these people would die with their loved ones. They would die on this ship in the middle of nowhere, far away from family and friends. Their sole purpose for being here right now was to make sure Andrew, my mother and I made it to safety. It made me sick to my stomach.

I excused myself to use the restroom and threw up everything I had just worked so diligently to force down out of politeness. This wasn't right. I couldn't do this. I couldn't go to the safe house. I didn't deserve it any more than any of those people out in the mess hall. The only reason I was going was because I was in love with the president's son and he was in love with me. I splashed some water on my face and looked into the mirror, prepared to go tell Andrew I wasn't going.

"E?" Mom pushed through the door and, upon sight of my dewy face, pulled a couple of paper towels from the dispenser and dabbed gently at my cheeks, her eyebrows pulled together in concern.

"Mom," I said, placing my hand on her arm and looking her square in the eyes, "I'm not going."

"Yes, you are," she said with authority.

"I can't."

"Eden?" Andrew called quietly through the door with a gentle knock. I opened the door and he tentatively glanced in.

"We're the only ones in here."

He nodded and crossed the threshold, closing the door behind him.

"Are you okay?" he asked, pausing before saying, "Of course you're not. Neither am I." He looked at me as if he wanted to fix it, but didn't know how. It was alarming. Andrew always knew how to fix it.

"Andrew, I can't go. It isn't right," I forced out. I wasn't going to cry. I'd cried enough. "I can't go just because I happen to be dating the president's son."

"Eden, I know it doesn't seem fair," Andrew argued. "But everything happens for a reason. Some greater force brought you and your mom to D.C. and into this life. That same force brought you to this aircraft carrier right now. There's a reason for that. We may not know that reason yet, but it's not by mistake. It's not just a coincidence."

His argument eerily mirrored his father's from only weeks before. And damn it. It made sense.

"We are being led to this safe house for a reason," he continued. "And who are we to mess with fate? How do you know that the entire survival of the human race doesn't lie solely on your shoulders? On our shoulders?"

"It can't. I'm just ordinary," I insisted.

Now Mom chimed in. "So were Martin Luther King Jr., and Gandhi, and Benjamin Franklin, and anyone else who went down in history as extraordinary. They were all just ordinary people who did extraordinary things. You are capable of extraordinary, Eden. There's a reason for all of this, for the safe house. And we are part of it, regardless of the reason."

"But all of those people…" I stammered.

"I know," Andrew said, taking my hand. He was at a loss for words.

My mom wasn't. "We will grieve for them, just like we will grieve for everyone else we are losing. But we can't turn our backs on humanity."

* * * *

Captain Dodge showed us to a small, outdoor living space carved into the gallery at the stern of the gigantic ship. It was cold, but the night was still, and I wanted to breathe in the fresh air as long as humanly possible. In just a few short hours, it would be years, possibly decades, before I would once again breathe fresh air.

Mom gave me a quick hug and excused herself to use a satellite phone. I had a sneaking suspicion that she was calling the president, but as I did earlier, I shrugged off the notion. The captain was all too eager to show her the way. It was pretty obvious he liked what he saw.

When they took their leave, Andrew and I laid side-by-side on the floor looking up at the stars. "It's so beautiful out here. You can see every star. I've always loved the night sky," I sadly reminisced. "It's so mysterious…I used to think about how there had to be other intelligent life out there. In the whole of the universe, Earth is tiny. Why wouldn't there be life in other solar systems, other galaxies? I knew there was so much out there to be discovered. It intrigued me."

Andrew nodded in agreement. "Whenever I was stressed about life as the first son or disgusted with myself and what I had become, I would go up to the third floor Promenade and lay just like this, looking up at the stars. And I would think about how enormous the universe is and how small I am in comparison. It always helped me realize how trivial my problems were in the grand scheme of the universe. It put things into perspective. Our problems are still insignificant in relation to the universe. To this asteroid, Earth is just another obstacle in its way, an inconvenience." We lay pondering this philosophical fodder.

"You know, today was the last day we would see the sun for years, possibly decades, and I didn't even think to look at it properly. I didn't listen to the birds chirp, or feel the grass under my toes for the last time…" My voice broke, catching me off guard yet again.

"Close your eyes, baby," Andrew whispered.

I looked at him, confused.

"Just do it."

I closed my eyes.

"Remember the day we ran on the White House track for the first time?"

"How could I forget?" I smiled at the memory.

"Can you picture the way I looked with the sun shining down on my hair? The way the tree felt on your back when I kissed you? The sound of the birds living in the tree above us?"

"Yes," I whispered. "Like it was happening now. My heart is sure racing like it was then just thinking about it." I placed his hand on my heart.

"It's all in here, Eden," he said, his hand still on my heart. "You can see the sun any time you want to, feel the breeze against your skin, smell the rain as it begins to fall, feel snowflakes on your nose..."

"Smell fresh cut grass," I mumbled.

"Mm hmm. Any time you want to see it, hear it, feel it, smell it...it's all there. Just close your eyes and take yourself there."

I turned over and kissed him one last time under the seemingly tranquil spread of the night sky—the night sky that would soon explode in a fury of self-defense.

Countdown: 2 Days
December 3, 2021

Shortly after midnight we stood under the cover of darkness next to the B-3 Spirit sanctioned to transport me to safety. Andrew pulled me into a tight hug and nervously stroked my back.

"It's only 32 minutes," I said, nestling my head into his chest, seeking out the heartbeat that was not only his lifeline, but mine as well. Our nearness calmed him and his racing heart slowed down a bit. He melted into me and began to quietly sing. "A new way to fly...far away from goodbye...above the clouds and the rain...the memories and pain..."

"Aww, Andrew. You've been listening to my Garth playlist. I'm so proud," I murmured into his chest. The words were from a little-known Garth Brooks song I had exposed a reluctant Andrew to over the past few weeks while living in the White House. He didn't want to admit it, but he was becoming a fan.

"And the tears that they cry..."

"Just don't sing the part that says, 'They all crashed and burned'," I joked through sniffles, trying to stop the tears from falling.

Andrew chuckled ironically and continued. "But they could leave it behind...if they could just find...a new way to fly," he finished in time to the tears flowing down my cheeks. "I'll see you in thirty-two minutes," Andrew whispered. He kissed me gently on the lips and walked away, not looking back. I knew it was because if he did, he wouldn't leave again.

I turned toward the jet, not allowing myself to watch Andrew walk away from me. This was ridiculous. It was thirty-two minutes. Why was I acting like this was the end of the world? I caught myself in the use of the old adage casually spoken by the masses throughout time. But in this case the answer was

214

simply, *Because it* was *the end of the world.* Shivers coursed through my body at the irony.

Jarvis descended the jet stairs from his preparations in the cockpit and handed me a helmet. He took one look at my tear-streaked face and asked, "Eden, are you okay?" He looked genuinely worried.

"Thirty-two minutes, Jarvis. I'll give you a million dollars if you get there in under thirty."

"I'll see what I can do," he said, laughing nervously. He gestured toward the unfolded staircase. "After you."

I walked under the wing to the belly of the jet and ascended the stairs into the recesses of the tiny cockpit that would carry me to my new life.

* * * *

"All set, Eden?" Jarvis asked from the front of the jet, where he sat next to the mission commander, who was introduced to me as Will. We all wore headsets so we could hear one another more clearly.

"All set, Jarvis," I answered half-heartedly, strapped tightly into my seat.

"Eden?" a voice I knew so well said into my ear.

"Andrew?" I exclaimed.

"Hey, Oxygen," he said smoothly.

"How did you...where did you...who..." I stammered.

"It was a surprise," he said and I could hear the smile in his voice.

"Oh, I'm so ready now, Jarvis!"

Several men chuckled at once through the headphones.

"Well in that case..." Jarvis gave a swift salute to the men on the ground, pressed some buttons, talked into a radio of some kind and pulled on a stick, jerking us forward like lightening.

"Holy crap!" I tried to yell as the air pressure smashed my helmeted head back into my seat, leaving my stomach where we sat only a millisecond before. The whole 0 to 165 in two seconds felt quite different than it sounded. I thought I would throw up, but I couldn't, because not one part of my body could move. I couldn't even close my eyes. The end of the flight deck and nothing but blackness appeared before me in the window so quickly I didn't even have time to register the fact that we made it into the air.

"And we have air," Jarvis announced triumphantly.

"Eden?" Andrew prompted, full of worry.

"I'm okay," I breathed. "That was freakin' awesome!"

More laughter sounded in my ears, including Andrew's.

"Andrew?"

"We're up, too," Andrew said, reading my mind. "So is your mom," he added, anticipating my next question.

I breathed a sigh of relief and took some time to enjoy the view. Well, what view I could see through the front window, which wasn't much. Another barely visible jet led the way. It really was difficult to see, even at this close range. "Andrew, are you in the first plane?"

"Nope. That's your mom's plane. You're in the middle and I'm bringing up the rear," he explained. "I wanted to keep an eye on you," he joked.

"Of course you did," I said light-heartedly, but in reality felt much better knowing Andrew had my back.

The next twenty-five minutes flew by much faster than I thought they would. With seven minutes remaining, Jarvis said, "Time to dirty up, Will."

I felt the nose of the plane point down, and we began our descent. I watched my mom's plane land and let out a breath. One down, two to go. Jarvis picked up a pen and wrote something down.

"Taking notes, Jarvis?" Will joked. Jarvis didn't respond. Was something wrong? My stomach dropped in sudden worry.

"Jarvis, is everything okay?" I asked, troubled.

No answer.

"Jarvis?"

Still no answer. I realized I couldn't hear anything in my ears anymore and panicked. "Andrew?!" I yelled.

Nothing.

It's okay, Eden. Calm down. They probably just turned off the headphones for landing.

The jet took a nosedive and gunshots fired.

What's going on? Are we being attacked?

Fear pulsed through my body.

Where's Andrew? Is he safe?

I strained in my harness to see out the window, not knowing whether or not I actually wanted to see what was happening. But it was not what was happening on the outside of the jet that made my skin crawl. It was what was happening inside. Will and Jarvis fought over control of the throttle, making the already bumpy ride even more unstable. Jarvis drew back his fist and easily took Will out with one effortless blow to the head. Relief spread through me. The enemy was subdued. Now we could land. I leaned back in my seat and waited for the nose to point down signaling our descent.

I yanked my helmet off and shouted, "Jarvis! What the hell just happened?"

"Eden, sit back," Jarvis barked. I slumped back in my seat in frustration. What the hell was going on? Why weren't we landing yet? Were Mom and

Andrew okay? I felt claustrophobia setting in. Only it wasn't from the tight confines of the jet. It was from being trapped in my own skin; unable to get to the people I loved.

"*Jarvis!*" I yelled again.

"*Shut up*, Eden!"

"Not until you tell me what's going on! Why aren't we landing?" I demanded.

Silence.

"Jarvis!"

"Shut up, Eden! So help me God, if you ruin this for me..." he snarled.

"Ruin what?" I insisted. "I don't understand what's going on!"

"I'll tell you what's going on. I'm saving my own ass for once, that's what's going on," he screamed. "Just do as I say and you won't get hurt."

I had never seen Jarvis like this. He was a completely different person. His face was contorted in fury, and his voice conveyed a hatred I never knew he had been concealing. This was not the Jarvis I knew.

He flicked a couple of switches and spoke into his microphone. "This is J.L. I have the location coordinates for the safe house. I repeat. I have the location coordinates for the safe house."

Fuzz...beep, beep, beep, "Meeting place is a go," beep, beep, beep, fuzz.

Fuzz...beep, beep, beep, "On my way. Prepare for landing." Fuzz...beep, beep, beep.

My entire body went cold and fear grasped my body like a vice. He was going to give the coordinates of the safe house to the man from the garage. The one who kissed me. I would know that voice anywhere. Even through the static of a two-way radio, it reverberated through my body like a jackhammer, shattering my soul. And Jarvis was going to give him the key to the safe house. The key to my demise. The key to the demise of everyone I loved...everyone I thought was safe from the end of the world. How could Jarvis do this? How could he be working with that monster? Jarvis wasn't just my protector. He was my friend. At least I thought he was. I had never felt so betrayed, so stupid.

I shook my head to clear it. I didn't have time to mourn my relationship with Jarvis. The people I loved needed me right now. My mom, my best friend, the man who was not only the president, but who had become like a father to me...and Andrew. They needed me. Humanity needed me. The future of mankind needed me. Jarvis could not disclose the location of the safe house. I had to stop him. But how?

A little voice in the back of my head whispered the answer.

You need to crash the plane.

I closed my eyes and pictured Andrew for a moment, just like he told me to. The sun was gleaming off of his brunette hair and his sky blue eyes were gazing into mine, full of love. My Andrew. He was so much more than the boy I loved. My feelings for him ran so deep, I couldn't even put them into words...there wasn't a word strong enough to describe what we had. A hot tear ran down my cold cheek as I spoke to him silently.

This is why God brought me to you, Andrew. The future of all mankind does depend on me after all. I'm sorry we didn't have enough time. But I have to do this. I love you...

I brought myself back to the task at hand by opening my eyes and leaving Andrew and everyone else I loved safely tucked into the safe house, content in the knowledge that I was going to save them.

I foolishly put my helmet back on and quietly unbuckled my harness. I craned my neck to try to see out the window the best I could, but all I could see was night. I had no idea how high we were. It didn't matter. My mind was surprisingly calm. I knew what I had to do.

I searched around the cavity of the plane to develop a plan. Planes were a foreign entity to me. I knew nothing about them. Surely I could find a way to damage the instruments panel enough to cause the plane to fall or take a nosedive. But Jarvis could overpower me with the flick of a finger. He was huge. He was a military man, a secret service agent. I was a waif in comparison. A feather to a boulder. There had to be a way to take him out. But how? I studied the contours of his body. The person I had become so strangely familiar with in the past few months. The curves of his ridiculously huge muscles, his shiny, bald head, covered at the moment by his helmet, the bulge of the gun at his waist...his gun... Was there any way to get to his gun? My eyes lowered to his belt in search of the familiar bulge. My heart palpitated at the sight of the dull black handgun grip sticking out of its holster on his right hip, beckoning to me. It was my only hope.

I closed my eyes and attempted to summon up some of the crime-of-the-week shows Mom loved so much and visualized how to work it. The cops usually just pointed and pulled the trigger. But what if I got the gun in my hands and couldn't figure out how to use it? And could I actually shoot Jarvis even if I could? My protector? No. My assassin. My enemy. I had to, regardless of our history. He was no longer my buddy Jarvis. He was a domestic terrorist. Shooting him was my only option. Humanity depended on it.

But how do I get the gun?

I would have to disorient him long enough to grab the gun from its holster. Could I kick him hard enough to distract him for a moment? If so, perhaps I could snatch the gun and shoot before he recovered from the shock. I stretched out my leg to see if I could reach him from where I was. I couldn't, but I was only inches short. I crept out of my seat the couple of extra inches I needed as slowly as I could move, working out toward the middle of the plane at the same time. I lifted my leg again, just enough to see if my kick would hit home. It would. I took inventory of my position. Was I stable enough to get a good kick? My bottom was only supported by about a quarter of the seat, but if I planted my left foot solidly enough and braced my arms against the seat and floor, I could probably gather enough strength to at least startle him long enough to get the gun.

I took a deep breath, braced myself, and kicked the side of Jarvis's head with all of the force I could muster. It made a sickening sound and knocked the wind out of him in an audible gush of air. As Jarvis's head lolled about and he swore, grabbing at his head, I swiftly grabbed the handle of the gun, whipped it around and pointed it at his head. Jarvis's shock froze him for the split second I needed to pull the trigger, pointing it at the last second at his chest instead of his head. I wasn't sure what the outcome would be if I shot him in the helmet. I needed to make sure to take him out. The resounding boom of the gun had the exact response I had intended. I watched in detached surprise with ringing ears as Jarvis slumped over and fell still.

I studied his body for a while, indifferent to the consequences of my actions. I never thought I would have to kill someone. That was reserved for murderers, police officers, and military personnel. Not for teenaged civilians. My total lack of remorse frightened me. Until I closed my eyes and summoned the faces of my loved ones. But my family and friends were not the only faces that flashed in my mind. They were joined by countless other blank, faceless silhouettes. The silhouettes of the thousands of people responsible for rebuilding the human race. I killed one to save thousands. To save mankind.

I opened my eyes and refocused my attention away from Jarvis and onto the instruments panel. It was a mess of foreign gadgets. The jet seemed to be on some kind of autopilot at the moment, because it didn't seem to notice the terrorist's demise. My eyes fell back on the gun, still dangling from my right hand. It rose of its own accord, pointed at the instruments panel, and fired. The jet jumped in response to its injury, throwing me up into the air. I landed with a painful thud. An involuntary groan escaped as I crawled back into an upright position. I couldn't tell if I had done enough damage with my first shot to make the jet fall from the sky, so I lifted my arm once again and fired a second shot. It hit home and the jet lurched again before steadying itself.

This jet was not going down without a fight.

I mustered up all the resolve remaining in my feeble, exhausted body and straightened up. I stared down the instrument panel as though it were a disgusting bug needing to be squished and pulled the gun's trigger. It clicked in mocking defiance. I squeezed the trigger over and over again, as if my efforts could magically conjure bullets into the barrel. I yelled in frustration and began to strike the instruments panel with the gun, over and over, grating my fingers between the cold metal of the gun and the hot epicenter of the jet.

"Crash, you son-of-a-bitch! Crash!" I screamed in tearful futility, falling to my knees in defeat. As though it were listening, the plane took an abrupt nosedive, sending me into the air. My head struck the ceiling of the jet, painfully jarring my neck and crushing my head against the innards of my helmet. I fell to the floor, limbs flailing and striking the terrorist, Will, seats, and anything else in their path.

"Eden!" a hoarse voice called.

It's okay, Andrew. I did it. The plane's going down.

The plane jerked, smashing again against my already pounding head. My eyes fell closed, too exhausted to endure the overwhelming pain pulsing in my head any longer.

"Eden!" the voice urgently called again.

I'm here, Andrew. You'll be okay now. Take care of my mom. She'll need you. I love you. I'll love you from the other side.

Everything went black, and I became the asteroid plummeting toward Earth.

* * * *

Where was I? I opened my eyes to utter darkness. I couldn't see a thing. I was disoriented and helplessly called out, "Andrew!" Then he came to me. He lifted me up into his arms and began to walk. It felt good in his arms; like home. I tried to find his face in the darkness, but something was burning behind him in the distance, shadowing his face. The light created a halo around his head. My angel. "Andrew," I muttered sleepily, nuzzling into his neck.

I let myself go under again.

Countdown: 1 Day
December 4, 2021

I awoke again, but this time I was surrounded by light. There was nothing but light. It didn't hurt my eyes though. Instead, it was comforting.

Am I dead?

I didn't care. If this was dead, I wanted to be dead. It was so peaceful. The aura of light enveloped me into its embrace, taking with it any negative feelings I had ever had. It was freeing. I had never felt so light. I was weightless, almost as though I was floating. My body began to drift toward a brighter spot in the orb of light like a moth to a candle.

"You shouldn't be here yet," an angelic voice told me.

But I want to be here. I like it here.

"Eden," I scarcely heard from far away. "Eden, please…" the voice sobbed. Who was it? The voice sounded familiar. It pulled on my heart, and for the first time since I woke up, I felt a tinge of regret.

Stop it. Stop talking.

"Eden…Eden I love you," the voice cried.

I love you too, I thought automatically. *Whom do I love? To whom does that voice belong?*

I paused in my journey toward the bright spot.

Why am I stopping? I want to go.

But part of me was drawn to the distraught boy's voice.

"You choose," the angelic voice commanded.

I searched my surroundings some more and my eyes fell on a room below me. It was a hospital room. No, not a hospital room. It had familiar hospital instruments, but it didn't look like any hospital room I had ever seen. It was dark, the complete antithesis of the light above me.

"Eden," a boy cried, draping himself over a bed. "Eden, please come back

221

to me." He was crying. His shoulders heaved in anguish and tears streamed down his face.

His grief filled me with sorrow.

Don't be sad, I tried to tell him.

He turned his face up, searching for something.

When he looked up, I caught a glimpse of the boy's face. *Andrew!* I thought in the form of a cry. *My Andrew...don't be sad, Andrew.*

He yelled up to me, challenging me. "Please, don't take her! You took my mother from me! Isn't that enough? You have to take her, too?"

No Andrew, she won't leave you. I'll tell her.

I floated down a bit to get a better look at whom he was fighting for. I jerked to a stop when I saw her face.

It's me.

Am I dead? Am I going to die?

"You choose," the angelic voice repeated, sounding farther away.

I looked up at the beckoning orb of utopia. It's light pledged happiness, freedom from pain, and safety. I looked down to the room below me. Its darkness intimated sadness, pain, and fear...but it also had Andrew. It had love. My love.

"Andrew," I said, through a hoarse voice as the light relinquished its hold and gave way to agony. An intense blanket of pain wrapped around me as I regained consciousness, gasping for air.

"Eden!" Andrew cried out through his despair.

"Andrew," I repeated. "I choose you," I said softly, before succumbing to the pain and falling unconscious again.

Countdown: 0 Days
December 5, 2021

I awoke to a familiar smell. The smell of soap, deodorant, and cologne. The smell of love. "Andrew," I murmured.

"Eden?"

"Andrew," I said again, tears beginning to form in my eyes.

"It's okay, baby. Don't try to talk. I'm here. I'm not going anywhere, you brave, brave girl." He was holding my hand and released it. I swiped my hand through the air, trying to relocate his hand, until I felt him climb into bed and wrap himself around me. "Am I hurting you?"

"No, but I wouldn't care if you were," I mumbled drowsily. "Hold me, Andrew."

"I am," he said, tightening his grip. "I've got you. Oh my God, Eden. Don't ever do that to me again."

"I won't. I'm not going anywhere. I chose you."

He kissed my neck, my cheek, my lips, my shoulder. It was not out of lust. It was to convince himself that I was there. That I was alive.

"Eden, I don't even know what to say. I can't even put into words my feelings for you. 'I love you' just doesn't seem like enough…"

"You don't have to say anything. Just hold me."

He pushed closer to me in response.

"How am I not in pain?" I asked.

"Medicine. Lots and lots of medicine."

"What's wrong with me?"

"We don't know. Everything seemed to be in working order, but you were in a coma caused by a pretty bad concussion. No one knew if you would come out of it. You just never know…"

Tara Tolly

I wrapped my arms around him with all the energy I could muster.

"You have some bumps and bruises that will probably be sore though."

"Where are we?"

"We're in the safe house."

"I don't understand. How did I get here? I crashed the plane."

"I know you did, you stupid, brave girl."

"Hey!" I said, a little too forcefully. Oh, there came the pain. Well, not exactly pain, just a strange sensation in my head. I groaned a little and Andrew released some pressure. "Please don't let go." He acquiesced and retightened his grip.

"The asteroid," I said, trying to sit up.

"In two hours. You're safe now. We're safe from it."

"Mom..."

"She's here. She just went to find something to drink."

"Dani?"

"She's here, too. She's in her room."

"Is your father here?"

He didn't need to answer. I could tell from the tightening of his body that he wasn't.

"He'll make it, Andrew," I said uncertainly.

"He's not coming, Eden." He readjusted his body so he could look at me. "But I don't want to think about that now. I just want to focus on you." He brushed my hair back and looked at me with glowing intensity, tears wetting his cheeks. "Eden, I thought you were going to die. I could feel the life leaving you. I couldn't lose you..."

I wrapped my arms around him and whispered in his ear. "I was almost dead, Andrew. I could see heaven. I could feel it. I wanted to go. It was so tranquil and free from pain and suffering."

He shuddered in fear. "You wanted to die?" he asked, betrayed at the thought.

"Let me finish."

He nodded, wiping his cheeks with the back of his hand.

"At first I didn't know living was an option. I didn't know who I was or whom I was leaving behind. But then I heard you, and you pulled me back a little. With each tear you shed, you pulled me back to myself, until I realized who you were and how much I loved you. Then a voice told me to choose."

He took in a sharp breath.

"I considered both options. It was easier to die. It was...peaceful. Andrew, I think it might have been Heaven. But Heaven didn't have you. I knew I loved you too much to leave you. I chose you."

224

First Sun

"You chose me over Heaven?" he asked in awe, looking down at me through his long, wet eyelashes.

"Yes," I breathed. "I'll always choose you."

He held me tight, as if I could still choose Heaven.

"Andrew?"

"Hmm?" he breathed against my neck.

"I'm not as worried about the billions of people who will die as I was before. If what I experienced really was Heaven, then they are about to go to a place where the best day on Earth they've ever had will pale in comparison to what Heaven has in store for them. I'm not afraid of death any more either. The only thing I'm afraid of now is living without you."

"Eden," Andrew murmured, holding me close. "You won't have to, baby."

Suddenly the door opened. "Andrew, is she—" my mom began to ask, but stopped when she realized I was awake. "Eden!" She ran to me and kissed my forehead and cheeks, crying tears of relief and joy. She scurried back to the door and shouted, "James! She's awake!"

Before Andrew and I even had the chance to absorb what her words meant, the president pushed through the door and was by my side, holding my hand in an instant. He kissed the top of my head and said, "Thank God," through the beginnings of his own tears.

Andrew jumped out of bed and made it to the other side in three swift steps. He stopped in front of his father and looked at him in disbelief. "Dad?"

The president cupped Andrew's face in his hands and looked into his eyes intently. "Drew, I couldn't abandon you. Not after losing your mother and possibly…" He glanced at me without finishing his sentence. He looked back at his son and gathered him into a tight embrace.

"Ahem, sorry to interrupt your reunion, but I have a patient to attend to," a male voice said kindly as he pushed through the door. I instantly recognized him as Dr. Frank, a doctor from a reality TV show documenting an emergency room in New York City. He was quite arguably one of the best doctors in the country. I had been a fan of the show since its premiere episode and was instantly a little star struck.

"How's my favorite patient?" he said, smiling.

"I have a feeling I'm your only patient so far," I said, blushing.

"Maybe not," he teased, putting a stethoscope to my chest. "I'm glad to see you awake. You gave us quite a scare. I thought I was going to have to treat Mr. Wellington here for a broken heart if you didn't pull through soon," he joked.

I looked at Andrew and he shrugged sheepishly. He came back over to my side and held my hand while Dr. Frank finished his examination.

"So what's wrong with me, Doctor?"

"Well, it's complicated. When you were first brought to me, you were in rough shape. You were unconscious and a CT scan diagnosed brain edema, swelling of the brain, just as I had suspected. I started you on an IV infusion of corticosteroids in hopes of reducing the swelling. All we could do at that point was wait and see how you responded to the treatment. Luckily, you responded well. I'm going to do another CT scan to see what we're still dealing with, but your level of consciousness is a good sign."

"Could I have died?"

Andrew squeezed my hand.

"That was a possibility, yes. The brain is a mystery. Despite modern medicine and all of the technology available to doctors, head trauma still eludes us. Different people react differently to treatment and to put it casually, you just never know."

"But how is it possible to survive a stealth jet crash?" I asked in amazement.

"Well, thanks to Will, you didn't exactly crash," Andrew said.

I looked at Andrew in confusion. "What? He was out cold. How was he able to do anything?"

"He—" Andrew began, but the president cut him off.

"Doctor, if Eden is out of imminent danger for the moment, would you please excuse us? There's a time sensitive matter we need to discuss."

Sensing the urgency of the situation, Dr. Frank nodded. He rested his hand on mine and with kind eyes said, "I'll be back to check on you soon," before slipping out the door.

The president swiftly fished his phone out of his pocket and texted someone before turning his attention to me. "Eden, could you please tell us what happened on the aircraft that made you feel the need to crash it?"

I told them everything that had happened in the jet from the moment I lost contact with Andrew. I realized at the end of my story that I had started to cry in the midst of the disclosure of Jarvis's betrayal.

The president was furious. He paced back and forth, fuming. I could tell through Andrew's body language that he felt the same way. Their reaction calmed me a bit. I no longer felt alone. Now that they knew, they could carry some of the burden.

"I'm so sorry, Eden," Andrew whispered into my ear in sorrow. "We trusted him with your life. That son-of-a-bitch will burn in hell."

For some strange reason, I felt a little jolt of defensiveness for Jarvis. It quickly subsided and was promptly replaced by hatred.

The president stopped pacing and studied me for a moment. "Eden, you said you shot Jarvis in the chest?"

"Yes. I was going to shoot him in the head," I said, shuddering at the thought, "but I changed my mind at the last second because I wasn't sure what would happen if I shot him with his helmet on. I wanted to make sure he would die."

James resumed his pacing, shaking his head in frustration.

"Did I do something wrong, Mr. President?" I asked, suddenly very worried.

He took a couple strides over to me and took my hands into his, looking meaningfully into my eyes. "No," he said firmly. "You didn't do anything wrong, Eden. You were very brave. Not many people would've risked their lives the way you did."

"Then what's wrong?" I asked.

"Secret service agents always wear bulletproof vests on duty."

I took in a sharp breath at this news and buried my face in my hands. "So he's not dead," I unnecessarily deduced. How could I be so stupid? Suddenly I felt very small.

"Probably not. At least not from the gunshot. A point blank gunshot to a bulletproof vest can knock you out cold for a while, but it won't kill you," he said, resuming his pacing.

"Sir, where's Jarvis?" I asked, suddenly cold.

The president's silence was chilling.

"Where's Jarvis?" I asked more forcefully, abruptly sitting up and causing my delicate head to spin.

"We don't know," he answered.

Before I could respond, the door opened and in walked the chief of staff with Will flanked by a small fleet of secret service agents. Will smiled at the sight of me and tried to come to me, but one of the agents grabbed his arm to stop him. The president halted them by saying, "It's okay. Eden's story matches his," and dismissed them with a curt nod.

Will rushed to my side and said, "Eden! Thank God you're okay! I was so worried...you weren't doing so well when I pulled you from the plane." His face glowed with warmth.

"*You* pulled me from the plane?" I turned to Andrew. "It wasn't you? It was Will?"

He nodded his head sadly. "We couldn't get to you fast enough. If it wouldn't have been for Will..." He vigorously shook Will's hand. "Thank you so much for saving Eden. I am forever in your debt." While I could tell he was genuine in this sentiment, there was also an edge to his voice. Did Andrew feel threatened by Will? The thought made me smile.

"Yes. I don't know how I'll ever repay you," I said, beaming in appreciation of my hero.

"Ahhh, it was nothin'." He waved his hand in dismissal of the notion that he was to thank for my survival.

"You're hurt," I said, worried. He had a large contusion on the left side of his head where Jarvis had hit him. "Have you been seen by a doctor?"

"Yeah, they sent Dr. Frank down to look at me. Which was rather nice of them considering I could've been the one responsible for this whole mess."

"You're not mad?" I asked in disbelief.

"Nah, they were just doing their job. I would've done the same thing."

I liked Will. It was the first time I got a good look at him. Before Andrew, I would have thought he was cute. He was blond with kind, light brown eyes. He was tall (but not as tall as Andrew) and built (but not as built as Andrew). His youth surprised me. He probably only had Andrew and me by two years at the most.

"Will," the president said gravely, bringing us out of our happy little reunion and back into the somber present. "We need to know when Jarvis was last seen. Was he still in the plane when you woke up?"

"Well, he was when I woke up the first time. But I guess that's pretty obvious, since the first time I woke up was right before Eden passed out." He turned to me. "I tried to keep you conscious by calling your name, but fuzzy as my head still was, I had to focus all of my attention on landing the jet. It wasn't easy. You did quite the number on it, Eden. It was a pretty tough landing, thanks to the shots to the instrument panel," he added slyly. "But if I wouldn't have woken up when I did neither one of us would be alive talking right now."

"I tried to crash it. I didn't think there was any chance of you waking up to land it," I admitted, embarrassment hitting me with full force.

Will shook his head in amazement. "With all due respect, Eden, you have quite the pair of balls."

We all chuckled lightly at his sincere attempt at a compliment. And somehow, this sentiment made me feel much better about my failure.

"You said Jarvis was there the *first* time you woke up. Did you pass out again?" the president asked.

"Like I said, it was a pretty rough landing. I hit my head again as the jet came to a stop. Doc said it wouldn't have taken much to knock me out again after the first head trauma. The next time I woke up, probably from the smell of smoke, Jarvis was gone. I kept an eye out for him as I, well, we," he corrected, smiling at me and prompting Andrew to step between Will and me, "vacated the vicinity of the jet. But he was nowhere to be seen. It was too dark to track him, which would've been difficult carrying someone anyway." Andrew reclaimed my hand. "Plus, my head wasn't in the best condition, either. I was

First Sun

barely able to get us clear of the plane before she blew and I passed out again."

We all fell silent as we processed this new information.

I broke the silence by asking, "Mr. President, is Will able to stay?"

"Of course, Eden. I'm not going to put the man who saved your life in harm's way. He may have to sleep on a couch in the rec room, but he can stay."

I nodded in thanks.

He turned to Will. "Will, Harry, my chief of staff, is out in the hall waiting for you. He's going to ask you some more questions to see if you can help in locating Jarvis."

"Of course, Mr. President." He shook my hand and Andrew's, saluted his Commander in Chief, and left the room.

The president began to pace around the room yet again to get his thoughts in order. I had come to recognize his decision-making process. I waited for the definitive nod of a resolute face that would inevitably follow the pacing. I didn't have to wait long. When his mind was made up, he stood his ground and began to defend his decision.

"Drew, you're not going to like what I'm about to say. But I need you to think about the implications of the situation at hand. Jarvis is at large with knowledge that could destroy everything we've set out to protect. It is my re—"

"I understand, Dad," Andrew said, cutting him off. He went to his father and put his hands on his shoulders. "The captain always goes down with his ship. I get it. Go find the son-of-a-bitch." The president took his son into his arms, hugging him like there was no tomorrow. There wouldn't be for most. But there was a chance there wouldn't be for any if they didn't find Jarvis.

The president finally let go of Andrew and came over to me. He took me into his arms. "I'm sorry I failed you, sir. I tried to save us...I failed..." I stammered in defeat.

"Eden, my sweet, sweet girl. You did save us. If you hadn't shot Jarvis, the safe house would already be taken over. Or gone. You bought us some valuable time. You are one of the bravest people I've ever met."

"But if I would've succeeded, you wouldn't have to leave..."

"Don't you dare blame yourself for Jarvis's betrayal. You did everything you could. Now you have to let me do what I can."

"Sir, please don't leave. Can't we just protect the safe house from within? The asteroid is going to hit soon. Nature will take care of Jarvis."

The president shook his head in disagreement. "Eden, we're far enough from the impact site that it may be hours after the collision before our side of the globe sees the effects. But when we do..." he trailed off and shook his head in dismissal of the thought. "Jarvis knows the exact location. Soon, his terrorist friends will as well, if they don't already. I can't risk any damage to the safe

229

house. These people are ruthless. They will do anything to get in. If they destroy the air seal they could compromise everything we've set out to accomplish here."

"But sir, aren't there others who can protect it?" I was grasping at straws and we both knew it.

"A true soldier doesn't abandon a mission. Besides, what makes anyone else's life less valuable than mine?" He shook his head in determination. "'President' is just a title, Eden. I'm still just a man with loved ones like everyone else. And I will sacrifice myself in a heartbeat to keep them safe."

I shuddered in fear and threw my arms around the president as tears streamed down my face in realization that he was saying goodbye. "Come back to us," I whispered. "Please. For Andrew, for my mom…for me…to finish what you started here."

The president hugged me back, then gently pushed himself away enough to look into my eyes. "I'll do my best, Eden. But if I don't make it back, please take care of my son for me."

"Always," I whispered. "Take care of yourself, James."

He smiled in response to my use of his first name and kissed me on the cheek. Before leaving he stopped and hugged his son again. He whispered something in Andrew's ear and Andrew nodded. The president pulled away and looked at Andrew in silent communication. They both nodded and the president was gone.

Andrew stood there frozen for a moment, then strode over to me, climbed into bed and crumbled in my arms. We cried together for some time. We cried out of fear for his father. We cried for the loss of our fellow humans. We cried for the end of the world as we knew it.

When neither of us could cry any longer, we just lay together, comforted by the notion that no matter who or what we lost, we still had one another. A knock on the door brought us out of our own little world.

"Come in," I croaked.

"Eden?" a familiar, but sad voice said. "I'm sorry to interrupt, but I needed to see for myself that you were okay."

"Dani! Boy are you a sight for sore eyes. Get over here!"

She thankfully ran over to me and hugged me, despite Andrew being wrapped around me. He didn't move.

"You look like shit, E." But she smiled in relief of my obvious wellbeing.

"Thanks, Dan. I can always count on you to make me feel better." But she did make me feel better, just by being there.

"Okay, I'll leave the two of you alone. I'm going to go keep Will company for the end of the world, if you know what I mean," she joked.

Andrew busted out laughing. "Thanks, Dani. I needed that right now."

"How much time, Dan?" I asked, putting an end to the laughter.

"Ten minutes." Andrew tightened his grip on me.

"You'll be okay? You can stay in here with us," I offered.

"No, that's okay. There's kind of a countdown party going on out there. It's totally sadistic, but oddly comforting at the same time. We're all in the same boat, you know? Plus, I wasn't kidding when I said I would keep Will company. He's hot." She smiled to convince me that she really was all right, even though I knew she wasn't. None of us were. "Plus, you need some rest."

"Okay, but come see me again later."

She crossed her fingers over her heart and hugged me again. As she left, my mom came back in. "How's my girl?" she asked, trying to smile even though I could see the heartache in her eyes and the tear stains on her cheeks.

"I'm fine, Mom. At least I am until these drugs wear off. What about you? Are you okay?" I didn't have to ask if she had said goodbye to the president. I had a hunch it was the source of her tears.

"I'll be fine." She rubbed Andrew's arm in comfort and he smiled at her in appreciation. "Do you want me to stay in here with you? Otherwise, I can follow Dani out to the countdown. It's a little strange, but for some reason it makes me feel a little better about everything. Plus, Harry's there. He has communication with James."

I smiled at the similarity of her description to Dani's. "It's up to you."

She looked from Andrew to me and said, "I'll leave you two alone. We're right down the hall. Let me know if you need me?"

We nodded. She hugged us both and headed to the door.

"Mom?"

"Yeah?"

"Leave the door open. The sound of voices is comforting."

The last couple of times the door opened I could hear a crowd of people, and just as Mom and Dani had said, it was oddly comforting. Even though we were leaving the rest of the world behind, we all had one another.

Andrew and I lay in silence for a while, both lost in our own thoughts.

"What are you thinking?" Andrew whispered, breaking the silence.

"A million things at once. But the loudest one is how safe I feel in your arms."

He repositioned us so we were lying on our sides facing one another, legs entwined. "Is this okay? Am I hurting you?"

"It's perfect."

"You know what I was thinking?" he asked.

"No, but I wish I did."

231

"I was thinking about how even though I may have just seen my father for the last time—"

"Andrew, he'll come—"

"It's okay. Because even though I know I may never see him again, I'm okay because I have you. You're my family now. You're my life." He smiled. "You're my Oxygen."

Ten, a chorus of voices ominously bellowed from down the hall.

My body stiffened.

"Look into my eyes, Eden."

Nine.

I did as I was told. His sky blue gaze instantly grounded me, just as it had on Marine One.

Eight.

"No matter what happens, we have each other," he said.

Seven.

He drew his hand up to my chest and rested it on my heart, not breaking eye contact.

Six.

I put my hand on his heart and felt the reassuring thud against the palm of my hand.

Five.

He leaned forward and kissed me gently on the lips, just once.

Four.

"Look back into my eyes, Andrew," I pleaded, fear gripping me.

Three.

"I'm here, baby," he assured me. He rested his forehead against mine, looking deep into my soul. "I'm always here."

Two.

My body relaxed once again when our eyes locked. In one second, billions of people would leave this place to be reunited with their creator. Others would escape the wrath of the initial blast, only to suffer to their inevitable ends. But here with Andrew, lost in his eyes, in my safe house, I could escape it all.

One.

Acknowledgements

Anyone I know or have ever met has contributed to the creation of this book in some way, shape, or form, because they have helped shape who I am today. So one can imagine how impossible it is to narrow those influences down to a concise acknowledgements page. But alas, I must do just that. Here's trying:

To Steven Tolly, my other half and real-life Andrew (minus the whole first son celebrity thing, of course) for his support through this rollercoaster ride called publishing. I could not imagine taking the ride with anyone else.

To my beautiful children, Bella and James Tolly, for being my muses. They are the great loves of my life.

To my parents, Dennis and Nancy Stecklein, for raising me with the confidence to know that I am good enough and dreams can come true. There are not sufficient enough words to describe how much I love them and appreciate all they have done for me throughout my life.

To my agent extraordinaire, Tina P. Schwartz from The Purcell Agency, for recognizing a diamond in the rough and encouraging me to polish that diamond up to shine for the world. *First Sun* would not be what it is today without her tireless commitment and passion. A girl could not ask for a better agent.

To Nancy Schumacher and Caroline Andrus from Fire and Ice of Melange Books, for recognizing the potential of *First Sun* and giving me the opportunity to share it with the world. Thank you for being a dream to work with.

To Lauren Hughes, who probably doesn't know just how influential she was in the fruition of my dream. She was the first person outside of my immediate family to make me feel as though *First Sun* was good enough to see the light of day. Without her cheerleading and enthusiasm for this story, I don't know if I ever would have thought it was good enough to pursue publication. For that, I can never thank her enough.

To Billie Friedman, the best unofficial editor a girl could ask for. Nancy will never know how much time Billie saved her! From plot holes to semicolons, she covered it all, and, I may add, is one heck of a shoe aficionado. But most of all, she is, and always will be, my "Be Fri."

To Annie Hester, for her unwavering friendship.

And finally, to my first readers (besides the aforementioned), all of whom built my confidence, brick by brick, each time one of them read and praised *First Sun*: Kristin Heggen, Jen Sauerbry, Brad Stecklein, Elizabeth Barrett, Emma Boote, Alaysia Pursell, and Madilyn Rink of Kennedy High School.

About the Author

Tara Tolly lives in Cedar Rapids, Iowa with her husband and four children (two human and two canine) where she spends her days shaping the minds of impressionable fourth graders and her nights and summers shaping the lives of her make-believe characters. She loves to escape the pressures of the real world by entering into the fictional worlds she creates within the depths of her imagination. When not immersed between the covers of a book (or in reality, the glow of her Nook screen) or typing away on her computer, she loves spending time with her family, running, and participating in other creative endeavors such as photography, crafting, and baking.

https://www.facebook.com/tara.tolly
https://twitter.com/TaraTolly
https://www.taratolly.com